The Edge of Life

Happy Reading!

Lena Gibson

Lena Gibson

Black Rose Writing | Texas

ISBN: 978-1-68513-171-5
PUBLISHED BY BLACK ROSE WRITING
www.blackrosewriting.com

Printed in the United States of America
Suggested Retail Price (SRP) $21.95

The Edge of Life is printed in Chaparral Pro

*As a planet-friendly publisher, Black Rose Writing does its best to eliminate unnecessary waste to reduce paper usage and energy costs, while never compromising the reading experience. As a result, the final word count vs. page count may not meet common expectations.

For Rob, who is my everything.

The Edge of Life

CHAPTER 1: KAT

Today would be a carbon copy of hundreds that had preceded it. Once, every day had seemed fresh, now each was another obstacle to overcome. Kat smothered the intrusive thoughts as she stress-bit the inside of her lower lip, a distraction while she searched the radio for something cheerful to get her through her Friday morning commute. Yesterday, she'd forgotten her phone at work and already she missed her music.

"*As asteroid 2025 NR hurtles toward Earth, scientists forecast...*" Kat changed the radio station. Nope. Not cheerful.

"*Forest fires rage throughout the Pacific Northwest and into Canada, ahead of the summer forest fire season...*" She pushed a different button.

"*April temperatures break the one hundred eighty-year record...*" She stabbed another button, searching for something less depressing.

"*Climate change...*"

"No," she said, pushing yet another.

"*Riots last night in Portland and LA mirror...*"

"*Flooding along the Columbia...*"

"*Reduced snowpack and high temperatures combine...*"

"*The mass shooting at Snake River Elementary was the fourth shooting this...*"

She wanted to scream, but fought the impulse and took a deep breath. "Last chance," she said with a final stab.

"Near miss forecasted for asteroid…"

"The umpteenth 'near miss' this year, blah blah blah," said Kat as she snapped off the radio. She forced her clenched jaw to relax. "How many million miles away for this one?" Rolling her eyes as she took in the now ominous morning sunshine. "Why can't one station play music?"

Tulips, daffodils, and heather blooms provided splashes of much-needed color as she passed the nearby houses and townhouses. Maybe flowers could help her be more positive. Spring had arrived and with it the promise of the upcoming summer vacation. Another six weeks of school until she was free. Though, with the doom and gloom predicted, there'd be nowhere left to go. The last few summers had been similar. Climate change, protests, and misery. Before that, the pandemic. She wished there was something to look forward to besides staying home.

Kat used to love her job, but now she couldn't wait for holidays, for time away from work. She kept the radio off and drove the rest of the way in silence. Arriving at the three-story stone building outside Seattle that housed the private school where she taught, she parked in the staff lot. Her sport model crimson hybrid Camry stuck out like a sore thumb in the expanse of black and white SUVs. It had been her only major purchase since Mark died two years ago. He wouldn't have liked her flashy car, but for her, its vibrant color had been the draw.

Her eyes swam with tears at the thought of her late husband. "Get a hold of yourself, Mrs. Davies. Time to be a teacher," she muttered. Collecting her book and lunch bag from the passenger seat, Kat blinked and checked her mascara in the overhead mirror. She pasted on a smile. Fake it till you make it. She might not be the same person she used to be, but she pretended.

Even when the rest of her life was difficult, this was the one place she needed to be friendly and pleasant, at least to the students. Her starring role was as her old self, the version that hadn't been widowed at twenty-eight. The parking lot filled as her colleagues arrived. Not wanting to walk in with anyone and be forced to chitchat, Kat hurried, glad that her sensible shoes made it easy to escape into the cool hallway inside.

She signed in and kept moving, not making eye contact with anyone. She bypassed the staff room and hustled upstairs, taking them two at a time to the second floor, where her classroom was located. Entering, she unpacked her tea, found the forgotten phone, and turned on her favorite playlist to block the incessant hum of the fluorescent lights.

She shifted into teacher mode and opened the window to reduce the ever-present underlying scents of dust, whiteboard marker, and stale lunches. She straightened desks, posted the schedule, and checked her email to ensure no last-minute changes were required to the day's plan.

When the students shuffled in, she greeted each by name and with a smile. Pouring energy into her performance, she ensured each student spoke at least twice that day, keeping a mental tally in her head. She called on the quiet students to ensure their inclusion and checked on the few who needed extra help. Her friendly teacher role had become automatic because she had done this for so long.

She also made side deals with two students to reduce their required homework, knowing it was a struggle. The last thing was a verbal "ticket out the door" math question. She personalized each, designed to be challenging enough to be of interest, but not so hard the student couldn't answer. Correct answers got a high five and a goodbye with their name that let each student know she valued them. The routine also kept the kids from giving her unwanted hugs.

She'd sorted the numerous crises for the ten-year-olds in their Kelly green and crisp white uniforms, pretending she was doing more than going through the motions. Her performance mattered. It wasn't the students' fault that her heart was numb and encased in ice.

Sipping tea, she marked the work needed for Monday and prepped her day plans for next week. She preferred to be a week ahead, rather than the one day required by the school. You never knew when life wouldn't go according to plan. She'd learned that the hard way.

At five, Kat scurried out to her car with a vague wave toward the other fifth-grade teacher from across the hall, who was also on her way out.

"TGIF," said Tracy. "That sounded like a great lesson on the rock cycle. Maybe I could borrow some samples next week. You have any weekend plans?"

Kat smiled on cue, the last toothy one until Monday. Her cheek muscles ached from over-use. "Not really. See you Monday." She headed in the opposite direction.

Getting in her car, Kat relaxed her face, massaging the tight muscles along her jaw. Once the tension eased a bit, she turned on the radio, checking traffic for the route home. Seattle and the outlying area were gridlocked at the best of times, let alone during Friday afternoon rush hour. She had to make it home; then the weekend was hers, hers to do with as she pleased. Her hands shook as she drove. All week she'd been anticipating peace and oblivion.

One nagging doubt plagued her as she drove. She couldn't shake the idea that she'd promised someone something, but she couldn't recall what. Her brow furrowed. It wasn't a birthday or her parents' anniversary. She hadn't spoken to them in months, so that wasn't it. The sense that she'd forgotten something persisted.

She parked outside her townhouse and hurried upstairs. Kicking off her shoes with a sigh of sheer pleasure, she threw her bag inside by the door and headed straight for the cabinet over the stove with the alcohol. She needed a drink.

She opened the fresh sapphire-colored bottle of Bombay gin, took down a large glass from the cupboard, and free-poured a generous measure into the bottom. She sliced a lime from the fridge into wedges and rinsed the knife and cutting board. The tonic, pre-chilled in the fridge, fizzed when opened, the sound making her mouth water. She swallowed in anticipation. She filled the glass three-quarters full and squeezed in two lime chunks, licking the excess from her fingers because she loved the tang. Adding four ice cubes, her drink was perfect.

Taking it in both hands, she breathed deep, inhaling the bubbling citrus scent. Without thinking, Kat tipped it back and gulped down half. The bite of alcohol was strong and delicious. Her hands shook as she let the rest wash down her throat. Setting down her empty glass, she sighed. With a deep breath, she made a second, stronger drink, ignoring the nagging voice inside that told her to go slow. The ritual was calming and her hands no longer trembled as she carried it to the couch and sat, putting up her feet. It was easier not to think when she drank.

She didn't bother with the TV, but stared out the window, though she didn't pay attention to the view. Sipping, she savored her drink, noticing how each swallow slid down her throat. She didn't touch a drop Monday to Thursday, but from Friday to Sunday she could do what she liked; she was beholden to nobody.

Three drinks later, Kat wobbled to the fridge to see if she'd bother with food. Fridays, she preferred to drink her dinner because cooking seemed like too much work. Each week, she told herself to order something if she didn't want to cook, but more often than not, she didn't. The first drink wasn't a problem, but after she had a second, it was never worth the effort to do more than make another drink, despite the twinge of guilt about wasting her life. She shouldn't be this way, but she didn't have a reason to change.

Her phone rang, but she let it go to voicemail. Three minutes later, it started again, the ringtone piercing and setting her teeth on edge. She glanced at the phone where it was charging and exhaled a mouthful of air in disgust before muting the sound. Nick knew better than to call Fridays. What the hell did he want? After a hectic week, she didn't feel like talking.

Her phone chimed with a text moments later. God, he was persistent tonight. She squinted, trying to read the jumble of words on the screen, but they were difficult to read.

"Shit," she said, deciphering enough to get the idea.

Be there in ten with pizza.

"Shit, shit, shit."

She unlocked her front door, staggered back to the couch, and sat while she waited for her best friend to arrive with dinner and a lecture. She sat up straight, trying to look sober.

Nick didn't bother ringing the bell, knowing she hated the loud noise. He entered, two large pizzas in hand. The rich scent of cheese, tomatoes, and basil filled her living room. It smelled better than anything in her fridge. Maybe this could work.

He took one look at her and set the pizzas down. His shoulders slumped.

"I'm already too late." He flipped open the top box and grabbed a slice.

"Too late?" she said, trying to focus on him while the room spun. Feeling proud for covering her inebriation so well, she lurched to her feet and tripped over her shoes lying on the floor. She crawled a few steps and got to her feet, her cheeks burning.

"Kat, you promised, remember?" said Nick, his mouth full. "One drink to relax, then we'd have pizza and watch a movie."

"Just had one," she said, concentrating on walking in a straight line. The floor buckled and swam as she made her way toward the pizza. She'd been stupid to think he wouldn't notice.

"Three drinks or four?" he said, lifting the bottle of gin. "Kat, what are we going to do with you?" His tone was concerned. "Can I help?"

"Can't do anything," she said as she chose a wedge of pizza with ham, pineapple, and bacon, her usual favorite. Her words might be flippant, but she was disappointed in herself. Nick was a trusted friend and deserved better. She wished she'd remembered their plans.

"I'm thinking that's true. You won't come to our place. You won't meet us anywhere; you don't answer your phone and as far as I can tell, all you do is work and drink."

She shrugged and took a big bite. She chewed while thinking of a reply, her brain functioning slower than usual. "I don't drink all week. I just need to blow off steam."

She scowled, feeling resentful. He had no idea.

"Kat, I'm worried about you. The only time you aren't alone is when I inflict myself upon you. You don't see anyone else. Do you?"

"Don't want to," she mumbled around another bite of pizza. The sauce was tangy, still hot, and oh so delicious. A niggling voice in her head called her a liar, but she squashed it and focused on the pizza.

"Are you looking forward to time off work, your summer holiday? What have you got planned?" He grabbed a slice and sat.

"Nothing much," she said with a shrug. She hadn't made plans because she didn't know what would help her feel more connected again. The look in his eyes made her cringe inside. He was up to something.

"We should plan something. We used to hike all the time."

The pizza stuck in her throat, and she glanced at her empty glass with longing.

"We should pick a day for hiking every weekend. Every Sunday? Start right away. No need to wait for summer. Jake can join when he's free. I have another friend who needs to get out, too. We should all go."

She didn't feel well. The pizza in her stomach had become a greasy lump. She set her half-eaten slice down in the box and walked on unsteady legs back to the couch, the room spinning.

Nick's eyes held concern as he put two slices of pizza on his plate and her partial piece on another. He carried them to the coffee table as he sat at the opposite end of the couch. At least she hadn't driven him away. Even in her foggy state, she recognized she needed to meet his effort's part way. She didn't want him to give up or think she was hopeless.

"Who else for hiking?" She didn't want to exercise, but it might be easier to agree. She could always cancel. Or hike and escape this place with all its unpleasant memories.

"A friend. You might have met him years ago at university."

"Ugh, this isn't a set-up, is it?" She wasn't ready to consider the idea.

"No way. I wouldn't do that without permission, and you don't like surprises. I want to spend time with both of you, and I don't have a lot of spare time. If I double up, I can see you twice as often." He nudged the plate in her direction.

He seemed sincere. She picked up the pizza and nibbled. "Lucky us."

"That's a resounding yes, then?" He perked up, his tone hopeful.

"I guess."

"Last week, you freaked me out."

"What happened last week?" She wracked her brain but came up empty.

"You don't remember, do you?" He slumped back on the couch.

She shrugged and shook her head. She took another bite of pizza, humoring her friend. Dinner was a good idea.

"You didn't answer your phone or your doorbell even though that morning you said you'd be here, and your car was parked out front. I wanted to tell you about my big discovery at work. You used to love to hear about comets and meteors and space dust."

"I would still like to hear." She eyed her drink where she'd left it on the counter.

"Kat, your door wasn't locked, and I came in and found you on the floor, passed out cold. I put you to bed and came back early on Sunday. We made this plan for tonight."

"I don't remember." She swallowed, her food tasting like cardboard as she touched her forehead, remembering the goose egg.

"On Sunday, you sobered up, and we talked. You admitted that you blackout every weekend. You agreed to try not to this weekend. I don't want to babysit you, but if I can help be a distraction until you break the habit, I will."

Tears leaked down her face at his words. She seemed to have no control. What was wrong with her? Maybe not remembering what she'd done was better. She was such a mess.

Nick took her hand in his. "Mark wouldn't want you to mourn him this way."

"Mark isn't here." It came out sharper than she expected. The usual filter had fallen off her mouth and emotions. "He doesn't get a vote."

"You're acting like you're dead, too." Nick squeezed her hand and let go. "I want to tell you about my cool discovery. If you forget, I'll tell you again Sunday. I want to share it with you like I used to."

"I don't want your pity time," mumbled Kat as she stared at the floor. She needed to clean. Crumbs and dusty balls of hair floated along the edge of the baseboards and she couldn't remember the last time she'd swept or washed anything other than a dish. Afraid she might have offended him, she forced herself to make eye contact and saw he was smiling. Why was he being so kind? She didn't deserve it.

"It isn't pity," said Nick. "I'm looking to get my friend back. This is purely selfish."

She didn't believe him, but got up to collect her drink. She could sip while she listened.

Nick followed her to the counter, his hands jammed in his front pockets. His eyes looked sad, and she wished she could stop hurting him. She stopped with the glass halfway to her mouth and handed it to him. He gave her a tremulous smile and emptied her gin and tonic down the sink; the ice clinking on the stainless steel.

She didn't speak, but the drink being gone came as a relief. She picked up the bottle and handed it to him with shaking hands.

He dumped the rest of the gin with a gurgling sound, the ice cubes bumping into each other as they swirled around the drain. She closed her eyes, concentrating on her breathing. It would be okay.

"You might be angry, but you need help." Nick's voice brought her back to the moment.

She looked at him and nodded. How did she explain she was empty inside?

"Can I have a hug?" Stabbing pains in her chest accompanied her request. From her, it was an unusual request. Most of the time, she preferred not to be touched. It shouldn't hurt to let herself feel.

Nick held out his arms and gave her a squeeze that loosened some of her pent-up angst and loneliness. After resting her head on his shoulder, she walked away. She needed to try harder to get her life back.

She took a deep breath and swiped the tears from her cheeks with her hands. "Let's hear about your space dust."

CHAPTER 2: RYAN

Ryan glanced at the clock. It was late enough that Nick should be awake. Dreading the task, he called his friend, who answered on the second ring.

"Hey, Ryan. What's up? You running late?"

"Nick, sorry. I have to cancel. I like the idea of hiking, but not this week. I just arrived at the office." Ryan ran his fingers through his hair, standing it on end. He didn't like to disappoint his closest friend.

On the other end of the line, Nick paused. "Again?"

Even though his friend sounded understanding, it still didn't make Ryan feel any less like a flake.

"Yeah, sorry. I'm up for a promotion soon. I'm on track to make partner in six years, so I need to keep up my hours. I could do lunch this week though, say Tuesday? My treat." He hated canceling, but he'd woken up at four and hadn't dared to wait around for a nine o'clock hike. He needed to keep his mind occupied.

"I'd like that," said Nick. "I want to talk to you about something. In-person, if that's okay. Something I found at work."

His discovery couldn't be that exceptional because Nick's excitement level seemed more muted than usual.

"Sure. We can text Monday to set up a place. Enjoy the hike." Ryan hung up and swiveled his black leather office chair to take in his cramped office. At least he had a window, as this was just about the

11

only view he saw nowadays. More downtown office towers filled the skyline, but it was better than the cubbyhole he'd used as a junior associate his first two years at Goodrich, Singh, and Hardcastle.

Though it was Sunday, he put his head down and worked, concentrating on writing the brief a partner wanted later this week.

He wrote and rewrote it a dozen times before he could no longer ignore his stomach rumbling, reminding him he hadn't eaten yet. He'd finished ahead of schedule, priding himself on getting everything done early. Checking his phone for the first time since lunch, the time was nine-thirty. He'd been here for fourteen hours with only a sandwich, but he'd driven in because it was easier to avoid distractions here than at home. Writing his hours on his timesheet, he gathered his laptop. He'd grab a bite on the way home. He couldn't remember his last home-cooked meal. Or rather, he didn't want to. It always led to him feeling foolish, rejected, and ended with crushing regret.

He drove home, the streets dark and quiet this time of night, making it an easier commute than weekday Seattle traffic. He collected his mail from the lobby on the way up to his seventh-floor apartment, his bag of chicken tacos in hand. The apartment was quiet and smelled of unwashed laundry with a hint of garbage. He hated coming home to an empty apartment night after night. He dragged one of his two kitchen chairs into position and flicked on the TV, wishing for a comfy chair instead of the rigid remnants that had been left behind.

The wall-mounted wide-screen TV and the surround-sound speakers were the only things in the otherwise barren living room. When Heather had annihilated him last year, she'd taken the couch and loveseat, lamps, coffee table, and end tables when she moved out. She'd taken the artwork from the walls and every symbol of their life together. Including the other chairs, the table, and... his heart; leaving him as empty and hollow as his apartment.

He hadn't gotten around to replacing anything. But he wasn't here often enough. Of course, she'd left the bed, the last thing he wanted.

He slept on it because it was softer than the floor, but he should have it replaced.

When he finished dinner, he sat for half an hour, letting his food digest before he changed into workout clothes and did four reps of his exercises, each with a dozen weighted arm curls and lifts, twenty-five each of sit-ups, push-ups, and squats. After a quick shower, he set an alarm for four forty-five a.m. as Monday was a run day. He had to wake early to clean up and be at work by seven a.m. He'd have to keep the pace up to get in his eight miles.

Before he fell asleep, he remembered Nick had mentioned a discovery at the observatory. He made a mental note to be sure to ask for details on Tuesday.

•   •   •

When Tuesday morning rolled around and Ryan's alarm woke him before work, he was covered in sweat and his heart pounded against his ribs. He'd been dreaming about Heather again. This time when he'd proposed, he was naked and in front of all their watching friends. When she'd said "no" she'd pointed and laughed, joined by everyone he knew. Their cruel laughter echoed through the room. His mom had shaken her head and turned away, her lip curling in disgust. The alarm had been a game show buzzer for the wrong answer.

Despite the venue changing, the dream wasn't much different from the nightmare reality. No one else had witnessed his humiliation, but he'd caught Heather cheating. In the subsequent fight, she'd laughed and said she would have refused his proposal. She'd lived with him for two years, but it turned out she'd never loved him. He hadn't expected the words that followed and tore through his soul. "Are you kidding me? I'd never marry an unfeeling bastard like you." It had shocked him to his core. He'd worked hard to create a better life for the two of them, but she'd only felt neglected.

He hadn't trusted himself since. His perception of reality and where he fit in relation to others must not be accurate. Shouldn't he have seen it coming instead of being blindsided? Perhaps that was why he worked so hard now. It wasn't enough to think he was working long hours; they had to be excessive to impress the partners.

He hopped in the shower, determined not to think about Heather anymore or to allow lingering thoughts of her to ruin his morning. It worked because his day went as they most often did, spent writing briefs that those above him on the food chain would take credit for until he left work at eleven fifty to meet Nick, as promised. They'd agreed to meet before the downtown lunch rush.

Nick was seated when he arrived at the hole-in-the-wall sushi spot they favored. His friend looked stressed; his forehead creased more than it should be at thirty-one years of age. Did he also look that weary?

"What's up?" Ryan slid into his seat after placing his order at the counter.

"I might need new friends," said Nick. "Ones willing to spend time with me."

"We can't all be that bad," said Ryan as he sipped his ice water.

"Between you and Kat, it's a tie." Nick held his hands up as though he surrendered.

"Kat, the bubbly elementary school teacher you tried to set me up with right after university? Didn't she marry some uptight guy named Matt or Mark or something? You haven't mentioned her in years. I assumed you'd lost touch. What's she doing wrong? Working too hard, like me?" He threw that out there, knowing that was why Nick worried. Broken-hearted Ryan, who lived at the office and had no life.

"Her Mark died two years ago. A heart attack at work. A heart condition that nobody knew about. He keeled over one day. They'd been married less than a year." Nick frowned and looked out the window.

Ryan felt like shit for not remembering. He recalled hearing about the tragedy. He hadn't meant to shove his foot in his mouth. "That's horrible. How does that make her a terrible friend?" He didn't see the connection, but his heart went out to the poor girl. They might have something in common now, if they hadn't in the past. She'd seemed like someone whose life had always been perfect.

"She seemed devastated and wanted to be alone, so I gave her space. I tried to reconnect a few times, but kept getting the brush off. Nobody had seen her in ages. We hadn't spoken in forever, and I thought she might need someone to talk to or hang out with, so I tried again." Nick's voice sounded strained, and he poured himself another steaming cup of green tea.

Ryan sat up straight. Nick seldom showed this much emotion. Perhaps he needed a friend to talk to if something was troubling him.

"What happened?"

Nick hesitated before speaking. "A couple of weeks ago, I got pushy and Kat and I made plans. When she blew me off, I checked on her and found her passed out dead drunk on the floor. She'd smashed her forehead, given herself a lump the size of an egg." He swallowed and looked out the window, his eyes moist.

Ryan pretended not to notice. Finding a friend in that condition would be difficult.

"That doesn't sound like the person you tried to convince me to date," said Ryan with a frown. He hoped it wasn't a setup now. She sounded like a real mess. At least he was productive in his heartache. He'd never been in better shape and had billed an extra four hundred hours last year. "If I recall, you warned me she was almost too happy and positive, if that's a thing."

"Not the case now. It wasn't then either, but I figured that would be your first impression because that's the face she shows to the world. The thing is, that isn't even the worst."

Ryan waited.

"I went back a couple of mornings later, and we talked. What I'd seen was the tip of the iceberg. I read between the lines and became horrified. It's like she's a different person. She drinks until she blacks out every night every weekend. For two years. How could I not have noticed?"

"You have your own life," said Ryan. "We're all busy. She probably didn't want you to know. If she hid it from you, maybe she hid it from everyone." She sounded like a disaster. He grimaced to himself; to be honest, he was similar.

"She hasn't lost her job because nobody knows or cares what she does on weekends and holidays. She's kept it secret because she holds it together during the week."

"It could be worse. She might have lost her job."

Nick shrugged. "It's bad enough. We made plans for last Friday night. She forgot and was smashed by the time I got to her house an hour after she got home. She didn't remember talking to me the previous weekend. I have to do something."

"You aren't her babysitter. It's been like two years. Isn't it time she pulled up her big-girl pants and moved on with her life?" Was that advice intended for himself too, to deal with his problems and move on? Ryan flattened his mouth into a frown.

"Easier said than done. When she doesn't want me to interfere, it kinda sucks. She's trying to drink herself to death. She didn't use to drink more than the odd hard lemonade at a barbeque."

"Maybe you saw her on a bad day?" said Ryan.

"Every Friday, Saturday, and Sunday? That's a lot of bad days."

"I can't picture that," said Ryan. "Thanks," he said to the server who dropped off their orders. He poured soy sauce into a dish and separated his chopsticks.

"Will you help me?" Nick dipped his sashimi in soy. "I was hoping you would come hiking with us, make it a group thing. Jake will come too when he's free. There's two coming Sundays when I'm busy with work commitments, and I need someone who will get her out of her house, whether or not she wants to."

"Maybe she wants to wallow," said Ryan as he ate. He didn't mean to sound unsympathetic.

"It's been two years. I don't know where the hell her family has gone, but they aren't helping. She's isolated and alone. That isn't good for anyone."

"Okay." Ryan's heart wasn't in it, but he owed Nick. Nick was awesome and had taken care of everyone. Back in their university days, they used to joke, "Nick's your buddy, Nick's your pal, Nick won't make you clean it up if you puke in his car." Nick helped people, and it appeared Kat was his new project, and Ryan owed him for kicking his ass into gear when Heather left.

"Thanks," said Nick as he popped another chunk of California roll into his mouth.

"So, let's hear about this discovery," said Ryan, switching to a happier topic. He wanted to show that he was a decent friend.

"It's that asteroid they're talking about on the news. Did you notice its name?"

Ryan shook his head. "Haven't there been like six already this year?"

Nick laughed. "Nope. Three. But the recent one, the one they're talking about this week, it's my discovery. Its name is the year, cause that's when I discovered it, and my initials. It isn't far away, but nobody had seen it before because the Sun was in the way. It's called 2025 NR. I found it and they've assigned me to watch it. I have to determine its final trajectory, where it will go after it passes Earth, and if it will be back."

"Is it one that will make that Sentry list you mentioned, the one that ranks potential threats?" Ryan leaned back to listen to his friend.

Nick shifted forward with a smile. "It's over 800 meters..."

• • •

Findings by Nick Rhodes as of April 15, 2025
I discovered 2025 NR on April 12, 2025, using a camera mounted on a telescope.
Preliminary Findings:
Estimated diameter: 825 m +/- 100 m or 0.825 km +/- 0.100 km
Estimated speed: 23.95 km/s +/- 5.0 km/s
Initial threat assessment: Add to the Sentry Table as a precaution.

<u>Recommended Action</u>: Further monitoring to increase data.

<u>Conditions affecting visibility</u>: weather, position relative to the Sun, phase of the Moon

Assess asteroid orbit for a minimum of fourteen days.

<u>Follow-up</u>: Observations after the initial window to increase the accuracy of orbit determination.

Calculate if, when, and where the orbital may intersect with Earth in the future (as defined by within the next 200 years).

Conclusion: There isn't enough data to make an estimate of the probability of an impact event on Earth.

CHAPTER 3: KAT

Kat waited on her couch, her knee bouncing and worrying at her lip as she thought about today's excursion. Nick was bringing a friend. He'd explained over the phone that his buddy Ryan worked too hard and needed to get out. She remembered the name, but they hadn't met. Nick had wanted to match them up eight years ago, but she'd just met Mark and turned down the suggestion.

The first hike had been for herself and Nick. They'd been gone for most of the day, driving toward Mount Baker National Forest, and they'd hiked a trail that Nick had chosen. Afterward, they'd gone for dinner, and Kat hadn't had a drink. She supposed she could have had one with dinner, but it didn't tempt her when she was with Nick. Drinking was something she did alone. She'd returned home to a bubble bath, a luxury she hadn't indulged in for far too long, then gone to bed with sore muscles, exhausted. Monday morning had been more tolerable without a hangover.

Her phone chimed with a text from Nick. *"We're here."*

She groaned, grabbed her daypack, and collected two bottles of iced water from the counter for her pack and another from the fridge. She checked she had extra Tylenol in her pocket. After being alone so long, it seemed odd to have plans for the second weekend in a row. Often, she went months without a social commitment. This was the fourth time in nine days.

Nick had arrived Friday night, the new ritual. She smiled, thinking of their evening. It hadn't been exciting, but it had meant a lot to both of them. She'd foregone drinking that night and he'd brought dinner. After they'd eaten, they'd watched the latest Marvel movie on Netflix. Nick's boyfriend, Jake, was a firefighter and worked Friday nights, leaving Nick free.

Saturday, she was left to her own devices, and she'd had a few drinks, but hadn't finished the bottle. A small accomplishment, nevertheless, it was something. No matter how her stomach churned, Sunday was for hiking. She was determined that she wouldn't cancel; it wouldn't be fair to Nick. Sometimes Jake planned to come if he was free, as well as this Ryan, who Nick assured her wasn't a set-up, just also in need of weekend outings.

Her head throbbed from yesterday's drinking. She remembered little after late Saturday morning. She'd woken up this morning on the kitchen floor, her cheek stuck to the tile. It wasn't the first time, but it bothered her more than usual. A shower had worked wonders, and she felt almost human, despite the pounding. She downed two glasses of water to clear her head. The third water bottle was for the car. She wanted to ensure she was hydrated for hiking.

She tied her hiking shoes and locked the door as she left. Despite herself, she was curious about Ryan. He'd been Nick's long-time friend, and she'd heard of him several times over the years. He was a lawyer, but she didn't know what kind of law he practiced. That kind of job sounded tedious, but to each their own. She trotted out to the orange SUV where Nick was at the wheel.

The passenger seat was empty, for which she was thankful. She'd get motion sick in the back seat on the windy roads off the highway. Ryan sat in the back on her side, her view blocked by her seat. Her first impression was that he was tall and had short hair somewhere between blond and brown. She didn't think they'd met, but she couldn't be sure because he was looking at his phone. She didn't glance at him more than once.

"Thanks for driving." She slid in, putting on her work persona for the benefit of the stranger in the back. "I'm Kat." She spoke over her shoulder toward the back seat.

"Ryan," said the voice behind her. "Checking my emails one last time before we leave the city."

His voice was flat and disinterested. He must be clear it wasn't a set-up, too.

"How's asteroid watch?" she said to Nick, dialing back the fake cheer.

"I've got more data, but I haven't run it through the machines for analysis yet. That's my plan on Tuesday, but it's a big one." He frowned, then glanced in the mirrors and pulled out.

Sometimes she had trouble reading people, but his eyes looked strained and tired. Perhaps he didn't want to talk about work today. It had been keeping him busy all week.

"I thought we'd go toward Baker again. Got another trail marked that opened this week. First hikers of the season. Listed as hard, but we're up for it."

Kat wasn't up for a strenuous hike, but she didn't argue. After liking the outing more than expected last week, she'd enjoyed having something to look forward to this week besides a gin and tonic, or six.

They drove for a couple of hours without a lot of chatter. Ryan seemed unfriendly and Nick wasn't his usual self, choosing to be quieter, perhaps overtired from work. The equivalent time spent with her mother and sister would have been more difficult to sit in recovery mode while the Tylenol did its magic.

Once, she would have filled the silence with stories about her fifth graders and questions about the hike, but now it was more effort than she wanted to expend. Being social took a toll. She closed her eyes, sipped water, and listened to the music Nick had chosen as today's road trip playlist. He'd always liked to make a list for each excursion. She'd forgotten that until last week's upbeat driving mix. Today's selection was more mellow for which she was grateful.

It was already warm when they stopped at the end of a rocky, bumpy road filled with potholes. They parked by the side of the road at the trailhead in the pull-out next to an open area filled with baby fir, spruce trees, and leafy bushes. They got out, and she slathered herself with sunscreen, using the window as a mirror. Stowing her half-full water bottle, she put on her hat and backpack. Her pack was light, with just her phone, keys, water, and lunch.

Kat would have been happy to take the rear, but Nick said, "Lead the way. You set the pace and we'll try to keep up." She wasn't fooled. They were in better shape and if she went first, they wouldn't leave her behind.

She glanced at Ryan as he came around the back of the SUV. "You don't mind?"

He shrugged.

She examined him for the first time and felt like someone had punched her in the gut. He was gorgeous, with golden-brown hair and a body that looked hard and fit; like a trained athlete with defined muscles everywhere she could see. His eyes were startling, a mismatched pair: one blue, one hazel. It was difficult to look him in the eye without catching her breath. She felt like an idiot to have such a strong physical reaction to someone she'd just met. Her cheeks burned, but she hoped he didn't notice. She was the slightest bit disappointed Nick wasn't arranging anything date-like. She almost gave Ryan a genuine smile instead of her patented fake grin. Hoping to center herself, she turned toward the trailhead.

The mountain trail started in the clear-cut area but was soon forested and shady as they headed to the Hidden Lake Lookout. They passed a couple of other groups of hikers stopped for water breaks.

Kat set a quick pace to start, not wanting to hike with strangers or be forced to go slow. The footing was uneven as they crossed a creek and climbed up the slope. She slowed just enough to place her feet with care when the footing became rougher. Once past the forested section of conifers and alders, the terrain became rocky, and the vista opened up. She could see a long way. She liked the varied terrain and appreciated the beauty as she climbed. The mountains were peaceful and undemanding.

Though it was late April, patches of snow littered the ground and, in the shade, still piled several feet deep. Ice crystals sparkled where they were caught by the sun, and slushy bits melted into the mud. They passed through clusters of granite slabs and alpine meadows, turning emerald green with recent growth. Later in the summer, they'd be filled with a riot of bright purple, pink, red, and orange, like the alpine areas where she and Nick used to hike.

Those had been happy days, and she wasn't sure why they'd stopped, but then an onslaught of less pleasant memories swept over her, overwhelming her with shame. She and Mark had always been busy with one of his projects and there'd never been time. Why had she let him dictate who her friends were? She didn't like to think of Mark and their troubles. He'd been controlling; it had been disguised by good humor and affection, but somehow, he'd always gotten his way. Strange that it had escaped her notice.

They stopped after a few miles to admire Mount Baker from a viewpoint while Kat reached for her water. Sweat drenched her clothes since she was unaccustomed to exercise. She gulped down her icy water, her face burning. It must be rosy from the exertion of the steep climb. Her heart thumped against her ribs, a hard rhythm that matched her gasping breath. The altitude made a difference. That, and she was out of shape.

She glanced at her companions. Nick didn't seem to have broken much of a sweat, though his cheeks were pink. Ryan looked like he was out for an easy Sunday stroll in the park. He didn't have even a sheen of sweat, and his breathing was normal. He took a quick drink and looked impatient to continue, pacing up the path ten feet to wait while she caught her breath. She lifted her chin, determined to increase the pace for the second half.

They hiked onward and found a shady section where the snow and ice lay thicker across the trail, reaching down the slope like a tentacle from the mountain's glacier above. If it hadn't been for the packed, dirty footprints through the ice, Kat would have been nervous. She had to be careful on the treacherous icy piece. This section would have been impossible earlier in the season.

It was early afternoon when at last they scrambled through a saddle between two peaks and found themselves with stunning views down to Hidden Lake and from Mount Rainier to Mount Baker, with a multitude of lesser peaks between.

It had been three hours since they'd left the roadside, and she was ready for lunch. This was an out-and-back hike, rather than a loop, and should be faster going downhill on the return. Her knees and ankles might feel it tonight and her butt was already sore from the sections that had been steep.

"Let's eat." Nick parked himself on one of the flat faces of a gray boulder overlooking the incredible view.

Ryan sat on his other side, and they unpacked their food while Kat sat apart on a different rock to their right, preferring space to being crowded together. The view from her vantage was no less spectacular. Her lungs burned, her legs felt like rubber, and she was glad for a break. Perhaps she would have done better if she hadn't been hungover. She was glad she'd made the effort to come, even if she wasn't looking forward to the descent.

An inquisitive chipmunk scooted around the base of the rock the men sat on. She said nothing but observed as it advanced in small bursts of movement. She flicked a few breadcrumbs in its direction and watched as it collected the tidbits. In the distance, a trio of birds circled below. It was like she was also in the sky.

She inhaled and took in the breathtaking view as she ate. The air was chillier than expected at this elevation as she cooled down. She wished she'd worn long pants or had another layer to wear while she sat and made a note to locate her zip-off convertible pants and a light hiking shirt with long sleeves for next time. Her old motto had been: wear layers. It was always colder than expected on a mountain during a break. She was already looking forward to next time.

She adjusted her waistband; she also needed a belt. Her hiking shorts were loose, and she'd lost weight. She'd never been so thin before, the result of too many skipped meals. Being on the mountain made her feel more relaxed than she'd been in years. She would try harder to be healthy and social. If it was difficult to do for herself, at least Nick would be pleased.

She leaned forward. "Ryan, have you been here before?" She broke the silence as she finished her sandwich and started on her cut-up strawberries. She wasn't making small talk, but was interested. Nick was one of the select people with whom she'd always felt herself, like there was no need to conform to a particular ideal. She extended that to Ryan almost without thinking. She was too exhausted to put on a show or mask.

Ryan shook his head and took a bite of his second sandwich. He seemed to be a man of few words. Perhaps he wasn't enjoying the hike. It was difficult to tell what he was thinking. If she concentrated, she could read some people; perhaps his experience as a lawyer helped keep his face from showing his thoughts. Still, his nonverbal dismissiveness put her teeth on edge. If she could attempt to be friendly, why couldn't he be civil?

"Jake and I came here two or three years ago, but in September," said Nick. "The meadows were insane. We might have to return in late summer."

"Count me in," she said, taking a bite. "Remember the bright red paintbrush and different purple lupins on Mt. Rainier about ten years ago? That's one of my favorite memories." She disliked thinking about the past, but leap-frogging over the Mark years wasn't so bad. A lump formed in her throat. She'd had a full life before marrying him. Why had she fallen apart without him? She didn't want to think about Mark, but she needed to try harder to enjoy her life.

They reached the car by late afternoon, and Kat's whole body was warm and thrummed with that post-exercise feeling. Her calf muscles were tight and on fire, but in a good way. She stretched, feeling self-conscious since Ryan was watching with an amused glance. She grit her teeth so she didn't say something rude. Perhaps he thought her a wimp whose hiking was too slow for him. It was odd, but she wanted to improve his opinion of her next time out.

"Going to be stiff tomorrow?" he said with a smirk and raised eyebrow.

She clenched her jaw tighter at his tone.

He might be beautiful, fit with broad shoulders and those disconcerting eyes, but he was annoying. He was also about six foot four and in another climatic zone. Somewhere with an arctic chill. Not once had he initiated a conversation, even if they'd been together for a solid eight hours and her only attempt had been shut down.

At dinner on the road home, she ordered lemonade instead of an alcoholic drink. Nick had an iced tea and glared at Ryan when he ordered a craft beer. She didn't care if Ryan drank; it had nothing to do with her. She arrived home and didn't take down the remainder of last night's bottle of gin. Leaving it in the cupboard, she soaked in the tub with a favorite book she hadn't read in a long time. Even if Ryan had been unfriendly, her excursion had been fantastic. Tears pricked her eyes, and she couldn't keep them away. She needed more weekends like this.

● ● ●

Findings by Nick Rhodes as of April 29, 2025

2025 NR was discovered on April 12, 2025. We monitored it an additional fourteen days with a telescope-mounted camera every three hours while in range.

Findings:

Estimated diameter: 900 m +/- 25 or 0.900 km +/- 0.025 km

Estimated speed: 26.22 km/s +/- 5.0 km/s

Initial threat assessment: we have added 2025 NR to the Sentry Table as a precaution. Rank eighth in concern.

Recommended Action: Further monitoring to increase data.

Report forwarded to superiors with a recommendation to speak to the government liaison with all relevant information.

<u>Conditions affecting visibility</u>: weather, position relative to the Sun, phase of the moon. Orbit remains difficult to calculate with precision. Assess asteroid orbit for another fourteen days. Seems to be both larger and faster than the original estimate. Possibly increasing in measurable speed.

Priority. Continue to follow-up observations after the initial window to increase the accuracy of orbit determination.

Send information to observatories in other parts of the world for additional monitoring capability and independent analysis.

Calculations indicate orbit will intersect Earth's orbit within the next forty to fifty days. Location and number of million miles away cannot be determined.

Conclusion: There is a minor concern that there could be a near miss or an impact event on Earth.

CHAPTER 4: RYAN

After they dropped Kat off, Nick turned to Ryan. "What do you think? Will you help?"

"She seems all right. Hard to believe you found her passed out on her floor only a couple of weeks ago. She looks too uptight to get blotto." He regretted uttering the uncharitable words as soon as they emerged; he didn't believe them. On the other hand, he had to admit, she'd looked delicious. He'd admired her ass as she climbed uphill, like a fine piece of art. Not for touching, just for display.

With rosy cheeks and hair disheveled by the breeze, he'd found her damn attractive, but he sure as hell wouldn't share that with Nick. He wasn't looking for his friend's interference or encouragement either. Ryan had no intention of acting on his attraction. Romance was the furthest thing from his mind, and he suspected it wasn't on hers either. Her cheery exterior hadn't fooled him. Her smiles had never reached her eyes. It was like she'd forgotten how to have fun.

"This is good for her. Next week Jake is hiking, but the week after I have an out-of-town meeting and Jake has to work," said Nick with a grimace. "Can you plan a hike for you two? I'll make sure she won't back out. You'll just have to collect her and hike."

To meet his personal quotas, Ryan would have to stay late a few extra nights at work, but he'd done that this week as well. He wanted to break twenty-four hundred billable hours this year. He was angling for a huge Christmas bonus, and wanted to have such a strong case for making partner they couldn't put it off another year. Not that being a junior partner would change his life, but it was a milestone accomplishment. Something he needed to keep as a sign of progress. He hadn't needed markers until Heather left, but he didn't want his life to be meaningless.

He'd promised to be helpful. "Sure." Ryan shrugged. He'd do this for Nick.

* * *

Ryan bowed out of hiking the next weekend with Kat, Jake, and Nick on Sunday, but swore on his mother's grave and the head of his unborn children that he would be available the following week. He wouldn't let Nick down. His friend had enough on his plate.

The following weekend, Nick had a classified meeting scheduled with government officials about his asteroid, some kind of briefing. His superiors had included him because he was the expert. Of course, Nick wasn't at liberty to share details with a civilian like himself, but Nick's elusive responses and tense tone caused Ryan's lawyer senses to go on alert and he couldn't help but wonder if there was a serious concern. Much more serious than Nick was saying. Briefing the president wasn't standard procedure for a discovery, no matter how interesting. The situation made Ryan uneasy, and he hated being in the dark about potential danger, so he played to his strength. Research.

Ryan started online. The asteroid had dominated the news again and was garnering international attention. It was the largest planetary body to come Earth's way since the extinction-level event that had taken out the dinosaurs over sixty million years ago.

He worried he was being an alarmist, but he decided to collect a more serious emergency preparedness kit, maybe store jugs of water and buy fuel and extra rations. The type of thing his survivalist grandfather would have done. If it turned out to be a false alarm, he'd take his stockpiled food and equipment when he went on vacation in early July. He was planning to leave town for a change of scene and head for his cabin in South Dakota. If he stayed in Seattle, he'd end up working from home.

Ryan pulled up outside Kat's place at nine a.m. sharp on Sunday. Parking, he realized there was a flaw in his planning. He didn't have her number. He couldn't text to say he was here. It shouldn't be a problem; the hike was at the usual time, but it wasn't like his friend to have forgotten important details. Meeting with the president must have thrown him. Nick's tired demeanor the last two times Ryan had seen him showed that he'd been more stressed than even exams and job interviews used to make him. He'd need to find time to talk with his friend so Nick could share or vent.

He waited a minute, but Kat didn't emerge from her house. Feeling self-conscious, he marched up to her door and knocked.

There was no answer.

He glanced at his phone. It was three minutes after nine. Nick's meeting started any second. Nick would kill him if he messed this up. Ryan sent a message to his friend, hoping it wasn't too late for assistance.

"Kat's not answering her door. Can I get her number?"

Nick's reply was immediate. He shared Kat Davies as a contact.

"Sorry, I forgot to share her information. This asteroid presentation has had me run off my feet all week. Wish me luck. I'll talk later. Thanks for doing this."

"Good luck with the meeting. We should go for drinks when you're less busy."

Ryan called Kat. No answer. He didn't leave a message. He stood on her porch for a minute, trying to decide what to do.

He wanted to leave, and irritation made him impatient. If the hike was canceled, he had work he could do. He didn't need this. He was about to turn toward his car when the memory of her desolate brown eyes flashed through his mind. If anyone understood the bleakness of heartbreak, it was him. That must be the reason that Nick had chosen him to do this. Not a setup, but perhaps someone who might understand what she was going through.

He sighed and rang the doorbell. There was no sign of movement inside. He tried the front door. It was unlocked.

Feeling like an intruder, he opened it and called, "Kat?"

No answer.

Breathing out a mouthful of air, he said, "Kat? It's Ryan. You ready to hike to Rachael Lake?" No sounds came from within the townhouse.

He stepped further inside, the awkward feeling intensifying.

An almost empty forty-pounder lay on the counter, the distinctive square bottle and blue color indicating that her preferred poison was gin. An end slice of lime lay on the cutting board beside it. He took a couple of steps farther. Half a dozen open cans of tonic sat beside the sink. Ryan frowned. It looked like she'd had a party last night.

A bright red puddle on the cutting board attracted his attention. Someone had cut themselves. Darker drops led in a trail across the room and down a hall where he assumed the bedroom and bathroom were located. He shouldn't continue, but she might be hurt or in trouble. Cursing Nick under his breath, he continued.

There were two doors, one on either side of the hall. He knocked on the left, praying he wouldn't have to pick Kat off the floor. He turned as the opposite door opened, releasing a blast of music from inside, and Kat screamed. She had a Band-aid wrapped around a finger on her right hand.

He backed up several steps at her angry expression. This looked bad. He was in her house and hadn't been invited.

"I'm sorry," Ryan said, stepping back into the living room. She was dressed for hiking and looked ready. She'd just been running a couple of minutes late and he'd made a mistake.

"What the hell are you doing in my house?"

"You didn't answer the door or your phone. I was looking for you." It sounded lame.

"And you assumed the worst." Her mouth twisted on her words.

He met her dark, blazing eyes with his own anger. "You were late, and I was trying to help. You didn't answer your phone and there's blood all over your kitchen floor. What was I supposed to think?"

"You thought I had passed out. Nick's charity case. I can't find my phone, but I'm ready otherwise. Crisis averted. Kat's not half dead and doesn't need your help."

Her eyes were bloodshot, but she'd showered. The wafting scent of her shampoo hit him in a wave. She smelled like citrus and vanilla, with a hint of summer flowers. In her righteous fury, she was stunning. It made his groin ache. He hadn't thought to take care of himself this morning, and his body was going to keep reacting to her presence.

Dressed in hiking-appropriate layers, Kat's hair was in a ponytail. She might have tied one on last night, but if it hadn't been for the carnage in her kitchen, he wouldn't have known. She was good at covering. For the first time, he was eager for their hike. For their sake, not for Nick's. His temper cooled.

"Didn't you see my water bottles and daypack by the door?" Her voice expressed irritation as she took a deep breath.

He shook his head. "I'm sorry. I shouldn't have worried."

"Damn right, you shouldn't. I'm not the one who's canceled twice."

Ouch. She had a point. Her voice was still sharp, but perhaps warranted.

"Ready then." He jingled the keys, feeling uncomfortable and hoping his attraction wasn't obvious.

She nodded, her eyes guarded, perhaps wondering if it was too late to back out.

Ryan turned for the door, wishing he hadn't entered without permission. "I'll leave you to find your phone and lock up. See you outside."

Minutes later, Kat emerged with her phone in her hand. She stood next to his SUV, and he opened the window. Her tense shoulders remained lifted.

"Everything okay?"

"Can I have a minute?" She held up her phone. "I just remembered it's Mother's Day. I should call my mom."

"Shit." He'd forgotten. "I need to make a call, too. Thanks." He opened his door. "You can have privacy in the car. I'll get out. I pace when I'm on the phone."

He hopped out and pulled up his mother's number. He steeled himself for a conversation, but she didn't answer. Instead, he left a message—short, sweet, and pretty standard. "Happy Mother's Day, Mom. Hope we have time to talk later. Going for a hike with a friend, but I'll call tonight after I get home. Hope you have a wonderful day." It was a relief to not have to speak.

He'd try to remember to call back, though it wouldn't be pleasant. Things had been worse than rocky between them for the last year. She'd been close to Heather and remained convinced that he'd done something stupid to drive his girlfriend away. She'd asked him several times if he'd cheated, which was preposterous. He wasn't that kind of guy. He'd told her the basics about what happened, and she didn't believe him. His mother had lunch with Heather every few weeks. When she'd dropped that tidbit last time they'd spoken, his vision had become a scarlet haze.

He took a deep breath and checked the car. Kat was still on the phone, crying.

He should stay out of it. He didn't know her and he sure as hell didn't like her, despite thinking she was stunning. She was a gigantic mess and prickly as a cactus this morning, but he didn't like to see anyone cry—it brought out his protective side.

He hesitated, opened the door, and slid behind the wheel, trying to catch her eye. She kept talking through her tears. You couldn't tell from her steady voice she was crying. She was acting like everything was fine.

"I said I'm sorry, mom. No, I didn't know you were having a special brunch party today. I'm sorry for interrupting your preparations. Yes, I understand why you didn't invite me. I'm sure you'll enjoy your day.

No, mom, you don't have to worry about me. I'm with a friend and we're going hiking. We made plans and are on the road."

There was a pause. "No, a friend of a friend. You remember Nick? One of his friends. I'm not driving, so I'm not in charge of that, mom. I just wanted you to know that I was thinking of you. No, I'm not trying to wangle an invitation and I'm not insulted. I get it. It's easier when I'm not there."

There was a long pause while her mom lectured her. He couldn't hear the words, but he recognized a guilt trip, having received them on multiple occasions. He couldn't make it worse, so he grabbed the phone from her, which earned him an open-mouthed stare.

"Hi. This is her friend, Ryan. It's my fault Kat had to call now. This is when I said I'd pick her up. I'd forgotten it was Mother's Day when we made plans weeks ago."

There was silence on the other end.

Then Kat's mother said, "You're real." From her tone, he guessed she was surprised.

"Of course, I'm real. There's a group of us hiking most Sundays."

"She can call me later. Tell her to do that if she can show some interest in my life."

Her nasty tone shocked him; his mother wasn't the only cold mom around. "Will do." He hung up the phone and handed it back to her. "Call her when you're home. She wants to hear about your hike."

Kat raised an eyebrow.

"Maybe take a picture or two and send them." He hesitated. "Why did she sound surprised, like she didn't think I was a real person?"

"I've been blowing her off for months. Said I was busy on weekends, but she was pretty sure I was lying. I was until the last month when it's been the truth."

"Why don't you want to see her?" The question slipped out before he thought. The answer was probably none of his business, so it surprised him when she answered.

"A bunch of reasons, but one is that they loved Mark and think he would want me to be happy, so they get my sister to try to set me up on blind dates. I'm not interested in dating. At all. So, I wouldn't go. My parents mean well, but I don't appreciate it when they're pushy and make me feel like shit about my choices. I haven't been easy the last while, but they believe nothing I say." Her tone was bitter. "If I won't take their advice, then they don't want me around."

He shot her a look, surprised to find her family's lack of understanding was another commonality they shared. Guessing there was more to the story, but not wanting to pry, he let it drop. There was always more with family. He opened the glove box and handed her napkins to wipe her tears.

"Ready?"

She nodded and took a deep breath. "Tell me about Rachael Lake. I've never been."

Grateful for the change of subject, he told her about the hike and Glacier Peak Park.

"Rachael Lake is off the Snoqualmie Pass. I thought we might like something challenging."

He started the car and headed for the interstate.

• • •

The planned hike was eleven miles on an out and back trail. Like the last time, two weeks ago, it was rated as difficult and had just opened for the season. The online information said the trail was best from June until October. May was almost June. It should be fine. If it wasn't, they could turn around and go for lunch somewhere else. The majority of the trail was supposed to be wooded. The only steep section should be the end if they tried for the mountain peak and Rachael Lake.

They couldn't drive as far as he'd planned because the mud became too deep and too thick for them to reach the parking lot, even with four-wheel drive. Ryan pulled over, and they hiked an extra couple of miles to the trailhead. He appreciated that there were no complaints. If it'd been Heather, she'd have whined all morning.

The beginning of the trail wasn't difficult, though they got mixed up twice, and floundered off the path. He consulted his downloaded map to get them more or less back on track. They crossed several slippery creek beds and snowy sections, but they were wearing proper hiking shoes and had no trouble. The route was passable if challenging.

A nagging thought about trekking poles or spikes for their shoes occurred to him as they continued and the trail grew more treacherous. He took the lead to test their footing. If the snow and ice were solid enough to hold his weight, Kat should be fine. He was debating whether to call it when there was a yelp behind him.

He turned to see Kat sliding down the slope, one hand scraping the snow, as she scrambled for something to grab. She gave another louder yelp as her ankle rolled and she slid into a tree well ten feet down, grabbing the top of the young tree to halt her sliding. Her eyes were wide and her breathing was ragged.

"You all right?" He tried to project calm. Her eyes filled with tears, but to give her credit, she didn't break down. She was tougher than she looked.

She nodded. "I just slipped." She worried her lower lip as she fought to catch her breath.

He hoped she wasn't injured. She didn't put weight on her ankle and bit her lip to keep from crying out.

He backtracked down the trail so he was at her level and inched toward her across the icy snow. "I'm ready to turn back. Conditions are worse than I expected." It had been a mild winter and warm spring; he'd expected more melt and less snowpack.

"I can do it," she said, her chin lifting in determination.

He raised an eyebrow in surprise. She hadn't put weight on that ankle yet. She clenched her jaw, dealing with the pain. He wasn't blind. Damn. He shouldn't have pushed so hard. He'd set the pace today. They were close to the Lake at the top, but the section that remained was steep and icy, and now she was injured. His first time in charge wasn't a resounding success.

He and Kat hadn't exchanged more than a dozen comments since they'd left the car, but now he needed more information. He'd try to be more specific.

"How's your ankle?"

"I'll be fine." Her injured foot was freed from the tree well, but she still wasn't putting weight on it.

That still didn't answer his question. "Let's turn around. We can eat in the last sunny patch. See how we feel after. It wasn't far."

"You sure? I don't want to ruin your hike." She straightened up, testing her foot, and winced when it touched the ground. "You wanted to get to the peak." She hopped a couple of steps. "You hungry?"

"My hike isn't ruined. I've enjoyed myself, but I could eat a horse, so yes. Lunch, then decision time." He stepped toward her and reached out his arm, which she ignored. She took two steps, then reached for his hand to anchor herself.

She released his arm once back on solid ground and they made their way to the chosen place to eat. Every step looked painful, but he let her navigate the trail on her own terms since she was being proud, or maybe stubborn.

They ate lunch near the trail, sitting on a trunk of a fallen tree. The wind had picked up, and the sun had disappeared behind growing patches of dark gray cloud that circled the summit. Her lips had turned blue, and she was shivering.

"We should turn back," said Ryan. "Regardless of your ankle, bad weather is coming. I don't want to be stuck in the open. The wooded part below will be bad enough."

"Do you think it'll snow?" She scanned the sky. "It's the middle of May."

Thick dark clouds spread overhead, and she was working over her bottom lip. He hated that something supposed to be fun and relaxing had become something stressful.

"It might. Are you almost ready? We need to get back to the trees before the storm picks up." He packed the remains of his lunch. He could finish his sandwich as they walked.

Their downhill pace was slow with all the creeks, rocky terrain, and slick sections with ice, now wet with rain. He helped where he could, but unless he carried her five or six miles, she had to do this herself. A few lazy flakes of snow twirled to the ground, but soon became sleet and rain. They pulled up their hoods and trudged onward. Ryan sent Kat ahead of him so he wouldn't go too fast and leave her behind. Once she stumbled, and he reached to steady her arm, but she caught herself without help and continued. She had a pronounced limp. Her ankle must hurt like hell. He admired her grit.

It took four hours to return to the car from the point where she'd slipped. There'd been no other hikers all day. Perhaps others had realized the trail was still treacherous. For the last hour, they'd left the threat of snow behind and walked through chilly drizzle. He would kill for a hot tea. It soaked him through his Gore-Tex coat and hiking shoes, and his icy toes squelched as he walked. He kept waiting for tears or complaints from Kat, but there hadn't been a word. She seemed to have gone inward to deal with the pain and arduous task. If he'd known her better, he'd have offered to carry her on the last part. As it was, she'd just refuse.

When they arrived at the car, he popped open the hatch. He threw his pack into the back and patted the edge of SUV. "Hop up. I want to look at your ankle." He grabbed a towel he kept in the back and dried his hair, then threw her the towel. She caught it with a small smile.

She didn't move, though she unclipped her pack and chucked it next to his.

"It's fine." She patted her wet hair and tossed the towel in beside his pack.

"You've been tough, but we're back now. Hop up. Let's take your boot off and I'll wrap it." He pulled out his first aid kit and unzipped it.

She hesitated, then did as he suggested.

"If we remove the boot off, it might not go back on." He kept his tone matter of fact. She seemed to respond better when he did.

She nodded; her shoulders set stubbornly. At her side, her fist clenched. He couldn't read the expression in her fathomless dark eyes. He cradled her foot between his hands and held her heel with one hand, unlacing the boot with the other, then eased off the boot. She winced twice, but it didn't prepare him for the sight of her swollen, purple foot. He let out a whistle. When he met her eyes this time, they were full of tears.

"That's ugly. I'm sorry we came somewhere so icy. I should have given more credence to the seasonal warnings." He couldn't believe she'd walked on with that. It might be broken. At the very least, it was a nasty sprain.

Her eyes appeared enormous in her pale face and showed signs of the strain it had taken to get off the mountain.

He peeled off her hiking socks and got her to wiggle her toes before he wrapped her ankle with a tensor bandage. "Tell me if it goes numb or is too tight. We should get a doctor to check your ankle in Everett on the way out. We'll hit a quick drive-thru for food first so we don't starve. I don't know about you, but I'm ravenous. Lunch seems too long in the past." He released her foot and supported her as she slid down.

"There goes the rest of your evening." She took one hopping step, her injured foot in the air. An involuntary moan escaped her lips.

He scooped her up, one arm behind her back, the other behind her knees, and carried her to the passenger seat so she wouldn't have to walk. She stiffened up but didn't protest. Her vanilla smell washed over him at the close contact. He tried not to breathe it in.

"I don't mind," he said, surprising himself. "I have nothing better to do." He wasn't even being polite. He was ahead with his work and he didn't mind the thought of spending extra time in her company.

Findings by Nick Rhodes as of May 10, 2025
2025 NR was discovered on April 12, 2025. We have monitored it with a telescope-mounted camera every three hours while in range for the last month.

Findings:

Estimated diameter: 900 m +/- 25 or 0.900 km +/- 0.025 km

Estimated speed: 27.05 km/s +/- 3.0 km/s

<u>Threat assessment</u>: 2025 NR is fast and large. They added it to the Sentry Table as a precaution. **Upgraded threat assessment from eighth to first.**

Since monitoring began, 2025 NR's orbit has been determined to be much closer than expected. It will be less than 2 million miles away when it passes Earth, well inside the less than five million miles to fall into the list of potential hazards.

<u>Recommended Action</u>: **Trajectory correction needed.**

DART-Double Asteroid Redirection Tests were inconclusive when attempted in April 2021, February 2022, and July 2024. As part of our Earth Defense Systems, a spacecraft already in orbit could smash into the asteroid to change its course. We have scant data on this method and some NASA pilots have concerns that this action could increase the chance of a collision because of the unpredictable nature of an object in motion, such as an asteroid. The size of this asteroid makes this method difficult. The force required may be too great. We will consult experts and run simulations ASAP.

A surface nuclear explosion in space. Could fragment the immense asteroid. Potential to minimize damage on any single impact, but dangerous to consider as fragments of unknown sizes could rain down over much of the northern hemisphere.

Coordinate with Russia and China to determine the best course of action.

Presidents and world leaders should be involved in emergency preparedness. Avoid the media and do not inform the public, or it could lead to widespread panic.

Conclusion: There is a serious concern that **in less than two weeks there could be an impact event on Earth.** The asteroid is massive enough that a full impact would be a catastrophic global event, rather than a regional disaster.

CHAPTER 5: KAT

Kat scowled as she bumped her injured foot on a desk in her class, biting back a curse. Since the injury, she sat at her desk or leaned against a stool for much of her teaching, even if her usual style had her on her feet almost all day. She hadn't broken her ankle, but the pain of the sprain kept her awake at night if she didn't take Tylenol. She hadn't remembered to tell Nick about her mishap and was a little surprised he hadn't asked about her hike with Ryan. He'd been busy all week, and she looked forward to pizza with him after work on Friday. He needed a chance to relax and reduce his stress level.

To reduce her drinking, she hadn't replenished her weekend gin and tonic supplies. She had enough for Saturday if she chose. Having a choice about drinking or not drinking made her feel powerful. For too long, it hadn't seemed like a choice, but a necessity.

She'd just reached home on Friday evening when her phone chimed. It was Nick. Her face lit up until she read his message.

"Sorry. Can't get away. Flying me to London on short notice. You should call Ryan."

Her heart plummeted. In the last month, she'd depended on Nick and Friday dinner as a reason to delay drinking until Saturday. It wasn't fair to rely on him so much and she'd already decided to make this week about him. It seemed she wouldn't have a chance.

"Good luck in London. Is there anything you can share?" Despite her news avoidance, she'd seen and heard snippets about his asteroid. Nick's sudden trip to London made her nervous, raising internal flags about what that might mean. She remembered enough about his job to know that this was something unusual. Had he determined the chances of an impact with Earth? Nick had said nothing he shouldn't, but the sense that it was serious, lingered.

"Ryan asked good questions, but I couldn't answer. I could be fired. Call him. Please."

She sucked in a deep breath. Text messages were sometimes difficult to interpret. They could be blunt or lack emotion, but Nick's message seemed full of emotion and hidden meaning. It was uncharacteristic of someone who was honest and open with information, knowing she often took things literally. The hair on the back of her neck rose. She shouldn't ignore his request. If he said to call Ryan, she would, because she trusted Nick's advice. Her pulse fluttered as she stared at the phone and she rubbed her sweaty palms on her knees. Before she lost her courage or went inside and made herself a drink, she made the call with shaking hands.

He answered on the first ring. "Ryan here."

She almost hung up. What was she doing calling him at six o'clock on a Friday night? He would think she was desperate or lonely. He might be out with friends and she was interrupting. Her chest tightened, and she spun the ring from her grandmother on her right hand.

"This is Kat." She felt stupid. Her name would have been on his screen. She stuttered, but forced herself to continue. "This is going to sound weird and pathetic, but Nick canceled our plans tonight. He said I should call you." She still sounded lame, so she tried to make the request a pragmatic one. "I think his asteroid is a problem, and he mentioned you asked good questions."

"He said that?"

"He did." Seconds of awkward silence ticked by while she held her breath. Would Ryan answer?

"I asked him about putting together emergency supplies. Adding to my earthquake kit. Any interest in making one with me?"

A weight settled on her chest at his revelation. Her voice shook as she said, "That was your good question?"

"I also asked him if I should go on vacation to my cabin. Nick said that it was an excellent time for a holiday."

Her heart rate picked up and her words caught in her throat. "When did he say this?"

"Fifteen minutes ago. I think they're monitoring his calls."

She hadn't answered Ryan's question and didn't know what to say as the uncomfortable silence stretched with Nick's unspoken message hanging in the air between them. Their mutual friend had issued an indirect warning, but neither of them wanted to say it out loud. It would be too real if the words were uttered. Kat needed to process this information.

"How's your ankle?" Ryan spoke first, for which she was grateful. A safer topic.

"It's been better. I've stayed off it more than usual and taken Tylenol. It's more mauve than eggplant in color today." She could have kicked herself for launching into detail. He might be just being polite. It was a wonder she could speak; her brain was overloaded. She wanted to go inside, make a drink, and chug it down. Then three or four more. She wanted to be numb instead of a quaking mess, but if she started, she wouldn't stop at one drink. Her hands shook and her car seemed too cold despite the pleasant May evening. The threat from Nick's asteroid was real.

"I'm glad it's getting better."

"Maybe I'll buy stuff too. I could use an emergency kit." She felt ridiculous and her cheeks burned, but Ryan had spoken with Nick, and he already had one started. He wouldn't judge.

"I can be at your place in forty-five minutes if I leave now. Why don't we make it an hour and I'll bring dinner? We can make lists tonight and shop tomorrow."

This was a generous offer. They were the only ones who knew about the impending disaster and in this moment, they'd become a team. Her hesitation was brief.

"I'll get dinner. Pizza?" If she ordered and picked up the food, she wouldn't go inside her place and drink until the fear lessened. She replayed Ryan's words about a vacation in her head and swallowed her fear. A band tightened around her chest, limiting her air. Ryan was going to leave town, but she didn't have anywhere to go.

"Pizza's good. Any kind. I'm on the way to my car." Ryan's voice had a hollow quality. Maybe he was in a stairwell or an elevator. The line went dead. He hadn't said goodbye or see you later. That seemed to be like him, a little abrupt. Her mouth went dry.

She shouldn't ask Nick anything else. He couldn't tell her anyway, but she couldn't help herself as she opened up her messages.

"Thinking of going on holiday soon. Suggestions?"

"Great idea. You and Ryan should leave the city."

His reply seemed innocuous, and like she and Ryan were a couple that would vacation together, not acquaintances who'd hiked together twice.

"After school is out for the summer?" Her vacation was a week and a half away.

The three dots that meant he was typing appeared and disappeared several times. She chewed her lip until it hurt while she waited, unable to pry her eyes from the screen.

His reply came at last.

"Why wait?"

•   •   •

"Why wait?" said Ryan, when Kat showed him Nick's text.

They sat in her spartan living room, each with a pizza box in front of them on the coffee table. She hadn't bothered with plates, so they ate off napkins. She'd eaten three pieces of Hawaiian without tasting anything. Or was it four? She looked down to count.

"If this is nothing, I could lose my job if I take off." Her voice cracked. "What about yours?"

"I'm worried about work too, but Nick wouldn't say anything if it were nothing. We can't tell anyone. Maybe call in sick if you're worried, but I suspect it won't matter." He picked up his fifth piece of pizza and put it back down.

Kat's stomach churned thinking of all the people who could use a heads up: her family, her students and their families. Everyone. Not telling seemed unfair, but it might not matter. She couldn't explain what she suspected and be believed.

"He said to get out of town, but I don't have anywhere to go." Her voice shook. She didn't want Ryan to feel sorry for her, but she couldn't keep her fear inside.

"I'm going to my cabin." Ryan hesitated. "You could come."

Was he asking out of pity? Her head snapped up, but he wasn't looking in her direction as he reached for another slice of pepperoni.

"Is it nearby?"

"Near the Black Hills in South Dakota. I'm leaving Wednesday. That should be enough time."

She hesitated, reluctant to commit to drastic action. Wednesday was just five days from today. This was happening fast, like a runaway train bearing down on them. Time to hop aboard or jump off the tracks. She couldn't wrap her head around needing to make this decision, but if an asteroid was going to strike, she wanted to escape somewhere safe. How could she be living in a disaster movie? These things didn't happen in real life.

"You don't have to decide now. Just soon. I can't imagine the lid will stay on this much longer. Nick's been flown to London. My guess is that world leaders are having an emergency meeting, and the president wanted him to share his findings. They'll assign top scientists to it who'll have some idea how to solve this or get more accurate information. That's when the news will leak. My plan needs to be in motion before the media spills everything. Supplies could be hard to acquire and people might panic."

Kat visualized the insanity from the pandemic when there were shortages, hoarding, and opportunists. She swallowed her pride. "If I come, what should I bring?"

"The cabin is stocked with years' worth of food and survival gear, but we'll have to drive there. It's over 1200 miles away."

"What kind of cabin is stocked like that?" She cocked her head, her curiosity trumping her fear.

"My grandfather was a survivalist and bought a doomsday bunker in a resort in South Dakota back in 2020, during the pandemic. He left it to me in his will. I've used it as a cabin; a destination in the summer or when I take a week off work. There's an entire community of bunkers. They use most of them like cabins, vacation destinations, although there are some colorful full-time residents. I spent time there last summer, Thanksgiving, and again at Christmas."

His mouth turned down at the mention of Christmas. She got the feeling he'd gone alone. Maybe he'd also been through trauma. Someone good-looking and smart like Ryan wasn't usually single or alone for the holidays.

"I should bring whatever I might need on a road trip?"

He nodded. "I imagine this asteroid strike will be along the Ring of Fire or in the Pacific. Nick wouldn't say to leave the coast otherwise. He knows about my grandfather's cabin. They'd be concerned about tsunamis, earthquakes, and maybe volcanic activity. Anything like that could mess up the power grid, or gas supply, at least short-term. We will camp along the way, not hotels unless we're lucky. It could take longer than the usual two days to drive. Maybe closer to a week if we encounter problems and have to take a longer route. It's hard to know what to expect."

"All these dormant volcanoes, all the way down the coast..." She shivered.

"Imagine any of them becoming active or several. There could be a dozen volcanoes down the coast of the U.S." He listed several. "Mount Baker, Mount Rainier, Mount St. Helens, Crater Lake... not to mention the seismic activity that could happen all the way along the San Andreas fault."

He'd done his research. She'd studied Earth Sciences, but hadn't expected him to have that detailed knowledge. "News like that should be on every broadcast. The entire West Coast could be in danger." Her voice sounded too high and her stomach clenched. She couldn't eat anything else tonight as the food inside her sat like a stone.

He said nothing but stared at her, one blue eye and one hazel.

"I'll come." She bit her lip so hard that the metallic taste of blood flooded her mouth. "Count me in." Her voice grew stronger. "We can divvy up our supplies."

Ryan nodded. She started to get up to grab a notepad and pen, but he waved her down.

"You should stay off that foot. Where will I find them?"

She directed him to a drawer in the kitchen.

They made a list of supplies and divided them into three sections. One for outdoor and hiking gear, including a tent and freeze-dried food in case they ended up on foot. They both had backpacks, sleeping bags, and Thermarests as base equipment. Another list for the grocery store for car camping necessities and non-perishable, easy-to-transport food for a week of traveling. The third list was for hardware store items for odds and ends, like matches and water purification tablets.

The only costly item would be the tent, but it felt satisfying to be proactive.

Kat and Ryan planned and discussed what type of clothing and personal items to bring, taking several hours. They made an arbitrary decision to include a week's worth of underwear, hiking and rain clothes, clothes for warm weather and cold, a hat, and a jacket. They would limit the other clothing to a couple of changes of shirt, pants, and shorts, needing to pack light.

"Should I bring a suitcase?"

"We should both bring one. But if we end up leaving the car, we should be prepared to switch the essentials to the backpacks."

"An extra toothbrush doesn't take much space." She tried to lighten the mood with her offhand comment and was relieved to see a small smile reach Ryan's lips.

Kat avoided thinking about the underlying reason for the trip and the careful preparations, but late that night after Ryan had gone home, it was hard not to dwell on her fear. She tossed and turned, waking several times from nightmares that left her heart racing with a growing sense of dread.

Saturday after breakfast, she met Ryan outside when he pulled up in his black SUV. She'd gotten up early and was eager for action to take her mind off of Nick's cryptic warnings. They visited three outdoor stores before they found a three-person, four-season, lightweight tent. The two-person tents were too small for Ryan's enormous frame. Even the one they settled on would be cozy.

Ryan bought the tent, and she paid for the camp stove and a backpacking stove and pots. If they had to leave the car, she'd be grateful for another way to cook besides an open flame. She paid with her credit card with a stab of conscience. If the worst-case scenario played out, she would get everything for free. She couldn't afford to buy everything if the disaster came to naught, and she had to pay the bill. They stopped at a bank to use an ATM and take out cash. Buying the supplies had been fun, if she ignored the reason they were doing this. It felt strange to prepare for a disaster that nobody else knew about.

After shopping, she and Ryan stopped for tea. Standing in line at Starbucks, she spotted one of her current students. The little girl hadn't seen her and was with her dad and swinging his arm back and forth.

"Please, Daddy, can I have a frappuccino? Please, please." The little girl tilted her head and batted her eyelashes at her father.

Her father laughed and caught Kat's eye. He winked and whispered to his daughter. Sara's eyes rounded in wonder as she stared at Kat, unsure of what to make of seeing her teacher outside of school. Kat was used to this reaction from her students. It was like they thought she lived in the school full-time. Many couldn't imagine that she had a life and home.

Kat waved, smiling to herself as Sara's jaw dropped.

As she and Ryan left, a wave swept over Kat, almost knocking her over. How could she pretend nothing was happening and say nothing to the people she cared about? If the asteroid collided, people like Sara and her father could be hurt, or die. Even if they survived, their lives would change forever. Perhaps there was a way to tell people, to explain. But she didn't think she'd be believed. Everything about it was unbelievable.

Kat teared up as she got in the car. Sara was a sweet girl and her class was filled with children she cared about. Knowing she couldn't help was a torment that, if things came to fruition, would haunt her forever.

Back at her house, Ryan came inside to help repackage their gear and have dinner so they could set up the tent in the backyard.

"I feel guilty ordering-in two nights in a row," she said. "I cook through the week and live on leftovers on the weekend, but I'm out. I'll shop Monday night and get the rest of the fresh food."

Ryan shook his head. "The sooner the better. How's your ankle?"

She'd propped it on the couch. It throbbed and was a spectacular mottled purple with greenish edges on the swelling. She'd been on it all day, shopping, and it ached more than it had since Tuesday. She shrugged and grimaced at the same time.

"Let's get groceries tomorrow. I'll help. It'll be quicker and we won't hike this week, anyway. Nick's still gone, and your ankle isn't ready."

"That's a good idea." She wasn't keen to be on her foot anymore, but Ryan's offer of help made her feel productive. He'd done more than his share already in asking her to come.

Ryan helped repackage their gear, and she ordered food so they could set up the tent. Ryan spoke with ease about the trip or when discussing the merits of one tent versus another, but was still almost a stranger. He avoided topics that seemed personal and shared nothing about himself. She didn't care. He'd offered to include her on his trip and let her in his shelter. If the worst happened, being in the bunker might be a matter of life and death. She tried not to think too hard about the reason for their preparations.

Kat ran through what she knew about him. He'd mentioned that he was a corporate commercial litigator and that his grandfather had left him property. He was the same age as Nick and herself, give or take a year. Thirty. Maybe thirty-one. They'd gone to university at the same time. He didn't seem like a sociopath or a murderer.

"What about Nick and Jake?" she said before Ryan left Saturday night.

Ryan looked up with his mismatched eyes. The blue one looked frosty while the hazel one seemed to warm her inside. "I sent Jake the info about xTerra."

"X what?"

"The bunker complex with the cabin is called Vita xTerra. Look it up if you like." She made a mental note to do that later, once he'd gone.

"Did Jake reply?"

"Just a thanks. If he knows anything about the real danger, he isn't talking either."

"Do you think they'll try to meet us there?"

"I hope if the president is looking out for Nick, they will include Jake."

She looked at the food and equipment littering the floor of her living room. In four days, this would be packed, then they'd leave. The sense of dread had grown to the size of an elephant that sat on her chest, making it hard to breathe.

• • •

THE SEATTLE TIMES
ASTEROID STRIKE IMMINENT!

The world braces as this story breaks, the leak from our source having been confirmed. Our source is quoted as saying, "Early this morning, at nine a.m. GST on May 19th, a Double Asteroid Redirection Test, or

DART, was employed for the first time in real circumstances. Despite their best efforts, no appreciable change in trajectory was noted for the massive asteroid approaching Earth."

Seattle's Pacific Northwest Observatory discovered the incoming asteroid, 2025 NR, in April 2025. Since then, it has been determined that it has an orbit that will bring it much closer to Earth than the original estimates indicated.

In early May, they predicted the asteroid could come as close as two million miles away. Today, the world learns that the asteroid poses a direct threat to civilization. The severity of the effects of such an event is unknown, but the asteroid is estimated to be the size of the meteorite that caused an extinction-level event for the dinosaurs over sixty million years ago.

Officials in London attended an emergency meeting of world leaders from the G7 countries where the leaders of Russia, China, and Israel have also been invited. A joint action committee has been made of top scientists from these countries. Utilizing the International Space Station, or ISS, they launched a spacecraft toward 2025 NR in order to attempt its redirection.

Failure may have been because of the asteroid's erratic orbit, increasing speed, or immense size. With the failed DART, the leaders say that Plan B will take effect. The contingency plan is to launch a series of nuclear strikes from multiple locations across the globe. The hope is that they can break the asteroid into smaller pieces that will disintegrate upon entry into the Earth's atmosphere, eliminating the threat to humankind.

Everyone should prepare for possible power outages and short-term communication failures. Scientists from across the globe race to calculate the most dangerous zones of the world, but based on the countries at the emergency summit, the focus appears to be the northern hemisphere. With meetings led by the U.S., speculation is for a North American strike, so the people of the U.S. may need to prepare for an impact event and its aftermath. Sources close to the president could not be reached for comment.

Tomorrow's special disaster edition will focus on Nick Rhodes, the scientist who discovered 2025 NR, and the science behind the upcoming nuclear strike. Find links below that focus on the social and environmental impact of an asteroid strike.

CHAPTER 6: RYAN

Monday morning came after a restless night. Ryan had shut off his alarm and slept later than usual. He could skip his morning run today. Flipping on the TV news as background noise after his shower, it alerted Ryan to the change in the world. Instead of the traffic report, the radio blasted a strident, panicked voice that set his heart racing. An unfamiliar voice replaced the regular DJ. The new one spoke too fast, his words almost incoherent. When Ryan's sleep clouded mind deciphered what he heard, it was chilling.

"*2025 NR will collide with the northern hemisphere in less than three days. Attempts to change the asteroid's path in space have failed. Launch time for the series of nuclear missiles known as 'Plan B' begins in thirty-six hours.*"

The report repeated every few minutes, each time seeming more unbelievable, even though this was the news he'd been dreading. The recorded voice played on a loop and the countdown had started while he slept. He checked the time—now less than thirty-four hours. The news seemed like science fiction and it was hard to comprehend that it was real. Instead of getting ready for work, he packed.

Ryan had prepared as well as he could, though he kept running over the lists and supplies in his head, hoping he hadn't forgotten something important. He and Kat had bought everything they could think of that they might need on their road trip. Last night he'd laid out everything for his suitcase and backpack, so now he stuffed it in. He just needed to do his bathroom kit, and then he'd be ready to leave.

"Can you be ready to leave today?" He rubbed the back of his neck. His muscles were so tight a headache was forming already. He took a picture of his baggage and texted it to Kat. Minutes later, a matching photo of her pile of gear arrived. He was pleased she was a planner and wouldn't cause a delay. They should leave soon. Now that the news had leaked, the situation might change in a hurry.

"What time?"

He was about to say, "Now," when he stopped, turned on a dime, and dashed into his bedroom. He didn't have the keycode for the bunker compound's gate. The gate combination changed every month, and he'd written it down at work. Just in case, he checked his bedside table. The notebook with the latest code wasn't there. They wouldn't be able to access Vita xTerra without it. He'd have to return to the office. Despite the heads up, he wasn't a hundred percent ready.

Ryan wanted to smash his fist against the wall. Leaving it at work had been an idiot move. He'd been trying to be so thorough. They needed to leave town.

"I forgot something important at work. We can leave as soon as I get it. I'll go now."

Ryan finished his bathroom items, shoving them in the kit fast. He was low on stuff here, too. Disgust filled him as he picked up his drugstore list from the bathroom counter. He'd planned to shop on the way to work today. He was out of Tylenol, low on toothpaste, and had wanted to talk to a pharmacist about antibiotics, to determine if there was something he could buy without a prescription. The code was more important.

Ryan sprinted for the elevator and headed downtown. He hadn't driven far when it sunk in that this delay was a serious mistake. He should have packed his vehicle so he could leave directly from work. He considered turning back, but it felt too late, so he pushed on.

Traffic was pandemonium. The commute took three hours instead of the usual forty-five minutes, and once more, he cursed his luck. He couldn't turn back, but stuck to his decision to proceed. He would stop at a drugstore after he finished at the office. Somewhere close to home. He'd be quick inside both places. In and out. Reaching the office tower, he parked underground, his footfalls echoing in the emptiness. A feeling of disquiet stole over him. It shouldn't be this dead during a workday. Had he made a mistake by coming?

When the elevator doors opened on the fourteenth floor, it, too, was empty. The usual morning bustle was gone. Nobody else had come in. Phones in two adjacent offices rang over and over with no one to answer them as he walked down the carpeted hallway. The secretary he shared with another senior associate had cleared her desk, leaving it bare. He darted into his office and grabbed the code notebook from his top drawer. Flipping it open, he checked he had the most recent code. It was there. He scanned the sparse room where he spent most of his days, but there was nothing else he wanted.

When his work phone rang, he jumped, but let it go to voicemail. His cell phone had been eerily quiet, but there wasn't anyone he wanted to talk to besides Nick, who remained silent. Leaving with his notebook clutched in his fist, another associate hopped in the elevator ahead of him, not speaking or making eye contact, slipping out with a cardboard box of her belongings and a marble sculpture from reception.

Back in his car, Ryan avoided the news, but sirens remained a constant reminder of the growing trouble as he clutched the wheel and headed home. He skipped lunch, his stomach growling, but unwilling to stop. While grateful he and Kat were almost prepared, this delay was killing him. He ran over their lists again in his head.

Yesterday, they'd repackaged the food into Ziploc bags, with meals for two people. Each bag held two breakfasts, four snacks, two lunches, and two dinners. Dehydrated pouches of food might not be satisfying, but it was the best way to take a week's worth of food. If they arrived at the cabin with excess food, they could eat it later. Better bored than hungry.

Ryan left the downtown building at one thirty. The countdown for the missile strike was down to twenty-seven hours. He wasn't sure if the timer seemed too fast or too slow, but it ticked inside his head. He couldn't wait to find out if the strikes were a success or a failure. It could go either way and deep down, he feared it wouldn't work. With conditions the way they were, it would take hours to drive home.

His regular commute seemed like nothing compared to the intense gridlock traffic. Angry drivers shouted at one another while making aggressive moves, cutting each other off, looking for any advantage. He held his breath at several near misses and was relieved to remain unscathed. While he would have preferred to be in the left lane, the fast lane was like Mad Max Fury Road and better avoided. He counted several dozen vehicles banged up and abandoned, parked half in the median between sections of the I-5, the other half on the shoulder. Scratched and dented ones whizzed by on the outside, moving fast.

Once he turned off the highway, groups of people stood roadside with large signs proclaiming the end of days. Written on the posters were dismal sayings, like *"Prepare to see Jesus," "Repent Sinners,"* and *"The End is Nigh."*

People weren't reacting well to the uncertainty and end-of-world scenario. They mobbed grocery stores and gas stations had lines that stretched for blocks. He was thankful for the two large jerry cans he'd filled and placed in his storage locker yesterday. There was another at Kat's. Everywhere was too busy. The drugstore would have to wait.

He passed several buildings on fire, their flames leaping ever higher, burning near the side of the road without firefighters on the scene. Smoke filled the air, and he lost count after six or seven unattended fires. His eyes teared and coughing made driving more difficult. Columns of dark gray rose from all directions of the city. Crowds of people loitered outside, some with cameras documenting the destruction, while others looked to be inconsolable and in tears. People were losing their homes and their jobs, while some treated it like a spectator sport. Not only was the air filled with smoke, but he swore he could smell desperation. It made him feel nauseous.

"You still in Seattle?" came a text from Nick just as Ryan pulled onto his street three blocks from home.

He snatched his phone from the charging pad. *"Leaving within the hour. Kat's coming."*

"This is my last communication. They've been monitoring my phone for a week. Jake's plane is almost here. Get out, now. I'm in DC and it's mayhem. Headed to a bunker just in case. Good luck."

It was a group text. Kat typed, *"Good luck to you, too."*

Ryan received a separate text from her. *"Scary out there."*

"Sorry it took so long. Traffic insane. Almost home. I'll leave ASAP. Can't believe this happened overnight."

"The school year is over, no matter what happens. Meet in Everett?"

"Yes, but it might take all night to leave the city. Good thing we drive hybrids. Impossible to get gas. Huge lines. Power still on where you are?"

"So far. You?"

"Car accidents all over Greater Seattle and fires taking out power in localized places. Traffic lights down in chunks. Nobody is fixing anything. Almost home. I'll head out when I'm finished packing the car." He'd be as fast as possible.

"I'll let you know when I leave. Be careful."

"You too." It was an immense relief that she had suggested to meet elsewhere. It would have taken too long to drive across Seattle to her townhouse. At least she felt confident to get out of her neighborhood on her own, despite the chaos. He wasn't sure what he would have done if she'd cried like Heather, who would have begged for help. He couldn't help but admire her tenacity and courage.

Ryan's building was dark, and the power was out. It was after six p.m. and the trip back home had taken five hours. His stomach growled with an intensity he couldn't ignore, anticipating dinner. He parked underground and headed for the stairs to the seventh floor, not wanting to chance the elevator. Emergency lighting lit the stairwell, casting just enough light to place his feet on the concrete stairs. He used the handrail to pull himself up as he hurried, running through what else he'd need.

The food and new purchases were all at Kat's. He kicked himself for not splitting it. If something happened to her or they couldn't meet, he was screwed. It was violent outside and getting dangerous. He wished they'd left town this morning. That would have been smart.

He'd seen several beatings, a couple of fights, and three roadside screaming matches in the last few blocks. Tempers were high. He hadn't wanted to scare Kat, but the sooner she was on the road, the better. It might not be safe for her to travel alone, but she was closer to Everett and he would take backways to wind his way around north Seattle and Bellevue.

Upstairs, he turned on the TV for the latest news, half expecting to hear something worse than this morning. It was the same, except the countdown—now at twenty-two hours. In the back of his brain, the clock ticked like a bomb with flashing red digits.

He packed his bag with snacks for the road and ate a couple of quick tuna sandwiches for dinner. He savored the tangy pickles and French bread, not knowing when he'd get something like them again. Bakery fresh bread was about to become a luxury. Dried food was often bland and canned would be monotonous, but better than the no-food option. He wondered if Kat knew how to make bread because he didn't.

Ryan made several trips down the stairs in the poor light to his vehicle, his footsteps echoing in the cement stairwell. He was uneasy about meeting others, but the stairs remained deserted. The elevator was running again, but he preferred to avoid people. To be cautious, after each trip, he covered his food and water jugs with a blanket before returning upstairs for another load. On some floors he passed, doors slammed. On others, it was eerie and quiet. He had a thought part-way through packing and sent Kat a quick text.

"Bring your bike and saddlebags if you can."

"Good idea."

He recalled that she'd mentioned taking a bike trip years ago with Nick and he hoped she had a bike rack for her car. He'd hate to ditch the vehicles, but at least they'd have options if problems caused the highways to be blocked. Retrieving his bike, he settled it on the rack. He saved his suitcase and backpack for last, as they held the most important gear and he was unwilling to leave them in the car unattended. The final personal items he'd packed had been four books he'd never read, a deck of cards, plus his favorite sci-fi paperback, *Ender's Game* by Orson Scott Card.

He looked around his bare apartment, stopping to consider if there was anything else he needed or brought him joy. He grabbed a framed photo of his childhood retriever, Sparky, and stuffed it in his backpack. His grandfather had given him a pocketknife when he was young, that went in his pocket. He hadn't carried it since middle school, but he liked how it felt. There was nothing to be gained by staying, so he stepped into the hallway and took a deep breath.

It was a weird feeling, locking the door to his apartment, not knowing if he'd be back. This could be for nothing, or could save his life. It was impossible to know which. He'd spent as little time as possible at home for the last fourteen months, but walking away from everything was harder than expected.

His phone chimed as he stowed the last items and drove out of the parkade. The message was from Kat.

"Leaving now."

He was relieved she'd gotten away at the same time; it was eight p.m. and almost dark. Blocks from his building, he had to slam on the brakes to avoid hitting a man running across the street and he broke out in a cold sweat. Square patches of the surrounding city were pitch black, with no lights. It made him uneasy. Rioters and looters thrived in the anonymity of darkness. Tonight, there would be more violence.

In the intervening hours since he'd gotten home, the streets had grown more ominous. Gangs of people wandered in groups, sometimes spilling onto the streets and interfering with the flow of vehicles. The traffic lights close to home were out, but many drivers weren't adhering to the four-way stop procedure, anyway. It was like a game of chicken to cross those intersections. Just go.

He held his breath and gunned it through when he neared the front of the line. Somehow, he made it through each unscathed, accompanied by cursing and loud honking. Driving etiquette seemed a thing of the past. This was more like a chaotic video game without visible teams or rules.

Reaching the end of the main street at the edge of his neighborhood, Ryan slowed when he recognized a slim young man who lived in his building. The man smashed an ax to the glass door of a corner store, breaking the glass from the edges of the doorway to remove the jagged bits. He vanished inside, followed by four shadowy figures with flashlights. People were becoming brazen about looting. Less than a minute later, they emerged, each carrying a couple of flats of beer, and disappeared up the street into the darkness as Ryan accelerated.

It was shocking how fast things had devolved, giving Seattle an apocalyptic feel. He shook his head, disappointed in humanity as a whole. Not everyone was out for destruction, but they seemed the majority tonight. He didn't feel great about himself, either. He wasn't stealing or destroying, but he wasn't helping anyone except himself and Kat. They were like rats abandoning a sinking ship. Another wave of guilt enveloped him, but he blocked it. If he didn't look out for himself first, nobody else would.

Ryan turned off the main street and zig-zagged his way through town, avoiding box stores and well-lit areas using side streets. There were fewer cars and fewer groups of people. Despite the late hour, box stores and strip malls seemed to attract wanderers and those looking for free groceries and alcohol. Crashing glass became a constant, accompanied by the ever-present sirens wailing. He felt for the firefighters, paramedics, and police teams who fought their losing battle with the desperate population.

The radio countdown said the missiles would launch in eighteen hours. The turnoff to Kat's neighborhood from the highway was in flames, blocked by a three-car accident, including a car flipped upside down on the off-ramp. He breathed a sigh of relief that he didn't need to take that route. It would have been impossible.

No sooner had he thought this, when he arrived at a dead end and had to backtrack to a busier street, forcing himself into the stream of slow-moving cars. He was glad his SUV had tinted windows, as his loaded vehicle could have been a target for looters. Every glance in his direction made him sweat.

For a while, he made steady progress, but once more, traffic came to a standstill. The apartment building at the end of the block stood engulfed in flames, this one with emergency vehicles blocking three of the four lanes. His head pounded in frustration.

A police barricade blocked the closest neighborhood streets, and they diverted him onto the highway on-ramp. He sighed when a sea of neon brake lights stretched before him as far as he could see. He switched his car to EV mode to conserve gas, easy at this interminable crawl, and settled in for a long night, telling himself to be patient.

The rest of the night remained tense, inching forward, his progress minimal. Several stretches with only a couple of exits took hours to pass. Wiggling his jaw back and forth, he tried to ease the tension in his face and to stay awake despite the boredom of creeping along. He didn't know where most of the people in the other cars were headed, or if they'd been last-minute grocery shopping, but it appeared that everyone in the Greater Seattle area was out, many roaming on foot, the rest in their cars and on the road. He'd never seen such horrendous traffic, not even on the dreaded Olympia to Tacoma corridor during holiday long weekends.

How was Kat doing with her drive? He hadn't received a message in hours.

•   •   •

The sun rose on Ryan's right and the traffic thinned at last. Crooked cars littered the side of the road, the vehicles perhaps out of gas, their occupants joining the roadside throngs. Turning off the highway, he passed a Walmart with a packed parking lot just after six a.m. Many of the parked cars looked quiet, perhaps the occupants sleeping, unable to make it home. It looked quiet enough he decided to risk his drugstore shopping.

A few blocks away from the Walmart, he located an empty street, away from the action. He adjusted the covering over his gear and double-checked the locks on his bike. He looked everywhere, reluctant to leave his vehicle if he was being watched, but the nearby park was deserted. He walked ten minutes back toward the store.

Outside the main entrance was a fight, and he almost left, but he hung back to watch. Five men milled about, ramming each other's half-full shopping carts and yelling obscenities. They'd attracted a crowd of onlookers. Weighing his needs for medication, Ryan used the wall of looters as a shield as he made his way to the front of the store.

A mismatched young couple leaned against the outside of the building, passing a large bottle of rye back and forth. The young man lounged in dirty ripped clothes and greasy, long hair in a messy bun. The young woman wore a tailored jacket and skirt with designer shoes like those Ryan had seen around the law office. Both had bleary eyes and slumped half onto one another, on the verge of passing out. They may have been drinking all night. A second empty bottle rested behind her back.

He sidled around them and snuck into the store, feeling like a criminal. There were no blue-vested greeters posted near the entrance or employees of any kind in sight. Nobody worked at the tills. He stopped in his tracks, aghast. Overnight, looters had ransacked the Walmart grocery shelves. It reminded him of the pandemic shelves of March 2020 when the hoarders had cleaned out sections of the store, but worse. Smashed boxes and broken containers littered the floor— signs of panic.

He wandered the aisles, checking out the situation. Was this typical in other stores? Canned goods and pasta were gone, except a few dented cans rolling on the floor. He winced at the noise when a split package of macaroni crunched underfoot; the sound echoing in the cavernous space and eerie silence. People had stripped bare the junk food and alcohol aisles, leaving entire sections empty. It was like the Grinch had left only crumbs.

The produce section was a little better. It figured that when the world was ending, people wanted junk, not fruit and vegetables. He grabbed a perfect yellow banana, peeling it right in the store to eat, savoring every bite. His chest was tight, both with the waste and the feeling of frenzy, the need to shop. Acting on impulse, he filled an abandoned cloth shopping bag from the floor with half a dozen apples and several potatoes. A bright red can of Pringles lay underfoot where it had dropped, wedged underneath the berry display. He stuffed it in his bag with several boxes of raisins.

Furtive movements in nearby aisles let him know he wasn't alone. He hadn't been trying to be quiet, but the hair on the back of his neck rose, so he detoured to Sporting Goods where he picked up a baseball bat. He liked how it felt in his hands; the hard wood solid in his grip. It would have to do if there was trouble.

He didn't own a gun and wasn't sure he wanted one. Violence escalated fast when firearms were involved. Shopping may not have been smart, but he'd wanted to get the last items on his list and the quiet Walmart had seemed ideal. Now he wasn't so sure. It was like a scene from The Walking Dead, minus the zombies. He couldn't relax as he continued through the store to the far corner, the real reason for his stop.

At the pharmacy, he didn't hesitate, grabbing several of each item: packages of non-drowsy allergy medicine, tubes of sunscreen and toothpaste, and bottles of Tylenol, Tums, Ibuprofen, and Aspirin. He was surprised this area hadn't also been ransacked. On a whim, he shoved several boxes of condoms, a small flashlight, and several packages of batteries into his bag of loot. It was getting heavy.

With a glance back and forth, he vaulted the counter and located a handful of bottles filled with antibiotics. He wasn't sure of their specific use, but they were variations of penicillin. He took them. You never knew what you'd need. The tight feeling in his chest grew as he made his way along the edge of the store, heading to the exit. He wasn't a shoplifter by nature, but there were no cashiers at the registers, but there was so little left and nobody guarding it, he felt obligated to grab what was available.

He peeked out the door toward the drinkers. The second bottle was empty and the sad couple had collapsed on each other. The scuffle outside had grown since his entry and he wasn't certain he could leave without getting caught up in the disturbance. Ducking back inside, he considered his options. Voices rose and become more heated. Instead of five fighters, dozens shouted and pushed, with more joining all the time.

Someone was going to get hurt, and he didn't want to be involved. He'd taken another step back when three gunshots rang out. He ducked, his heart pounding. Almost dropping the bag in his haste, he gathered it to his chest. He needed to get out of here. He shouldn't have taken the risk. Toothpaste and Tylenol weren't worth his life.

He couldn't use the main entrance, so he looped his bag over his shoulder, leaving his hands free to open doors and hold the bat. He slunk into the washroom hallway and walked until he found a door marked Staff. Resting his ear against the door, he listened. Nothing. It was unlocked, so he eased it open.

He locked the door behind him, the click of the deadbolt louder than he liked. He was on edge, his senses alert for anything dangerous. With the lights off, it was dim, but there was a window that let in enough light to make out the contents of the room. It looked like a lounge, with a long table and a dozen chairs. There wasn't another door, but the window could be an exit.

A coffee maker filled the room with its aroma—perhaps on a timer. The machine's orange light beckoned, but he was already jittery. He'd just decided to find an exit somewhere else when voices approached in the hallway.

Several people, maybe four or five. He was outnumbered and didn't want to chance that they were friendly. He held his breath and froze. Someone tried the door. He tightened his grip on the bat. He didn't want to hit someone, but he would if he had to defend himself.

The door shook, rattling in its frame. The door was solid, and the lock held.

"Locked," someone said, and the footsteps continued down the hall. Several more distinct gunshots sounded nearby, making him flinch. He couldn't go back into the store. It would have to be the window. He moved a chair beneath it, taking care to be quiet, each move precise and deliberate. He stood on the chair and unlatched the window without a sound. Pushing it open to its fullest extent, he stuck his head out to look at the surroundings.

It opened onto the empty loading dock at the back of the building. He was in luck; there were no people in sight. He dropped his bags outside, then the bat. Almost before their noise could be registered, he slithered out the window. When someone yelled, he was half in and half out.

He dropped, scraping the skin on his chest in his hurry, grabbed his loot, and ran. He didn't wait to determine if they'd directed the shout at him or if they'd followed. Running as fast as he could, he left, expecting gunshots to follow. His feet pounded the pavement as he fled, the bag over his shoulder and the bat in his hand. He was fast and fit. When he looked around before slowing, he was alone.

Looking over his shoulder every few steps, he returned to his vehicle at a fast walk, sweating more than he should from the brief exercise. Everything appeared to be undisturbed in his car. He snatched up an apple, threw the rest of his acquisitions onto the passenger seat, hopped in and locked the doors, the clicking sound a relief. His heartbeat was still too fast as he departed.

He took a deep breath; he was almost to Everett, perhaps another half hour.

Despite the close call and his hurry to meet up with Kat, he needed a minute to take stock of what he'd taken. The condoms seemed stupid and presumptuous, and he was embarrassed at the impulse that had guided him. Checking that he was alone, he stopped, hid them in his suitcase, and threw the boxes in a dumpster, where he ditched the packaging and his apple core.

He hadn't thought to check his phone in hours and removed it from the charger. It was on silent mode and there were messages he'd missed from Kat. He let out a sigh of relief.

"It's crazy out there," said one. *"Traffic at a standstill,"* said another. The last was from fifteen minutes ago. *"Just outside Everett on Highway 2 near Snohomish. Parking behind an empty office building near the road out of town."*

As he read, he received another message. *"Please let me know you got out of Seattle."*

Feeling guilty that he'd missed her messages and neglected to let her know about his progress, he sent, *"Sorry. You're right, it's nuts. Send me the address. I'm close."* He added, *"Highway 2 was a good call. Interstate is a nightmare. Glad we decided not to take I-90."*

He snapped on the radio for the first time in hours, holding his breath, bracing for the bad news.

The DJ's voice was shrill and hurt his head. He turned the volume down.

"Mayhem across the U.S. has closed several major highways. The interstates are closed in many places by roadblocks. Citizens are urged to return home. Nobody knows when, where, or if the approaching asteroid will strike. You are more likely to be safe at home than on the road. The government is urging everyone to stay inside."

He snorted. Nobody was following that advice.

The countdown to the missile strikes was eleven hours, the ticking clock continuing.

Ryan changed the station.

"Martial law and curfews are being implemented in most major cities in the wake of destruction and chaos as the countdown continues."

He tried another station and listened to REM's "It's the End of the World." Someone had a dark sense of humor that he appreciated. After the song, they played a news segment.

"Several religious groups have declared this the prophesied end of the world. Many claim to have forecast this day for decades. Last night, a mass suicide by one such group took place in Texas, where three hundred people stepped off a twenty-two-story building in Dallas."

Not wanting to hear any more, he clicked off the radio.

His phone vibrated as someone called. He wasn't worried about getting a ticket, but missed the call while navigating around a three-car accident, one lucky enough to have an ambulance on the scene. He gave it a minute and checked his voicemail, expecting it to be Kat.

Instead, it was his mother, and his chest tightened.

"Why haven't you called? Your stepfather and I were hoping you could help defend our house. There are looters up and down the street. We have Heather with us. Don't you care about any of us?"

Here was the guilt trip he'd expected. He hated when she did this, but it was effective and made him feel like shit, even if he should be immune after all these years.

His parents didn't call unless they wanted something, often money. He'd put himself through university and law school, working odd jobs and long hours. He'd earned scholarships and bursaries. His family had never supported his decisions, and they'd never been close. The only one who'd been on his side was his grandfather, who'd passed away last year.

Now his ex was with them. He didn't want to know whose idea that had been. His mother and stepfather lived in Olympia, the opposite direction from where he was headed. He didn't wish them harm, but he didn't feel obligated to help. He'd chosen not to warn them because they wouldn't have believed him or would do what they'd chosen to do now. Panic and drink. Having Heather with them wasn't the enticement they thought. He'd drive a lot farther than xTerra to avoid seeing her.

He took a deep breath and called them back, hands free, keeping his eyes on the road.

"Hi, Mom. I can't talk for long and I'm not driving to Olympia. They've closed the interstate and besides, I don't think it would be safe to travel that far. You've seen it outside." He felt a pang of guilt for lying; he was planning to travel a lot farther than the next city. He paused, thinking of what to say.

"We're all going to die and you can't drive an hour or two to see your mother?"

"We don't know the asteroid is going to hit or if it does, where. My being there won't make a difference if it hits." His voice was tight with barely restrained impatience. He didn't have energy for this shit.

"Don't you care about us?" His mother's voice was shrill.

"It's not that, mom. Tell me about the looters." He tried to sound concerned as his fingers clutched the wheel.

"Well, maybe they're not looters. The neighborhood kids and their friends milled around outside all night. They won't go away. It isn't safe, I tell you. We invited Heather here because we know you'd never let anything happen to her."

In the background, Roy said, "Someone get me another beer."

His stepfather's voice was slurred even though it was still early morning. At their house, anytime could be beer o'clock; it wasn't just the impending disaster. This was every day. Ryan hadn't walked to university, but ran, needing to get away from home. Nick had been his roommate first-year university and soon became his new family. He'd taught Ryan that not all families were nasty and drunk. Some families were kind and supportive of their son's choices. Today was another example of what he owed Nick, who'd been a staunch friend.

"Mom, Heather and I broke up over a year ago." He couldn't believe what a bullet he'd dodged when he'd discovered her in bed with two other men. One of them had been her ex, another someone from her work that she'd dragged home for playtime. In his bed. The bed she'd left behind when she'd moved out. Ryan had come home with a surprise engagement ring that evening. It had been a surprise all right, just not the one he'd planned. He'd told no one the details, just that she'd cheated. She'd proven one thing: he was better off on his own.

"Don't you have something you want to say? You still owe her an apology."

"No, mom, I don't. Look, I can't talk. You're going to have to take care of yourselves."

"I raised you better than this. You're a selfish asshole who thinks only of himself. I don't like the man you've become, all Mr. High-and-Mighty, thinks he's better than we are."

Her words were like daggers piercing his flesh. He should be desensitized. She'd slung similar insults before, but it stung as much as ever. This was his mother.

"Goodbye, Mom. Take care. I hope things work out." He ended the call as she resumed berating him. Guilt stabbed him. Maybe he should have shared Nick's warning. He didn't wish them harm, but he also didn't want them to share his bunker. They didn't know about it because he hadn't told them about his inheritance from his grandfather.

One stipulation in the will had been that he keep it secret. It had been easy. Ryan hadn't wanted them to interrupt his holidays or his peace. Even Heather didn't know because she'd left before his grandfather had died. He didn't owe her anything. He didn't know what would happen. No matter what they'd done, it wasn't right to add to their panic. Knowing how serious it was would only make it worse.

At least, that's what he told himself. He gripped the steering wheel tighter and kept driving.

CHAPTER 7: KAT

Kat waited behind the empty office building in Everett for Ryan to arrive. It was hard to sit still after the grueling night of driving. Jittery, she couldn't relax, shifting positions several times as she tried to lean back and rest. At every noise, she popped up, heart racing, to peer out the windows, but there wasn't anything to see. Ryan had said he was close.

It was still early, but nobody had arrived to unlock the building. If this was your final day on earth, would you go to work? No way. These last couple of days, she should have been having sex, eating ice cream, and rewatching her favorite movies. Instead, she'd been packing for a 1200-mile road trip to an underground bunker halfway across the country with someone who was little more than a stranger.

She'd been worried all night when she hadn't heard from him. She'd even fired off a text to warn her family. Her clothes were damp from the constant slick of sweat, her antiperspirant long since gone. Her nerves jangled, and she hadn't been able to drive farther without a rest. She'd turned the radio on several times to distract herself from the traffic and roadside violence and had been appalled by the change in people's behavior within a matter of hours. This was the reaction to a potential impact? How much worse would it be if there was an actual disaster? She and Ryan were banking on at least a partial collision, but she'd never hoped to be more wrong.

She wanted to believe in science, after all, her undergrad degree was in Earth Science, which was how she'd met Nick. She hoped the missile strikes would be at least a partial success and blow the asteroid into tiny bits that would burn up in the atmosphere upon entry. Nuclear strikes in the upper atmosphere hadn't been attempted in the past. There was no margin for error, which made it difficult to believe that it would succeed. There wasn't time for a second chance. The asteroid had to be close before they could nuke it; technology wasn't advanced enough for a different strike further away. This was a last-ditch, panic effort to save humankind from extinction—from going the way of the dinosaurs.

It might not work. It could be too little, too late. Her heart hurt to consider the end of modern civilization and the innocent creatures that would die.

Kat monitored the time, knowing the scheduled missile strikes would begin at six p.m. today. She and Ryan planned to head east, if they could find their way past the roadblocks. She'd chosen Highway 2 as the best of the options to keep off the interstates.

They'd agreed to take Ryan's SUV for the main journey, but she didn't want to unload her Camry yet. She stayed hidden, with her doors locked. Every time a vehicle drove past her location, she froze and slouched lower in her seat. She'd strapped her bike to the back, making her feel conspicuous, but she was glad that Ryan had suggested it at the last minute. With her sore ankle, biking might be easier than walking if they had to leave the vehicle at some point.

She yawned. It was approaching eight a.m., and she'd been awake and on edge for the last twenty-four hours. She'd also gone nine days now without a drink—a new personal record.

Despite the terror of the unknown, she hadn't felt this alive in years. Since Mark's death, she'd wanted to feel nothing. Her life had felt like a tragedy. Strange how it took a disaster to snap her out of her depression. Her hands shook. She might have left living too late. Friday night she'd been tempted to seek oblivion in a bottle, but making lists with Ryan had been productive and an excellent distraction.

Her jaw creaked with another ear-splitting yawn. Her eyes were filled with grit, but she didn't dare close them while she was alone. She needed sleep but would wait. For now, she needed to keep watch. She ate a granola bar and washed it down with lukewarm iced tea, grimacing at the taste in her mouth. Hoping to feel a little better, she freshened up by brushing her teeth, smoothing her hair into a new ponytail, and applying new antiperspirant.

With time to kill, she grabbed the pile of paper maps she'd found in a box of Mark's things and shoved in her glove box, and opened one of Washington state to examine to keep her mind occupied. What was taking Ryan so long?

The maps were ten years old, but many roads and highways should be the same. If there was an asteroid strike, the power could go out, and they might lose cell service. They might not have access to the internet, Google Maps, or GPS to navigate. Maybe ever. It depended on what happened to the Earth today. She'd always been good at thinking of worst-case scenarios; now it might be useful.

She exhaled hard when Ryan arrived. It was about time. If he hadn't shown, she didn't know what she would have done. She might have gone looking for a bottle of gin since she'd left hers at home on the counter. She'd considered packing it for a rainy day, but at the last minute decided against squirreling a bottle away. A deliberate choice not to be a drunk on what could be her last days.

She felt like hugging Ryan, but she didn't know him well enough for such liberties. They weren't quite friends, and he seemed too standoffish for random affection, even if her feeling was derived from relief. Instead, she stepped out of her car on rubbery legs and strolled over to his window where he handed her a Granny Smith.

The sour apples were her favorite, and he flashed her a dazzling smile. How could he look so composed and handsome after that harrowing night with no sleep? Her eyes must be bloodshot and her look haggard.

"Hope you like apples and potatoes. That's all I found at the store this morning, that and a dented can of Pringles for a treat. The junk food aisle was cleaned out."

She still found it hard to meet his eyes when he spoke, but his words startled her into a direct gaze. Maybe it was in her head, but his blue eye seemed like it had laser vision and saw every worry and terror she tried to keep hidden.

Her eyes opened wider as his statement sunk in about shopping. There was a three-second delay in her tired brain. The metallic taste of blood flooded her mouth after she chewed her bottom lip. She'd seen what the store parking lots had looked like and avoided them like a Black Friday sale at the mall. She'd never been more grateful for his suggestion about shopping before the news had broken. If she'd followed her routine, she'd have been caught in the shopping frenzy or had to go without the planned food. Their supplies were a new wealth.

"You went shopping?" Her tone was full of incredulity. "That was dangerous."

"It was stupid. Go ahead and say it. I needed to get things, like Tylenol and antibiotics. I meant to stop Sunday on the way back from your place, but it was late and I put it off." He shook his head. "When gunshots started, I was in the store. I bolted and slithered out a window. I ran away." He shook his head. "Unless places are abandoned, we should make do with what we have. I've learned my lesson."

"Me too. I'm glad you're safe." She paused. "My drive was both hectic and boring. How about you? Any problems other than traffic, religious fanatics, and thieves?" She bit into the apple, the juice dribbling down her chin. She couldn't even eat because she was so tired. The tart fruit was delicious—though it made her teeth ache. Crunching the apple, she took another bite, this time keeping it all in her mouth.

"Other than the population going crazy and violence spreading like wildfire? No."

Her chest tightened again with thoughts of the interminable night. Today wouldn't be better, though perhaps more civilized in the daylight. Unless it was worse. She was glad they headed for the mountains, beyond city limits, where she hoped it would be peaceful.

She hesitated. "Could we find somewhere quiet to sleep for a few hours? Not here. We're still too close to the city, but maybe not far down the highway? I'm exhausted."

"I need sleep too, but I agree. We should push a little farther. We can find somewhere to pull off, maybe at a campground. I doubt I'll nap more than an hour or two if we stay in the car. It'll be cramped, but better than nothing. Let's keep both cars until then. Your car is less likely to be vandalized if we leave it somewhere quiet. The mess will spread beyond the cities today. Everyone is on edge with the missile countdown."

She walked back toward her car.

"I'm glad you made it here," Ryan said, his words coming out in a rush as he stepped out of his car. His voice seemed to contain warmth and not just relief, and her tension lessened a notch. Something about him made her feel safer.

She leaned inside her car and grabbed a paper map before spreading a section on the hood of her car. "Retro maps." She pointed and spoke over her shoulder. "Money Creek Campground is less than fifty miles. Want to try that?"

Ryan joined her and studied the map, his solid presence next to her beside the car. Up close, he smelled like pine trees and caramel, enough that it was distracting.

"Sounds good. I like your paper maps, by the way. Good call. Everyone relies on the internet too much and we might not be able to use it for much longer. I'm turning my phone off for a bit. Save power. There's no one else I need to talk to." His voice trailed off.

The sadness of his tone pulled at her and she recalled Mother's Day. Had his luck with his family been as bad as hers?

They got in the vehicles and departed, with Ryan in the lead. She was past tired, leaving her nerves jangled. Soon after they resumed driving, she got a second wind, perhaps the energy from the apple kicking in, and hoped it would last until they found a safe place to sleep.

Money Creek Campground was part of the Mount Baker/Snoqualmie National Forest. They reached it in less than an hour, passing fewer than a dozen cars on the highway in that time. In the campground, tall trees rose above shaded campsites by the river. It was a weekday and dead quiet. It surprised Kat others weren't here, but she was relieved that they had the campground to themselves. They chose a site distant from the road and parked the cars in a pull-through drive that would be easy to leave in a hurry in case of emergency.

"Sleep in the cars or set up the tent?" said Ryan, surveying their chosen site. "I'd rather be able to stretch out to sleep, but it might not stay this quiet." Echoing her thoughts, he said, "I'm surprised more people haven't had the idea to leave the city. Staying in our cars could be more secure."

"I vote for the tent," she said, gratified to be included in the decision-making. She liked that he was take-charge without being bossy. "I didn't have any luck resting in the car while I was waiting. If I can sleep for a few hours, I'll feel like a new person."

They unpacked the tent from her car and set it up in the shade, hidden behind a bank of bushes on one side and the leafy trees near the creek. She found the sound of the flowing river soothing and hoped it would lull her to sleep. Ryan tossed the Thermarest mattresses inside to self-inflate and removed the sleeping bags from their stuff-sacks while Kat ferried supplies from her car to his SUV, packing them with the other boxes and gear. She didn't want to leave her car, but it wasn't practical to take both vehicles. If this turned out to be a false alarm, they would return and collect it. His SUV held more gear, had four-wheel drive, and was better if they had to leave the main roads.

Not wanting to light a fire or set up the camp stove because they were keeping the camp minimal, she planned food to eat that didn't need cooking. She checked Ryan's cooler and made ham and cheese sandwiches for when they woke up. Best to eat perishables first.

They crawled inside the tent, with the fly left unzipped for better air circulation and visibility. She'd be too warm if she slept in her sleeping bag, but lying on it was more comfortable than she expected, although Ryan was close, and lying shoulder to shoulder was tight. She preferred more personal space than was possible in the lightweight backpacking tent. Someone with his stature took up a lot of space and made the interior of the tent seem small.

She unzipped the doors to the vestibules on either side to create an illusion of space. In the confined area, she was more aware than ever of the difference between their sizes. His frame extended from one end almost to the other and his sleeping bag filled the length. In contrast, she owned an extra short sleeping bag because it was lighter to carry on backpacking trips, and she and Nick had been obsessed with keeping their packs light.

Kat was too keyed-up to sleep. Much to her annoyance, Ryan fell asleep within minutes, and she was jealous. She was relieved he was a quiet sleeper and didn't snore, which would have made sleeping even more difficult. She stared at the inside of the tent where the aluminum poles crossed at the top and took slow, deep breaths. Her heart seemed too loud, so much so that it roared in her ears. She imagined cartoon sheep jumping a fence, but it didn't work as her mind constantly wandered back to her worry that the world was ending. The worst part may be the uncertainty.

She couldn't keep her eyes closed, and each time they opened, the sun overhead reminded her it was daytime. She should be at school with her class, not in a tent on the road to South Dakota. Besides her busy thoughts, small forest noises were the major distraction. She identified many as the breeze in the trees, birds, or small creatures rustling in the nearby bushes.

Kat became sticky and sweaty and shifted positions several times, hoping she didn't disturb Ryan with the rustling of her sleeping bag. She hated wearing the same clothes for multiple days, but there was no point in changing until she woke up. Taking several more deep breaths, this time forcing her eyes to remain closed, she focused on the sound of the water. At last, it lulled her to sleep.

• • •

Kat awoke with a start, disoriented and confused. Her mouth was dry, and a sheen of sweat covered her skin; she didn't recognize where she was at first, and her brain was slow to clear. Once again, her heart raced too hard, pounding like it wanted release from her chest. She was alone in the tent and footsteps crunched outside in the gravel. She sat up and controlled her breathing. It was probably Ryan.

"Ryan?" Her voice sounded shaky. She shouldn't be so fearful without reason, but it spoke to how uncertain and life was right now. Every out-of-place noise seemed like a threat.

"Good, you're awake," said Ryan, rounding the front of his car and becoming visible through the tent's mesh.

His hair was wet, and he'd changed into dark jeans that hugged his lean frame and a pale blue T-shirt that not only showed off his wide shoulders but matched his blue eye. He looked like Steve Rogers. Her physical attraction to him seemed like an interesting distraction from other, more fearful thoughts.

"I was coming to get you. There's a shower in the building two hundred yards down, on the right. Take a minute to go clean up. I feel a thousand times better for having had a shower and a rest. We can eat and pack when you're done."

"Thanks." She scrambled out of the tent, glancing at her phone with a double-take. It was almost three in the afternoon. Three hours and fifteen minutes until the missiles launched.

Ryan laughed. At her startled look, he grinned. "I did the same thing twenty minutes ago. Our power nap was almost six hours. We must have needed it."

They hadn't driven far enough from the city for her liking, but now they'd have the energy to travel far tonight—enough to leave the coastal region. The missile strike was in three hours. On clear quiet roads, they could be hundreds of miles further by the time the asteroid struck.

She collected her towel, bathroom kit, and clean clothes and headed to the shower on shaky legs. She was terrified by how little time they had before the missiles. The brick building had a faint aroma of mildew overlaid with the scent of pine-scented cleaner and dirt. Bits of tree detritus scattered the brown-tiled floor and spider webs decorated the corners of the ceiling, but she didn't care.

Monitoring the long-legged spindly spiders, she turned on the water and stripped down before stepping into the warm water. She let it stream over her for a minute before lathering the soap, as she tried to wash her anxiety down the drain. She would have loved to take a longer shower, but they needed to drive. She washed her hair and dressed in fresh clothes without wasting time. Clean and rested, she felt like a new person, ready to tackle the rest of the journey. Or at least the afternoon. In a few hours, they would learn if the missile strike would be successful. Uncertainty made her stomach churn once more—best not to dwell on the unknown.

At the campsite, everything from inside the tent had been squared away, and she helped Ryan pack the tent. Unable to help herself, she checked her messages and voicemail before putting her phone in her backpack, which she shoved in the back of Ryan's SUV. Her shoulders slumped and her lips pressed together at the lack of news. Nick had said he'd be out of touch and she hoped that he and Jake were safe. She hadn't expected other messages, but it was telling that despite having cell service, there was nothing. Besides this morning's warning, she'd sent messages to her mom and sisters yesterday, telling them she was thinking of them and to take care.

She'd been a mess the last couple of years and she couldn't blame them for not wanting to deal with her and her problems. She'd blown them off dozens of times and burned several bridges the last two years. But even before Mark's death, their relationship had never been close. They would never understand how she expressed emotion. Now, she was getting a taste of her own medicine.

Ryan wasn't much for talking, which suited her fine, and it was a pleasant change to be a passenger instead of the driver; her nerves remained shot from the drive last night. Once underway, she enjoyed watching the forest at the side of the scenic highway. They left the mountain region and forests for the drier, inland plateau, with fewer trees and stretches of open plains. There still wasn't much traffic, though the odd car traveled toward the coast.

A radio station from Seattle reported anyone found looting faced jail time. She huffed, thinking of the destruction she'd witnessed overnight. It wasn't likely they'd be able to catch anyone. Either that, or they'd need to lock up the entire city. A curfew of five p.m. was imposed; an hour before launch time. The authorities must want people home, not causing mischief or destruction, though how would they enforce the new rules? Perhaps the highways had settled, and the police had turned out in force to curb the violence.

They were almost to Wenatchee, where they'd either turn south to I-90, or north to stay on Highway 2. Soon they'd have to choose, and the ball of dread in her stomach wouldn't dissipate. She voiced her opinion because there were pros and cons for each route.

"It'll take longer, but how do you feel about staying on Highway 2? We'd drive a little farther, and we'd have to turn south on 200 to reach Missoula, but we'd avoid cities. Spokane and Coeur d'Alene could become jammed like Seattle. We could get stuck for hours."

"I agree. We should stay off the interstate," said Ryan, to her surprise. "Sounds like many are closed, anyway, and we should avoid further delay."

It was less than two hours before the launch when they drove through Wenatchee. The streets were almost deserted. People must have stayed inside, glued to their TVs to watch the news and spend time with their loved ones. She shot Ryan a glance. Perhaps he had similar thoughts. Leaving town, they came to a roadblock where two black and white police cars blocked the highway, leaving just enough room for a car to pass between them if the officers stepped aside.

Ryan stopped beside the officers and unrolled his window. Kat sat up straight.

"Curfew is less than an hour away, folks," said the officer on the left. "State your business, please. We're restricting highway travel. Not a lot of services on this road beyond Wenatchee."

Kat jumped into the conversation. She played the flaky blonde; she'd prepared for this moment for the last half hour, practicing her lines in her head.

She flashed a vapid smile at the police officer. "We have reservations at the Lincoln Rock State Park campground." She'd chosen it from her map because it wasn't much farther up the road. "We must be almost there. Everyone was all like, it's the end of the world, 'let's party,' but I like talked to my boyfriend and convinced him to, you know, like, go camping instead."

The officer turned to Ryan, who shrugged. He shot her an amused glance.

She brought her best smile back and leaned forward to show off her cleavage while she spoke, resting her hand on Ryan's thigh. "Don't you think camping sounds way better than being with a crowd for the end of the world? Somewhere fun for just the two of us. What would you like to be doing?" She wet her lips. The young officer's gaze didn't leave her mouth.

The officer cleared his throat and glanced at his partner. "Girl's got a point."

The second officer shrugged.

"Carry on. If the world doesn't end, maybe we'll see you back this way in a few days."

"Thank you, officer," she said with a flirtatious wink.

The two men moved aside. They proceeded past the barrier as they continued north.

"What was that?" Ryan sent her a sidelong glance. "They thought you're taking me out there to fuck my brains out. That was an impressive piece of acting. Or terrifying."

"Sex would be a better way to die than jumping off a building, if you ask me," she said, lifting one shoulder. She acted every day to fit in; how was this different?

"I'm not arguing. I'm in awe," Ryan said, blushing, which she found interesting. "That isn't a side of you I've seen before."

"Teaching, acting, same thing," she said with a deep exhale. "What side is that? Did I lay it on too thick?"

He laughed, something she hadn't heard often before. "We're too early to stop at Blowjob Park for the countdown, but we can find another when it's time."

"I wasn't suggesting parking, for real," she said, feeling a wave of panic that he might think her role play was real.

"That wasn't what I meant, either." The tips of his ears turned pink. "I want to stop and listen to the final countdown, so we know the outcome. Whether or not the missiles work, it's a big moment in history. I want to be paying attention, not thinking about road conditions like whether a deer will jump in front of us, or what speed I'm driving. I'm a little rattled at the whole concept of the asteroid strike and want to take a minute. Five minutes won't make a difference in the grand scheme. If the missiles fail and the asteroid smashes here, it won't matter if we're at the side of the road or driving full tilt."

It was the longest speech she'd heard him make, and she agreed.

"If it's just for a few minutes, I'd like to stop, too. Would you like me to drive until then?"

"Later. I'm good. I want to hear the launch and wrap my brain around the enormity of the moment."

She nodded in agreement; that was precisely what she wanted.

A few minutes before six p.m., Ryan pulled off the road, leaving the car running while she flipped on the radio. Her heart was stuck in her throat while they searched for a signal.

Time slowed as she wiped her damp palms before she scrolled through the radio signals to find a station that was clear and broadcasting in the area. At a crackle, she stopped and zeroed in on the signal. They listened to a two-minute countdown that stretched for an eternity. Kat gripped Ryan's hand when it reached thirty seconds until launch. She was shaking. Ryan flashed her a nervous grin at the contact, but didn't speak.

"We should watch. There must be a live feed somewhere," said Ryan. Without dropping her hand, he set his phone on the console between them. His other hand trembled. They leaned together over the small picture when he found a live video. It was hard to see anything.

"*Three, two, one, launch,*" came the radio voice. "*The nuclear missiles are on their way. Official confirmation of missile launches from America, Russia, China, and Israel.*"

Kat held her breath while they waited with the radio on, hoping for an update. The radio fell silent as the world waited.

"*Reports say the missiles are on target,*" said the voice with a strained quality.

A short commentary summarized how the nuclear weapons were supposed to work. It droned on, but Kat didn't absorb the information. Sweat dripped from her forehead, and her mouth felt like a desert while they waited for the missiles to strike the asteroid. The screen went blank. There must be nothing new to show. They focused all their attention on the radio, where the silence became deafening.

Six minutes later came a distinct voice; the Vice President of the United States.

"*The missiles have struck 2025 NR. Repeat, the nuclear missiles have struck 2025 NR. The asteroid has cracked into several pieces as scientists who have monitored our Sentry Defense Program had hoped.*"

The Vice President didn't sound as pleased as those words might indicate. The hair on her arms lifted. There was more.

"*Several pieces of the asteroid remain large enough to cause significant damage when they strike the Earth. Prepare for impacts of varying sizes across western North America, eastern Russia, China, and Japan. Pieces will rain down through the middle and northern latitudes. Smaller, more erratic chunks knocked from their original trajectory will strike the Midwest, Mexico, and Brazil, starting in the west and moving to the east. Stay inside. Retreat underground if possible, if your location is within a strike zone. Your local emergency broadcast systems will sound after this broadcast in regions most likely to be affected.*"

Kat took a deep breath, thinking it was over, but the voice continued.

"*Residents of the western United States of America need to prepare for the worst. The single largest piece, maybe as much as a third of the meteor, remains intact. The estimated time to the Los Angeles area impact is less than one hour. May God have mercy on our souls. Let us pray for those in California.*"

Ryan switched off the radio. His mouth was flat, his face expressionless. "We need to drive. Every mile might count. Even with optimal driving conditions, the bunker is two to three days away." Despite his urgent words, he didn't put the car in drive. He stepped out of the car and retrieved her phone, passing it to her as he sat down.

She waited for him to say something, but he didn't. He turned his phone over several times in his hand before putting it on the charger without making a call or sending a text. He took a deep breath and pulled off the shoulder. Driving as far east in the time they had left.

Kat's heart lodged in her throat as she tried to process the information in the message. The asteroid impact would be in less than an hour. Would they feel the California impact here? California didn't feel very far away. Her shoulders hurt from the tension. The horror story version of events was about to play out, and for all their preparations, she wasn't ready. She turned on her phone and sent a last message to her family.

"I love you," followed by a purple heart. She left her phone on for five minutes while Ryan stared out the window and the radio fell silent. She was heartbroken when there was no reply. Maybe the systems were busy, or nobody in her family was near their phone. Ryan's phone also remained blank and silent.

Both phones buzzed. She jumped when the anticipated warning of the Emergency Broadcast System arrived via text.

"Seek shelter."

Her hands felt icy as she turned off her phone and the floodgates opened. Her hands folded together in her lap and tears leaked down her cheeks. All of those people were going to die. There was no way to save Los Angeles and the population of the surrounding area. There was no time left to evacuate. Even if they'd known the impact site days ago, there wouldn't have been time. Perhaps that was why the government had been slow to share information. They'd known that it wasn't possible to save everyone. The President and top scientists, like Nick, had used the time to get somewhere safe. The Vice President had stayed behind.

The missiles had been their last hope and only a partial success. A successful strike might have saved the planet from a catastrophic extinction event, but it hadn't been enough to save everyone. She and Ryan were in peril; the western states were a danger zone.

"It's almost the worst-case scenario we discussed." Her voice sounded clinical and remote. "The whole Ring of Fire thing."

"Can you check the route around Spokane? So we can stay off major highways." Ryan's voice sounded detached, too.

Discussing traffic seemed so trivial. Bile rose in her throat.

"It can be a traffic bottleneck. I want to avoid it. I'd hate to be stuck on Division Street. Something smaller even than this highway. Maybe another campground or an empty building in case we need to take shelter." His voice shook on the last word as he clenched the wheel.

"Pull over." Kat covered her mouth with her hand. Her stomach roiled. Ryan looked at her and screeched to a halt.

She fumbled for the door handle, flung open her door, and lurched into the ditch. She heaved the contents of her stomach into the tall weeds. The driver's side door opened, and Ryan joined her. Without a word, he handed her a stack of fast-food napkins, and she wiped her mouth with shaking hands. He passed her a water bottle, and she rinsed her mouth and spat. When she was cleaned up, he surprised her by pulling her into an embrace. His hard muscles and solid presence grounded her, allowing her to catch her breath.

"I'm scared too," he whispered against her hair. "Me too. We've got each other." He held her for what seemed a long time, perhaps as long as a minute. Maybe two. "You okay to go now?"

She nodded and took a deep breath. "I'm fine. Let's go."

"We can do this," said Ryan. "We'll find somewhere safe."

His kindness and confidence were unexpected. That she would have liked to have stayed in his arms even longer surprised her. Their connection helped ease the panic and some of her everyday loneliness.

Just as they turned to get back in the car, the sound of a large vehicle roared toward them and careened around the corner. Startled, she jumped off the road and Ryan flattened himself against the door as a large navy-blue pickup with a skull and crossbones on the back window sped past. The driver made no attempt to swerve around them, and air rushed past her face. Clearly, someone else who didn't care about speed limits anymore.

She intended to thank Ryan for the hug, but he'd stepped out of reach as he climbed back behind the wheel and shut his door.

"Ryan, I..."

"We should go."

His words brushed her off, like he hadn't just been kind, or they hadn't connected. They'd just been together through something traumatic. Was he one of those men who didn't like to show their feelings? An asteroid was about to strike, and the Earth was out of options, but Ryan pushing her away left her feeling more alone than ever. Or maybe she was reading him wrong, and they just needed to drive. He was being practical.

Kat swallowed her hurt feelings and climbed back into the passenger side and didn't speak, her throat blocked by a large lump.

Maybe he was panicking about the distance they had to travel to reach safety.

Back on the road, she unfolded the map with trembling hands. It was hard to see with wet, blurry eyes. She hadn't been aware that she was still crying. She hated feeling weak, so she wiped her eyes and concentrated on her job. He was the pilot; she was the navigator. They didn't have much longer before the asteroid would strike.

They drove for less than an hour.

Orange streaks appeared like trails of fire in the sky. They were too bright to watch. There was a massive booming sound to the southwest, and the trails passed overhead.

A closer, roaring sound whooshed through the air with twin streaks of fire. Ryan slammed on the brakes, skidding to a stop sideways across the road. Kat covered her head and smothered a scream. A sound she never could have imagined ripped through the atmosphere and the vehicle rocked.

A shockwave, followed by an echo of another farther away. Ryan placed a shuddering hand on her back, connecting them once more in this terrifying moment. A deep rumble came from within the Earth while the ground shook with a grinding noise. The road buckled, flexing up and down in waves, rocking the vehicle. Another vibration caused the earth to tremble again. The earthquakes continued longer than she would have imagined possible, having never experienced them before. It was several minutes before they stopped and time resumed at its normal speed. Only then could she breathe.

Ryan was as white as chalk; she must be a matching color. Her breath came in ragged gasps as the earth groaned and shook in a series of aftershocks following the original impacts. There had been at least three crashes. The largest impact had been first and seemed far away. California? Seattle? The second and third had been close, each collision crashing almost simultaneously. A grating noise continued at the edge of her hearing as the ground shuddered again.

More distant meteor streaks had passed overhead at a shallow angle, disappearing over the eastern horizon as pieces of asteroid rained down beyond their line of sight. The cracked and broken road appeared passable. At least here and right now. She had no idea what they'd find as they traveled.

"When the volcanoes erupt, the ash will be like snow. We need to get farther away. At most, we have a few days." Kat's voice was unsteady. "There will be volcanic activity soon, I'd imagine. The Cascades are going to erupt as the pressure builds underneath with shifting tectonic plates. It's a matter of hours, days at most."

Ryan turned on the radio and rotated through the dial in both directions. There was nothing but static.

"The power could be out in most places, making it hard to broadcast." Her uneven voice sounded small.

"We should go." Ryan put his RAV4 in drive and pulled away from where they'd stopped for the impact.

They had to keep going, or this would be the end.

CHAPTER 8: RYAN

Ryan glanced at Kat while he drove. She'd pulled herself together, though only moments ago she'd been in turmoil. Her cool composure might be an act as she seemed to be a consummate actor. How she appeared and what was underneath or in her head might not match. His stomach tied in knots, becoming queasy, but he clenched every muscle to keep going. The asteroid pieces traveling east must have struck by now. If he thought about it much, he'd fall apart, so he avoided giving free rein to his imagination.

Since they hadn't felt additional impacts, the pieces must have been smaller or crashed farther away. There'd been no additional collisions or shock waves, but there'd been at least a dozen trails blazing across the sky. Maybe more.

At the edge of sight, pale yellowish-orange streaks raced past. The image of the falling meteorites had burned into his retinas; he hadn't been able to rip his gaze away. He didn't know what mess they'd be driving into, but they needed to be far from ground zero. He looked to the south. They were only a couple of hundred miles from Yellowstone. Would it be stable? He glanced in the rear-view mirror. Mt. Rainier remained visible. He'd read that ash from the eruption of Mount St. Helens back in 1980 had been three to four inches deep in Spokane, Washington. They were still too close to the mountains. He didn't want to drive in that kind of mess.

Web-like cracks covered the road, and he drove with care, avoiding uneven patches, broken chunks, and holes in the surface. His speed was much less than the limit of seventy miles per hour. If it was this bad now, what would it be like later? He revised his estimate of driving time to South Dakota. Three days might be optimistic.

As the miles flashed by and evening approached, his chest tightened with uncertainty. Night driving with poor road conditions on an unfamiliar road might cause an accident. He wasn't sure what to do. Stop and risk the volcanic fallout or push on and chance an accident. His usual method of dealing with problems was to avoid and push through, but that didn't apply to this situation. He could work as hard as possible and it might not be sufficient. It was out of his control. Going the long way and stopping overnight set his teeth on edge, but were the smarter options.

He didn't dare drive into areas of dense population, worried about civil unrest and violence. He was reluctant to get stuck in traffic or behind roadblocks. The route Kat suggested veered north, a route that would avoid both the main part of Spokane and Coeur d'Alene. It was a longer distance and would take longer, but there were lakes and campgrounds in quiet areas where they could stop for the night and regroup. They wouldn't be able to purchase gas or additional supplies, but they could make do after the mess in Seattle. The fewer people they encountered, the better.

He ran some quick calculations in his head. His hybrid engine required little fuel, and he estimated he could travel close to eight hundred miles on a single tank of gas. They would need every mile they could eke out, with a twelve-hundred-mile journey to xTerra. They also had three full jerry cans. With the detours, that might not take them the full distance to South Dakota, but they still had their bikes and their feet. If necessary, they could trek on foot.

His research convinced him the bunker would be necessary for long-term survival. This was the calm before the storm. There would be worse to come than the actual collision. He'd researched asteroids after Nick's warning and believed civilization would change forever after such a catastrophic impact. Earth's ecosystems were already at a tipping point because of climate change. This would be the final straw.

After the intense volcanic action, he suspected there would be extreme weather and limited crops for years. He wasn't a climate change expert, but he'd done more research than he cared to admit. He didn't want to consider what civilization might look like without sufficient crops for several years. Millions, maybe billions, would die of starvation and he didn't intend to be one of them. He appreciated his grandfather's massive stockpile of seeds and gardening implements, in addition to several years' worth of canned and dried food. If it came to it, he could become a farmer and grow his own food.

"Want me to drive?" Kat's voice interrupted his thoughts.

He shook his head. "I'd rather drive than be a passenger. I hope you don't mind."

"I dislike driving, but I'm willing to take a turn whenever you want a break."

"Noted. I'm good for another few hours. Tomorrow, you can spell me off. Why don't you check the map and choose a campground on the lake, somewhere near where we turn south again?" They should stop tonight. They would make about four hundred miles today, even with the delays.

"I found somewhere, but there's a long bridge. It should be okay as long as the bridge is sound." She chewed the edge of her lip. "The road buckled and cracked. We can hope that the bridge didn't."

She kept the map section showing where they were open on her lap. It looked like she marked their progress using the roadside mileage signs. She bent over and examined the map in the fading light.

"Let's try the Sam Owen Forest Service Campground on Highway 200."

"How far?" Now that he'd decided to stop, he didn't want to drive half the night.

"About a hundred and fifty miles."

He nodded. Barring further complications, that would take them until about ten o'clock tonight. After their extended nap, they shouldn't expect to travel farther. He worried about the damage to the bridge, but didn't voice his concerns. It would either be fine, or they'd have to backtrack.

If they drove around the lake, they could aim for Missoula, Montana, and return to the interstate or go south and around. His thoughts drifted like tumbleweed on the wind and he couldn't keep up. It was quiet, but Ryan didn't feel like playing music. He was too tense to enjoy it, even if it might provide a distraction from his worries.

The glow of a brilliant sunset painted the sky in his mirrors. The orange and pink dimmed, and the darkness deepened. Would there be adequate light to examine the bridge and its structural integrity at night?

The sky had darkened to deep purple twilight—the color of a nasty bruise—when they reached the near shore with the bridge and Ryan stopped the vehicle. The lake was almost black, with the faintest silver sheen from the half moon's reflection. He was about to step out with a flashlight and inspect the near section of the bridge when a white pickup truck rattled off the structure. It slowed down where they'd pulled off the road and a man wearing a cowboy hat unrolled his window.

Ryan did the same. "How did the bridge hold up in the earthquakes?" Had the truck come across or returned because they'd turned back?

"It's good," said the man. "Solid construction that accounted for seismic activity when it was rebuilt in 1981. Back then, they made things to last. Those tests and upgrades were worth their weight in gold. It's our fourth bridge on the same site, but this one should last another century. It would cut folks in these parts off from civilization if the bridge went."

"Thanks. We were debating if it was sound since we can't see it." Ryan pointed to the darkened overhead lights.

"Power's out in Sandpoint. Most of Idaho too, I reckon. You folks from around here?"

"Washington," said Ryan, not wanting to mention Seattle. If the roads were closed, it might be a problem for some that they'd fled.

"Good for you for getting out. If you're from the coast, you must have been before they closed the roads. Sounds like thousands of cars ran out of gas, blocking traffic and jamming the freeways. Bet it's a nightmare now. Martial law. Everyone is supposed to stay home. They've sectioned off several cities in the West, sending the military to keep the peace and enforce curfews. No one's allowed out after dark. I'll give you two some leeway, but I need to know if you're planning to stay or carry on?"

Ryan and Kat looked at each other with matching horrified expressions. News of the outside world was as bad as expected, but it was worse to have it confirmed.

"Passing through, but camping for the night." Ryan squinted and determined that the shadow on the truck door was a star. This must be the sheriff.

"Where you headed?" The sheriff's eyes flicked inside their car.

"I've got family in Helena," said Kat, once again making things up on the spot. She'd never mentioned family in Montana.

"Drive safely," said the sheriff. "There are washed-out places at the far end of the lake where the road's down to a single lane. Best be driving that part in daylight."

Ryan nodded and eased the gas pedal down, inching forward. He was glad the man trusted them enough to talk and let them through. "We'll find a campsite soon. Stay overnight." He wouldn't always be so forthcoming, but the lawman seemed trustworthy.

"Thanks, officer," said Kat with a big smile and fake cheer in her voice.

Her sugary tone set his teeth on edge, and he was glad that wasn't how she sounded most of the time. It reminded him of Heather when she wanted something. He liked Kat better when she seemed natural, without putting on an act. Driving onto the bridge, Ryan couldn't see beyond his headlights—he missed the streetlights of the city—so he kept his speed slow.

Kat clutched the handle of her door and peered into the darkness, perhaps as intently as he did.

The bridge extended along the water, low like a causeway. It seemed stable, though the tires hummed with a distinct noise on the surface that differed from the sound of the rough highway. Ryan felt like a kid, holding his breath as he guided them across. Kat's breath whooshed out after they reached the far side and left the bridge. He shot her an amused glance. It wasn't the first time they'd been on the same page.

• • •

Sandpoint, Idaho wasn't a large town at the best of times, and it wasn't quite tourist season. He didn't expect to see many people and wasn't disappointed. At night, with the lights extinguished, the rest of the town was almost invisible. The businesses along the main street were closed for the night. The restaurants were dark and many buildings had boarded up their windows.

All three gas stations had signs that read, *"Out of gas."* The town had a ghost town feel, like it was deserted. With no gas, residents would soon be cut off from the outside world. Maybe they were home, conserving fuel. There were no big cities nearby. Ryan drove the empty streets, following the signs for the turnoff onto Highway 200 as the road curved around the north end of the lake.

Half an hour later, Ryan almost missed the turnoff for Sam Owen Forest Service Campground, but the light from his headlights caught the pale sign in the dark at the edge of the thick coniferous forest at the last minute. The darkened office check-in building was deserted.

They followed the loops of the dirt and gravel campground road, choosing a site on the water side of the peninsula in an unoccupied section. On the upper side, there'd been two trailers parked next to one another. Nobody was about when they drove past, but he would rather give them space and camp elsewhere. It was late enough that perhaps their inhabitants had already gone to sleep. Both trailers were long and sleek, unhitched from full-size pickup trucks. Tarps stretched above their cluttered tables and firepits, giving both camps a semi-permanent yet messy lived-in feel. Maybe people lived there for the spring and summer and had set up weeks ago.

The campsite they selected had the obligatory blocky wooden table and the standard flat spot for their tent. Tall trees separated the sites, giving them a private feeling. He'd felt sweaty and gross since afternoon and he didn't see a place to shower. In the morning, he might jump in the lake, even if it would be cold as it was not yet summer.

Today was the twenty-first of May, a day now burned into his brain. If they lived through this, it would be one of *those* days. People still asked, "Where were you September eleventh?" He'd been six years old, on the way to school. His teacher had explained what had happened. Everyone who lived through the asteroid and its aftermath would also have a story. He hoped his had a happy ending.

He and Kat set up the tent, working as a team as if they'd camped together dozens of times. He was thankful for this morning's practice. Setting up camp in the dark was always complicated, even with the light of the headlights streaming into the camp.

That thought reminded him of a distant memory. On an overnight hike, he and Nick had put up the tent at night, in the snow, spending a restless night clinging to the mountainside as they slid inside their tent, aided by gravity. The next morning, they'd discovered a young fir tree poking the underside of their tent. No wonder it had been uncomfortable.

"You hungry?" Ryan remembered only now that they'd skipped dinner. Right after the asteroid, he hadn't been hungry. On cue, his stomach growled. His last meal had been the midafternoon sandwich, a lifetime ago.

Kat's eyes and teeth gleamed in the yellowish glow as she laughed. "I could eat."

He liked that on a day like today, she could appreciate little things, like food. It would have been hard to be with someone crying or miserable all evening. After her tears at the time of the impact, she'd been under control. Not that he blamed her for her initial reaction, just that the doom and gloom part wasn't all she thought about it. Her attitude and change of topic had helped him to deal as well.

"Can you finish setting up what we need for sleeping? Like bedding and suitcases? I'll make food. Anything you don't eat?" He didn't think anyone would come out of this a picky eater, but now, they had options.

"Just peppers. Red, green, yellow. I hate all of them. Peppers are poison." Her nose scrunched up in an adorable way and a deep heat rose within that he stamped out. Now was not the time.

"Noted." Peppers gave him heartburn, so there had been none in his fridge to bring.

He set up the camp stove with the fuel bottle on the picnic table and checked the ice packs in the cooler. They were still frozen, except at the edges. The food should be fine overnight and maybe tomorrow, but not much longer without fresh ice.

He made an omelet, using half of the ham and eggs, plus a generous sprinkle of grated cheese. They could finish the eggs and cheese at breakfast, and there was bread for another meal. He located his camping lantern and turned it on high so they could see without the lights from the car. He didn't want to deplete his battery, especially with no one else around to jumpstart them if he miscalculated the power drain.

They ate a quiet dinner facing the lake, looking up at the stars as they sat on opposite ends of the picnic table's bench seat. The sky was clear and the half-moon was a pale glow, hidden behind a drift of clouds in the inky black sky. As peaceful as it was, it was disconcerting not to see lights. No planes or glow from distant cities. It was darker than regular camping. This was what it might have been like thousands of years ago, before "progress" happened. The planet felt immense when you couldn't see the edges.

They did a quick clean-up after they ate and got ready for bed. With the daylight gone, there was a chill in the air and he was glad he wore a jacket. It was late enough that he shouldn't have trouble sleeping, even if they'd rested at midday. It would be light by five a.m. and he wanted an early start.

Once they were tucked into the cozy tent for the night, Ryan couldn't fall asleep. The dark pressed against his eyelids. He relived the moment of the meteors crashing to the ground and followed by the series of earthquakes; his brain kept running scenarios. If the volcanoes erupted, they might feel more tectonic movement or shifting. It wasn't something he wanted to live through again. It had been disconcerting to feel the earth, which was supposed to be solid, so unstable.

"You asleep?" He kept his voice pitched low enough that if Kat was asleep, he wouldn't disturb her—unless she was a light sleeper. Which he didn't know. His chest had a tight feeling that wouldn't stop, making it hard to relax. He wished he could shut off his busy mind.

"Too much in my head," she said, an echo of his thoughts. Her voice was quiet and close; the tent seemed smaller.

"Me too."

A pause followed, one heavy with unspoken thoughts, and then she said, "I know a guaranteed way to sleep."

He recognized the sound of her biting her lip in the dark by the way her voice changed. He turned in her direction, but she was only a vague shape and a scent of vanilla and something floral in the darkness. If only she knew what biting her lip did to him. Shocked at the thought, he wanted to bite her lip, too. He became hard in an instant and shifted, cursing to himself as his sleeping bag rustled with his uncomfortable movement at such a powerful reaction. That wouldn't help him sleep.

"What's your plan?" he turned onto his side to face her, expecting her to say something about counting sheep or doing multiplication tables in his head—some sort of teacher wisdom.

The next thing he knew, her lips were on his and his skin felt like it lit up from within as heat rushed through him. The groan that escaped his lips embarrassed him. Her kiss wasn't soft, but wanting, like she wanted to devour him. It made him think thoughts of debauchery. His cock strained at his boxers. He pulled back, reluctant to stop, but confused. She couldn't be serious. It was a bad idea; he wasn't looking for a girlfriend.

"What was that for?" His voice was breathless. She must know how turned on he was. Could that be her distraction?

"I'm out of practice, but I thought it was obvious."

She sounded amused, like she was smiling.

The sound of a zipper released her from her sleeping bag, and moments later, she fumbled for his and slid in next to him, her lithe body touching his. He held his breath.

"Is this okay with you?" Her voice was soft and uncertain.

God, she was serious. "This will make me sleep?" His voice was incredulous.

"Eventually." Her hands found his erection and closed around it. He swore he could hear her grin as she sucked in a breath and slid her hand down its length.

"Are you sure this is a smart idea?" He wished he could take the words back; he wanted this. It had been a long time since he'd had sex. He'd craved a woman's touch for months, which was part of why he exercised so much. Too much pent-up frustration and sexual energy.

"Oh, it's a great idea. Inspired by my talk with the cops this afternoon. All afternoon I thought about what I'd like to do before I died. This was top of my list. Part of me is that girl who needs this. It's been too long and I want to feel good and lose myself for a little while. I really want to fuck."

His cock jumped at her unexpected words. He hadn't been with anyone since Heather and he'd never slept around, just had a few serious girlfriends. Was she offering casual sex?

"Condoms are in my suitcase." He didn't mean to blurt, but that's how his strangled words emerged.

She gave a naughty chuckle, and tugged his shorts to his knees, then he kicked them off, breaking contact for a few seconds to pull off her T-shirt and wiggle out of her pajama bottoms. Sexy, naked Kat asking for what she needed. He loved it. It might be the biggest turn-on of all.

Ryan wanted to roll her over and take her. This was like a dream come true. A desirable woman climbing into his bed, no strings attached. He reached into his suitcase by his side in the tent's vestibule, groping until he pulled out a couple of packets, still attached, and slid them under his pillow where they'd be easy to find.

"Do we? Oh shit. Bloody hell. Oh." He was at a loss for words and his thoughts became incoherent. He couldn't remember what he meant to ask as her hot, wet mouth was on him, his cock in her mouth while her fingers teased his balls. He couldn't think beyond partial words. Everything outside the tent ceased to exist. It wasn't important anymore. The restricted feeling in his chest floated away. He lived for each stroke of her mouth and touch of her hand.

She played for a long time, but stopped before he came. He nudged her onto her back and slid a hand between her legs. He'd never felt anyone this wet on their own. She was swollen and drenched from blowing him. He felt like a king. Or a god. Or at least damn lucky. Heat surged through him again. She'd brought him so close to the edge that it was difficult to remain in control.

"What do you want?" he growled. God, his balls ached for release, but waiting was fantastic and would only make it better. This was no tease who'd string him on after revving him up. She wanted him, too. He marveled at the revelation.

"Fingers first, please."

She whimpered as he slipped one into her glorious pussy. He slid it inside, rubbing her clit at the same time with his thumb. The only thing lacking was that he couldn't see, but the dark had its own anonymous magic.

"More. Please, more."

The sound of her pleading voice almost undid him, but he did as requested and added a second finger.

She pulsed around him, crying out as she shuddered with each movement. He needed to feel this from inside. When her orgasm subsided, he kissed her, his tongue flicking into her mouth with desire. She clung to him and moaned, reaching for his cock again. He was still hard as steel.

"Put one on. I need you inside me." She stroked his length.

It was a challenge to concentrate on anything except the feel of her hand, but with her help, he unrolled the condom. He slid up her silky-smooth skin in the dark, liking how she felt beneath him. He stroked her body and took her breast in his palm and squeezed. She made a delicious squeak.

He throbbed as the tip of his penis grazed her wetness. It knew where it wanted to be. He didn't need to guide as it nudged against her opening.

She whimpered.

He grabbed her hands and pulled them over her head as he poised to take her, pushing while she squirmed. He eased inside, stopping every second before advancing another fraction. The slowness stretched into exquisite agony, the opposite of what he wanted, but so much better. He hesitated, savoring this moment, though he couldn't wait to plunge inside to his fullest and ride her hard. He shook with the effort of holding back. He wanted this to last forever, to imprint on his mind. An image of Heather writhing underneath her other boyfriends flashed through his mind, and he almost stopped.

"What are you waiting for?" Her voice brought the desire rushing back, and her hips rose to claim him. She enveloped him and he shuddered at her hot tightness. She ground her hips against him and held him inside, as deep as possible. Rubbing the back of her, she throbbed around him. It took only seconds before she cried out again, heat flashing through them both and surrounding him while she rode the waves of ecstasy. She shuddered beneath him, the intensity rocking him to his core.

As soon as her spasms slowed, he thrust the way he wanted. All the way in, sliding his full length out, then in. It was better than he could have dreamed. He increased the speed as she moaned and rocked with him, finding the perfect rhythm. He didn't last long; it was too close to the surface. His orgasm shook him as he thrust. Once, twice, and the third time, hard. She came with him, quivering everywhere. When it was over, he was drained. All the tension and worry had left his body. His limbs grew heavy; it was the most relaxed he'd been in months.

"Hell," he said, trying to catch his breath. "I've never..." His words trailed off. He didn't know what else he could say. He kissed her again, their lips soft. The perfect ending.

He cleaned up in the dark and yawned as he lay flat, already fading toward sleep.

"Mission accomplished," she said with a matching yawn as she slid her naked body into her own sleeping bag with a zipping sound.

He missed her soft skin against his. He would have liked to feel her sleep against him and was surprised at the depth of longing he felt for their connection. It was just sex, but it had been life-changing, brilliant sex. His body thrummed with contentment and he felt alive. He couldn't remember the last time he'd felt that way. He'd spent a lot of time going through the motions, not really living.

Before he drifted off to sleep, a question flashed through this mind. Was this a onetime thing or the start of something incredible? Awareness left him before he could ask.

CHAPTER 9: KAT

Kat woke to a pleasant soreness between her legs and the realization that she may have been rash, but the sex had been incredible. Half asleep, she touched herself, replaying last night. She stretched, feeling satisfied. She couldn't believe she'd pounced on Ryan. That wasn't her usual style. Her cheeks burned. She hadn't woken up yesterday planning to have sex with him. The idea had grown throughout the day, but she hadn't expected to act on it so soon, if ever.

She spun her ring, hoping things wouldn't be awkward between them this morning. Yesterday, he'd pulled back as soon as they'd shared a moment. Would it be the same today? She looked to her right. Ryan was still asleep. His wavy golden hair was tousled and his cheeks flushed. Without the cover of darkness, she wouldn't have had the courage to proposition him. She couldn't imagine being brave enough under the intense gaze of his mismatched eyes that made her gooey inside. She was a coward at heart, so probably not.

If she stayed in bed any longer, she'd wake him and beg for another round. She wasn't ready to consider what that meant. Instead, she opted for distance.

Sliding out of her sleeping bag, she grabbed her swimsuit and slid into yesterday's clothes. There was a chill in the air that pebbled her skin as she slid her feet into her shoes and slithered out of the tent without making much noise. She wanted to feel clean and jump in the lake. It might be cold, but she didn't care. She wouldn't stay in long.

It was daylight already, but the light was soft and fragile after dawn, leaving the lake peaceful. If Ryan continued to sleep, she'd make him breakfast. Remembering the trailers on the far side of the campground, she hid behind the truck to change into her bathing suit, even if she'd rather swim naked. She didn't want to give anyone ideas. A naked woman swimming on her own was a sketchy idea in general, but if the veneer of civilization had fallen here as much as in the city, it was riskier than usual. It seemed silly to feel suspicious of strangers on a quiet morning, but that might be the dangerous reality.

At the edge of the lake, she dipped her fingers in the still water, sending shallow ripples outward. In the silence, she felt as if she could be alone in the world. She almost scrapped the swimming idea because of her uneasy thoughts, but decided to go for it. She wanted to swim and wouldn't be here ever again; why waste an opportunity? She dropped her towel and her stack of clothing onto the dock and walked to the end, where the dark green water yawned beneath her, its depths obscuring much of the sandy bottom. Without thinking too long, she dove in, rocking the wooden dock. The cold water was shocking and stole her breath, but it wasn't painful.

With powerful strokes, she swam back to the dock and climbed the metal ladder. Once on the dock, a strange sensation prickled her senses, and she turned, searching the shoreline for the source of her unease but couldn't see anyone. It almost seemed like she was being watched, but there was no sign of anyone else near the lake. Shrugging off the feeling, she shivered.

Returning to the business of getting clean, she soaped herself and shampooed her wet hair before jumping into the lake again, leaving a slick of foam and bubbles. She swished her hair and rubbed in the conditioner, this time staying in the water. She was turning blue as she prepared for a final rinse when the dock shook with a rumble. Ryan raced to the end and jumped over her head, pulling his legs up in the air.

"Cannonball," he shouted just before he landed in a curled ball on the surface of the water, sending a gigantic spray of white water into the air.

Water dripped down her face and she spat out the lake water. If she hadn't already been wet, she'd have been annoyed. As it was, she grinned. He surfaced and shook his wet hair, flicking water all around, his grin lighting up the campground.

"Something make you energetic this morning?" she said with an answering smile. Her breath caught for a second, a pang of guilt for flirting. The end of the world was serious, and they needed to continue their journey. She ducked underwater and rinsed her hair so she could avoid seeing if he reacted to her words. She wasn't adjusting to the temperature of the water; it was cold, so she hurried, reminding herself she wasn't in trouble or harming anyone by being pleasant.

"Morning," Ryan said, treading water nearby when she returned to the surface. "I wasn't sure I was brave enough for the cold water but saw you'd survived."

She'd worried that it would be awkward between them this morning, but Ryan treated her the same as he had the last few days. Not close, like the fleeting moments on the road, but normal—like a friend. She couldn't decide which of his eyes was her favorite. Today it was the warm hazel one.

She swam to the ladder. "It's chilly. Don't stay in so long you get sick. I'm just about frozen." She flashed him another smile so he wouldn't think she was leaving because of his presence and climbed out to cook breakfast. Her skin was bumpy with gooseflesh as she shivered, even surrounded by her towel as she dried off. Once more, she got a funny feeling, one that made her shoulder blades twitch. She turned back, but Ryan was underwater, so it wasn't his gaze she sensed. It must be her imagination. Heading back to the shore and camp, she made tea. They would warm up faster with a hot drink inside.

In the distance, an engine revved and screeched away, but no vehicles disturbed their side of the campground and once more, it fell silent.

●   ●   ●

Kat and Ryan didn't waste time after eating and packing before they hit the road. Driving out of the campsite, they got a shock. The two trailers they'd driven past in the dark looked like someone had smashed their way inside. Someone had left the doors flung open and belongings strewn across the ground. Something wet the ground with a dark streak. Another vehicle had been here, leaving a set of wide tire trucks pressed in the damp ground. Bile rose in Kat's mouth. Who would do such an awful thing? Her shoulders twitched at the memory of being watched in the lake. Had the person who had done this been watching her this morning?

Ryan stopped beside the trailers.

"What are you doing?" Her voice shook.

"I want to check if everyone is okay." He left the engine running as he hopped out.

Walking to the first trailer, he stepped inside and came right back out, shaking his head.

She opened the door to follow, but he said, "You should stay in the car."

Though she didn't like being given orders, it might be smart to listen because she trusted his judgment. She closed her door.

His reaction to the second trailer was the same. He got back in the driver's seat, his face white as a sheet of paper. Without a word, he drove away, leaving the campground.

Ryan set his shoulders—like granite and his mouth fixed in a flat line. He didn't seem to want to talk about it. The air became thick with tension when he didn't speak. Shuddering, he took a deep breath, ran a hand through his damp hair, standing it on end. Still, he said nothing, and the silence stretched until it became uncomfortable. It was painful not to know what he'd seen. Her imagination created horrible scenarios until at last she had to ask.

"What did you see?" Her words seemed to break a spell.

"Nobody's there now, but there was blood everywhere. Ransacked cupboards, like someone wanted supplies." His voice sounded remote. "I don't think the owners put up much of a fight. Did you hear anything this morning?"

She shook her head, more in dismay than denial. "A truck maybe, just after you jumped in the lake, but nothing before that. Nothing concrete."

"Anything at all?"

"Before you jumped in the lake, I sensed someone watching. Was that you?"

He shook his head. "I jumped in as soon as I got up." He stopped talking for a few minutes before continuing.

"I don't understand what's happened to some people. I didn't think they'd change in a matter of days. Some people have become their worst selves overnight. I don't want that to happen to us." He glanced in her direction.

She nodded. "Me either. I hope we can keep being ourselves and also survive. Us making it to safety shouldn't take away from anyone else."

• • •

The first two hours were quiet, but they relaxed as the morning remained uneventful, and they didn't see other vehicles. It seemed like a regular road trip on a quiet road instead of a frantic flight toward shelter. Ryan's steadying presence made it easy to forget the seriousness of their journey.

Throughout the third hour, the air became smoky, and it increased as they drove southeast. Kat worried about the reason and her shoulders tightened. A dozen packed buses and a steady stream of packed cars drove in the opposite direction on the broken road. The radio remained static on all stations, so there was no way to determine the source of the smoke unless they came to the fire. Kat rotated the dial from one extreme to the other every ten minutes, hoping in vain for news.

She turned on her phone, but once again, there were no messages. She powered it down, trying not to feel hurt by her family's lack of communication. Perhaps she should be more concerned about their well-being, but it was a relief not to be forced to talk to them and justify leaving. The sky became hazy, with limited visibility as the smoke thickened further. The blaze could be huge, or the direction of the wind could carry the plume. She hoped for the latter.

Abandoned cars littered the side of the road in more frequent intervals once they rejoined the interstate. Soon, they passed several at a time in clumps. Each time, Ryan slowed for Kat to check their windows, but all were empty. Where had all the people gone? The world seemed too quiet, like it too was holding its breath.

They were perhaps half an hour outside Missoula when the roadside cars started spilling onto the highway; the groups becoming larger. What had these people known that she and Ryan didn't? At first, it was just the slow lane, then both lanes. Were they going to be able to continue?

Ryan maneuvered his RAV4 onto the roadside shoulder and back several times like a slalom course, making Kat glad that he was still the driver. Her car wouldn't have had the clearance to get in and out of the chaotic mess.

The blanket of smoke grew thicker and darker, with billowing black plumes blacking out the horizon. The line of buses and cars had been leaving the fire.

"Not sure we want to go much farther," said Ryan, reducing his speed. "If we're driving slow like this, the smoke is going to make us sick. Can you look for another route? Even if we have to backtrack. We'll have to go around Missoula to get to South Dakota."

Kat pored over the map, but it was difficult to tell if any of the smaller roads would connect somewhere ahead to get them past the burning city. The air was hot and dry, making her eyes itchy. Even in the car, the air tasted like smoke, and Kat's throat hurt; she sipped her water to keep her mouth and throat moistened. She passed the open bottle to Ryan as he drove. Germs weren't a consideration when they'd shared more than a water bottle in the dark.

Her cheeks flamed, remembering last night's passionate kisses. The memory must be written all over her face, and she wished she could hide her blushes. Remembering that she'd seen cloth masks in the vehicle's center console, she dug them out. It had surprised her when Ryan had added masks and goggles on the list, but now she was grateful. She would be safe from embarrassment and reduce the amount of smoke making it to her lungs.

She slipped two masks free of their packaging and passed one to Ryan. He took it with a smile and slowed to fasten it in place, but didn't stop. They drove around a bend in the road to see a roadblock ahead manned by the military. Her chest tightened. There were almost a dozen khaki army vehicles blocking them from proceeding. Soldiers milled around in front while thick smoke hung in the air, reaching toward where they'd stopped.

She looked beyond the soldiers at the wall of black plume rising into the air behind the barricade; the fire was close. At the base of the hazy billows, the bright orange of flames glowed. The entire city of Missoula was on fire.

Kat couldn't take her eyes from the flames. There must be hundreds or thousands of homes lost in the blaze, and thousands who were now homeless. Her breath hitched in her throat and she fought tears. The poor families had lost everything. The abandoned cars took on new meaning as she hoped they had taken the people of Missoula to safety. Her heart went out to them. The sight of the fire stripped away the adventure feeling of their journey once more, leaving her feeling stone sober and scared.

Ryan parked in the middle of the road because there was nowhere else to go.

"Want to stay in the car, or walk ahead with me? I want to find out if they'll talk about what's going on or the best way around this mess." He unhooked his mask and shoved it in his pocket.

She raised an eyebrow, surprised he'd removed his filter for the filthy air.

"It might make them uncomfortable if they can't see my face. People are pretty tense. I don't want them to misunderstand." He reached for the door handle. "You can leave yours on. You don't look threatening." He said the last with a wink, the first sign of his old self after the gruesome scene in the campground.

"I'll come." She wanted to hear first-hand about the extent of the fire and its cause. It must not be safe for anyone past the barricades, except perhaps the firefighters. They'd wondered where the closer meteors might have crashed. This could be one of those places. She shuddered at how close it had been.

Kat stepped from the vehicle. The air was hotter and tasted like ash, even through the mask. Breathing through the thick cloth was too warm as she wasn't used to wearing one anymore, but a filter for the air was a great idea, so she left it in place.

Ryan approached one guard at the main roadblock, keeping his hands visible at all times. The soldiers kept their rifles in a ready position but didn't aim them in their direction. Their presence seemed precautionary, not aggressive, as the men and women in uniform didn't appear threatened by the newcomers. The soldiers watched their every move.

"Good morning," said Ryan, addressing his remarks to the closest group of six soldiers. "We camped in Idaho last night and haven't had news since before the meteor strikes. We were hoping you could fill us in."

She held her breath, hoping someone answered.

"The I-90's closed," said the closest man in fatigues. "All civilian traffic is being diverted. You'll have to turn around. Missoula is an asteroid crash site."

Another said, "Two meteorites hit. One downtown, one outside to the east. The highway's impassable. We emptied the stranded cars and sent the refugees by bus to Spokane. No vehicles are allowed beyond this point. You'll have to turn around, head back to Spokane, where they've set up a refugee center. The fire has been burning since the impact yesterday and the survivors evacuated from the city. Most went to Spokane, Coeur d'Alene, or fled south last night if they had fuel."

"We're hoping to travel east," said Ryan. "To go around the city."

Several of the soldiers shook their heads. One man stepped forward to speak.

"Not here. I'm in charge of this outpost. The interstate is closed on both sides of the city. Nobody in, and there's nobody left to come out. I suggest you head back to Washington or Idaho. There's another roadblock south of West View Park to prevent southbound traffic. There's no way through or past Missoula. It's too dangerous."

"Captain," said a young soldier running up. "The Colonel is on the radio. He'd like to speak to you. Says it's urgent."

The captain nodded and strode toward the barrier. The others drifted in that direction too, leaving the young soldier who'd brought the message behind.

"Any updates on the West Coast?" Ryan asked the messenger. It wasn't much louder than a whisper.

The soldier glanced toward the soldiers gathered at the other end of the barrier who'd followed the captain.

"Here, I'll point out the best route." The young man spoke in a loud voice as he walked toward them, pointing off the road to the north. He lowered his voice. "That's you back there with the bikes?"

At Ryan's nod, his volume increased once more when he said, "Do you have enough fuel? I'll check."

He followed them toward the SUV and Kat furrowed her brow. This must be a ruse for his companions. They didn't need him to check their fuel.

The young man pointed again, as though still explaining, while under his breath he said, "You've got bikes, which gives you options. Drive back a few miles, take the exit to West View Park. We blocked all the major roads from Seventh and West View onward. You could try to make it through by bike if you're set on getting past Missoula. The highways are closed, but if you stick to side streets in the residential areas and stay alert, you might make it. Not everywhere is on fire yet, and we only have personnel to block main roads. Forces are spread thin with martial law in the big cities and dealing with the evacuees. There's nobody to fight the fire, so the sooner you get past Missoula, the better. By tonight, it will be impassable."

Her guess was correct; he was giving them vital information.

"I wouldn't be surprised if we're ordered to fall back to safer positions by afternoon."

Kat's breath hitched. The fire would keep burning without firefighters. No wonder the inferno had spread. It was worse than she'd thought. How many had died in the initial impact? How many because of earthquakes or fire? She hoped the evacuation had come in time for most of the inhabitants. Shaking, she stumbled back.

"Is there an estimated death toll?" asked Ryan, reaching for Kat's arm.

His warm hand grounded her in the moment, keeping despair at bay.

The young man shook his head, his expression bleak. "That information is classified. But it must be high. The meteorites blasted in hot and fast yesterday, and there was nothing anyone could do. I heard the big one downtown caused a firestorm on impact."

Tears filled Kat's eyes, and she turned away to wipe them.

"Other news?" Ryan's eyes were intent on the helpful young soldier.

The young man shouldn't be so free with his news, but perhaps he needed to unburden himself. The sad news would weigh anyone down.

"We've been told to expect volcanic activity up and down Washington, Oregon, and California. Mount Baker, Mount Rainier,

Mount St. Helens, and Mount Hood are active and steaming. Crater Lake is steaming and bubbling. At least one of them is going to erupt. Maybe all. Nobody in living history remembers more than one eruption at a time."

The young man glanced back toward the barricade and swallowed hard. "Off the record. Once you can, go east. Get as far from the coast and mountains as you can. There were medium-sized strikes in New York, Georgia, and Texas. The whole country is a mess. Millions of dead and homeless. They've set up refugee camps outside the cities and hope that people can make their way there. Smaller strikes were scattered across the country, cutting off major routes. It's a colossal shit-show. Power is off in most sectors because the grid couldn't handle the surges. They overloaded, and there's no timeline for getting it back on. Hundreds of cell towers were smashed or are wrecked without power, and there's no way to know when they can fix those either. There isn't other help coming. We're it." The man's eyes looked frightened as he took a huge breath in conclusion.

"Thanks. We appreciate your honesty." Ryan stepped away and reattached his mask as he opened the door to his vehicle. "C'mon Kat. We'll have to head back." She missed the warmth of his hand on her arm.

Were his words serious, or for show? There was nothing to go back to. Violence. The murder scene by the lake. Fire. Death? Her chest tightened further and it was all she could do not to sob. She pressed her lips together and clamped down on her jaw. If she had to speak, she wasn't sure she could keep from bawling.

Climbing into the vehicle, they turned around. Ryan raised a hand in thanks to the soldier as they turned around, headed north, and crossed back to the proper side of the highway. He waved as she looked back, the soldiers standing at their posts. The soldiers looked so small and insignificant. Just like them. No one here would see their families again.

CHAPTER 10: KAT

Kat's deep thoughts continued as they drove for several minutes. At the Westview Park marker, Ryan exited, heading for a quiet neighborhood instead of continuing up the highway toward Spokane or back toward Idaho. Ahead, in the distance, soldiers blocked the road where they'd been told. She and Ryan turned right again, searching for a workaround.

She reached for the radio dial and resumed her search for a signal. There was nothing.

Each time they tried to return to the main roads that led around Missoula, the road was barricaded. After seven or eight failed attempts that took them farther from their intended route, Ryan pulled over to examine the map. He ran his hands through his hair, standing it on end, and let out a deep sigh.

"We're not having luck going around." They were his first words since the young soldier's horrifying report. "The only routes through Missoula are the two highways, but they're both blocked."

"Is there another way if we turn back?"

He shook his head. "We can't go back. There's only forward. My grandfather's bunker is prepped to the hilt. He has everything."

"I looked up xTerra, like you suggested. It surprised me they built it from a decommissioned military base."

"I can't think of anywhere safer. With civilization crumbling, food supplies will diminish. We have to get to the bunker."

After another couple of failed attempts, they parked in an empty church parking lot. Kat checked the street signs, an automatic response in case they could return in the future, even if she had a feeling that would never happen.

"If we go left, there's the fire. We've tried everywhere on the right. To get anywhere, we would have to cut across the parks, the field, or the golf course that are all fenced. That means we need the bikes, which isn't the news I hoped for, but now I believe what we were told," he said, leaning back against his door. "I'd like to have gotten farther before switching to the bikes, but we can't wait. They can't put out this fire. It could burn for weeks." Ryan moved to the back and unlocked the bikes, settling each on the ground.

The tight feeling worsened, but she ignored it, even though it felt like a car was parked on her chest. This was going to be excruciating and slow. Biking to South Dakota?

They removed items from their suitcases and packed what they could into the bikes' saddlebags. Kat kept her books and most of her clothes, but discarded most of the personal items from her apartment—except a framed photo of her family and jewelry from her grandmother. She'd rather live than have a bunch of keepsakes. It was interesting what mattered when it was life or death as she sorted her belongings.

She ran through the six P's again in her head. People and pets. She had Ryan, no animals. Papers. She had her birth certificate and passport. Prescriptions. She'd had her birth control renewed; the hopeful two-year supply was stuffed in the bottom of her backpack. She also had her sunglasses and assorted vitamins, and a stocked household first-aid kit. PC. She'd brought her laptop, even if it wasn't useful right now. She'd stocked it with her favorite movies. Personal items. She had little of value. The final P was plastic. She had credit cards and cash, though she had no idea if either would be usable.

Between them, they had enough dried food for at least a week. She reduced her shoes to a pair of sandals and hiking shoes, leaving her boots in the truck. If she needed boots in the future, she'd have to buy or scavenge. She filled the canteens and water bottles from the big water jug in the back. It was still half-full when she returned it to the hatch. Maybe someone who needed water would find it. Then it wouldn't be wasted.

Ryan checked over both bikes and added air to the tires with his portable pump.

"Ready? Nothing else to do."

He cast a look over his shoulder at the wall of menacing dark-gray smoke and she turned as well. It looked closer and blacker. More menacing, like it was chasing after them. They hadn't ridden far when Ryan deked down a side street, farther from the main street where they'd been told the roadblock was located. She followed him as they headed south, cutting through a park on a paved trail, and ducked through a schoolyard. Her bad ankle was stiff, but not too painful as she pedaled.

In the distance, army vehicles blocked the road, soldiers milling in front of the parked jeeps. With increasing frustration, they struggled to discover a way through without being stopped. As they turned around, Kat spotted a broken fence and a wide set of muddy tracks running through the section, where a vehicle may have forced its way through. Someone had tried a quick repair, restricting the size of the gap. They cycled through the narrow opening, which led onto a golf course, staying away from the highway until they were well past the matching northbound roadblock and it had disappeared from sight.

It was eerie and quiet, riding through the abandoned streets and neighborhoods. It was scary to think that these homes might all burn because the fire raged unchecked. Were other cities in a similar situation? It sounded like the evacuees were filling up other cities in the area. What would happen to the refugees long-term? Many were now homeless.

They didn't see a soul as they cycled; at least the soldiers must have done a thorough job with the evacuation. At last, Ryan directed them back toward the smaller Highway 93 out of town, also known on the map as the Bitterroot Trail. She released a breath when they returned to the main road without incident.

Cycling far was difficult with the poor air quality. Kat struggled to draw a full breath and her lungs labored. Her eyes watered from the acrid smoke and made her mask damp. The cloth clung to her face, making it yet harder to breathe. Despite the headache and fatigue, desperation lent strength to her muscles.

They rode all day, leaving the burning city behind as they traveled south for hours before turning east once more at Grantsdale. The tight feeling in her chest remained, caused by the urgency to find shelter and the thought of joining the homeless, on the road forever, rather than the air pollution.

Generic small towns seemed much farther apart by bike than they had by car, no longer flashing past in an instant, but forcing her to notice how quiet they'd become without milling people walking the sidewalks or children playing. She and Ryan earned each mile they traveled.

As daylight waned, they stopped at a rest area to look at their map and have a quick break. A couple of semis had parked in the truck area, though they didn't see the drivers. They'd seen two other vehicles since leaving the burning Missoula, both heading north—the opposite direction.

"Let's stay in the Georgetown Lake area." Ryan tapped the map.

"Lots of campgrounds," she said, her shoulder leaning on his.

"With what that soldier shared, I'd rather search for a cabin or a motel. Something more solid. Maybe try that for the next couple of days. They might not have power or running water, but at least they'd have walls and a roof. We're going to be on the road longer than we first planned."

Her heart sank at his words, but he was right. She'd avoided thinking about how much farther it was to South Dakota.

"Do you think the volcanoes might erupt tonight?" She pictured the videos of Mount St. Helens and its famous explosion in 1980. She'd tormented herself by Googling the eruption last weekend.

"Tonight, tomorrow, a few days. It could happen anytime."

Her mouth pulled flat and she chewed inside her bottom lip. "How much longer should we ride tonight? An hour?" The light remained hazy, but sunset should be in about an hour.

"Sounds about right unless you want to stay here. We could stay in the restroom." He raised an eyebrow in inquiry and she shook her head. She hated the idea of sleeping in a filthy roadside bathroom, even if it had a roof.

"Can you wait for dinner until we've found a place? We don't have much more light. I'm even less a fan of riding in the dark than driving. The earthquake damaged the road. I'm surprised we haven't seen more power lines and trees across the road."

Her stomach gurgled. "I can keep going." They were looking at another late dinner. She wished they could stop, but his reasons to travel farther were valid and convincing.

"Let's go," she said, pushing her bike toward the exit and climbing aboard. When she glanced back, Ryan was right behind.

The rest of the ride was quiet that evening. Kat's butt was sore, her ankle stiff, and her legs rubbery as they neared Porter's Corner. She was ready to rest. Sundown had been half an hour ago, and they'd turned on lights on their helmets and the bikes, but her eyes ached from the strain. They needed a place to stop.

The sign for cabins, a resort, and several inns on Georgetown Lake was providential, and incentive to ride a little further. They could sleep in proper beds just off Route 1 in a cluster of buildings overlooking the lake. It was difficult to know which buildings were occupied this time of year with the lights on the roadside signs turned off, but they could figure it out when they arrived.

When they stopped, Kat did some quick calculations in her head using distance increments from the paper maps. They'd driven about a hundred and seventy miles before leaving Ryan's SUV before noon, then cycled another hundred and fifteen miles. The bunker was still far away.

Several darkened motels sat near the roadside. They were rundown and dingy but would be better than nothing.

"If we can't find something better, we'll return here," said Ryan. "I'm done in."

She appreciated she wasn't the only one. On their hikes, she'd noticed that he was more fit than she was and she was proud of keeping up the pace today despite her sore ankle. Unbidden, the memory of sliding her hands over his hard abs and across his smooth chest popped into her head. A memory was all it would remain because she was too tired to proposition him again tonight. The idea was appealing, if unrealistic, because of her exhaustion.

Five minutes later, they found a sign for a resort that said, "Cabins." They turned up the hill and stopped at the darkened office fifty yards from the road. They'd found functional electricity for the first time since before the asteroid yesterday. Lights illuminated half a dozen up-scale two-story log cabins in two rows above them—their porch lights, glowing yellow spheres that beckoned.

Ryan knocked on the office door, receiving no response. He peered in the window, his face and hand almost against the clear glass. Inside remained dark.

"Nobody's there."

Her disappointment was thick enough to choke her. She swallowed it. There was no point in getting upset.

He turned the door handle, but it was locked. He shook the knob, and the door rattled and shook in its frame. "This isn't that solid."

Kat didn't know what he was planning, but without warning, he kicked the door. It splintered inward. The wooden frame cracked and freed the latch. She cringed at the idea of breaking and entering. She looked for security cameras, but there was nothing. With everything else happening, this should be the least of her concerns. It was absurd to care.

Ryan flicked a light on and ducked inside, coming out a minute later with a key ring in his hand and half a dozen paperclips in the other. He pulled the door closed despite the splintered frame.

"Cabin Six." He pointed to the second row, and they pushed their bikes to the front of the cabin. The cabins were two-story, rectangular boxes built from what looked like thick square pieces of lumber. Each had a compact lower porch and another upper deck above with windows that faced the lake. Up close, they weren't as large as they'd seemed from below, as they were wider than they were deep, but they'd be a lot bigger than the inside of the tent. They were a lot nicer than many of the rustic cabins she'd slept in when hiking.

"What's with the paperclips?"

"When they're straightened, I can pick locks. I thought that might be useful another time, so I don't have to kick holes in doors." He shoved the metal clips into his pocket.

It made her feel uncomfortable that they'd be breaking into more places. Hopefully, only places that were deserted.

An ancient spruce tree shadowed the end cabin and the porch light's yellow glow was inviting. She crossed her fingers, hoping that meant there was electricity inside. She longed for a hot bath or shower, anything to wash away the smoke and sweat before bed.

Ryan tossed her the key as they unloaded the bikes. "Why don't you check it out?"

She trotted up the steps to the porch and unlocked the front door. She flicked on the light switch and did a little dance on the threshold when the overhead bulb turned on, flooding the room with a warm yellow light. The inside of the cabin looked cozy.

"There's a kitchen and a living area. A loft upstairs. Lots of space to bring the bikes in." She went out to help lug them up the shallow wooden stairs, determined to do her share.

The main room featured a kitchen at one end and a small living room with a quiet patio that would be awesome for watching sunsets over the lake. The cabin would have been perfect if not for the surrounding chaos. For a split second, it had seemed like a vacation rental where they could sleep in and lounge for the day. Somewhere they could explore and stay for a long weekend. She visualized drinking a gin and tonic on the deck and realized she'd gone eleven days now without drinking. This was the first time she'd wanted one, and not for the usual reason. Still, she was glad she'd left that behind because she liked herself better sober.

They propped the bikes against the wall in the living room, tucked out of the pathway. Kat drew the curtains on the large front windows to make it less obvious that this cottage was occupied. It was like the blitz during the Second World War, with all of London and the surrounding countryside keeping their lights hidden, so they didn't reveal their position to the German bombers. Maybe she'd been reading too much historical fiction.

While Ryan located food packets, she searched the cupboards for a pot to boil water or a kettle. That's all cooking would entail for the rest of the journey. She found a pot and clattered through the drawer to find a matching lid before turning the stove to maximum.

Ryan held up two dinner options. "Beef stroganoff or lasagna?" They had double of all the freeze-dried options so they could eat the same meal.

"Stroganoff. Lasagna tomorrow?" She smiled and went to explore the rest of the cabin. It didn't take two people to watch water boil. The stairs wound around in a tight spiral, with treads spread like a fan. Upstairs was a loft bedroom with a king-size bed overlooking the lake with a view in three directions. She hauled back the curtains to see the moon rising over the lake, casting a silvery path on the shining water.

Next to the bedroom was a bathroom with a deep soaker tub. Kat sighed, pleasure and want infusing her body. She couldn't wait to wash away the nasty fire smell from her hair and the sticky feeling from riding all day.

Back downstairs, she examined the loveseat; it looked like a pull-out. She removed the cushions and unfolded a double bed. With a lump on one side and springs sticking through the threadbare mattress, it didn't look comfortable. Quite the disparity between upstairs and downstairs mattresses.

"Sleeping options," she said, returning to the table. "King-size bed upstairs and that." She pointed, unable to keep the derision from her voice. It looked like a piece of junk. "Which I don't think you'd fit. So that's me." At least she'd be clean and inside.

Ryan laughed. "That would probably break the back of anyone unfortunate enough to sleep there. We can both sleep upstairs. Tons of space."

"You're sure?" She bit her lip. She didn't want him to think she was clingy or a sex maniac. Tonight, she was tired. She wanted to rest her weary body and sink into oblivion.

"I don't need to sleep alone. It was nice having you there last night." His eyes widened. "Not just the sex. Which was good. Amazing, actually, but that's not what I'm angling for. I just mean..." His voice trailed off and he took a deep breath. He ran his hands through the front of his hair on either side. "I mean, there's no reason for either of us to sleep on that deathtrap in the living room when there's a spacious bed upstairs, big enough for two."

She restrained herself from laughing. It was a relief to hear him babble and see the tips of his ears turn pink. He seemed more human and approachable.

She cocked her head to the side. "Are you sure?" She wanted to see if he'd blush again and grinned when his cheeks flushed.

"Please sleep upstairs. We both can."

She laughed. It wasn't that funny, but it was a relief after the last tension-filled days.

"I sound like an idiot, or a teenager, don't I?" He too laughed while he shook his head and poured the boiling water into the waiting bowls. Handing her a spoon, he said, "For poking fun at me, you can stir your own gourmet meal."

Hot food and good humor made the evening pleasant—as did the prospect of bathing.

Though the stroganoff was freeze-dried, it was appetizing enough. It was satisfying, even if she wasn't quite full. If they were cycling to South Dakota, she'd be fit and lean when she arrived. They were approximately halfway, so traveling by bike, it would take another five days. Maybe six. Dinner was quick, as they were both hungry. She wondered about the etiquette of licking her bowl and decided she didn't know Ryan that well yet. He might be horrified if she showed her barbarian side. She flicked a glance in his direction and restrained herself.

While Kat washed their dishes after dinner, Ryan plugged his phone into the charger, taking advantage of having electricity. She dried her hands and did the same. He read messages that left him scowling. She checked again that her last ones had been sent. They sat on Read, so they'd been received, but there'd been no response.

She had no way of knowing how her family was; she sent another message, hoping they would answer by morning before she and Ryan set out again. Of course, if the satellites and cell towers were destroyed, her message might not get to its destination. It might be several days before they could charge the phones again, especially if they camped. Finding electricity here had been a stroke of luck, but they shouldn't count on it tomorrow or in the days ahead.

She stared at the words and how little she'd said. *"Hope you're safe. I love you. With my friend Ryan. We're safe so far."* She didn't tell them where she was, afraid they'd say she'd abandoned them. Guilt washed over her. She couldn't bear to watch their lack of reply and shut down her phone, her throat aching as she suppressed her feelings. Maybe they were saving their charge and had their phones powered off. She moved the charger across the room out of reach. She didn't want to torment herself by checking for messages that were non-existent.

"Mind if I have a bath? I won't be too late or in your way."

"Of course not. I want to shower before bed, too." Ryan's face became granite-like once again. He looked down and grimaced, breaking the illusion of stone. "I smell like a chimney sweep."

He looked like he was trying to keep the mood light, but his message had made him quiet. He didn't seem close to his family, either.

Kat went upstairs with a lump swelling in her throat. Should she ask Ryan about his family? He might think she was prying. He seemed unhappy, and she was curious about his story. She knew little beyond

Nick's mention of a nasty breakup last year. She also considered him her friend and wanted to be there if he needed it.

Running a hot bath and brushing her teeth in the steam-filled bathroom normalized the evening as she luxuriated in the hot water and rinsed the smoke smell from her long hair. It felt good to be clean without freezing, unlike her dip in the lake this morning. After the events today, this morning seemed like days ago. The last shower in her apartment on Monday morning seemed like another lifetime. After twenty minutes, feeling relaxed, she got out and slipped into pajamas.

Ryan had stretched out on the far side of the bed, shirtless, where he read. "Hope that side's okay?"

She tried not to be obvious about her admiration of his broad shoulders and heavily muscled biceps while she folded back the duvet. Whatever his workout regime had been, it had been successful. "I don't care about the left or the right. I'm tired enough that I could sleep almost anywhere. Possibly even the deathtrap downstairs, but I'm glad you don't mind sharing. This is great." She slid into bed and sighed.

"I won't be long," he said with a tired smile, grabbing his bathroom kit and towel and heading to the bathroom. The sound of the shower soon turned on.

Kat left on the overhead light but found herself nodding. She wasn't waiting for Ryan to sleep. Too exhausted to read, her muscles thrummed from the day's exercise, and her sore ankle throbbed. The bed was so comfortable it was like she was sinking into a cloud and it was impossible to stay awake. The last thing she remembered thinking was that she should have stretched. She might be stiff tomorrow.

CHAPTER 11: KAT

Kat startled awake with a gasp, her heart racing and a scream caught in her throat. The house shook, causing the windows to shudder and the dishes downstairs to rattle. Books crashed off the shelf on the main floor, hitting the hard floor. The grinding earthquake noise had returned. The bed was flat and empty, with Ryan standing near the window where the moon shone.

"In an earthquake, you're supposed to stay away from windows." Her voice shook, but her inner teacher couldn't help but recite information from the dozens of earthquake drills she'd performed. The real thing was still different. The noise was so much worse than what she'd expected.

"It's okay. This place is sturdy. Not even cracks in the windows. Come see." He beckoned her with a toss of his head. The earthquake slowed, then stopped. The night became silent as the grinding subsided.

Despite his reassurance, she shook all over but joined him, the wooden floor chilly on her bare feet. The view was worth the discomfort. The moon over the lake was disappearing, like it was being consumed by a fast-moving storm of dark clouds. She'd seen nothing like it and it made the hair on the back of her neck stand up. It was both terrifying and incredible. It reminded her of a nature movie taken with time-lapse photography; it didn't seem like it could be in real-time.

The clouds moved too fast and looked wrong. She shivered. With her sleep-fogged brain, it took her a minute to realize what was happening. Volcanic activity must have caused the seismic activity.

"That towering plume of volcanic ash is devouring the sky."

She must have uttered the last words aloud because Ryan said, "Spewing a ton of ash into the atmosphere. This was one of my biggest concerns." He couldn't seem to take his eyes from the sight of the expanding cloud of ash, either.

"I have a dumb idea," Kat said, her voice hesitant as she looked up at him. "Should we fill the tub or pots and pans with water in case the power goes out? Maybe the water comes from the lake and will get filled with ash?" Her voice was unsteady. This would cause devastating pollution for the birds, fish, and small creatures that would die. Humans weren't the only ones who were going to suffer.

"That's genius, not dumb. I'm glad one of us is thinking right now," he said as the last of the moon vanished behind the thick, rolling volcanic cloud, the light outside snuffed out. He trotted down the stairs to the kitchen and filled pots while she ran water into the tub.

When they returned to their separate sides of the bed, she was wide awake, her brain spinning despite it being four a.m. when she should be tired. So much was changing and society wouldn't return to the way it was. What would the world look like when she awoke? Every day it got harder to imagine it returning to normal. Part of her had hoped Ryan would be wrong, that the seismic activity was finished and that the volcanoes wouldn't erupt, but his fears had come true.

"I can't sleep."

"Me either." His voice seemed far away—once more challenging to read.

"Tell me about you," Kat said, reaching an arm across the empty expanse in the enormous bed. It felt like a risk. What if he shot her down? "You're my companion for the end of the world, my new best friend, and I don't know you." She scooted a few inches closer and touched his warm arm, wrapping her hand around his bicep, wanting to feel him, to connect like they had in the truck the day before when the asteroid had hit. Ryan was strong, calm, and solid. She needed that.

It was dark, with the stars covered and the moonlight extinguished. Thinking too much made her chest tight while she waited for him to respond.

He said nothing at first. Had he gone back to sleep? She loosened her grip, but his hand covered hers, locking it in place.

Ryan cleared his throat. "What do you want to know?"

"Tell me something awful, then something nice. Things a good friend would know."

He was silent for several seconds. She didn't think he shared much about himself with many people. Maybe Nick. Maybe no one.

"My girlfriend, Heather, almost ruined me," he said at last. "Is that awful enough?" His voice was sharp. "She lived with me for three years. I paid off her student loans, purchased her new furniture, and paid for our vacations. I got her everything she asked for. We were supposed to get married. I even bought an engagement ring." He laughed, a horrible mocking sound that broke her heart.

Kat pictured the disaster coming in his words. He wasn't engaged; Heather had broken him. It must have been horrible. She tightened her grip on his arm, offering support.

"I was so blind. I came home to surprise her with free hockey tickets to see the Kraken. When we got home, I was going to propose. He hesitated as his voice cracked.

The bad part was coming. It was like a movie unfolding before her, so vivid she pictured it in full color. Ryan's eyes aglow with happiness, the sparkle of the ring, and the pieces of his heart smashed.

"I found her fucking her ex in our bed. She'd been seeing him the whole time." His voice was bleak. "They'd picked up a stranger to play with too, something she said they liked to do from time to time. Called him her exciting new boy-toy. She made me feel like being with me had never been enough."

"That's awful," Kat said, squeezing his tense arm. "Heather was stupid." He made a sound in his throat that she couldn't interpret in the dark. How had Heather failed to see what a catch Ryan was? Sometimes he was distant, but other times he was kind and caring. If Ryan was her boyfriend, she'd never treat him that way.

"What's your horror story? Your husband dying?" His voice was still thick with emotion.

He tucked a lock of her hair behind her ear, and she swallowed in the darkness. Imagining both the blue eye and the warm hazel one gazing at her, taking away her loneliness.

"It should be, shouldn't it?" She paused. "From the outside, that's what it would look like—the reason I fell apart." Her voice was softer when she resumed. "Mark was a bully. He didn't hurt me, but he disapproved of everything I did, said, wore, or listened to. He mocked my differences and insecurities, calling them excuses. He made me feel stupid and worthless, like I didn't matter. He discouraged me from seeing Nick and Jake, or my girlfriends. I wasn't told I couldn't. He just made it clear that he needed to be the most important. He undercut my relationship with everyone, except my work colleagues, who I wasn't close to."

Kat hesitated, taking a deep breath. "The worst was that my family believed what he told them about past wrongs and hard feelings, even though they were invented, out of context, or blown out of proportion. I wasn't close to my family, but we drifted farther and farther apart. Even before he died, I lost myself and didn't know how to find myself. I didn't like myself anymore." She hadn't felt her tears start, but they streamed down her face and slipped onto her damp pillow.

She didn't know if Ryan could tell she was crying, though she hadn't tried to hide it. She couldn't believe she'd said so much. Something about Ryan and the days they'd just lived through brought her pain closer to the surface than she'd allowed. Most of the time, she smothered thoughts of Mark.

"I was lost too." Ryan's voice sounded thoughtful. "That's an accurate description. My life since I kicked Heather out revolved around working out and my job. It kept me from thinking and let me be numb."

"That's why I drank." It was easier than she'd thought to be honest. Like last night's sex. It was easy to be brave when nobody could see her face. "I'm supposed to miss him, but I'm glad he's gone." It was the first time she'd spoken that sentiment aloud.

She waited for Ryan's judgment, but none came. It came as a relief that he offered no opinion, just accepted her words. "What about your nice story?" Her voice hitched. She didn't enjoy talking about Mark, but her admission was freeing. Maybe Mark's hold on her was almost gone. She'd liked herself better the last eleven days than she had in years.

"I have a better idea." Ryan moved closer and took her face between his substantial hands and wiped her tears away with his thumbs.

He knew or had guessed that she was crying. His lips were soft, and she tingled all over at the warm current that passed into her, thawing something inside. Maybe the icy wall around her heart. He kissed her forehead and pulled her against him in a hug, his arms around her. She didn't always like to be touched, but he made her feel safe.

"They're gone and can't hurt us anymore. We're better off without them. Let's go back to sleep. The world will be different in the morning."

Kat turned, and he spooned her, wrapping his arm around her. His fresh peppermint soap smell enveloped her, as did his warmth. She relaxed against him, letting some of her worries dissipate, at least for now. Tonight, this connection was better than sex and just as intimate.

He spoke into her hair, his breath warm on her neck and cheek. "We didn't quite break and we aren't lost forever. Maybe we can find our way back together. We'll just take it one day at a time."

She sighed, feeling content, and closed her eyes. She was safe in his arms, no matter what was happening outside. She shouldn't feel this way. Fires raged, people were dying, and volcanoes were spewing toxic gases and ash into the atmosphere, but a sense of belonging suffused her, one missing for as long as she could remember.

"Something nice is this moment, right here, right now," Ryan squeezed her tighter. "We're together."

CHAPTER 12: RYAN

When Ryan woke the next morning, he and Kat were still intertwined in bed. He didn't move, as he enjoyed the sensation of the warmth of another person—her warm breath and silky skin next to his. It had been too long since he'd felt that, or wanted it. The last couple of days were the most he'd connected with anyone in as long as he could remember. He'd tried to resist, but he craved this kind of closeness.

His relationship with Heather had been distant and superficial. It had been about the right clothes, the right restaurants, and impressing her friends. There'd been no substance. Too bad he hadn't realized sooner. He'd felt foolish when she'd cheated on him; he'd been used. Ryan hoped he hadn't said too much last night and scared Kat off.

He gave Nick credit. His friend's hunch may have been unerring to try to set them up in the past. Kat was a better match than he could have expected. A lot of the extra bubbly, happy-go-lucky version he'd glimpsed in the beginning seemed to be her public persona or an act, not the real her. Or it was how she used to be. It sounded like her relationship with Mark had changed her as much as Heather had changed him.

He relished the sensation, lying next to her for a few more minutes before admitting that he needed to get up. He'd rather stay in bed, but there was too much he didn't know. Rolling onto his back, he stared at the wooden beams in the ceiling, missing her closeness at once. He needed to check the situation outside, but dreaded what he might find. He took a breath and pushed to a sitting position, easing into wakefulness. The coffee maker waited downstairs, so he swung his feet to the floor. Forcing himself to move.

Last night, the lake across the road had dominated the spectacular view, but was now lost in a bank of impenetrable white. It should have reminded him of a winter wonderland, but instead it was bleak and apocalyptic—like the dense fog of a horror movie. They needed to discover something about the world beyond the cabin. He had a hand-crank radio in his bag. Today he'd break it out and search for a signal. He hadn't wanted to stop long enough yesterday to mess with the radio when they had mileage to make. He'd disliked leaving his Toyota behind, but it had been the smart choice. Still, they could have used it now. Biking added days to the trip ahead, days he didn't want to be on the road and away from shelter.

He glanced at Kat. Her hair was wavier than usual from sleeping on it wet, and for once wasn't pulled into a ponytail, and her cheeks were rosy with sleep. Her messy hair and no make-up held a natural beauty that made his balls ache. She was so fuckable and had no idea. He was rock hard this morning and should escape before she woke and noticed.

He slipped out of bed, tugging on his pants before trudging downstairs. He put on coffee and water for her tea, grabbed his mask before sliding on shoes, and stepped out onto the porch. His heart sunk at the sight before him, though it was much as he'd expected.

Outside seemed a different world than the one they'd ridden their bikes through yesterday. The sun's light was weak and faded, with the sun only appearing as a pale orange glow behind hazy skies—much like seeing it through thick smoke, but worse. Light gray ash fell from the sky, interspersed with small chunks of ash and cinders. Small black bits littered the porch and stairs amid the accumulation of finer dust. It swathed the ground in a blanket of debris like dirty snow.

He brushed off the stairs with a broom, discovering the ash was already three to four inches deep.

Shading his eyes, he looked west. There was no break in the whitish-gray sky; it extended as far as he could see with more powdery ash falling, twirling like distorted snowflakes. The birds and insects were silent. The gentle sound of waves lapping on the shore was gone, as was the wind. Unnerved by the silence, he didn't want to stay outside alone.

Ryan was thankful for Kat's quick thinking. They had water for a couple of days, but they shouldn't stay here long, though he didn't know how they'd leave. They wouldn't be able to ride the bikes on roads covered in thick drifts of ash. He'd have to think of an alternative. Maybe they could stay here a couple of days and hope it rained enough to clear the roads. He pictured the mess that would make—an ash slurry covering the road. That wasn't the answer. He wished he had information about how many of the volcanoes had erupted and what kind of sustained ashfall they might face. If it was going to spew ash for days, they'd be better off to continue on foot. Maybe. That might be drastic. They were still too far from South Dakota.

He turned back to the house, stomping his shoes to remove the powdery grey clumps stuck to the bottom. He flicked the switch and the porch light still turned on. He'd been afraid they would have lost power in the earthquake last night, but they had electricity—which bought them time.

He might hike back to the general store at the north end of the lake that he'd seen advertised near the turnoff to the campgrounds to see if he could gather additional supplies. It wasn't far. Seattle's buying and hoarding frenzy might not be the norm in the country, though they'd stayed out of the stores. He and Kat could perhaps supplement their food and save the freeze-dried rations. They might need it to stretch, as there was still a long distance to travel.

Plans and thoughts swirled through his head. He hated sitting being idle. He needed something to do. Kat was up and making breakfast when he entered.

"It's like snow out there. Slow-moving now, but there are several inches of powder on the ground and getting deeper. The road's buried."

"We can't ride in that." Tightness by her eyes showed her feelings about the delay matched his.

He shook his head and filled her in on his thoughts of a trip to stock up.

She'd opened a day's worth of oatmeal, two packets per bowl. The smell was too sweet when she poured in the water, but his stomach gurgled with hunger as their meals had been irregular.

"Can I walk to the store with you?" she said, surprising him.

He'd assumed that she'd read or watch movies and rest her ankle.

He shrugged. "Of course. I'm not going far, though. Just back a couple of miles."

"What if it isn't open?"

"We'll deal with that when we get there." He wasn't planning to leave without additional supplies, one way or another. He touched the paperclips in his pocket.

They didn't waste clean water on the dishes, instead wiping them with paper towels.

Ryan located his small blue radio and cranked the handle until it showed that it had a full charge. Raising the antenna, he spun the manual dial, starting at one end and scrolling through all stations. He turned up the volume, not wanting to miss a distant or partial signal. He'd rotated three-quarters of the way through the range when a crackle interrupted the white static of nothing. Slowing, his sweaty hands quivered as he homed in on the elusive signal, noting the numbers so he could find it again.

A practiced radio voice grew clearer, and he wiggled the dial to sharpen it.

"Stay tuned for further details in the days to come."

It sounded like part of a recording. Finally. His heart pounded in his chest.

Kat moved closer and sat across the table to listen, meeting his eyes with an optimistic look and a slight smile. There was a pause, and he held his breath, hoping the broadcast resumed.

"*This is the Emergency Broadcast System,*" the voice said. Hope surged through him at the voice from the beyond. He'd been feeling like everyone else had disappeared, that they were alone.

"*This is a message for everyone in the Western United States. Transportation and communication have become dangerous and limited in the wake of the asteroid strikes and last night's volcanic eruptions of Mount St. Helens, Mount Rainier, and Mount Shasta in the Cascade Range. Further eruptions are expected from Mount Baker and Mount Mazama, more commonly known as Crater Lake, where a cinder cone volcano has grown from beneath the lake that fills the caldera.*"

This fit the news that the soldier had shared yesterday. He wished it was more positive. "No wonder there's so much ash." His tone was tight, and he kept his voice low enough he didn't obscure the sound of the broadcast.

"*Military forces from across the country have been deployed to aid evacuations in the areas most affected by lava, mudslides, fire, and clouds of toxic gas. Expect ashfall to continue for several hours up to several days in the coastal zone, which includes a distance of about five hundred miles stretching east of the mountains on one side and to the ocean on the other. Reports about the status of the civilian population of the West Coast will not be forthcoming for several days as crews assess the initial damage. There is no news from the Greater Seattle area, but it is believed to have sustained significant damage.*"

He and Kat exchanged a glance.

"Several days?" She reached for his hand and clutched it, her fingers like ice.

"*Citizens are urged to stay home. Conserve food, fuel, and water. The government predicts it will be at least a week before it clears major routes utilizing snow clearing equipment. Avoid drinking water from contaminated sources. If you have no alternative, strain the water through a tight cloth and boil it before drinking."*

"Glad you figured that out last night." He squeezed her hand, reminded of acidic water in an old disaster movie about a volcano. The lake had become acidic and burned on contact. Perhaps they were far enough from the eruptions that it would be different.

"The death toll in Greater Los Angeles, which consists of Orange, Ventura, Los Angeles, San Bernardino, and Riverside Counties, is unknown. Conditions are too dangerous for estimates, as military personnel must maintain safety protocols and remain in safe zones outside the direct impact zone. The asteroid strikes, fires, earthquakes, and shockwaves may have killed twenty to thirty million people."

Kat's sharp intake of breath and the tear she brushed from her eye made him sorry he'd found the signal. He held his breath, hoping it ended on a more positive note.

"Casualties following last night's eruptions are also unknown, but estimates are in the hundreds of thousands. All branches of the military are coordinating rescue efforts. Please be patient and stay tuned for further instructions in the days to come."

The message repeated, and Ryan clicked it off. His shoulders ached from tension and his head pounded. He didn't want to talk about the staggering number of deaths or the worry about their families. It wasn't the right time.

"Let's go shopping." He got to his feet. Kat was biting her lip again, which was damn distracting. He could tell she was thinking. "Out with it."

"We won't stay here for a week or more, are we? Even though we're past Missoula and the worst area, the ash will continue to get worse. Maybe we can borrow a vehicle."

"Borrow? You mean steal one?" His eyebrow raised; she had the makings of a criminal yet. "There was a vehicle parked behind the cabin office, though I didn't get a good look at it in the dark. Maybe the keys are in the office. Even if it doesn't have much gas, we might get far enough that the ash will be less. It would be better than biking."

He hadn't considered grand theft auto, but if they could take the bikes too, it might work to leave this region before resuming cycling. Kat spread the map on the table.

"Maybe we could return to the Interstate. If the road will be cleared anywhere, that's where. It sounds like they'll use snow removal equipment."

"Smart. Okay, Operation Food, then I'll check the vehicle for the possibility of leaving tomorrow. If it doesn't work, we should stay another day, maybe two, unless you object. See if the ash stops falling. We have power and water, at least for now."

Despite the look of snow, the air outside was hot and dry with a burnt smell that scorched his throat and made him want to take shallow breaths. They wore long sleeves, hats, and masks to minimize the contact of ash on their skin because they didn't know if it was dangerous.

$$\bullet \qquad \bullet \qquad \bullet$$

It took close to an hour of walking to reach the small roadside store. To his surprise, the bright pink neon sign in the front window read, "Open."

Finally, a sign of life.

The bell jingled above the door as they entered, stomping the powder from their hiking shoes. The shelves here were probably more sparse than usual, but they weren't bare, which was a relief. Behind the counter stood an older man with a bushy white beard, his long gray and white streaked hair tied back in a ponytail. He and a petite woman further down the counter wore matching tie-dye shirts, like hippy Santa and his wife.

"See, Mary. Customers." He drummed his knobby hands on the counter. "We aren't the only ones alive in the county. What can we do for you folks?" His voice sounded friendly, but his eyes were watchful.

One hand stayed below the counter, maybe resting on a gun or another weapon. Perhaps there'd been trouble with thieves, even this far from the cities.

"Good morning. Nice to see people. I can't believe you're open."

"We live in the back. Gives us something to do." The man's eyes flicked to Ryan.

"It's been so quiet out there. We've been on a bike trip for over a week," said Kat, with her fake cheerful voice. "It's been a rough couple of days and then we woke up to this." She waved a hand, indicating the mess outdoors.

If Ryan hadn't known better, he'd think her smiles were real.

"We got stuck at a cabin nearby where we took shelter for the night. We were hoping to buy food. We can pay."

"You poor things." Mary's feathered earrings swung as she swished from behind the counter. "Riding bikes in this disaster." She bustled across the room and enveloped first Kat, then Ryan, in bosomy hugs.

They exchanged startled glances. Mary's hair smelled of spices, like she'd been baking, which her next words confirmed.

"I made fresh cinnamon buns this morning. How does tea and a bun sound? My treats would cheer anyone up."

"You're too kind." Tears filled Kat's eyes.

They were genuine. She might be able to cry on demand, but that was a superpower he hadn't yet seen. A cinnamon bun sounded divine.

"We were hoping to find a lift to the interstate or get some extra supplies, since otherwise we're stuck until they clear the ash," said Ryan. "We can't ride our bikes. It's a mess out there."

"You're in luck," said Mary, glancing over her shoulder. "My Burt was planning a trip to Three Forks, about ninety minutes up the highway. Supply run to our daughter's family. Tomorrow or the next day."

Burt's bushy eyebrows rose as his wife volunteered his services. His mouth turned down. He didn't look keen to take strangers.

"Might not be for a few days. Mary and I will discuss it. Later. The radio said to hunker down, not to waste fuel." His voice was gruff. "I might not be leaving when you want to go."

"Since when have you listened to the government?" said his wife, her voice dripping with scorn. She turned to Ryan and smiled up at him. "You look like a nice young couple. He can give you a lift. You don't seem like that man who was in yesterday afternoon."

Ryan and Kat exchanged glances with raised eyebrows again and moved through the store while the older pair bickered. Ryan tried not to listen, even if he cared about the outcome. Their whispers were brief but mentioned the man who had come with a gun and a pickup. A sudden image flashed through his mind of the only other vehicle they'd seen heading in the same direction. The truck with the pirate flag. With the road closures at Missoula, was it possible it could be the same truck? His thoughts flashed to the smashed fence and tire tracks, to the campground yesterday morning, and the blood-soaked campers. He'd tried to block that image from his mind.

"I'll be right back with the hot water for tea and fresh cinnamon buns," Mary called before disappearing into the backroom through an orange curtain.

"What did you folks do before doomsday?" said Burt, keeping a wary eye on them as they moved about the store.

Kat took the lead again with one of her bright, cheery smiles. "I'm an elementary school teacher and Ryan's a lawyer." She rested her hand on his shoulder. "I try not to hold it against him." She winked and removed her hand, though her touch still zinged through him.

"Not the summer vacation you had planned, then?" said Burt, his expression softening in the face of her positive attitude and infectious good humor.

Ryan marveled at her ability to put strangers at ease.

"Definitely not. The bike trip to Ryan's cabin seems lucky now, other than the ash. We started in Seattle. Good thing we left when we did. If we'd waited until now, we'd have been trapped."

"That was lucky," said Burt. "Nobody's getting off the West Coast now. Sounds like mayhem. What about your families?"

"We haven't heard anything." Kat's voice sounded small and sad. "We keep trying, but nothing yet."

Ryan hadn't shared the contents of his last messages. His mother had laid one more guilt trip on him and when he hadn't responded, she'd gone back to nasty. Heather had sent an apology, saying she'd do anything if he'd pick her up—that she missed him. Perhaps her ex had ended their relationship. He'd replied that he was alive and shut off his phone. He didn't want to talk to his family. They'd sent their messages before the asteroid strike and the volcanoes. There was no way of knowing if anything else would get through with the damage to the cell towers, but he hoped they were okay.

Mary reappeared with a pink takeout box and two steaming to-go cups. "It's just water, but help yourselves to tea and milk or whatever. On me." She gestured to a counter where the coffee and tea fixings were located.

"Thank you." Kat peeked into the box. "Oh. The kind with cream cheese icing. You've made my week. These are my absolute favorite."

Mary beamed, her creased face looking thrilled. Burt shook his head, perhaps resigned to driving after all. "If you're short of reading material, I have a couple of books you might like." Kat followed Mary to a shelf at the far end, where she read the back of a few paperbacks.

While she deliberated, Ryan chose a couple of cans of soup, a half carton of eggs, a brick of cheddar, and a loaf of bread with a decent best before date. He grabbed a small jar of peanut butter and one of raspberry jam. Breakfast, lunch, and dinner had just improved.

"The machines aren't working. Hope you have good old-fashioned cash. Many don't carry it anymore," said Burt, moving to the till to ring up the purchases by hand.

When Ryan paid with a crisp twenty-dollar bill, some of the tension left Burt's shoulders.

"Yesterday, two customers left yelling when they couldn't use their credit cards."

"I don't blame you for just asking for cash," said Ryan, pocketing his change. "I couldn't help but overhear that you had a problem yesterday." He left the thought dangling like bait.

Burt latched on. "A young punk came through yesterday and robbed the store. Took all the beer, junk food, and cash from the till—which wasn't much. Snatched a few boxes of ammunition and some odds and ends." Burt's voice hardened. "I'd have shot him myself, but he had his gun on Mary. Our neighbor stopped by and interrupted, and the punk split. I'm just glad he didn't get trigger-happy and kill us all."

"Did you see which way he went?" said Ryan. "Or what he drove?"

"Big navy-blue truck with a Wyoming plate. I wrote it down fast, but nobody answered at the sheriff's office. I'll keep trying." Burt's fist clenched on the countertop.

That sounded about right. Would there be more trouble from him as they continued? Ryan hoped not.

Mary joined the conversation once more. "I'm just thankful nobody got hurt and that we have electricity. Both the travelers yesterday and the radio say it's out most places. We have an old-style wood stove we can use for cooking if we have to."

"If we stay longer, I can split wood or carry stuff if you need help," said Ryan.

Burt shook his head and waved a hand. "If I decide to go to Three Forks the day after tomorrow, it'll be early. You could throw your bikes in the back of my truck and ride up front with me." He glanced at Kat and lowered his voice. "If you were traveling alone, I'm not sure I'd go for it, but I've always been a little paranoid. Have to admit, your girl, she's a sweetheart and has won me over. I'll consider giving you two a ride." He shot a look at his wife, who tidied items on the nearest shelf with a smug look.

Ryan glanced over his shoulder, where Kat was preparing her tea. She smiled at him, somehow filling him with hope. They made a good team. For the first time today, confidence filled him. They'd get to his bunker.

He leaned in as he spoke to the store owners, not wanting Kat to hear. "She's terrific company. I'm glad I asked her along for this trip. It would be a lot more stressful and less fun on my own. Especially the way things have turned out." He smiled and relaxed his shoulders. The admission was more for him than for Burt and Mary. It was the truth, and it lightened him to say it aloud.

"Where will I find you two the morning I leave?" Burt's shoulders dropped as well.

"We're up the road at *The Trees Resort*, Cabin Six," said Ryan. "Across from the marina."

"Anyone manning the office?" said Burt with a sharp look. "I'm pretty sure Theo headed south toward Utah when the news broke. He has family down there."

Ryan shook his head, wondering if Burt would change his mind.

"Make sure you leave it in decent condition." His gruff voice softened again. "But I understand. Any port in a storm, or so they say."

"I'm so glad you're considering letting us drive with you," said Kat, handing Ryan his hot drink. "We'd be so grateful. Riding our bikes in the deep ash would be slippery like snow. It would be easy to get hurt."

"Perfect amount of sugar. You're a lifesaver," said Ryan after his first sip. It was scalding, but would cool on the return walk. He nodded to Burt and left to look at the map books, leaving Kat to handle the store owner.

She flashed him a smile that took his breath away as he left Burt, who was falling farther under Kat's charm while they discussed his daughter and grandson. Ryan was confident that the ride would be firmed up after their chat. He browsed the magazines while he waited. One had a special about the asteroid and a two-page feature on Nick. He hoped Jake had made it to DC in time to join him in the government bunker.

After five minutes, he collected Kat and the groceries. She didn't relinquish the baking, but tucked the box under her arm in a proprietary fashion.

"We'll see you Saturday at eight," she said over her shoulder as they left the store.

The ashfall seemed less when they followed their footstep trail back to the cabin, but a thick, white curtain still blanketed the sky.

CHAPTER 13: RYAN

Back in their cabin, Ryan put the groceries away and sat at the table, drinking the remains of his warm tea. It had been too hot at first, but he'd been careful not to burn himself and had looked forward to drinking it. He checked the radio, but the bleak message of destruction on the EBS remained the same as earlier that morning. He cleared his throat, trying to clear the lump.

"Maybe we could watch movies this afternoon or play cards to pass the time. You're going to go nuts sitting around today." Kat's eyes were sympathetic. She must be feeling the desperation of the situation, too. They needed a distraction, or the time between now and Burt's ride would seem endless.

He nodded. "Cards would be great if you can find some. Mine are buried."

"If we get to your bunker, will you be able to stay inside without going stir crazy?" Kat cocked her head to the side.

"Unlikely, but there's a gym, a theater, and a library. These are not minimalist cement bunkers, but luxury cabins. My grandfather spent years prepping for the end of civilization. He was certain climate change would get us all. Don't worry about me, I'll make the best of the situation. We'll be able to go in and out if we need to. We won't be locked inside, but we'll have the security of knowing the compound is safe. We'll have water, power, and supplies, regardless of what happens out here."

"Maybe you'll come out of this even more buff, like convicts who spend their time lifting weights and doing pushups." Her dark eyes twinkled.

He laughed. "You'll be an expert on at least two new hobbies or historical events. Or maybe you'll write novels." He wouldn't be surprised if she were a writer. It hadn't occurred to him before, but someone as fantastic as she was at inventing stories might write.

"For this evening, why don't we each choose a movie, so we have options. The DVD selection is… interesting."

"I want to check out the truck by the office after my treat, but that shouldn't take too long. Either it works, or it doesn't."

"Your treat?" said Kat with a wide-eyed look that was too innocent. "What treat is that? I have a box with two lovely, fresh cinnamon buns. What do you have?"

She covered the top of the pink box with her hands. He looked her in the eye, then snatched the box and bolted. She chased. They circled the living room and the kitchen, stopping twice on opposite sides of the table. He was more out of breath from laughing than from the exercise. He opened the box and slid a finger into the sticky icing and licked it off. He held it away from her at arm's length—taunting her.

"Oh my god. So good," he said with a sigh as the sweetness filled his mouth.

She glared and lunged at the box, and the side of his mouth twitched. He lifted the goodies over his head where she couldn't reach and stared down at her in amusement. He expected her to climb on a chair or give up, but she grabbed him by the balls and smiled. He swallowed and looked down at her as he lowered the box of baking. She didn't hurt him, but she could have. Someone had taught her to fight dirty.

"Since you asked so nicely," he said with a cautious grin. "We can share."

She released him with a broader smile and took the box, placing it on the table where she flipped the lid and removed a giant cinnamon bun—the one whose icing was undisturbed. With a quick glance, she swiped icing from the other one and sucked it off her finger. Desire rocketed through him. From the look in her dark eyes, she knew what sucking on her finger did. Evil woman. The air became charged.

"You play dirty." He took her wrist and tugged her closer, but not so hard that she couldn't refuse. He wanted her to be a willing participant for this first daylight kiss. "You missed some," he said as he bent down to capture her lips with his. She tasted sweet, of icing with an undertone of just her, the vanilla-like scent he craved. He didn't want to stop kissing her and tangled his hand in her hair, hauling her closer still. Her lips were soft as her pliant body molded against his, giving him all sorts of ideas about how else they could pass the time. He was breathless when he stepped back.

"As I was saying," he swallowed. "I'll eat my treat, then I should check the truck." She looked like she, too, was struggling to regain her composure. She bit her lip and looked up at him with her big brown eyes that looked almost black. They were the kind he could drown in.

"Maybe there are other treats you'd like later."

His eyes didn't leave hers as he caressed the side of her face and cupped her jaw. "I'm going to take you up on that, if you're sure, because that's a tempting offer." Last night's talk had made him feel close to her, but tonight he was interested in something physical.

"I wouldn't offer if I didn't mean it," said Kat. "Later it is."

Her flushed cheeks added to her desirability. He traced her bottom lip with his thumb, right where she always bit. He backed away and pulled out a chair. She took a deep breath and sat, unrolling a section of her cinnamon bun from the coiled dough, ripped it off, and stuffed it in her mouth.

"Oh my god, it's so good." She closed her eyes as she chewed.

The sexual tension in the room dropped to a manageable level.

Ryan grabbed plates from the cupboard and joined her. They sat together and enjoyed their pastries while they finished their tea.

"Mary's an angel." Kat popped the last bite of sticky goodness into her mouth. "This might be the best thing I've ever eaten."

Ryan finished and washed his hands. He seldom indulged in such decadent food, but had to agree; it was delicious. He drained the last of his tea and tied his shoes, wishing he was staying inside, but knowing whether the truck was viable would prey on his mind. Burt's offer was an option but limited in scope, with a ride only to the next town. Their own vehicle might get them a longer distance.

Outside, the air smelled strange as he trudged down the hill to the office. Not just scorched, but unpleasant. Perhaps methane or other gases traveled with the ash. He kept his mask in place, determined to hurry.

The splintered door frame of the office wasn't obvious unless you were close, but he'd pulled the door closed to camouflage the damage. He'd left the door unlocked so they could return the key without additional damage. The light bulb in the office was dim, and the blinds were closed, but he located a set of Ford keys in a drawer. They might be for the rusty blue truck out back.

It was an older model that didn't have a key fob, but the Ford key fit the driver's side door. Inside, the truck smelled like old plastic and mold, and when he tried to start it, the engine didn't turn over. He swallowed his disappointment, released the hood latch, and got out to check under the hood.

From the corner of his eye, he spied something that darted away by his feet as he lifted the lid with a screeching, reluctant sound. An avalanche of ash fell off the hood on both sides. To his disgust, there was a rat's nest that filled one side of the engine compartment, and the battery was missing. He dropped the hood, making sure it latched.

He hated having to rely on someone else's goodwill, but this option wouldn't work. There might be a chance later to find a vehicle, maybe from a used car lot, but gas could be a problem if stations remained closed or sold out. The supply trucks would have a challenging time getting through. Or they might not be on the road at all right now. Ryan returned the truck keys to the drawer inside. He felt grungy from being out in the pollution; he needed a quick shower.

Back in the cabin, Kat had located a crib board and a deck of cards. She shuffled the cards and raised an eyebrow with a smile. His shower could wait. He'd rather spend time with her and put off dealing with their problems. He changed and shook off his clothes on the porch, keeping them nearby in case he went out again. They spent the next couple of hours playing crib. Kat won their best of seven tournament, four games to his three. She played fast, barely glancing at her cards to decide what to keep and what went to the extra hand. He tried to keep up, the speed making the games fast and exciting. He couldn't remember a better time hanging out with anyone on a quiet day.

The afternoon flew by. Now and then, he'd look up and find her watching him. The anticipation of later curled his toes and swirled through his veins.

"Soup and grilled cheese for dinner?" said Ryan. "Save the just-add-water lasagna?"

"Sure. Then a movie?"

He nodded. And then it would be later.

•   •   •

Dinner was quick and easy to make and clean. They continued to be careful with the water. They used what came from the tap for washing, but for cooking and drinking, they used what they'd run last night before the ash. Ryan watched what poured out of the faucet to be sure it didn't have debris or a strange smell. He couldn't tell the difference, but better safe than sorry. When they left, they would fill the canteens from the supply upstairs in the tub.

The movie choices were limited. There were a few children's movies he wasn't interested in, some bad action movies he'd already seen, and a few classics from the '70s, and '80s that were more promising. From these, they agreed to watch Star Wars: Episode 5, The Empire Strikes Back, agreeing that it was their favorite Star Wars movie. He wasn't a fan of episodes one to three. Episodes seven to nine were good, but seemed somehow contrived. The original trilogy was the best—even with the Ewoks.

He slid next to Kat as the credits rolled at the end. He couldn't wait any longer. Perhaps it was the light in her eyes he'd seen at her favorite parts of the movie or how she'd said key lines of dialogue a second or two before the characters, as though she couldn't help herself. It didn't matter why, but he wanted to devour her, and he was through being patient.

The little noises she made as they rearranged themselves on the couch drove him wild. She tasted amazing as he slanted his mouth across hers and kissed her, her body the perfect combination of hard and soft beneath him. His skin was electric, and his lips tingled when he stopped to catch his breath, feeling drunk on lust.

"I still need a quick shower. Care to join me?" He kept the question casual, but he hoped she would. The fun had started, and he wanted it to continue rather than stop. He blamed himself for delaying his shower.

"Sure," she said, biting her lip.

At close range, he couldn't resist and he bit her lip too, tugging at it with his teeth. Firm, but not to injure. He let go as she arched beneath him with a hitch in her breath.

"What was that for?" Her eyes looked darker than usual.

"That drives me crazy," he said with a groan. His voice had a husky sound. She must realize how turned on he was. Why try to hide it? "That makes me wild. I can't take it anymore." To emphasize his point, he nibbled again to demonstrate, leaving his mouth buzzing and electric too.

She laughed. "My nervous habit turns you on?"

"Like you wouldn't believe." He grinned. "I know. It's weird."

"I'm going to say lucky," she said, sliding off the couch and from beneath him. He wasn't sure she was headed to the shower until she headed for the stairs. His heart rate increased.

He took her hand partway up the stairs, his pulse galloping. This was moving fast, but he wanted her so much he had trouble seeing or focusing on anything else. Throughout their card games and the movie, he'd imagined her naked. It wasn't dark like the tent and he was excited to see all of her, which until now he'd only fantasized about.

She turned the water on, and when it warmed, she dropped her clothes and stepped into the shower, turning away and tipping her head back to wet her hair. He couldn't take his eyes off her. Her curves were fantastic and he couldn't wait to get his hands on her. She was slim and fit, and her tight body gave him many bad ideas. He was rock hard when he tossed his clothes to the floor and followed her into the hot water and steam. She slathered herself with fruity-smelling soap.

He ran his hands down her slippery sides, then reached from behind to cup her breasts in the palms of his hands. She arched her back and pressed her ass against him. He rolled a nipple between his thumb and forefinger. She gasped, so he did it again a little harder. Then she picked up the bar of soap and lathered it in her hands. She turned with a smile and slid her soapy hands across his chest and shoulders, then down to his hard stomach while his anticipation mounted. Grabbing his cock without hesitation, slid her hand from the base to the top. With her other hand, she played with his balls while she stroked.

Ryan couldn't breathe. Leaning back against the wet shower wall, he let her play while his desire built. Every moan on his part made her eyes light up. He couldn't keep himself from touching her too, feeling her slick skin beneath his hands. Their fun exploring each other was getting him off, too. He was trying to decide between spinning her around and taking her in the shower or suggesting they move to the bed when she turned off the water.

"Will you take me to bed?" She looked so serious.

But her words went straight to his groin. Stepping out, he threw her a towel.

He scrubbed with his own fluffy towel.

She hung up hers in record time.

"Run," he said with a smile as he snapped his towel in her direction. Naked, she bolted for the bedroom with him hot on her heels.

He caught her partway across the room and scooped her into his embrace. She wrapped her arms around his neck and kissed him with enthusiasm, leaving no room for doubt or any thought except her. The world fell away, leaving only her clean smell and the feel of her mouth and skin. Her lips were soft, but she wasn't hesitant. He lay her down on the bed and lost himself to the moment, unable to keep his hands off her delectable, smooth skin. He wanted his mouth everywhere, then he fantasized about where else her mouth would go. It was like a dream come true when she took his cock in her mouth.

She left him cursing and gasping as she slid it down her throat in long, even strokes. He wasn't sure how much more of this he could stand. He'd been celibate for over a year, except for the night before last, but even his dreams hadn't been this erotic. This experience was what he needed. He was a second away from losing control when she stopped and smiled at him. Her puffy red lips and disheveled hair were riveting. He wanted to mess her up more.

"Grab the headboard." He gave her a light smack on the ass, liking how it sounded, and she squeaked in a way that left no doubt she'd enjoyed it too.

She grinned and, without a word, did as requested. He loved that she didn't ask questions and trusted him. He'd be happy to return the favor sometime, but this was what he needed right now. A counterpoint to the tenderness last night. A primal need to feel in control of something. The outside world was crazy, but here they were apart from it and in their own world.

He slid behind her and tapped her with his hard cock. She shuddered all over, breaking out in goosebumps. He loved seeing her in this position and did what he'd been dreaming of since the first hike. He kissed her ass and slid his hand between her legs. She was swollen and drenched and slippery. Just what he wanted.

He swirled his finger at her entrance and bumped her clit a few times, avoiding longer contact. He wanted her to ache the way he did, to hunger for him. She cried out each time and wiggled her ass. He slid underneath and tasted her, slow licks at first, but building intensity to match their earlier kissing.

He slid a finger inside her, and she cried out—tightening around it. When he added a second, she pulsed around him, coming on his hand while he licked her pussy. It was such a turn-on; he remained hard, waiting for his turn. When she finished shuddering, he didn't give her a chance to come down from the orgasm high, but rolled on a condom and put himself at her entrance.

"What do you want?" he whispered in her ear while he leaned over her from behind.

"Please," she said, her arms shaking. Her shoulder muscles were solid and defined, but her knuckles were white.

"Please what?" he said, pushing his tip inside, teasing. It was almost too much for him, but he forced himself to hold back a little longer.

"Please fuck me."

The words shot straight to his core, and he thrust into her, unable to contain himself even a fraction of a second longer. She was hot and wet and wild, wriggling against him with each thrust as he buried himself. His orgasm was coming like a freight train. It wouldn't be stopped, only delayed. He gathered her hair to the side and pulled at the tangled mass, and she came apart around him.

He thrust into her again as she shook and quivered and screamed. His voice felt raw as he slammed into her again and came hard, each thrust riding a wave that broke over him as he pounded, unable to stop. She still shook, her own orgasm aftershocks pulling at him again. He rested his head on her back, spent.

When they dropped to the bed, drained and exhausted, she rolled to face him and he kissed her soft and slow. Once more, feeling connected in a softer way.

"I knew you'd be delicious," he said. "How soon until we go again?"

He told himself that it was just sex, but he wasn't so sure when they dropped into an exhausted sleep cocooned together.

CHAPTER 14: KAT

Knowing they had a ride the following day, Kat enjoyed their downtime playing cards, packing and repacking their gear, and checking the radio. The Emergency broadcast remained the same. After a quiet day, they retired upstairs for more mind-blowing sex. Kat had never felt voracious before, but for once she didn't care what her partner thought. Ryan might think she was promiscuous or a sex fiend, but it didn't matter. She was determined to be herself.

She wanted to feel alive, and this sex accomplished that better than she could have imagined. Ryan had no way of knowing that Mark had considered her a prude. She'd been worried about being judged and had never relaxed enough to ask for what she needed. For once, she wasn't trying to please anyone else.

Not that the experience hadn't been pleasurable for both of them. She smiled as she remembered Ryan's expression the first night at the cabin. He seemed pleased with the new arrangement that included benefits. The sex was freeing and incredible.

Her alarm sounded, and she slipped from the warm bed and across the chilly room into the shower. She was going to bike all day and get sweaty, but she didn't know when she'd get another chance to enjoy hot water. If she was living in the moment, this was another thing she had to make the most of, even if she hurried. They didn't have time to fool around with Burt coming in an hour and the cabin to straighten.

It was important to her that they leave the cabin clean and in good condition. When they were ready, Ryan returned the cabin key while Kat watched their stuff. Their loaded bikes waited on the porch where they stood looking at the view. Ash no longer fell from the sky, but the acrid smell of scorched stone remained, so she kept her mask in place. Visibility had improved, but not enough to see across the lake.

It was seven minutes past eight when Burt arrived with a honk. They'd discussed options if he didn't come, but she was relieved to see him. She wasn't sure what they'd have done if he hadn't arrived.

"Morning," said Burt. "Appreciate you being ready."

"Did you hear from your daughter?" she asked.

He shook his head. "Not going to worry, probably just the bad phone connections right now. But it doesn't hurt to check on her myself."

Ryan loaded the bikes into the bed of the black truck while Kat slung the backpacks against the cab. Burt had attached an angled snow plow blade to the front of his truck and cleared the road as he drove.

• • •

The drive itself was uneventful, and Kat enjoyed sitting instead of cycling to start the morning. Burt knew the roads and had switched to snow tires even though it was late May. Between the plow and the tires, his truck gripped the road, and it took less than thirty minutes to reach the interstate. The highway was empty, other than the odd derelict car at the side with smashed windows covered in white powder. Somebody must have smashed the windows for fun.

By the time they reached the outskirts of Three Forks another hour later, a dusting of ash coated everything, but it no longer lay in several-inch drifts. She was glad they were getting farther from the eruptions as they'd traveled east. They'd have to be careful on the bikes, but it should be possible to ride.

Burt stopped the truck at the side of the desolate highway at the junction with Route 287 to West Yellowstone. They'd decided to chance cycling across the National Park and the Thunder Basin Grasslands beyond as the most direct route to South Dakota, rather than diverting south to look for a car. The shorter route outweighed the risks of going around. Ryan and Kat lifted out their bikes and backpacks and thanked Burt, who honked again as he pulled away, the black truck disappearing in a dusty cloud of ash.

Kat turned away, her arm covering her face, and closed her eyes. She dug out her goggles and put them on. Ryan grinned before getting his gear out, too.

"We look like ants," she said, adjusting her pack and pulling her sleeves lower to minimize contact with the fine powder.

When the dust settled, she unfolded the map and showed Ryan what she'd been thinking about their ride today.

"We should be able to get to West Yellowstone tonight. There may still be power and water. It isn't that far and may be on the same grid. We could try to sleep in a motel again, instead of a campground. There haven't been many tourists, or maybe they've gone home. But, near such a big tourist attraction, there might be people, and I'd feel safer with a door we can lock."

"I like your thinking," said Ryan, "But first, I want to check around town. We might find a used car lot or something abandoned. It may be our last chance to find wheels."

He and Kat rode into the small town, its quiet streets laid out in grid formation. There was an autobody shop, but when they peered inside, they couldn't see vehicles. Some houses looked occupied, but no children played outdoors. The few vehicles they saw were family vehicles outside homes, and it didn't seem right to steal from someone else who would need it. Abandoned vehicles might be a possibility, if they could find something with keys. An oversight was that neither of them knew how to hot wire a car. After a short but fruitless search, they returned to the highway. Even for a car, they couldn't afford to waste time.

"Will we need to ride until dark to get to West Yellowstone?" asked Ryan.

"I think so. It should be about ten hours of riding. That puts us at between eight hundred fifty and nine hundred miles in total." Her chest loosened, thinking that they would be two-thirds of the way to their destination, even if the final third might be the most grueling.

The further east they rode, the clearer the sky became, clearing enough to see patches of blue behind the hazy, ash-filled sky. When the light dimmed right after a glorious sunset, they were outside West Yellowstone and they pushed on. A few stars twinkled in the darkening sky.

All the other towns they'd passed through in the last four days had seemed empty. People had stayed away from businesses and hunkered down in their homes where she and Ryan hadn't seen them. West Yellowstone was the opposite. Bright lights and noise emanated from the center of town and pulled them in like a tractor beam. Reaching downtown, a pair of fancy hotels were lit up, as was a restaurant, and the bar across the street. Music poured onto the street from the bar that was hopping. A small crowd of people stood out front, talking and drinking. Its sense of normalcy was jarring.

Kat's first instinct was to be annoyed at the loud music because she often found noise overwhelming, but mouthed the words to a popular song as they drew nearer.

"Want to go check out the bar after we eat?" Ryan raised an eyebrow as he spoke, his hazel eye warm and amused.

"Only if you do." Her mouth filled with the imagined taste of gin and she swallowed, but she didn't want to drink anymore. Today was day fourteen.

"If you need a drink, we can find you one." His eyes showed sympathy, not judgment, although he knew she'd struggled with alcohol.

She shook her head, surprised that he'd anticipated her thought. For all she craved the taste of gin and limes in odd moments, she wasn't interested in drinking. She'd quit, and it was important to stick with her decision. "That's behind me, but I don't mind if you do." She hesitated. "Sounds like they're having fun."

"I like a beer sometimes," he said, "but I'm not interested in being wasted. Will that bother you?"

She shook her head. Her decision was for her; he could decide for himself what he wanted. It wasn't her place to say what he could and couldn't do, but she didn't want to look after drunk Ryan. But he'd just said a beer.

They dismounted from the bikes in front of a white hotel beside an enormous log building that was a restaurant. The lobby was well lit and the red *"Vacancy"* sign was lit. There were six cars parked in the lot. The idea of spending time with other travelers seemed odd after their days of isolation.

"I'll wait with the bikes." She took the handle of his bike and leaned hers against the building. Kat waited until Ryan returned. He held up a card key, a thick white bundle tucked under his arm. Sheets and towels?

"You won't believe this. The rooms are free. They're giving away overnight stays to anyone stranded or on the road. The whole town is full of wayward travelers. Most had signed on for jobs during the tourist season. Some were early tourists. A few others are like us and just passing through."

"Free?" It sounded too good to be true.

"Free. Everyone in town is concentrated here, staying in these five buildings. The bosses split, leaving the seasonal workers here to run the town. Anything goes."

"Is there a catch?" She couldn't keep the doubt from her voice.

He shrugged. "They ask that we don't make a mess. They gave me clean sheets and three towels."

"That's incredible." She'd never heard of anything like this.

"I said we're just staying one night. No matter how fun they make it, we have somewhere to be."

"How does it work?"

"The rule is if we wanted to stay longer than overnight, we would have to pitch in. Take a shift somewhere." He took his bike and walked toward the wing of the hotel to the left. "We've got ground floor rooms at the back, so we can wheel the bikes inside to keep them from being stolen. I'd rather not leave them outside, even locked up. It might seem like a fun place, but I don't trust anyone." He hesitated before adding. "The blue truck was through a few days ago, and the driver hurt someone. He found the front desk girl from the other hotel after hours and raped her. He left town the next morning, but they keep security there now. No one walks alone at night. Sounds like it was the same day he robbed Burt and Mary's store."

"He's gone now?" At Ryan's nod, Kat said, "Do they know where he went?"

He shook his head. "I won't leave you on your own if that makes you feel more comfortable."

That would help. She took a breath, determined to forget about the guy in the truck. She hoped they wouldn't hear anymore about him, but she just knew that wouldn't be the end of him. At least he wasn't here now. "Then this sounds perfect. At least for tonight."

"The restaurant is serving hot food. Not from their real menu, but they have either steak, chicken, or Beyond burgers tonight. The cooks from all over town take turns for a few hours each night. We're expected for dinner in not too long. The food is free too. There are supposed to be buffet-style salads and side dishes, and whoever is there will cook whatever we choose from tonight's options. There's a breakfast buffet as well until ten. We can eat before we leave."

"They won't be able to keep up the party and freebies forever." Kat followed Ryan to the rear of the hotel and room 125, where he swiped the card. "They'll run out of everything."

"The town has made it a holiday. They wanted to have fun one last time. End of the world and all." His voice sounded strange, and he hesitated before speaking, like maybe he was fighting to speak his mind or had a secret. It was hard to tell when she couldn't see his face. "Oh, there's another surprise at dinner, if you want to participate."

This time, he sounded amused, and she recognized the quirk at the corner of his mouth as he pushed his bike into the room.

Inside was a standard hotel room with two Queen-size beds. It looked and smelled clean, but the biggest difference from normal times were the unmade beds, though comforters were folded at the end of each.

Kat and Ryan threw their belongings on one. They fixed the sheets onto the other, pulling the clean white linen taut. She loved the feel of clean, fresh sheets when she got into bed. They spread the comforter on their chosen bed, making up only one. She liked the idea that they were sleeping together again without more discussion. They'd been enjoying each other's company. Why change?

They propped their bikes against the front window on the inside and removed the saddlebags before shoving the bikes together so they wouldn't crowd the limited floor space.

"It's after eight. Want to freshen up and eat?"

Kat salivated at the thought of a steak. "I'm starved." Her muscles thrummed from riding all day, but her ankle was improved after two days of rest. The idea of a hot meal gave her a second burst of energy.

"You don't need to change," said Ryan. "At least not for dinner. Apparently, that's part of the fun. Someone raided the town theater where they put on plays and borrowed costumes so everyone can dress for dinner."

"That's hilarious."

At the log cabin's entrance, they were met by a young woman with a dozen ear piercings and sleeved tattoos on both arms—the dark ink swirled in intricate patterns on her skin. She wore an old-fashioned gown with an empire waist, like something out of Pride and Prejudice or Bridgerton, the flowing material in soft yellow color contrasting with her tough, tattooed look. She'd twisted her brown hair up and looked gorgeous.

"You two are new tonight. They tell you about dressing for dinner?" At their nod, she said, "Men's stuff is in the sitting room that way." She pointed. "Lady's things this way." She indicated a bright hall. "First door on the right. Bring your street clothes back. I've got shopping bags to stow them while you eat. Have fun and see you in a few minutes."

Kat was hungry enough that she wanted to hurry, but the racks of bright clothing sent a thrill running through her. She'd play along. It had been a long time since she'd either played dress-up or dressed for someone special. She hurried to the racks and flipped through the choices, looking for something pretty. There were several options, but she narrowed it down to two dresses that were beautiful.

One was like the hostess's dress in orchid purple and was low cut. The second was turquoise with a full skirt that swished. When she tried on the purple, it seemed made for her. It was knee-length and fitted through the body. It flattered her figure, though it showed a lot of skin. Why not? The color was also a favorite. She'd never dared to wear something like this at home. It would have made her anxious, being too bare or too dressy for most occasions. Here, it was the perfect dress.

"What the hell?" she said to her reflection in the mirror. She didn't have matching shoes, but there was a bin with a selection of heels where she found black ones in her size.

She hurried back to the hostess, who showed her where to stash her clothes for the evening. Ryan stood waiting by the bar. Kat had been nervous about the sheer dress and how much cleavage it showed, but the appreciative look in Ryan's eyes made it worth it. He looked like he wanted to devour her on the spot. She smiled and took in his ensemble.

He wore a white dress shirt, black dress pants, and a black and charcoal satin vest. He looked like he belonged on a movie set. She'd forgotten how tall and gorgeous he was; he'd just become Ryan, but he was stunning, handsome—with Captain America shoulders she admired.

He bowed and stuck out his elbow for her to hold. "Shall we?"

"Want me to take your picture?" the hostess said as she held out her hand.

Kat passed her phone to the young woman who took a couple of shots. Ryan surprised Kat by twirling her closer and kissing her in the last photo.

The hostess sighed and handed back the phone. "You two are so cute. Have a great time. The food is at the end. Steak, chicken, or veggie burgers? I'll let the cook know."

"Steak. Medium rare."

"Same," said Ryan, placing his hand on the bare skin of Kat's back. A jolt of electricity surged through her at his touch. The feeling intensified as his touch lingered.

"Pick anywhere to sit. There's no one else here now because most people ate earlier. When you're finished, please clear your dishes. If you stay more than twenty-four hours, you're expected to help with dishes, laundry, or food the next day."

Ryan and Kat stepped down three steps to the hardwood floor of the main dining room with twenty tables covered in clean, white tablecloths. On each, gleaming silver cutlery, a jug of water, and glasses shone in the soft light.

"This is incredible," said Kat, admiring the room. This was one of the fanciest dates she'd been on, and there was no cost.

They chose a square table for four by the window, though it was too dark to see anything outside. It was quiet without other diners and felt odd without menus to peruse. These new oddities were preferable to what lay beyond the town. Kat pushed the thoughts aside and focused on her gorgeous dinner date.

Ryan sat beside her rather than across from her and poured two glasses of water. "Let's find salad or something. I'm starving. You must be too."

Not only were they going to eat proper food again, but it meant they were saving another travel meal for the extended trip.

At the far end of the room beside the kitchen, a long table was set up with a stack of clean white plates, cut vegetables, and a small salad bar with a selection of dressings. By the kitchen door, a second table was stacked with a dozen cleared plates from previous diners.

They returned to their table where soft music played overhead and candles had been lit. The hostess was going all out to set the mood.

"Are you trying to seduce me? Fancy clothes, candlelight dinner, private dining?"

"Is it working?" Ryan's hand rested on hers. "In all seriousness, they might try to help me win you over. I mentioned you were someone I was trying to impress."

She leaned into him and stroked his thigh under the table. "In case you hadn't noticed, I haven't been playing hard to get."

He turned, his mismatched eyes looking intense in the flickering light of the candles, and her insides turned to goo under his gaze. He stroked the back of her hand with his thumb. Currents shot through her with the contact. She imagined blue sparks of energy jumping between them that must be visible to anyone who saw them.

"I wanted to take you on an actual date. At least once. This is the best I can do. Dinner, then dancing if you like."

Her chest tightened. A date. She wasn't good at dating or social activities. She shrugged the thought off; life wasn't like that anymore. She was reinventing herself. This date wasn't like others she'd had, she was already comfortable with Ryan.

"I thought you were beautiful when I met you for our first hike," he said, his voice pulling her back to the moment. "I could tell there was something special about you, but I didn't think I was interested in dating."

"You did not. You barely spoke to me." Her tone was incredulous. She'd never guessed he was interested in anything about her that day.

"I watched. I listened. I admired."

"I was a mess back then." Her voice sounded breathless.

"Me too. Strange to think that was only a month ago." His face seemed serious.

"It feels much longer. It's not the same world anymore." She blinked back tears. She didn't know how they'd snuck past her guard.

"It won't go back to being the same. This is still the eye of the storm. I don't think most people know what to expect next, but I

161

suspect the bigger storm is coming. Food and fuel shortages, more fires and power outages, climate problems, and extreme weather. We need to be somewhere safe to stay out of it for as long as possible." Ryan twirled his fork as he spoke.

"Most people are playing it safe and hanging out at home. Maybe it won't be too bad." Despite her words, even she didn't think that was true.

"And this group is throwing a party, which may be a smidge delusional." His tone had become serious.

"Maybe places like this can become refuges, where people will work together to survive the tough times ahead, or I'd like to think so," said Kat, looking around again at the beautiful restaurant. Abandoning it would be a shame.

The hostess walked toward them, carrying two plates with enormous steaks and baked potatoes. Kat's eyes widened in appreciation.

The young woman set the food down in front of them.

Kat had never been served such a thick and juicy-looking steak, cooked to her specifications. Her mouth watered at the aroma. It must be twelve ounces of meat. She'd never been able to afford a meal like this, not on a meager teacher's salary. To eat it all would make her a glutton, but this once it would be okay.

"We're using up the good stuff first. Can I get you two anything else?"

"No, thanks. This is perfect." Kat couldn't wait to dive in. She sliced the first piece from the edge, revealing the pink inside. It melted in her mouth as she closed her eyes and savored the rich flavor.

"Not planning to go vegetarian then," said Ryan, the near corner of his mouth twitching in amusement. He sliced into his steak too and took a bite. "This is amazing."

She and Ryan ate dinner while they talked and laughed. She told him about teaching, the things she liked. He talked to her about the rush he got when arguing a case in court. It had been ages since she'd thought of her job in a positive light. Knowing she made a difference to some of her students used to make her job satisfying. She'd lost that when she'd lost herself.

"We both performed as part of our jobs," she said, thinking how similar she and Ryan were in unexpected ways. It made her warm inside to think that he might understand her. What would have happened if she'd let Nick set them up eight years ago? They'd never know, but perhaps they were better suited now. They were good together.

When they'd finished eating, Ryan leaned back and brushed an errant lock of her hair from her face, sending tingles through her skin, like sparks. He was more attentive than ever.

"Would you like to check out the party? I have a feeling it's going to be pretty wild. But, it should be safe since we're together. If it's too much, we can leave anytime you want." His mismatched gaze met hers and fire swept through her at his understanding.

She'd never been daring and hadn't been a partier during her university days or since. Ryan understood her reservations. Small talk and crowds had always intimidated her. But the strains of music from outside made her itch to dance, to let loose and blow off steam.

"What about you?"

"I'm curious as much as anything." His gaze drifted toward the party sounds.

"Will you dance with me?"

"Of course," said Ryan. "I'll dance for as long as you want, but I'm hoping you save some energy for when we're back in our room."

His words made her cheeks flame. It had been so long since she'd felt that excitement and returned it in spades. Mark had demanded or expected physicality, but their relationship had been without that electricity that buzzed whenever she and Ryan touched, whether accidental or deliberate.

They planned to change back to their own clothes, but the hostess passed them the bags with their regular clothes, saying, "You look great. Keep what you're wearing. Nobody knows how long this party will last. If you like the clothes, you might as well keep them. If you're on bikes, I doubt you brought anything fancy. It'll pack up small."

"Thanks. I love this dress." Kat smoothed the silky fabric of the skirt.

"I'm done here. Maybe I'll see you at the bar. Have fun." The young woman smiled and waved as she exited.

It was strange standing in the empty restaurant. No other patrons, no staff. They left, leaving the door unlocked.

CHAPTER 15: KAT

Kat shivered. After the warmth of the restaurant, the chill evening air caused the hair on her arms to rise. The driving beat of the music drowned out other night noises and thrummed through the ground towards them. They stopped by the room to drop off their regular clothes and continued across the street to the bar. The music grew louder as they approached and apprehension ate away at her. She bit the inside of her cheek, caught herself, and stopped. Crowded bars and noise weren't her usual scene.

Ryan dug in his pocket and pulled out a small package and handed it to her. At first, she didn't understand. Turning the cardboard over revealed it was a new set of earplugs. She looked up, grateful for this thoughtful gesture.

"Thank you." Her eyes welled up, overwhelmed by how something small seemed monumental. Mark would never have realized that the music might provide too much stimulation at once. Rolling the bits of foam between her fingers, she stuck them in her ears. The relief from the sound was immediate and muted the intensity. Ryan held out his hand for the container and shoved it back into his pocket.

He took her hand and squeezed.

It was nine-thirty, and the party seemed busier than when they'd arrived in town, the outside crowd larger. The air seemed full of sickly sweet flavored vape clouds rising into the air, and she held her breath as they sidled past.

The unattended doorway stood open, so they walked into the darkened room where the walls were painted black. There was no cover, no bouncer, no security of any kind. The sound swelled, and the beat rocked the building, making it difficult to speak. Without earplugs, it would have been too much. Black overhead lighting lit the dance floor; everything white glowed, the room awash with a sea of lilac and neon blue. Teeth and eyes glowed in near-indigo faces, some with unearthly patches of color where the dancers wore lipstick or other makeup. She'd never seen anything like it.

Gyrating dancers crowded the dance floor in various states of dress and undress, their skin illuminated in shades of pink, blue, and purple, often flecked with a mottled effect—perhaps from a variety of cosmetics. The right-hand side of the floor held a group of ten or twelve dancers, naked or almost, limbs and bodies entwined, undulating together. Kat's eyes widened and she averted her stare. She'd expected wild dancing, not public group sex. Maybe they were just dancing. She turned to ask Ryan his opinion.

His gaze flicked to the dancers and back to her, then he cupped his hand around her ear and spoke. "Yes, they're having sex, right here. Does that shock you? Still want to stay?"

She sucked in her breath, and spun the ring on her right hand, then shrugged. She wouldn't let anyone else drive her out; the dancers weren't hurting anyone. Maybe she should be appalled at their actions, but she wasn't. Shocked maybe, but with no judgment attached. She glanced at them again. Did they care they were being watched?

A young man knelt near the edge of the seething mass of skin. A pair of interested eyes above him held her gaze for three seconds. The vibrations of the music made her feel connected to everyone inside.

The blue speckled hand holding the back of the young man's head pulled away, beckoning to her and Ryan—asking them to join in the fun. Kat's cheeks flamed. Shaking her head, she slipped her hand into Ryan's and looked up at his amused smile. Warmth spread up her arm.

They strolled toward the bar, weaving through the scattered groups standing and drinking. The room smelled of equal parts spilled alcohol, sweat, and sex. She'd never noticed sex as a public scent before, but it was strong enough to fill the space and made her ache in unexpected ways. She didn't want to join the group action, but had to admit that it added to the atmosphere.

She appreciated it wasn't smoky inside. Anyone who wanted to smoke or vape must be outside.

The bartender, who wore a full Ironman costume, complete with mask, slid a bottle to Ryan. He left it on the counter and shook his head. She looked up at him, surprised.

"Changed my mind," he said.

"Something to drink?" the masked man said to Kat, shouting over the music.

"Nothing. I'm good." She shook her head, unsure if her voice had been loud enough.

"Bit of everything else. Hard and soft drugs, edibles if you prefer."

Kat shook her head. She hadn't tried drugs, and despite the end of the world party, she wasn't interested. She'd spent so much of the last two years in an altered state with few memories; it wasn't for her. She didn't care what anyone else did, but she was done with that type of high. She'd take the kind from exercise or sex; that would be enough.

Perhaps reading her mind, Ryan squeezed her hand. She looked up at him and smiled. She'd told him to have a drink and was pleased she'd been telling the truth about it not bothering her. Still, she appreciated he was sensitive to her situation. Drinking wasn't a temptation, after all. He tugged her toward the dance floor. They stayed near the edge, where she felt safe, and the dancers were clothed.

The first few steps felt awkward. She closed her eyes and let the beat of the music fill her chest. It didn't matter that she wasn't the world's best dancer. She loved to move. They danced to several songs with a heavy beat, and she worked up a sweat as she let loose, sometimes lost in the music. She didn't care who watched. Every time she glanced up, Ryan was there, his eyes locked on her. Every move she made, he followed. Weaving through the people, staying with her as he matched her step for step. A constant smile pulled at her face. This was living.

The air between them became charged until she could no longer look away. When a slower song came on, at last, Ryan swung her into his arms and she wrapped her arms around his neck. His quickened heartbeat thumped against hers. They were hot and dripped with sweat, but that didn't seem to matter. They swayed to the music, her body against his, losing herself in the feeling of togetherness. She tilted her face up and he kissed her. It was soft as a whisper, teasing her lips to respond.

As the kiss deepened, the rest of the room fell away, and his hands slipped down to cup her ass through the gauzy material, practically leaving his fingerprints on her. He tugged her closer so she could feel that he was hard as iron, as turned on as she was. His lips grew more demanding, and she gasped when his mouth left hers. He sucked on her neck right below her ear and she trembled.

It wouldn't take much to lead him into a darkened corner or join the throng in the shadows, if that's what she wanted. For a fleeting second, she considered those options, but it chased the thoughts from her head as Ryan's lips returned to hers, hungry for her. They left her shaking and breathless as the song ended.

Without a word, Ryan tugged her outside, and she followed, her body tuned to his. His eyes shone in the streetlamp's light overhead, moths flitting around it. "Do you trust me?"

It wasn't what she'd expected him to ask.

She nodded. The night wasn't over yet, though she ached for him. She tingled everywhere, and her lips felt almost bruised. She fantasized about being pushed against the wall at the side of a darkened building and taken there. Part of her still thrummed, hoping to be manhandled. She took out her earplugs. They weren't necessary outside.

Ryan took her small hand in his large one and led her down a street until they were two blocks from the bar. The noise of the party became less but not gone, allowing them to speak at regular volume. This far from the bar, there was no one else in sight.

"This looks like the one," he said, a pleased smile on his face. "The hostess mentioned it." There was another hotel here, one not chosen as party headquarters or to remain open. The roadside sign was lit, but the building was dark. He led her behind the hotel and opened the gate in a tall wooden fence. It clicked as it closed, separating them from other night wanderers and their eyes.

Before them spread an outdoor pool that shimmered in the pale moonlight. Water dripped from a rolled-up pool cover.

Ryan steamed as heat from dancing dissipated in the cool air. "Want a swim?"

A swim to cool off was an excellent plan, for now.

"We don't have bathing suits." She shivered and bit her lip.

"Do you care?" Ryan's eyes dared her to deny him this fun.

She pulled her dress over her head in one fluid motion and tossed it onto a nearby lounge chair. Ryan kicked off his shoes and removed his vest, his fingers quick. She stepped closer and unbuttoned his shirt. Though sweaty, he smelled good, and she inhaled his fresh, outdoorsy, masculine scent. She kissed his chest and slid her hands inside his shirt, untucking it. He sucked in a breath as her cooler hands touched his heated flesh.

She smiled, stood on tiptoe, and gave him a quick kiss. She stepped back and wriggled out of her underthings while he took off his pants. She dipped a toe in the water and glanced over her shoulder. It should be safe. She was covered in goosebumps, though the water seemed warm. They were standing near the deep end.

Without further thought, she dove into the crystal water. Ryan followed a split second behind, popping up a couple of meters further down the pool. He ducked under and continued swimming. After the heat of dancing and the day's ride, the refreshing water seemed incredible. She ducked under the surface and surfaced, slicking her hair back with one hand. She'd never skinny-dipped before. When Ryan came back after swimming, she grinned at him. They stood in the middle of the pool.

"Good idea?"

"Great idea." She smiled.

"You're not sorry you left with me instead of joining the group thing back there?"

She shook her head. "It looked... fun, but not for me. I'm only interested in you."

Ryan grabbed her around the waist with one muscular arm and tugged her closer, but gave her a chance to get away if she wanted. She threw her arms around his neck, her breasts pressing against his bare chest. Held close against him, every breath in sync as they kissed.

She didn't know how long they stood in the middle of the pool, half in and half out of the water in the chilly night air. This time when Ryan's mouth left hers, he took one breast in his warm mouth, circling it with his tongue before taking first one nipple into his mouth, then switching to the other. She moaned as he sucked; tendrils of desire teased her core.

He was hard again and responded to her touch. It didn't matter that they were outside and in a public place. It seemed like they were alone. She wanted more. She pulled Ryan toward the edge of the pool and pointed to an upright plastic chair.

They jumped out of the water.

"Lean back." She grabbed a towel from a stack on a nearby shelf, spreading it to protect her knees from the rough concrete, and knelt between his legs. She cooled off without a towel, but it didn't matter. Inside, she was molten. She took Ryan in her mouth with long, hard strokes, designed to make this quick. She quaked, more turned on than she'd thought possible. Reaching between her legs, she was slippery and swollen. Ryan's voice interrupted.

"This whole evening has been foreplay. I need to be inside you." He reached for his pants on the deck and pulled out a condom. He must have planned when he'd changed, hoping their evening would go this way.

Maintaining eye contact, she gave one more stroke before helping him with protection. Standing, he pressed her against the hotel wall behind them and thrust into her. She cried out and bit his shoulder to muffle the sound.

"You good?" he whispered, his ragged voice in her ear.

"So good," she said, her breath rough.

She wrapped her legs around him, and he boosted her up with his hands and thrust again, though this time one of his arms protected her back from the wall. She'd done nothing like this, nor had she been with anyone strong enough. He was right. Everything before this had been foreplay. This was primal. Quick and dangerous—proof that they were alive.

She shuddered, her vision fading as sparks exploded in her brain. Her voice broke the surrounding silence, though she couldn't believe they were her passionate cries. She'd seldom been so uninhibited, except with Ryan.

"Come again, Sweetheart," he said between hungry kisses. "I'll go with you."

His words were like magic. The heat in her core spread like wildfire as she pulsed around him again, each thrust taking her farther from herself until they cried out in ecstasy together.

"You're amazing. That was incredible." He let her down, and they stood trembling in the shadows, foreheads pressed together while they waited for everything to calm within. They forgot their worries and their journey, lost in each other, at least for tonight.

CHAPTER 16: RYAN

The next morning, after a quick breakfast, Ryan and Kat hit the road and with the journey, came a return to reality. Overcast skies had rolled in overnight, bringing the scorched smell to remind them of the volcanoes and devastation behind them. Ryan didn't like how far they still had to travel; it made him uncomfortable. The man at the hotel desk had mentioned that Yellowstone was still safe, but to beware of bison, grizzly bears, and moose. He'd also reported that some geysers were unpredictable and to stay on the roads and trails.

The fastest route to xTerra went through Yellowstone National Park. Their goal was to make it to Cody, Wyoming—near the other side of the park—by nightfall. It would be their longest cycling day yet, at well over a hundred miles. He eyed the white sky and scant drifts of ash. At least the conditions improved the farther east they traveled.

Ryan and Kat didn't stop for the roadside tourist pullouts at first. Urgency caused his chest to tighten as he pedaled, and he debated what to do. He didn't want to be caught in the rain with all the dust and debris in the air that could be toxic. But Kat had never experienced Yellowstone and, despite their hurry, Ryan wanted to share a few special sights with her. Maybe one stop would be okay.

Ryan chose a set of gorgeous sapphire pools near the road to show her, directing their bikes onto the empty gravel paths and boardwalks for a ride-by. They couldn't linger and they didn't have time to play tourist, but he couldn't allow this to be a wasted opportunity.

Out here, on the road, he kept waiting for the other shoe to drop and the situation to worsen. It was only a matter of time. They'd been lucky with the people they'd encountered. That wouldn't always be the case. The consequences of the asteroid impact were brewing like a storm, waiting to strike. The longer it took to gather strength, the worse it would be. People would become desperate, even out here. Good times wouldn't last forever, and the bunker would provide safety.

If they'd been able to keep a vehicle, they would have arrived at the shelter by now. He gripped the handlebars tighter, his knuckles turning white.

They needed a car but there weren't car lots in a National Park, and Three Forks had been a bust. The only way to get a car would be to steal one, and he couldn't steal from someone who needed their vehicle. He and Kat hadn't fallen that far. That eliminated family vehicles and left them without options. He sighed. Even if they stole a car, they would have problems with fuel. They had to keep cycling. The tight feeling in his chest and shoulders remained throughout the morning.

After a couple of hours, he relaxed and attempted to enjoy the here and now. He was wasting this chance to see the park with Kat.

The air temperature was warm as it was approaching June. Regular years, Yellowstone would swarm with tourists from across the U.S., Canada, and abroad. Instead, it was eerie and quiet. A couple of RVs parked in roadside lots, but people were scarce and kept to themselves. It was easy to imagine that everyone had vanished, leaving them the last people on earth, other than those partying in West Yellowstone.

Thinking of the dancing throng and the idea it had given him, he smiled at Kat, wanting to make this trip memorable today as well.

As a teenager, he'd come here with his family. To distract himself from the family drama and conflict, he'd tallied the different license plates he saw. His final total had been forty-eight different state plates, plus eight Canadian provinces. He'd missed only Hawaii and Rhode Island. He'd cheered for Vermont, Alaska, and the half dozen he'd found when they'd parked at the Visitor Center near Old Faithful. Thinking of the drunken parent arguments, the rest of the trip had been a disaster. The search for the license plates had kept him sane. Today, the plates were local—Montana, Idaho, and Wyoming, and his vehicle count was at seven as it neared noon.

Early wildflowers at the park's roadside bloomed in a tangle of yellow, white, and purple, filling the air with a wonderful fragrance; the delicate scent of flowers strong since it didn't have to compete with exhaust. If he'd been inside a car, he wouldn't have been able to smell the flowers or the mineral-like aromas of the hot pools, and the fields of flowers would have flashed by before they were appreciated. Riding a bike had advantages.

He forced himself to breathe deep and look around, which loosened the tight feeling in his chest. Kat wore a dreamy expression as she took in the beautiful sights, not needing a reminder to enjoy herself. They should stop to appreciate this spectacular and unique place. Maybe they wouldn't make it to Cody tonight, but they could camp whenever it got dark. He'd prefer a roof overhead, but he didn't mind camping since they were prepared and were beyond the main ashfall zone.

Without the crowds, it was peaceful in Yellowstone. Hawks circled, riding thermals and hunting small creatures—like the red squirrels and striped chipmunks that zipped across the road ahead and disappeared into the tall grass. Yellow, orange, black, and white butterflies fluttered in ones and twos, lighting on flowers, drifting onto bushes, or hovering over the asphalt. The loudest sound was the hypnotic whirring of the bikes' tires on the paved surface of the road.

Near the Norris Geyser Basin, Ryan left the road and bumped across the gravel corner of a massive parking lot. It looked odd without hordes of cars and the usual crush of people—much bigger than he remembered. He exhaled with a whoosh as they rode into the last section. The expanse of dirt and gravel remained empty. The park wouldn't make their quota this year.

Acting on impulse, he said, "Let's stash the bikes and take a quick walk. It'll feel good to stretch our legs. I was here years ago and there were a couple of geysers that were supposed to be impressive, but irregular. I want to check them out. You okay with that?" At her nod, he said, "It might take forty-five minutes to an hour." They shouldn't stop, but he wanted to do this for her.

She cleared her throat. "I thought we were in a hurry?"

"We are, but we shouldn't miss everything. We've been rushing and I don't know when or if we'll be back. I want to enjoy something with you that I found joy in when I was young. Find you some bubbling mud and wildlife."

Her smile made this decision worthwhile.

She looked around. "It seems like we're alone, but you never know."

They walked the bikes to the thick bushes past the trailhead. When they were sure that they were alone, they hid them behind a large park sign with a map for the various trail loops below. With the bikes stowed, he took her hand, liking how it felt in his, and they walked along the dusty trail, carrying their backpacks. They could have hidden them with the bikes, but it felt wrong to leave everything. When you had few belongings, the remainder was precious.

He would have liked to take her to Old Faithful, but it was in the wrong direction. Without a vehicle, it would take too long to travel so far out of their way. It would add a day or two instead of an extra hour.

A rumble started below the edge of the hill and an enormous spray of white water erupted into view with a rushing sound. The column of water was several meters across. He didn't remember seeing anything that size, other than Old Faithful, and they hurried to get closer. Another geyser sprayed upward to the left, and a third in the distance. Steam rose through cracks in the ground that crisscrossed the land like spider webs. The valley was hot and filled with steam.

Close to the first geyser, they stopped well behind the guard fence, now drenched and lost in the hot mist. He craned his neck to see the apex a hundred meters in the air—very cool.

"This is more impressive than last time. Seems like Yellowstone has increased seismic activity, too."

"It's an incredible display of geothermal activity. Do you think it's safe to be here? Or will it be like that movie, 2012, when the whole place disappeared, awash with lava?" They'd watched it after making lists one night a couple of weeks ago.

"Probably not very safe, but I doubt it's like the movie. We can't stay; I wanted to remember what it was like and didn't want you to miss everything in the park. Yellowstone is a one-of-a-kind place."

"Thanks for stopping." She kissed him, her lips soft on his.

They watched the geysers for a few minutes, then returned to the bikes, where they ate a picnic lunch on tables near the parking lot. Steller's Jays and Whisky Jacks landed near their table in the small pine trees and hovered, hoping for their attention to wander. One bird, bolder than the rest, landed at the end of the table and hopped closer until it was within arm's reach. It tilted its cheeky head, showing its dark eyes as it inched forward, one hop at a time. Kat broke off a crumb of her granola bar and set it near the trusting bird, who scooped it up and flew away, its blue under-feathers shimmering in the sunlight.

After a quick lunch, they got back on the bikes, slowing once to ride past pools of bubbling white mud. Watching the bubbles was mesmerizing, even if they spared only a few minutes.

● ● ●

It was afternoon when Ryan first noticed a low moaning sound in the distance, like a buzz of stop-and-go traffic. But that made little sense because there were no cars. His heart rate quickened. It must be a herd of bison. He'd hoped they'd find some at this side of the park.

"What's that sound?"

"Bison, I think. Lowing." He was glad he had an answer when her eyes lit up and her voice became animated.

"I've never seen wild bison."

"When we get closer, we should stop. We don't want to startle such gigantic animals when we're out in the open."

She nodded, but put on an extra burst of speed.

The sound was unfamiliar, but unmistakable. The Yellowstone herd was supposed to be impressive, but last time he'd seen only a dozen animals roadside. Until you were up close, they looked little different from shaggy cattle, but they were huge—a whole different scale of bovine.

Bikes didn't offer the protection afforded by a car. He swallowed his nervousness. They would need to maintain their distance from the giant beasts. He didn't think they were as unpredictable as moose, but it wouldn't hurt to be cautious. His step-father had told real-life horror stories of moose attacking cars, and even trains. He and Kat should remain safe if they went around the bison. Being on bikes would make it easier to go off-road than in a car.

They stopped at the top of the next rise, dropping their bikes in the ditch to hike up a knoll for a better view. A valley spread out before them in rolling waves of emerald green and dirt brown. Bison scattered across the sloped expanse, but lower down, a massive swath of dark brown was so thick he couldn't distinguish individual animals. A trampled track a couple of hundred meters wide stretched behind the herd. Were grizzlies and wolves that preyed on young bison also nearby? He couldn't see any, but that didn't mean they weren't present. It would be interesting to observe them from a safe distance, but he would prefer to avoid a close-up encounter with a grizzly.

A few bison roamed on and beside the road, but the herd congregated on the right near the water source. He and Kat sat on the hill and waited for the animals to leave the road. Kat snapped a few pictures with her phone and of the two of them. They didn't have to wait long before the herd moved on. Several steaming piles scattered the highway to mark the creatures' recent passage.

If he and Kat were careful, they shouldn't have trouble now. But the volume of the bison increased when they approached. Their lowing vibrated in his chest, much like the dance music last night. One massive male tossed its head and snorted in their direction, but didn't charge. Who was he kidding? This wasn't safe, but it was exhilarating.

Ryan held his breath as they cycled past the enormous, prehistoric-looking creatures with giant heads, but the creatures seemed immune to their presence and didn't startle in their meandering.

As they passed the last of the grazing herd, Ryan and Kat shared a grin for the once-in-a-lifetime experience.

If it hadn't been for the tragedy of the asteroid impact, he never would have experienced this adventure with Kat. Having her along had brought so much to what could have been a lonely and terrifying journey. Last night had been magical, and today her eyes had helped him to appreciate the beauty of Yellowstone in a whole new way.

• • •

When the sun went down, the temperature dropped, reminding him they were at high elevation, and Ryan's hands grew cold where they gripped the handlebars. They should stop while they had light to set up camp. There were no campgrounds in this section of the park, so they'd have to find somewhere on their own. Cody wasn't far, but they'd ridden enough for today. The Yellowstone road was smoother than the highways in Montana; the asteroid earthquakes appeared to have caused less damage here. Despite the shorter distance traveled today, he wasn't sorry for their short breaks.

They'd been cycling along the highway above the river, which would be convenient to replenish their drinking water. He hoped it was still safe to drink, but they would filter and boil it first, just in case. They stopped at a day-use picnic area and set up the tent, away from the road but near the washrooms. They tried the water pump for the first time and had no difficulty. After boiling water for dinner and replenishing their canteens, they ate their meals in silence, listening to the surrounding woods and the small rustling sounds of wildlife within while the last of the light disappeared.

The Grand Teton mountains to the south and west blocked most of the sunset, allowing only streaks of orange above their glowing snow-covered peaks. Once the sun's light had disappeared, they snuggled closer together to preserve heat as the temperature plummeted. Last night, they had slept little; tonight, they should rest and try to make up time in the morning.

"Should we worry about bears?" Kat said as they got ready for bed.

She repacked the clean dishes while moths flocked to the lantern and Ryan batted several from his face as he collected the light. Overhead, the shadow of a bat caught his eye as it swooped through the air, searching for insects. He considered his answer before he spoke.

"Bears are always a concern in Yellowstone." Like most animals exposed to humans, they'd lost their fear, which made them dangerous. However, he chose his words with care. He didn't want to terrify Kat before bed. Imagination was difficult enough to keep positive during the day without additional night-time danger.

She raised an eyebrow in what he considered her sexy teacher look, perhaps wanting more information.

"No food or cosmetics in the tent. Just to be safe. Nothing scented."

"I can't believe toothpaste and antiperspirant would smell good to a bear."

He smiled; an image of a bear snacking on a bar of soap and frothing at the mouth appeared in his mind.

"My stepfather once told a story from when he was young. His family was camping in an old canvas wall tent—the kind with no floor. At night, they packed the food into the car where it would be safe, but they didn't consider their personal items. While they were sleeping, a bear slit the tent open and stole the toothpaste. They didn't hear a thing."

"Oh my god." Kat's eyes were aghast in the lantern light.

"Another time, he was hunting mountain sheep with his brother. In the night, a bear stole their sheep horns from a stone cache along with a gamebag full of meat. They slept through the bear tossing the rocks aside and dragging everything away."

She said nothing, but her eyes were huge.

He squeezed her icy hand. He may have gotten carried away with the stories, but he had so few pleasant memories of his stepfather that he'd wanted to share. "There may have been alcohol involved with that kind of deep sleep." He'd shared little about his family, but Kat could be trusted. She wouldn't mock or judge.

"Was it just a story? Or do you think it happened?"

"I'm not sure." Ryan shrugged. "My stepfather sometimes played fast and loose with the truth. It could have happened to someone he knew and he 'borrowed' the story. But, he exhibited a healthy respect for bears and made me promise to always put my toothpaste with the food. Whether up a tree or in a car."

She collected her toiletries bag from the table, put it in her pack, and gave it to him to hang. He threaded the packs together with rope and raised them several meters up a tree.

That night, they were too exhausted to do more than cuddle and kiss, but they faced each other and spoke in whispers like giddy teenagers for an hour before falling asleep. Their breath warmed the tent and made it cozy instead of crowded.

Kat drifted off first, and Ryan listened to her quiet breathing and the night sounds outside. He identified the wind in the trees, the odd scurrying rodent, and an owl's hoot and the quiet gurgle of the swift-flowing river further away. His brain stayed on alert and it was difficult to relax despite his tired muscles.

He must have dozed off because a loud snuffling noise near the tent awakened him. It came closer, and his heart raced. It was hard to keep his breathing normal. Kat rustled in her sleeping bag as she tossed and turned, perhaps sensing something amiss while dreaming. She woke with a gasp, and he touched her mouth with his hand. He couldn't see much, just a vague outline of her shape in the dark and the whites of her eyes. She was tense and shook. He slid behind her and pulled her closer.

He whispered, "We have nothing in here it will want. If it's a bear, it won't be interested."

She snuggled into him, her back to his chest and his arms and legs wrapped around her while they stared into the darkness together.

There was a clacking sound, like rocks hitting one another, and a shuffling sound of movement. Ryan was almost positive it was a bear, but he didn't want to scare Kat more than she was already. Or himself. His imagination ran amok, with images of their tent becoming a bear burrito.

Despite Roy's stories, he wasn't experienced with bears. The sniffing moved toward the tree where he'd hung their packs. A scratching sound caused the hair on the back of his neck to rise. At a loud cough or grunt outside, Ryan held his breath, tightening his grip on Kat as they waited for the bear to leave. It was hard to track the passage of time, and the bear in their camp took an eternity to move on.

Sometime later, silence fell outside the thin walls of the tent. His heart still thumped like a jackhammer, and he wasn't sure if he'd be able to fall asleep again. He checked his watch to find that it was only two-forty-five in the morning.

"I think it's gone." Kat let out a big breath. "I'm glad we have nothing in here but ourselves. Either that or the smell of your hiking shoes scared it off."

He tickled her ribs, the impulse being too strong to resist while she was in his grasp. She squirmed away with a laugh and dove back into her sleeping bag.

He missed her warmth as he slid back into bed. Kat was amazing. What they'd shared and experienced was like something from a story—the two of them versus the apocalypse. Was Kat her real name? Maybe it was short for something. The question would seem out of the blue, but he wanted to know.

"Is Kat short for something?"

She laughed and clamped her hand over her mouth, as though unsure if it was safe to make noise. "That's what you're thinking now?" She whispered; her breath warm on his face as she turned to him to speak. "We had a grizzly in our campsite, and you want to know my name?"

"Mm-hmm." He saw the humor, too.

"My full name is Katana. Like the sword. My mom used to say it suited me because I was so sharp." Her voice sounded sad.

"Was that a good thing?"

"I never could decide."

Ryan hesitated, not sure if he should push for more detail. If the situation was reversed, he might share with Kat after everything they'd been through.

"What's the story with your family? I couldn't help but notice they haven't replied to your texts. Even before when they could have."

Her breath came out in a rush.

"Mark turned my family against me." Her voice sounded small. Perhaps his question had been too personal. "They took his side and didn't understand my feelings when he died. I didn't talk to them after the first time. It hurts that they see him as a paragon instead of a bully. We aren't close, as you've seen. They've had a hard time relating to me. They're all extroverts and didn't respect that my brain works differently than theirs."

"Do you wish you'd told them about the bunker? Or at least about leaving the coast?" He lived with his own guilt in that respect.

Her shoulders raised as her whole body looked as tense as a plank. "I tried, even though we'd agreed not to. They said I was being an alarmist and my mom hung up on me."

He smoothed the hair from her wet face in the dark. Her family had made her cry. Anger and protective feelings surged through him. He didn't like to see her hurt.

"I didn't tell mine. I didn't want them to come to the bunker with my ex. I suppose that's selfish, but I expected them to look after themselves. Just like they've always expected me to look after myself. There's been no word since they sent nasty comments before the asteroid." He paused. "I don't know if they're alive." His throat threatened to seize up if he continued to talk about his family. They'd always been a difficult topic.

He'd tried not to think about it. Even if he wasn't close to his family, the grief and guilt would eat at him if he let it. Maybe tomorrow he'd turn on his phone and see if he had messages. How many cell towers had been damaged by the asteroids or the volcanoes? There might be some that were operational, like pockets with electricity.

"Do you wish you'd told them? Now that we know how terrible it is back home?"

"No. I don't want them with us." He lay in the dark trying to sleep. Kat was so different from Heather. She put on an act for those they interacted with, but he believed he was getting to know the real her. She was different in a good way. She had depth, and it felt genuine.

In the morning, they ate a hurried breakfast of instant oatmeal and got back on the road, passing through Cody by nine a.m.. It was as quiet as the other towns they'd come through, adding to the apocalypse feel of their road trip. Tonight's progress goal was Kaycee, Wyoming. The black dot on the map looked small, but there should be a motel or two. He wouldn't mind an actual bed again tonight, even if that made him spoiled. It would be more than a hundred and sixty miles today, but they were making good time without roadside attractions, other than what they saw from their bikes.

CHAPTER 17: KAT

Ryan and Kat wheeled into town as it neared dark. With the lack of sleep last night, her bleary eyes took a minute to adjust to their change in scenery. They'd had another full day's ride and Kat wanted to stop. She rubbed her eyes. *Kaycee, Wyoming: Population 284,* read the sign on the outskirts of town—another small town they expected to find abandoned. They'd pushed hard to make it before dark, racing circling storm clouds. Closed gas stations stood empty, while stores were boarded up, the lights off. Smashed doors of an IGA yawned—the dark opening like a giant's maw with jagged teeth. The store may have been gutted. Another example of the asteroid impact bringing out the worst in some people.

Shards of glass fanned the parking lot in a large arc from the store toward the street; a pool of dark liquid spilled near the edge of the glass. Was it blood? Oil? Or something else? In the fading light, it was impossible to tell, but the state of the town made the hair on the back of Kat's neck rise. It had a different vibe than the other small towns through which they'd traveled.

They'd planned to eat another late dinner tonight after they'd set up camp; they just needed a place to stay. Her stomach growled at the thought of food. Eating dehydrated meals was less satisfying than cooked meals, and the portions, while sufficient, weren't generous—especially considering the energy expended biking.

Her heart plummeted at the sight of the deserted Siesta Motel. Several of the doors had been smashed open, the rooms open to the elements. Someone else had come through and trashed the small motel. Each building they passed looked more forlorn than the last, dark with unlit signs and vandalism. She would almost welcome a "No Vacancy", as a sign of normalcy in this desolate town. She'd been looking forward to a hot shower and a soft bed more than she should have. When they couldn't find anywhere to stay, they stopped to confer near the edge of a boarded-up pet food store. Spray-painted on the closed Kaycee General Store, the words *Slains* rose in blood-red letters a foot high. Eight-foot metal fences had been erected around both gas stations, the gates padlocked.

"What about the city park? Sagebrush Park." She'd seen a sign when they'd entered the town. "It might have washrooms and a flat spot for the tent. It won't kill us to camp another night." She sighed. She wouldn't get a proper bed tonight.

"We can try." Ryan's tone was flat as he scanned the nearby buildings.

They'd agreed to try for a hotel, so he must be disappointed. It was getting easier to read him. He seemed like a comfortable friend now, as though she'd known him a long time—like Nick. But he was more than a friend. She caught herself as her thoughts wandered back to the image of a bed. Neither of them had gotten much sleep last night after the bear; they'd been too on edge. Ryan must be exhausted, too.

They turned and made their way towards the park. The city streets grew dim as the wind picked up. The overhead streetlights didn't turn on as the evening grew darker and the stoplights weren't working. Instead, the traffic lights swayed and creaked overhead, making a high-pitched whine. If she'd been in a vehicle, she wouldn't have noticed the sound, but from her bike it was clear. The power must be out, as it had been in so many places. They'd be eating by lantern light again, but at least their food would be quick and easy.

Most of Sagebrush Park wasn't suitable for camping, being covered at one end by a large lot filled with thick sagebrush. The other end beside the closed Kaycee Highschool might be more promising. The empty school side of the park had a large grassy field surrounded by a running track and several sections of bleachers.

Kat and Ryan rode behind the school building, where more than a dozen giant RVs with awnings, carpets, and picnic tables in a row. This more established camp was using the school to block the wind. Past the RVs, they'd set up half a dozen faded tents. Between them stretched a flapping tarp that covered an outdoor sleeping area. A couple of occupied sleeping bags and two overflowing shopping carts completed the scene.

Remembering the feeling as they came into town, she was unsure about approaching the group ahead, and once more her hackles rose.

Dozens of people sprawled in the camp; there could be more if the tents were full. Three vans and a trailer had parked beside the building, blocking the entrance to the public washrooms. This was more people than they'd seen in days, which made Kat shift on her seat and look down. The vibe was different from West Yellowstone. A mix of retired people sat near their fancy, behemoth RVs with out-of-state plates, a few youngsters lounged by their tricked-out camper vans, and what looked like a homeless community congregated together—a strange combination.

Were some people residents who'd banded together for protection, or were they tourists? If the latter, where had the townspeople gone? The houses had looked deserted, with few cars. Perhaps they'd hunkered down out of town, waiting out the unrest or for the strangers to move on?

Ryan raised his hand in greeting to the people around fires in three above-ground metal fire pits like those she'd seen for sale at Costco; no one acknowledged them, though several people stared in their direction. The orange flames cast a glow over the camp and a dozen inhabitants who warmed themselves by the fire watched them with hostile expressions. Their unfriendliness contributed to Kat's uneasy feeling.

Feeling their watching eyes, she and Ryan rode their bikes across the grass to the far corner by a few large evergreens which could help block the rising wind. Kat's legs were rubbery when she got off the bike, as though they would buckle at her first several steps. She took a deep breath, massaged her calves for a moment, and forced herself to keep moving. She was determined to do her share. While Ryan was unpacking, she chose a spot for the tent at the opposite end of the field. Twice she glanced over her shoulder, back toward the other camp. She hoped this was far enough from the others to ensure privacy. The unfriendly vibe from the group made her uncomfortable, but they'd found nowhere else to camp on their ride through town.

Ryan must have sensed her unease, and he turned to talk, facing away from others. "We could keep looking. Just rest for a minute. Eat dinner. Move on."

"I didn't see anywhere else to camp, but I'm on edge and this doesn't feel right." Before Ryan replied, she added, "It's late and we're both tired, but we should be alert."

They erected the tent in the last of the daylight while fighting gusts of wind, which whipped her hair from its ponytail and into her face. They boiled water for their dinner, which was soon ready. The garlic and basil scent of spaghetti wafted from the steaming bowls. She almost burned her mouth on the first few bites, but the icy breeze soon cooled her food so once more she was eating cold rations. They huddled in their rain jackets while they ate at a picnic table they'd dragged near the tent. The tree branches behind them tossed in the wind and her thoughts turned to the prospect of an uncomfortable night listening to the whistling wind. Not to mention the unfriendly neighbors.

"You got extra food?" A scruffy-looking man dressed in several layers of mismatched clothing emerged from the darkness as though conjured. "They don't leave us much."

His demanding voice startled Kat, causing her to jump and her throat to tighten. Lightning crackled and thunder crashed—the storm was closing in.

"This is all we've got," said Ryan's confident voice. "We expected to find stores open in town, but no luck."

She hoped the other man would get the hint and leave.

"Can I have some? We didn't have much for dinner." The man stepped closer, and the stink of unwashed clothes and smoke permeated the air.

Leaning away, Kat tried not to gag from the potent smell as she twirled her last bite of pasta. Her hand trembled and her skin prickled with the first drops of rain. She tried not to look at the filthy man beside her, who was giving off bad vibes.

She and Ryan didn't have weapons, other than the baseball bat leaning against the picnic table. Her brow tightened. This could escalate into a larger confrontation. Something about this situation seemed wrong and had the potential to go south without notice. Her chest tightened. They'd already set up the tent, and it was almost time for bed, but she wouldn't be able to sleep. She wanted to leave, even if it meant braving the storm.

"You look like you can spare something." The man took a belligerent stance closer to the table, his stubbled jaw sticking out in defiance.

The persistent man stood over her and it became hard to think. She needed him out of her personal space. For the first time on their trip, she worried about having a meltdown. She concentrated on her breathing.

"Sorry, this is our dinner," said Ryan, stepping up, the bat in hand.

In the lantern light, his solid frame was much larger than the stranger, but the constricted feeling in her chest worsened. She hoped she could defuse the confrontation.

Standing and moving back, Kat took a breath and forced a smile. "We biked from West Yellowstone yesterday morning, two hundred miles. You should have seen the party that town was having. They even still had power. How long has it been out here?" Kat was proud that her voice didn't quaver.

"Days, I think," said the man with a shrug. "We don't pay much attention to things like that. We didn't have power before the asteroid, except in the washrooms. Others in the fancy RVs might miss it more." His voice made those folks sound weak.

His gray and rotten teeth were grim in the stark lantern light. He could also use a shave, though it was difficult to tell if his face was just stubbled or caked with dirt. She tried to tell herself that she was being ridiculous and that this man was harmless, but something about his aggressive stance and unwillingness to leave set off her inner alarms. This could get ugly. She wanted him to leave so she could relax in the tent and escape the weather. That was now impossible.

"Where'd you come from before?" The strange man stroked her sleeve.

She flinched and shrank away, using it as an excuse to set down her bowl. The man snatched it from the table and jumped back a few feet, but didn't leave. His eyes dared her to object, though she said nothing.

Ryan positioned himself between her and the man, making use of his superior height to be intimidating. Her chest tightened. What could she say? This wasn't the time to flirt or act cheery, though it often de-escalated situations. She didn't know how to act. Pretending to be normal wouldn't be helpful. The wind gusted through the camp, shaking the trees. The tent flapped with sharp cracking sounds. Would the stakes hold?

Crashing noises in the bushes next to the trees caused her to stare in that direction. She couldn't see anything unusual. She turned back and the man grabbed the second bowl. Licking it with wet grunting noises, he polished off Ryan's dinner. She should feel bad that this stranger was that hungry, but she couldn't find it within herself to feel sympathy tonight. Instead, the taste of bile filled her mouth.

A woman broke through the screen of bushes and joined them.

"If you stay in our park, you have to feed us," said the woman. "We were promised if we guarded this road, we could have what we wanted."

Who'd promised? Kat didn't know what she was talking about. She was about to ask when she noticed what the woman wore. She didn't match her companion.

The newcomer wore a red designer rain jacket and polka-dot rain boots. Something about her haircut and the cut of her clothes said she had money. Perhaps a woman from the RVs. She picked up Kat's backpack, unzipped the main pocket, and reached inside as though entitled. Kat sucked in her breath and bit back hot angry words, afraid to make things worse, as the woman removed the last of the food Kat carried—the package with tomorrow's meals.

Her bike's saddlebags in the tent had another couple of days' worth of food and Ryan's had enough for two more days. They needed all of it, as they were still days away from xTerra. Kat held her breath, hoping the woman didn't continue her search.

The woman smiled a shark-like smile that didn't show her teeth, her dark eyes gleaming in the white light.

"I knew they were holding out on you," she said to the first man who handed her the remains of Ryan's dinner. She shook her head and he resumed his licking. "Your mistake was asking."

She turned to Ryan. "We're not beggars, we're thieves, and we've inherited this town. People looked down on us for too long, dismissed some of us as too old or unimportant. Many of us were on the road a long time, living a nomadic lifestyle because we didn't fit in anywhere. However, we've found a new place to settle. We answer only to the Slains."

Kat's mind flashed back to the red lettering in town. Before she could ask, the woman continued, turning to include Kat in her speech.

"We make the rules. I suggest you move on at first light. Head back wherever you came from. We don't need you prissy do-gooder types. You're not our kind."

Kat bit her lip and clenched her jaw. She wanted to respond, but the man grabbed Kat's wrist and she froze, her heart stopping. His tight grip hurt as he clenched.

"There's something else I'd like," the man said, setting the empty bowls on the table.

Ryan pried the man's hand from her arm. His eyes fixed on the other man's face, staring him down, his knuckles white on the half-raised bat.

"Keep your hands to yourself." Ryan's voice was a growl.

His eyes were darker than Kat had seen before and his voice was hard. If she didn't know him, she'd have been terrified. He was a big man who had the strength to back up his anger. The look on his face made the scruffy man and the woman in the expensive red slicker step back. For the first time, they looked concerned, glancing at each other and shifting their feet, poised to flee.

The woman returned Ryan's stare for three seconds before she looked away and broke the silence. She swung her arm in front of her companion.

"Leave them be. The woman's spoken for. They can sleep in our park by providing us with breakfast. Stan, thank our guests for their generosity. Time to head back to our camp."

The man swallowed and muttered, "Thanks for the food." One of his hands twitched as he backed away from Ryan, and his eyes cut to Kat one last time before he turned. She flinched at his look of hatred.

The strangers trudged across the field toward the camp on the far side, and Kat lost them in the darkness. The only visible sign of those by the fires was the glow from the metal barrels. A distant cheer erupted when the visitors arrived back at their shabby camp. In all likelihood because of the stolen bag of food. If they were that excited over a few dehydrated meals, maybe they'd been starving. That didn't mean she forgave their behavior or trusted them to stay away.

"Can we leave?" Her voice shook and it took effort not to cry. Since they'd been on the road, she hadn't often feared people, but the terror from the last night in Seattle had returned. She'd been terrified and alone; today she wasn't but her chest remained tight. She and Ryan weren't hurt, but she still felt the place on her arm where the man had gripped her wrist.

"Let's take down the tent. We'll wash the dishes later." Ryan looked like he was calming down, but the set of his shoulders remained tense. "Are you okay?"

"I will be. I'm too tired to go far, but I won't sleep this close to that lot. No matter what she said, I don't trust him to stay away."

"We're going to stay at a motel tonight."

The wet wind and rain reminded her how good it would feel to be inside.

"They're wrecked or closed."

"We'll find a room. It doesn't matter if it's closed. I'll break in somewhere again, otherwise I won't sleep either. Not without a solid door and a functional lock." His voice had a steely ring, for which she was grateful.

They stuffed sleeping bags in their packs, dismantled the tent, and packed everything in a matter of minutes, hurrying to leave and find somewhere more secure. When they finished, they shut off the lamp and departed in the dark. For light, they used the scant light of the moon where it shone through a thin patch of boiling cloud, but it wasn't enough to relieve the dark that pressed inward.

Relying on memory to make their way back to the street at the edge of the park, they kept the bikes quiet, hoping the wind covered their small noises. They avoided the other camp by the bleachers and the stadium by cutting through the school parking lot.

Lightning forked through the sky, illuminating the west, thunder crashing on its heels. The rain began in earnest, and Kat's shoes squelched at every step while her clothes became drenched and clung to her chilled frame. It soaked her to the skin. Shivering, they walked beside the bikes back into town, not wanting to risk riding on the slippery pavement in the dark. Images appeared in her mind of acid rain eating her clothes and skin. That wasn't how it worked, but this rain might be unhealthy.

"There might be another motel on the other side of town. We should have kept looking." Ryan leaned in to speak in her ear, his voice pitched low for her alone. The hissing wind snatched his words away despite his care, and she strained to hear what he said.

Sneaking away in the dark kept her tense. Every noise and shadow became a potential threat, but they had no further incidents as they returned to the small downtown core. Water gurgled, covering the street in a flow several inches deep. At the edges of the street, overflowing storm drains roared, the deluge proving too much for the small roadside grates to handle at once.

Quiet and darkened houses stood in a row at the southern edge of town, near the highway. Behind them was an inn. The main building near the street resembled a large white house. The L-shaped motel surrounded a courtyard parking lot behind it, with eight rooms that provided some shelter from the wind. The windows were dark, with no sign of candles or lanterns within. She shook the knob of the office door, but it was locked. Ryan might break the door down, but it would be obvious to anyone searching. He must have another plan.

Ryan pointed to the rooms as they retreated toward the empty parking lot.

In the end, they chose a room at the back of the building with an outside entrance. A rocking awning provided little protection as they stood in the driving rain and wind to assess the exterior doors it covered. They were in luck; the Inn's rooms took keys, not electronic key cards. Taking a few steps to the right, Kat maintained a view of the street, standing lookout while Ryan picked the lock using a hook-ended wire made from a paperclip.

Though dark, he must have seen her questioning look, because he chuckled. "I got locked out a lot when I was a kid," he said as he jiggled the wire one last time and the latch popped open. Giving the dark street a last look and seeing nothing, she joined him. The gusting wind and rain shoved her toward the shelter of the building and the waiting door.

Once inside, the relief from the sound of the storm was welcome. It was pitch black, and the lights didn't work, but that was what she expected.

Locking the door by feel and flipping the deadbolt, Kat allowed herself a deep breath. She swallowed in relief, her heart lighter with a locked door between herself and the unfriendly group at the park. Using a flashlight, they pulled the blackout curtains shut to cover the window in full before turning on their brighter lantern. Inside featured shabby brown carpet, which was threadbare in places, and scratched wooden paneling, but the room smelled of lemon cleaner and the beds were made. It was better than sleeping outside.

They should have running water, even if it wouldn't be hot. She kicked off her shoes and ran for the bathroom, where she turned on the shower. The water hissed, then turned on. As expected, it was cold. She jumped in as Ryan followed, rinsing the rainwater and ash from their skin. She hated cold showers and was quick.

Grabbing fluffy white towels, they giggled like children as they wrapped the towels around their chilled bodies. Even this was fun with Ryan. She put on her pajamas, wishing she had thicker fall sleepwear instead of light summer-weight fabric. Still, the clothes were dry because she kept her spare clothing inside plastic in her backpack.

Kat wound her towel around her wet hair to keep it contained. Adding her tallest, thickest dry socks to the ensemble made it quite the look, but she wasn't here to put on a fashion show. She appreciated that Ryan limited himself to a single smirk.

She shivered as they draped the damp tent over the second bed to dry and parked the bikes by the front window. They washed, used filtered tap water to brush their teeth and refill their canteens before they hopped into bed. The room had no heat, but at least they were safe and dry. It was also small enough they would heat it with their presence.

Kat's teeth chattered as she snuggled against Ryan, who tugged her closer, sharing his body heat. Though he was cold, she was worse, except for his feet, which were like blocks of ice. While she lay there, trying to warm up enough to fall asleep, the evening's events replayed in her head. She must have tensed up because Ryan spoke.

"I was ready to hit him. He wouldn't have touched you again." His voice was soft.

It surprised her that he seemed emotional talking about the incident in the park.

"I'm glad you were there." Tears escaped of their own volition and trickled down her face, making her pillow damp. She'd been terrified but was now safe, and letting them flow was a release—a way to let go of her fear.

It made her feel cared for, knowing that Ryan wouldn't judge her for crying. It wasn't the first time he'd seen her tears. She felt comfortable being her real self, instead of hiding her feelings behind false smiles the way she always had with her family. They discouraged open emotions at home and later, they'd made Mark angry. She'd worked hard to keep them to herself, but here it wasn't necessary. Not with Ryan.

Tears were a genuine reaction to the situation, and he'd been scared, too. It wasn't every day he threatened someone with a baseball bat. His instincts had been protective. Mark wouldn't have stood up for her the way Ryan had. As the tears subsided, she allowed herself a smile and turned to give Ryan a chaste kiss as thanks.

"Thank you," she said, looking up at his beautiful eyes from her safe place in his arms. "I'm sorry I cry so much these days."

"Don't worry about it," he said, holding her tighter. "There's been a lot to cry about."

Once she was warm, it was still difficult to sleep, though Ryan seemed peaceful. Her mind replayed the incident at the park again. Should she have done something else? Was there a way she could have changed the outcome? Even now, she couldn't think of a different solution than Ryan's show of strength and their departure. The woman had said something Kat couldn't quite remember, something odd about answering to someone. She wished she'd paid more attention.

Outside, the wind whipped branches and debris against the windows. A draft whistled through the edge of the door with a faint hiss and thunder crashed. Rain splattered against the building and drummed on the roof, making a waterfall from the eaves at the corner. She was thankful to be inside and dry. No matter how waterproof the tent was, it would have been a miserable night. Perhaps the unfriendlies in the park had done them a favor by driving them away. Thinking of it that way helped her to relax and fade off to sleep.

CHAPTER 18: RYAN

They slept later than Ryan would have liked, which meant less time on the road today, but they were close enough to the bunker that with a little luck, he and Kat should reach xTerra late tomorrow.

Stepping outside, he revised his estimate. He looked around with a sinking feeling as pale sludge covered the town, stuck to his shoes, and collected on the bike tires. He sighed as he surveyed the ash coating; it would be more important than ever that they shouldn't drink water without boiling, straining, and purifying. He was looking forward to reaching the bunker and the water purification system it contained.

As predicted, the ash and debris-covered road slowed their pace, but they pushed on. Several downed power poles also impeded their progress where they'd fallen across the road. The storm must have been more extreme than normal. An ominous sign of deterioration, reminding him they needed to hurry.

It had tempted him to check the park before they left town to see how the inhabitants had weathered the violent storm, but he didn't want further interaction. He and Kat could have come out of the situation a lot worse than losing a day's food. In his head, he replayed the moment when he'd picked up the bat—intending to use it. He hadn't expected the rush of blind rage when the man had grabbed Kat. Ryan's body had claimed her. "Mine," it had said, a primal reaction to those that threatened him, or those he cared for. He wasn't quite ready to examine what that meant.

Thanks to Burt and Mary, he and Kat had more food remaining than expected after six days on the road. He'd thought it overkill when planning to take seven days' worth of food, but this morning was the seventh day on the road and they weren't at the bunker yet. Three dinners and four breakfasts and lunches remained in their travel packs. It should be enough. They'd been lucky, despite the obstacles.

It was late afternoon when they arrived in Wright, after biking only seventy miles. A slow day, what with the sludge and the late start, but they'd pushed as hard as possible. It wasn't dark, but the day had remained overcast, with clouds and ash-filled skies, with no true sunshine breaking through. They had a decision to make. Continue and camp or find shelter in another motel? Without threatening dark rain clouds, he was tempted to ride a little longer; every mile counted.

"Ride farther and camp, or stay and find a roof?"

"We only have a hundred and twenty miles left and the rain might hold off tonight." Kat had pored over the map for days and had memorized everything. "We should reach the bunker the day after tomorrow, even if it's slow like today. I hate to say it, but we should keep going. We have another couple hours of riding time before dark."

They biked through the town, which was twice as big as Kaycee, though not a bustling metropolis. Like everywhere else they'd been, the streets were deserted. Twice curtains twitched as they cycled past. People were inside some houses but staying isolated. Several board-covered store-fronts had been spray-painted with red letters that read, *"Slains Brothers,"* including all three grocery stores, the pharmacy, and the hardware store. The gas stations had also been fenced, chained, and marked.

"The name's familiar. Where have we heard it?" Ryan's voice echoed on the quiet street.

"The last town. That's a little weird." Kat frowned as she rode, her eyes searching side to side.

Was the name a coincidence? Probably not.

Whoever the Slains brothers were, they'd claimed the useful businesses and their contents. The glass windows remained intact on the places they'd painted, while the others had been destroyed. Broken glass littered the sidewalks and the interiors were gutted.

Shaking off his misgivings, they cycled east, determined to reel off a few more miles. They'd ridden for almost an hour when they crested a hill. Ryan cursed inside at the sight before them. He should have been paying more attention to the road ahead, instead of the scenery and distracting thoughts of Kat.

A hundred yards ahead, blocking the way forward, eight men, several with rifles, stood by four pickup trucks parked across both lanes of the small highway. He and Kat skidded to a stop and glanced at each other. The telltale navy-blue pickup with the pirate flag was on the far right. The Wyoming plate made sense; this must be home. The prospect of meeting the jerk who'd left destruction and mayhem in his wake made his stomach roil.

"Hold up. I have a bad feeling about this," he said under his breath. "Give them what they want and hope they don't take everything." He dismounted and walked his bike toward the barricade.

Kat gave an almost imperceptible nod before she pulled off her mask. She put on her biggest smile as they walked their bikes toward the men, stopping thirty feet away.

"Perhaps you could be so kind as to tell us how much farther it is to Gillette? We might have taken a wrong turn in the last town. We haven't seen it on the mileage signs. The internet isn't working for Google maps. It's easy to get lost out here." Kat's chipper voice sounded wrong and drew too much attention.

Ryan avoided rolling his eyes. She sounded like a ditz. It could work.

"I'll say you did, lady," said one man with long hair, relaxing his hold on his rifle. "Don't you know north from east? You're going the wrong way. There's nothing out here for miles."

Several of the men glanced at each other, making Ryan's hackles rise.

"I'm so glad you're here to help us. Imagine if we'd kept going the wrong way?" Kat smiled. Her lower lip quivered for a second and her eyes moved from the man to the truck with the flag. Would the men notice her subtle nervousness? They didn't know her like he did. His grip tightened on his bike.

"We've closed the road," said a man dressed in a faded *Ozzy* T-shirt and grubby jeans.

His graying hair was long in the back and his red Wyoming ball cap covered the shorter hair in front. Ryan didn't trust him, especially when he couldn't see his eyes. He didn't think this was blue-truck-guy. He was too old.

"Tourists and drifters aren't welcome in our territory." Ozzy's gravelly voice had a no-nonsense quality.

"Oh, we're not either of those," Kat said with a revolting giggle and vapid wave of her hand. "If we're looking for Gillette, what direction should we go? Everything's confusing when my phone doesn't work. We're just passing through and don't want to be a bother." She pulled her iPhone from her jacket pocket and held it up, turning as if trying to get a signal.

She wasn't noticing the subtle clues that she was making this worse. He wished he could pull her away and run. His chest tightened, but he maintained his outward calm.

A different man spoke. "Not through here. Not north of here, either. My brothers and I have laid claim to this county."

He was older than all but Ozzy, and the other men turned toward him in deference when he spoke. Several nodded with his refusal. This must be the leader, perhaps one of the Slains brothers.

Ryan's heart rate increased as he addressed his next remarks to the man in charge. "We'll head back. We'll stay on the road and abide by any rules you want."

"Road's closed." The leader looked Ryan up and down. "You're a big guy. How'd you like to join our militia?"

Ryan hadn't been expecting that offer. Despite the man's easy manner, Ryan was certain it wasn't a request.

"Your militia?" Ryan kept his tone even because he didn't want to offend the array of men with rifles. Kat shivered beside him and her smile disappeared.

"We're gathering up a few strong men and plan to hold this part of Wyoming."

Ryan kept his face as neutral as possible. "I appreciate the offer, but I have to decline. Kat and I have family in Rapid City who are expecting us."

"You're going to disappoint them," Ozzy said, stepping forward, a hard look in his eyes. "Our offer wasn't a suggestion."

Ryan shook his head. "I don't want any trouble. We'll ride back the way we came and find another route."

"If you aren't staying, you have two hours to get off my land." The leader's voice was flat and his face held no expression. "If you're still on land I claim after dark, we'll shoot you and take your girl. No harm to us."

"We should anyway," said one of the others with a sneer. He stepped forward from the far right. "I like her. She has nice tits." He gave Kat a creepy once-over look that undressed her with his eyes, making Ryan's blood boil. "Saw her swimming one morning back in Idaho at a campground."

Ryan gripped the handlebars tighter and tried to keep his rage at bay. So, this was the guy who'd wreaked havoc along their path. His bile rose at the memory of the campers he had found. He needed to keep his temper down. They couldn't win this fight.

They'd be hard-pressed to be gone by dark, no matter the direction they took. How much land did the Slains claim? Remembering the Slains cronies' comment last night meant at least the entire ride back to Kaycee. Maybe more.

"Shut up, Bob. We're working this out." The leader's eyes flicked to the younger man.

Judging by the strong family resemblance, he might be Bob's older brother or uncle, making the young creep another of the Slains brothers.

"You're right, we don't want trouble. We'll turn around and leave your territory." Ryan nodded to the men and jerked his head to the side for Kat. Giving in to them about backtracking rankled, but he didn't see an alternative. He wasn't joining them, and he and Kat couldn't go forward.

Kat had realized as soon as Bob had spoken that she couldn't work her magic on him and had stopped acting. Her simpering smile had disappeared as they reversed the bikes and rode back toward Wright. Her shoulders tensed and she fought back tears.

Once they had ridden out of sight, they stopped on the shoulder. He said, "You ok?"

She nodded.

"I don't trust them. They're likely itching to make me pay for turning down their offer. We need a way around them. If not here, north toward Gillette. It's out of our way, but I don't see an alternative. We'll get off the road before dark and hide until morning. I don't know where the county boundaries are and how far around Wright they're claiming the land, but I don't want to return to Kaycee and that lot there."

"They know this land better than we do. Plus, they've got rifles and the numbers. I don't want trouble," she said, putting on a burst of speed. "Maybe we should look for somewhere along here to hide and wait for them to drive by. Then we can sneak back this way and hope it's the last direction they check."

"That sounds too risky," said Ryan. "I'd rather take a chance on another route, even if we lose most of today's progress."

"Maybe they'll leave us alone if they can't find us right away."

He wasn't convinced it would play out that way, but he could hope.

His doubt must have shown on his face, because she started shaking. "They won't let it go," she said, a hitch in her voice. "They're going to follow, and I doubt they'll wait until dark. If they wait too long, they won't find us. They won't risk losing their prey. They'll be coming before dark."

He gave her a sharp look. "What makes you think so?"

"The creep from the campground," she said, biting her lip. "Bob blew me a kiss and mouthed the word, 'later.' To him, this is a game. He's given us a head start to make it a good chase." Her voice was tight with fear. "He's all about his fun." She hesitated again. "I thought I must have been mistaken that first morning on the road. I sensed someone watching me when I was standing on the dock, but you came out and the feeling went away. Plus, there's the other stuff we heard about him. He scares me."

She had missed cues in the group dynamic, but she was right about Bob.

"There aren't a lot of places to hide. It's so open. I haven't seen a tree all day, just sagebrush and chunks of black volcanic rock. We should try heading north, since they're blocking the southern and eastern routes. If they come after us sooner, we can jump off our bikes and hide. Maybe there will be something there. There isn't a lot of light left. We should use it to travel as far as possible."

He didn't think Kat agreed, but she didn't push back. She flattened her mouth and increased her speed, as though trying to outrun her fears.

He didn't want to force an altercation with armed men, but it was important to reach the bunker. It was getting rough out here. The memory of the red paint splattered throughout the town flashed through his mind. He didn't want to belong to a group like that, one that took what it wanted, be damned to anyone else or the law.

Ryan also didn't want to risk their wrath or be caught on the original highway, still within the boundaries of their territory. He also wasn't about to ride back to Kaycee to take a different highway and waste the whole day, today and tomorrow, even if outnumbered.

"We'll get past Wright and hide away from the road. It won't be dark for another hour after that. We'll have to skip dinner tonight so they can't find us with the stove's flame." They were so close to the cabin it was frustrating to make a detour, but they had no alternative. He'd try to keep it minimal.

She nodded. "Let's break the reflectors off the bikes. They shouldn't be able to find us in the dark." He liked her smart idea.

They made it as far as Wright without pursuit and turned north on Highway 59. He watched for the curtains to twitch in the houses close to the road, but the occupants stayed hidden. Ryan breathed a sigh of relief. Riding this route was going to add time to their trip, but it was better than wasting an entire day. The Slains might have already lost interest in them, but deep down, he didn't believe that. He and Kat wouldn't escape without hiding, but he wanted to be far away. Maybe there'd be somewhere better further along.

About five miles north of Wright, he felt a distant rumble on the highway behind them and it was growing closer. The sun was down, but it was not yet dark and there was nowhere to hide. The men hadn't waited. His stomach clenched as though someone had punched him. He'd misjudged the seriousness, and Kat had been right. They needed to hide right now. They were in trouble.

"Ditch the bikes, run, and hide," said Ryan, pulling over at the side of the road. He scanned in all directions while Kat did the same. "You go right. I caught sight of a drain back there. Some kind of culvert going under the road. I'll move the bikes and make for the buildings on the hill. We'll find each other later. I promise."

"Separate?" she hesitated, her eyes looking wide and fearful. "Why can't we both hide in the culvert?"

"It looked small and I won't fit. Even for you, it'll be tight. If it's impossible, keep going in that direction. Maybe they won't find you if the bikes are further up the road."

The panic in her gaze made him reconsider, but her chances of having enough time to hide and getting away were better if he caused a distraction.

"If they find me, they might beat me, but they could do worse to you." Bile filled his throat at the thought of the rough men getting their hands on his Kat.

She didn't argue, but turned off the road onto the shoulder on the right. He grabbed her bike and ran between both bikes up the road another hundred yards. He turned left and laid the bikes in the tall grass, hoping they wouldn't be visible from a moving vehicle. When he looked back, she was gone. Separating might buy them extra time.

He tore his backpack off and threw it over the barbed wire fence while the roar of the approaching truck increased. It must be close. He looked around, certain they'd see him, but the loud truck still wasn't in sight. He separated the wires and slid between. Scooping up his bag, he ran.

A house stood nearby on the hillside, but he couldn't count on help from that quarter. Anyone who lived this close to the Slains brothers and their friends either was with them or would be too scared to be involved. He looked across the road and released a tight breath. She wasn't visible. Had she fit inside the culvert?

The rumble of the truck's engine arrived as Ryan flattened himself against the ground and held his breath. Prickly grass poked his skin. The men must have missed the bikes because the truck raced past, its brake lights disappearing around a distant corner. They'd be back and when they were, they'd be more careful.

He remembered the creeping sensation the first time they'd come through town. That solved the mystery of how the Slains had found them already. Perhaps someone in Wright had tipped the men off about the direction he and Kat had gone. He should have considered that. The bikes weren't so well hidden they'd remain out of sight during a careful examination. It filled him with regret. He should have tried Kat's way. The Slains might have missed them, thinking they wouldn't hide so close by, and they could be on the way to the bunker.

Pushing himself up, Ryan grabbed his backpack by the straps and sprinted toward the buildings on the hillside, hoping to hide in the barn or a shed, or behind one of the parked cars in the yard. Behind him, the truck noise grew louder again—it hadn't been gone long— but this time it drove at a slower speed. He dropped to the ground again, hoping he hadn't been seen in the fading light. His heart drummed against his ribs in a painful fashion. He was still out in the open and without protection. He hoped that Kat had done better.

Laying on the ashy ground, his head turned to the side, wishing he had his mask on; he tried not to inhale the fine volcanic dust and to ignore the thicker damp sludge sticking to his clothes. Behind him, a dog barked. The barking moved closer and his heart sank to his toes. Its alert would attract attention.

On the road, a shout came from someone sitting in the back of the truck.

"Hold it. Bikes on the left."

Someone thumped on the back window, and the pickup skidded to a stop. Angry voices carried to him through the twilight as they flung open the vehicle doors. Men hopped out of the cab, slamming two doors, and three more leaped from the box, landing on the paved road with a series of thuds. Someone inside the front honked the horn, giving three short blasts, then held the horn down, the sound blasting through the evening. Perhaps some kind of signal to other searchers in the area. The bitter taste of fear filled his mouth. More than one truckful of men was committed to this game.

Ryan remained still, unsure what to do. Why did he and Kat matter so much to these men? They didn't have much of value or look rich. They were just two people on bikes with limited supplies. Maybe this was a power trip or about impressing the other men—a show of strength. Or he was being punished for refusing to join. His face grew stony. Most of all, they wanted Kat.

The dog barked again from a much closer position, but Ryan didn't dare turn his head to look, afraid it would attract more attention. A mid-size heeler bounded into view with a growl.

Behind the angry canine came slow, measured footsteps and swishing of the dry grass as someone stalked toward his position. Ryan held his breath and held still.

"King, stop your barking," said a deep voice.

The dog stopped but ran to where Ryan lay. He licked Ryan's arm and looked at his owner with a whine.

"I see you. Get your ass up. I'm guessing that fuss down there is about you."

"Please, sir. We just wanted to pass through on the highway."

"I can't help you. The new Slains militia says nobody in or out of their town. I'm staying out of their way. I have a family to think of. Give them what they want and they might let you go unharmed. You'll just lose your stuff, but in the big picture, stuff doesn't mean much. When you've joined them, you can thank me."

Ryan understood the man's words in principle, but he couldn't give up Kat.

The man hollered, "This what you're looking for? King and I found this jerk skulking around up here."

"What they want is my girlfriend," Ryan hissed. "If you find her, please don't turn her in. She means a hell of a lot more than anything else I have. Please, look out for her if she comes looking for me. I can't let them find her."

Ryan pushed up to a crouch, ready to bolt. He whirled away from the man whose face showed regret, as did the slump of his shoulders. Leaving his bat lying on the ground, Ryan sprinted. A baseball bat would do nothing against armed men, just get him shot sooner. He ran parallel to the road, away from the house, glancing back just once. Still no sign of Kat, but a trio of men from the trucks pursued. He had to give her a chance to escape.

At the crack of a gunshot, he hit the ground and rolled, his chest heaving. No pain. He wasn't hit, but he could have been. Another shot whistled over his head and he froze, sucking in his breath. Too close. He didn't dare get up. The next shot could be the one that struck him. They might stop shooting if he didn't run.

Options ran through his head, but there weren't many. These men might be hunters with expensive rifles and excellent marksmanship. He was better off waiting and making his stand here, hoping it was enough of a show to distract them from finding Kat. He didn't know if they'd realized yet that she'd gone a different direction.

He had to use his brain, take the beating, and hope they didn't do too much damage. A knot of fear blossomed in his stomach while he waited for the men to catch up. He hadn't been punched since he was a teenager, but once upon a time he'd known how to take a hit.

It wouldn't be long until dark. Maybe Kat would escape if the men couldn't see to search. Headlights approached and a second truck joined the first on the road, bringing additional men. Several shadowy figures crossed the fence and headed in his direction, joining the ones with guns that were close, wading through the grass and shrubbery together as they neared. From their voices, at least two of the hunters ran toward the house, perhaps thinking Kat had split from him once they got this far. He had to hope that she'd found a better location to hide than he had, whether or not she'd fit in the culvert. Her side of the road had looked like another barren field. It would look like nobody would even try to hide in that direction.

The men by the road chortled when they pulled both bikes from their respective ditches and tossed them into the back of one truck. If they survived this, he and Kat might be on foot for the duration. The idea of walking to South Dakota was daunting.

"Damn," he muttered. Not only would they be traveling the rest of the way on foot, but without the bike carriers, they'd also run short on supplies for the several extra days on the road. Kat had some remaining food in her pack, but he wasn't sure how much. And the lamp and extra fuel for the burner had been on the bikes.

"You, City Boy. Get your ass off the ground and act like a man. Hands toward the sky."

Ryan took a deep breath and got to his feet, his hands open and in the air. He didn't want any further misunderstandings—this had already gone wrong.

From the voices he recognized, the leader had remained on the road and the man from the navy-blue pickup must be searching somewhere else. Ozzy and several others he didn't recognize were here on the hillside. His knot of worry for Kat made his stomach ache.

Seven men surrounded him, forming a loose circle; the man from the house and his yappy dog were gone. Sensing the men at his back made his shoulder blades twitch. He couldn't guard against all directions at once, but his muscles tensed, waiting for an attack.

"We decided to check on you. Asked some of our good neighbors in Wright," said Ozzy in his gravelly voice. "You didn't leave toward Kaycee as instructed. That was your only chance."

The Slains had known where to look from the eyes in town. Confirming that felt like an additional blow; strangers had been willing to throw them to the wolves without cause.

"You disobeyed a direct order from John Slains. That was stupid. We're going to take your shit after all. Bob Slains wants your girl, and she won't like it when he finds her. The way he tells it, he's raped a dozen young women between here and Seattle. Nobody to stop him now, unless his big brother steps in. No police anywhere, from what I understand. If you were one of us, you might have been able to keep her. At least for a bit. You should have joined us when you had the chance."

Fear for Kat made Ryan break out in a cold sweat and he ground down on his teeth until his molars ached.

"Give us your pack."

His backpack lay next to his feet, where he'd left it when he'd dropped to the ground. He stepped away from it, cataloging what he might lose. With the bikes and saddlebags already confiscated, he'd lost most of the cookware, his warm jacket, and the remaining potatoes, but he didn't protest with three guns trained on him.

"Jim." Ozzy jerked his head toward Ryan.

One man stepped forward and unzipped the pack, tossing the contents, piece by piece, to the ground. It felt like a violation. This was everything that he owned until he got to the bunker.

At first, it looked like everything was rejected. Ryan clenched his jaw.

"Well," said another, sounding impatient. "Anything good?"

In the dim light, it was difficult to read expressions on the men's faces, so Ryan relied on their voices and body language to gauge the threat level.

"Mostly clothes. A couple of books," said the man pawing through Ryan's stuff. He sounded disappointed. That wouldn't be good.

"Plus a ridiculous number of condoms. Ha. You aren't going to need these anymore." He tossed them into the grass.

Ryan's blood boiled, but he remained cool on the outside. Survival was more important than pride or his belongings. He hoped they left the tent.

"We don't need more tents or another sleeping bag." Jim shook his head. "A headlamp, some batteries, nothing good." Unzipping the smaller pocket, he reached in. "Score." He'd discovered the inside pocket with Ryan's thick roll of cash.

They could have the money. He had no idea if it would be useful.

"A phone too, but that's useless." The man flung Ryan's phone into the sagebrush. It landed somewhere to his right—hard enough it may have shattered.

Another man moved closer and kicked the pile of stuff from Ryan's backpack. He was one of the younger guys who'd stood near Bob at the original roadblock. Picking up several long strips of condoms, he waved them around before throwing them into the darkness. "Bob won't want condoms. He rides bareback."

The crowd laughed and closed in around Ryan, cutting off his field of vision. The air became charged, thick with impending violence.

"Where's the girl?" said one man, stepping up to Ryan's face, his gun pointing toward Ryan's head, the sling over his bulky shoulders.

Ryan stared back without speaking. If they shot him, they wouldn't get answers. The man wasn't quite his height, but he was older and wider. He stood too close as an intimidation tactic. Ryan's stepfather had done that until Ryan had gotten taller than Roy.

Ryan shrugged. The inevitable was coming.

He stared the man right in the eye, letting him know he wasn't afraid. It wasn't much, but he was determined to salvage his pride.

The first punch smashed his stomach and Ryan doubled over, but refused to fall. The second was to his face and stars swirled like a cartoon dust-up. It wasn't like fighting toe to toe in the movies. Two punches and he was almost done. It was all he could do not to crumple. He took a deep breath, unable to restrain himself. He screamed and fought back, coming out of a crouch to ram one attacker with his head.

Roaring in frustration, he elbowed Ozzy in the face and punched another man before the mob moved in. He whirled around as he searched for a way out, swinging, hoping to hit anyone or anything. He connected several times, somehow staying on his feet as he reeled from one side of the circle to the other.

It surprised him nobody fired a gun, but they maybe didn't want to shoot each other or waste the ammunition when the odds were so tilted in their favor. Seven to one, he'd already lost. It was just a matter of time.

Ryan landed a few extra punches before the men coordinated their efforts and he went down. He curled up on the ground, protecting what he could while they kicked. Four of them participated in this part of the group beating while the others cheered. Fiery pain shot along his ribs when they stopped. He didn't dare move, afraid they'd broken his ribs. He ran his tongue across his teeth, his mouth filled with blood. One tooth was loose, but nothing had come out. Not yet.

"The prick's got nothing worthwhile besides the cash and he won't give up his girlfriend. We'll have to find her ourselves. She can't have gotten far. I doubt she's that smart." It was Ozzy's distinct voice.

That's where they were wrong. Kat was plenty smart and if she'd evaded them this long, they wouldn't find her. He had faith in her abilities.

The men moved away, still talking amongst themselves.

"I hope the chick has better stuff."

"They haven't found her yet, but I'd like a turn. Bob will have to share."

"He won't like that." The voices faded as they spread out, searching the hillside parallel to the road.

Ryan's stomach churned. So much for civilization. These men seemed to have lost the veneer that must have governed their lives until last week. He ached everywhere, but most along his right side, where there was a burning stab of pain.

Someone hollered from down the hill, perhaps across the road, and Ryan's heart stopped. He pushed to a sitting position and struggled to peer through the dark purple, velvety twilight, hoping to see what had happened. The road was invisible, except for the bright glare of the trucks and their blaze of headlights that hurt his eyes. He lurched sideways, pain shooting through his ribs at every breath. He spat into the tall grass, suspecting it was filled with blood. He checked his teeth again. Still there.

Where was Kat? Had they had found her? "Don't let them take you, Kat," he yelled, his throat raw from his earlier screams. "Stay hidden." It was a long shot that she would hear, but it might mean they'd keep looking on the hillside instead of elsewhere.

Ryan groaned, trying to remain on his feet. His face stung like it had been bashed too, and his lower lip was swollen.

One of the retreating men turned and dashed back up the slope. Ryan couldn't get out of the way. A gun cracked and a bullet whizzed past his head—a little high. It became hard to breathe as the darkened shape of the man's charge continued.

The man muttered as he approached. "Stupid prick. I don't want to kill you, but I will if I have to. Stay down. Let them think you're down for good."

Ryan couldn't move as the butt of a rifle smashed toward his head. At the impact, everything went dark.

CHAPTER 19: KAT

Kat raced down the bank and off the road, her tired muscles acting on the extra burst of adrenaline provided by fear. Ryan planned to take off uphill toward a farmhouse and its outbuildings. It looked too far. He'd never make it. With her heart in her throat, Kat hurdled the row of sagebrush that marked the edge of the field, coming down hard on her sore ankle.

A flare of pain erupted, causing her to stumble as it shot up her leg. Gritting her teeth, she fought the dizziness that assailed her and scanned ahead on the right side. That's where the culvert should be, though she hadn't seen the entrance. If not, she hoped there'd be somewhere for her to duck out of sight. She didn't like the idea of the culvert; the thought of being so confined and trapped had fear clawing at her throat.

She had to hurry. Every second counted. Her breath came in gasps.

Her panicked gaze found the culvert; at last, a stray gleam of waning light caught the silver gleam of its metal. Her heart racing, she stared at the small opening and swallowed. She might fit. She couldn't see any other possibility. Turning, she slid in foot first and belly down as she reversed inside, holding her pack like a shield, with her arms out straight like Superman. Her backpack was too precious to leave behind.

It was awkward as hell as she scooted backward through pools of stagnant water and mud. The foul smell made the air thick with the stench of rot, and the ceiling was slimy where her hips and shoulders brushed against it, but the image of the leer on the young tough's face right before he blew her a kiss kept her moving. His obsidian eyes had seemed dead and her blood froze at the thought of what he'd do if he caught her. She'd downplayed the visceral reaction she'd had to him, not wanting to upset Ryan, but Bob made her skin crawl. There was something wrong with the way he'd looked at her. Any humanity he had, had been stripped away.

She breathed through her nose and clamped her lips tight, trying not to let anything splash into her mouth as she retreated further into the metal drain.

Her clothes grew soaked and the entrance became a faint charcoal circle. She kept scooting back, though the pipe was a tight fit, her shoulders brushing the curved sides. After about twenty-five feet, she stopped, keeping her face behind the pack as both a chin rest to keep her face out of the muck and cover.

She fumbled at her side and removed a handful of sticks poking her hip and arranged them in front of the pack, trying to obscure its appearance from the outside and from anyone searching. Her pack contained her sole possessions and all of their remaining food. She wouldn't give it up without a fight. Her sore ankle throbbed, but she was thankful to have hidden—gross as it was—in this drain.

Even with a flashlight, she didn't think anyone would see anything past the pack. She might be safe. She prayed a stray shine or a reflection wouldn't give her away. Her heart thudded against her ribs, as though trying to escape. She tried to twist and check behind her for the far exit, but it was too tight to turn. Was she vulnerable to discovery from the other direction? It remained dark, the far end either well-hidden or too distant, to be a worry. She shouldn't move. She didn't want to make a sound.

Her breath seemed loud, contributing to her fear that they would hear it from outside, the metal tube amplifying every sound. She struggled to slow her breathing, to relax and be quiet. She stifled the urge to sneeze, suppressing it with the back of her hand, pushing it against the space between her top lip and her nose until the feeling passed.

The culvert was too narrow, and she hoped the men would dismiss it and move on. Better yet, she hoped they'd drive by and give up, allowing Ryan and herself to reclaim the bikes and escape.

Tires screeched, something banged several times, and there were loud shouts, but she couldn't make out the words. The pipe and earth around her muffled sound from outside. Soon after, a piercing horn signaled from the road. Her heart sank. Perhaps they'd seen the bikes or found Ryan. Her legs trembled with the urge to flee.

Deep in the tunnel, she was blind to what was happening outside and her imagination added fuel to her terror. She wished she could see what was happening or help, but she didn't dare move. Ryan had been right; he never would have fit in here. Holding her breath, she listened to the drip-drop of water above, straining to make out the voices beyond for clues. The sagebrush crunched as someone fought their way through, coming closer. She held her breath.

Boots clunked as they ran on the hard surface of the road, and two gunshots rang out. She covered her mouth with her hand, pressing her horror inside while her whole body shook. She lay straight as a pencil, but she wanted to curl up in the fetal position and cry. Time seemed to slow down, then stop. What if they had shot Ryan? He could die. Staying hidden was too hard. Part of her wanted to give up, so she was no longer in the dark, alone.

She shivered again, waiting for additional shots, holding her breath until her chest ached. Silent tears streamed down her hot cheeks. Outside was quiet at first, then the angry voices resumed, but further away. At last, she exhaled, her chest aching from holding her breath for so long. She rested her face against the fabric of the pack, a plastic clip dug into her forehead, but she didn't care.

When the gunshots had rung out, she'd had an epiphany.

She loved Ryan.

She wasn't sure she wanted to continue without him. He'd become important to her, and there was nothing casual about her feelings. She wasn't just having fun; she'd been kidding herself. She wasn't one for casual sex, and it didn't seem like he was either. Her feelings were intense and real, no matter how fast they'd grown. They'd been forged by the challenges of the last two weeks. He had to be all right. She needed him. They needed each other. They had to reach the bunker together.

A beam of light swept across the front of the culvert and she froze again, her next breath caught in her throat. She ducked lower, pressing herself into the stagnant water and the cold metal beneath, willing the men to move on. She was drenched from her chest downward. Cold continued to seep upward, soaking her with icy water that chilled her to the bone. She had to survive the next while, even if later she would be miserable.

The light moved closer and hovered near the entrance. She bit her lip hard, tasting blood in her mouth.

"Check this out," said an excited voice. "Here kitty, kitty. Come out, Kitty Kat."

She shuddered at the voice. The creep who'd blown her a kiss was here.

Bright light shone straight inside the metal drain and she shut her eyes, praying that the backpack wouldn't be recognizable—an anonymous mass in the dark.

"Something's blocking the pipe," said the same voice.

It didn't surprise her that Bob was one man searching for her. Her gut clenched and her bowels liquified. It was all she could do not to wet herself as she trembled.

"Hold the light."

She flattened further and held her breath.

"There's no way anyone crawled in there," said a second voice as it came closer. "That's too small for anyone except a kid."

"She wasn't that big. She might fit," Bob said, his voice chilling. "I wish we had something long enough to prod that mess back there, to make sure it isn't her."

"That's twenty-five feet back if it's an inch," scoffed the second man. "No way she's in there. Smells like something crawled inside and died. Can you imagine a pretty young woman climbing into a dark tunnel with a rotting raccoon carcass? I can't." He laughed. "Not even to get away from your ugly face."

"Hey, Kitty Kat. You in there?" Bob called, ignoring his friend's gibes. "You want a real man? We can spare your boyfriend if you come out and spend some time with me. Out on the road is no place for a pretty young thing like you. You need someone better to care for you. A real man who can keep you safe. Keep you satisfied." His cajoling voice sounded like he believed his own lies.

His voice echoed all around. She ground her teeth down until her jaw ached, but she didn't speak even though her body trembled. They didn't know she was here, they only wondered. She squeezed her eyes closed and didn't dare move a muscle. Her last breath seemed ancient—so long ago an eon had passed.

"I've got an idea." The second man spoke to the creep with the light. "C'mon."

The light retreated, but from their thumping footsteps, they hadn't gone far. She took the opportunity to breathe, though her chest remained tight. Their footsteps stopped. They'd only gone as far as the road at the furthest. The bushes crackled where the men had pushed through, but the gravel slope to the road remained silent. They were still close.

Shouting came from a distance and she raised her head a fraction to listen, trying to make out something, anything. She hoped that meant that Ryan was still alive and that he hadn't been killed. She covered her mouth to remain quiet when she thought she recognized his angry voice. Hope raced through her. He might be alive.

A dog barked several times, but not from close enough that she was concerned, though she prayed it wouldn't investigate the action on the road and lead the men to her by accident. Scenarios ran through her mind where she was caught and dragged out of the pipe and raped. She tried not to think of anything except remaining silent.

The crunching footsteps returned, bringing the light. A sound rang out inside the culvert a few feet in front of her. Then another pinging sound, and a third. Several more projectiles whizzed past as the men threw pebbles into the blocked drain.

One soared over her head, missing by perhaps an inch. Several ricocheted through the culvert, passing behind her. Another glanced off her shoulder, leaving a sharp stinging sensation. She stifled a scream when something moved on her leg, transferring its weight onto her. Her breath caught in her throat as she prayed it was her imagination. She couldn't take much more. Perhaps the stones had disturbed something deeper in the drain behind her. Something alive. Her skin crawled and her eyes filled with tears.

Something moved again, and she clenched all over, twitching her leg to make whatever it was go away. She didn't dare do more to make it leave, as it was the lesser of the evils. Was it a rodent? It was horrible to hope for a rodent instead of something worse. A faint scratching sound moved closer, scraping the inside of the culvert beside her. Something scratched her side through her damp clothes, then crawled on her back toward her hair, its weight now on her shoulders. She couldn't turn her head to look. Claws dug into her skin as it made its way forward. She cringed. It seemed too heavy to be a rat. Was it a raccoon? A possum? She had no idea what monsters might lurk in the dark tonight.

She was terrified that there were more critters. In her imagination, the pipe behind her filled with a horde—soon she'd be swarmed and eaten. Tears streaked her face, and she pressed her fist into her mouth to keep from screaming.

A pebble struck the water in front of the pack and the creature scurried forward, scratching her sore shoulder in its haste to investigate. The beam of light landed on it and she saw it. A rat as big as a small cat, the tip of its ropey tail resting only an inch from her mud-covered hand. Her stomach clenched to think of sharing the culvert with something that size.

"Holy fuck," yelled Bob. "What the hell?"

The night rang with his shout.

"Shit, it's just a rat, but look at the size of that monster," said his partner. "It could almost be a possum. No way that chick is back there."

"She's out here somewhere," said the creep. "I wanted some fun. She can't be far."

"Well, I'm not waiting around all night."

"I'm not done."

"Yes, you are. It's time to give up and go home. Your truck is back at your place. If you want her so bad, come back tomorrow when it's daylight. This is too fucking hard."

"I said, I'm not done. If you help, I'll share. I bet we can make her scream."

Bile rose in her throat and her stomach lurched again. It took all her willpower not to throw up.

The two men continued to argue outside the culvert, but the granddaddy of all rats had disappeared. It must have slipped out of the drain while the men were distracted. She wished she could do the same, but it would be foolish to move even when their discussion took them closer to the road. Until they drove away, she wasn't safe.

Suddenly there was another shout from further away, perhaps across the road and up the hill. Her heart restarted, thumping hard in her chest. It sounded like Ryan had called her name. He must know she hadn't been caught. She ground down on her molars. Making sure she didn't answer.

Another gunshot rang out.

Silence settled over the countryside for ten heartbeats. Twenty. She waited for another distant sound, but nothing came. The argument at the roadside broke out again, breaking the silence.

"Fuck you, Bob. Don't touch me again. Get in the goddamn truck."

She couldn't make out the other curses.

Perhaps the argument would lead to violence. Sounds of a scuffle broke out as gravel crunched.

"What happened up there?" called a deep voice on the road.

She strained to hear the complete answer.

"Asshole got what he deserved," called a raspy voice from someone approaching.

Once more, tears leaked from her eyes.

"Not before he elbowed you in the face. Knew he'd be a tough son-of-a-bitch. Any sign of his girl?"

"He wouldn't give up anything, not even to save his own ass."

"Nothing down here. Time to give up." That was the leader's deep voice that she recognized. When he spoke that way, it was obvious.

"Fuck all of you. I'm still looking," said Bob.

"You're wasting your time." There was another punching sound nearby.

"Kenny, Bob, stop bickering now," bellowed the leader. "We're done here tonight. I'm hungry and want dinner. Everyone, back in the trucks. Dragging this out is a waste of time. That ignorant jackass regrets not having joined us, I'm sure. That's enough for me."

It took several minutes to gather all the men and for them to load into the trucks. She listened to their voices but couldn't make out their words, as what they'd said about Ryan getting what he deserved, replayed in her head on a loop.

Kat waited until both trucks roared to life and drove away, the vibrations in the ground diminishing as they became too faint to discern. Silence settled over the road and field, and at last, she took a deep breath. She listened as hard as she could, straining at the darkness. It was quiet except for the faint dripping of water deeper in the drain, but she couldn't make out noises from outside and the pressing heavy silence.

What if everyone had left except the star of her future nightmares? She shuddered. She'd be hearing Bob's voice the next time she slept. What if he'd refused to leave and waited just beyond the culvert? She remained frozen for a length of time. Perhaps an hour. Perhaps more. She couldn't tell how long she waited. Her teeth chattered, and she shivered as the cold seeped into her bones, her adrenaline displaced by exhaustion.

Kat gave herself a mental pep talk to kick herself into gear. She needed to stop being a coward. She'd have to save herself. To move and to determine what had happened to Ryan. Remembering the final gunshot and the subsequent silence, she feared what she might find. Her delay may have already been too long. What if he was shot and bleeding out? Maybe he needed her help. He could be lying in a pool of blood. That gave her the strength to move. She pushed the pack forward, the sound scraping in the culvert. Stopping, she strained as she waited to be discovered, but outside remained silent.

She had to believe it wasn't a trick and forced herself to continue.

Pushing the pack again, she slithered ahead, her hips banging and scraping on the uneven metal. Her clothing was soaked through, contributing to her chill. Crawling on her elbows and belly in the pitch dark, she made her way closer to the end of the dark gray patch that was the exit. It seemed farther away than when she'd squirmed inside.

When she reached the mouth of the culvert, she shoved the pack to the ground and, swallowing her fear, she stuck her face out and took great gulps of fresh air. She slid the rest of the way out, her limbs wet, her clothing stuck to her as she shivered in the brisk night air. Her chest ached as she tried to hold in her sobs, but they couldn't be stopped. She was alone in the dark, cold, hungry, and covered in wet filth.

Her exhausted brain was in turmoil, but she reminded herself she was unharmed and alive.

It took several minutes to get a hold of her emotions. Her throat ached from crying as she looked up, trying to find something as a reference in the expanse of darkness, but thick clouds or ash obscured the moon and stars.

Her gaze settled on the distant house on the hillside, which was almost dark. A single bright light illuminated the porch and a dim square of yellow shone, perhaps behind blinds or a curtain from an upstairs window. What time was it? How much time had elapsed since she'd hidden? It seemed like hours, but it might not be that late. Should she risk asking for help?

She decided no, but would use the single point of light ahead as a guide. She was in rough shape after her ordeal and her sprained ankle was painful, but Ryan might be worse. The Slains hadn't been gone long, and she hoped they weren't coming back. Blood drained from her face. They might come back at daybreak to resume their search. She needed to hurry. The bikes had been taken. She and Ryan would have to leave on foot and stay off the road. She refused to think that Ryan wouldn't be able to travel. How far would they walk tonight while injured? It would have to be some distance.

She rummaged around in her pack, pulled out her first aid kit, and wrapped the tensor bandage around her ankle before replacing her socks and shoes.

She didn't think she'd been frozen in the culvert for hours, though it had been difficult to gauge the passage of time. Her chest heaved again with attempts to keep her sobs at bay as they threatened once more. If she gave in, she wasn't sure she could stop. She longed to find a bar to break into and drink herself senseless. A strong gin and tonic in her hand, the citrus smell, and the bite of alcohol on her tongue. Peaceful oblivion that would follow. The pain and fear would be gone, but she was better than that. The last week and a half had shown her she wanted to live.

Steeling herself to what she might find, she got to her feet. She didn't know if Ryan was dead or alive, but she had to find out.

CHAPTER 20: RYAN

It was dark when Ryan regained consciousness. It took him a few minutes to be sure that the attackers were gone and that the road below was silent. He listened for signs of Kat, but there was nothing. Not a breath of wind, a cricket, an owl, or a sound from the highway. It seemed like he was alone. He'd taken a beating and was sore, but he pushed himself to a sitting position to catch his breath and assess his injuries. His head spun, and the raised bump was painful to the touch. The raised butt-end of a rifle was the last thing he remembered.

The knuckles on his right hand were swollen and split, a metallic blood taste lingered in his mouth, even after he spat. Groping the ground nearby, he tried to locate his canteen, but all he found was grass and dirt, his hands coming away gritty and ash covered. He grimaced and tried to brush the powder away.

He listened for sounds that might mean Kat was searching for him. After a brief rustling in the sagebrush, he couldn't hear anything else. Perhaps the light feet of a mouse. The men might have found her after they'd knocked him unconscious. He froze, paralyzed by the idea, and his chest tightened. She had to be okay. He wasn't ready to be without her. He should go look for her. How long had he been out?

He couldn't call for her, or the man from the house with his dog might return. He couldn't risk being turned over to the Slains' men. If Kat was out there, she might need him. He swayed to his feet, shooting pains in his ribs on both sides. Damn, this was the last thing they needed. He took a careful breath, followed by a few deeper ones. Maybe just bruised. He shuffled a few steps on the slope of the hill, trying not to lose his balance.

Shame washed over him that he'd taken a beating. Never mind that Slains men outnumbered him and that he'd tried to avoid the confrontation. Those things might make him feel better later. But it was too soon. He needed to find Kat, but he couldn't see his hand in front of his face. The starless night remained black like the inside of a cave, except in the house's direction, where a single light shone like a beacon. Someone must have lamps inside. He tried to use its light to help locate his belongings, but he couldn't. His stuff remained scattered.

He took two steps and tripped, crying out with pain as he landed on the hard ground, jarring his arms when he broke his fall. He patted the ground, hoping to find his backpack. If he could get to his pack or the belongings strewn near it, he would have his headlamp.

The sense of urgency to find Kat was building again. He lay down for a second when a wave of dizziness passed through him. His stomach clenched. He might throw up, and his head spun again. He fought the feeling but lost, as once more, he slipped into unconsciousness.

CHAPTER 21: KAT

Kat slung her pack on, ignoring the dampness, and scrambled through the thick layer of sagebrush that separated the field from the road. She fought her way up the gravel slope to the road and stood on the smooth surface. It felt too quiet and exposed on the highway. She had to keep moving. If she stopped, she didn't know if she'd be able to start again. Ryan had crossed the road and ran toward the house, so she headed that way.

She tripped several times over sticks, rocks, and bushes that were impossible to see in the dark. Her ankle pain returned with a vengeance, shooting pains accompanying each step. Gritting her teeth, she climbed the slope. It was impossible for her to be quieter. She crouched low while walking, hoping to make herself small in case someone looked out from the house. She remained in the blackness, afraid to use her headlamp for the same reason.

Kat wasn't as high as the house when a dark figure appeared, walking straight for her. She stifled a scream. A man held a leashed dog and a rifle in his hands. She froze, waiting. They'd caught her like a mouse in a trap.

"If you're looking for your friend, I don't think they shot him, just roughed him up." His voice was little more than a hoarse whisper.

"You're not one of them," she said, her voice shaking with relief.

"I'm not. They couldn't find you or you would be worse off."

"I hid in the culvert. I'm just cold and wet."

"The culvert?"

"The drain across the road."

"You're brave. My dog won't even go in that foul place." He hesitated. "Will you tell your man that I'm sorry?"

He turned his face away, not meeting her gaze. "Before you ask, I can't help much. But, here, take my light." His voice trembled as he spoke.

He pressed a flashlight into her icy hands. She fumbled for the switch.

"Wait until I'm back in the house to turn it on. He's about two hundred yards to the right, parallel to the road. He's unconscious, but I couldn't see any gunshot wounds. I think they missed in the dark. Or they may have taken a final warning shot before they knocked him out. I gathered up some of his stuff, the parts I could find. Not much to salvage. A tent, a sleeping bag, and some clothes."

Kat nodded, picturing Ryan unconscious not too far away. Tears filled her eyes. He might need her. She turned to go.

"I'll leave clean water out by my stairs. Take it when you leave. I don't want to see what way you go, so give me a few minutes to put it out. When the Slains brothers or their men return in the morning, I can truthfully say that I don't know where you went. I'm sorry I can't do more. I have my family to consider." He disappeared into the shadows, his footsteps receding. She watched as he stamped the ash from his boots on his porch and lantern light poured out from inside as he opened the door.

"I can't see anything out there," he said to someone else inside before he closed the door. "King must still be unsettled after the earlier commotion."

Kat counted to a hundred, then flicked on the flashlight, keeping the beam low to the ground. She hurried in the direction that the man had indicated, making better progress now that she could see. She still jumped at shadows and her breath sounded loud, but she hurried, ignoring her sore ankle. She was going to have to be tough to get through the night. Hearing a low moan, she turned to the right and climbed the slope, moving toward the sound.

She froze when she found Ryan sprawled on the ground. She focused the light near him so she didn't blind him with the light if he opened his eyes. There was blood on the side of his head and new bruises on his face. His knuckles were swollen and red; he hadn't gone down without a fight. He looked hurt, but his eyelids twitched. He was waking up.

Her breath whooshed out in relief.

His open pack was about six feet away, his belongings in a heap. Dozens of packets of condoms lay scattered beside it. She covered her mouth as a laugh rose inside her, though none of this was funny, it was a relief. At least he hadn't lost everything important.

She crouched beside him, placing the light on the ground, and touched his arm. "Ryan," she said, her chest tight once more as she tried not to cry as she looked at his battered face. "It's me."

He groaned again and his eyes fluttered open. "Kat. Are you okay?" His voice was groggy, but he knew her. She was relieved, as well as touched, that his first words showed his concern for her.

She stroked the hair from his forehead, feeling a raised welt on the side of his head. Her hand came away sticky with drying blood. "I'm here."

"Did they hurt you?" She swallowed to keep the tears at bay. There wasn't time for more. She'd done all the crying tonight that she would allow.

"They couldn't find me," she said while he pushed to a sitting position. The statement downplayed the danger and fear she'd lived through, but that too could wait.

She wanted to throw her arms around him, but she didn't want to hurt him. The dim yellow light showed that his lip was split and swollen and one cheekbone was discolored and puffy. His movements were stiff, and he held his ribs as if they ached. She hoped they weren't broken. She broke out in a cold sweat, thinking about Bob returning too soon.

"The drain was filthy and I stink." Her voice shook despite her attempt to be strong.

"I was scared they were going to hurt you." His voice became more normal with each passing second, which gave her hope.

They might make it out of here after all.

"They didn't want much of my stuff, just cash, so they scattered the rest. We were lucky. What they really wanted was you, even if they devoted more manpower to me. Perhaps they thought I'd give you up or change my mind and join them. I was never doing either." His jaw clenched and he wore his stubborn face.

"I'm alright." Her voice still shook. Alright was a relative term.

"Then splitting up was worth it. They sent a lot of men to deal with me."

"I heard shots and I panicked; I was certain you'd been shot."

"I hit the ground when they started shooting. I had images of them being hunters and didn't dare run like prey. They beat the hell out of me because I didn't have much to steal. The last shot missed in the dark, on purpose. The shooter smashed me with his rifle and told me to stay down." Ryan's hand touched the lump on the side of his head.

"They took the bikes."

"I know. We'll have to continue on foot." His voice sounded resigned.

She said nothing about the pain in her ankle. He must hurt all over. But it could have been a lot worse.

"The man from the house was going to leave us water, and he gathered up your stuff. At least whatever he could find in the dark."

He shrugged and winced at the motion. "The farmer feels bad for turning me in the first time."

"He feels guilty for not helping us."

Kat hesitated, feeling like a coward. She wanted to tell Ryan her revelation, but it didn't feel like the right time. She didn't want her feelings to be a distraction when the most pressing issue was escape. They still had days of hard traveling, and it would be awkward if he didn't reciprocate her feelings. Instead, she repacked his backpack and helped him to his feet.

Shining the light around the small clearing, she couldn't see anything else. His phone was a loss, as it was his last tie to his family. That would suck, even if they weren't close. At least she had the option to reach out, if her family still lived. She hadn't spared them a thought when she'd been trapped and hiding. Her thoughts had been of her own survival. Hers and Ryan's.

She threaded the straps of Ryan's backpack over his arms so he wouldn't have to bend or move much. His ribs were a concern, especially if they were broken. His face looked strained by the pale light of the flashlight. He couldn't hide all the signs, even in the dark. This was going to be difficult. They were going to hike all night.

"We need to stay off the roads," she said as they limped toward the house. "They might drive them again first thing in the morning." Her voice trembled when she said, "That Bob guy said that he'd be back. He wouldn't leave until the leader ordered him to get in the truck."

"Sorry I didn't get you that hot meal tonight," he said. "I know you were looking forward to it."

"I'm glad they didn't shoot you," she said as they came level with the house.

She flicked off the flashlight as they approached the side of the stairs and used the glow of light from the window to navigate. Ryan's baseball bat, two canteens, and a gray woolen blanket were tucked beside the wood stairs. A corner of a white piece of paper stuck out from under the pile. Stooping, she picked it up and held it to the light.

"Head east across the grasslands. They can't drive there."

He'd included a simple, hand-drawn map below. It marked the house and the culvert, which was marked with an X in black Sharpie. Arrows indicated the direction beyond. It looked like the man recommended a path due east when they would reach highway 116 South which would cut perpendicular to their trail. There they would hike south and rejoin Route 450 East. Perhaps then it would be safe. It depended on how much effort the Slains put into the search.

Kat picked up the canteens, which were full and heavy. She put one in each pack, then she picked up the folded blanket. Beneath it was a metal thermos. With shaking hands, she unscrewed the lid to find that it was full of steaming hot tea. She took a long sniff, then closed the lid even though she was tempted to drink the scalding beverage to ward off her bone-deep chill. It could be their reward in a couple of hours; the hot tea would help them make it through the long night of walking.

Seeing Ryan's upturned eyebrow, she said, "Tea. Let's save it as an incentive for every few miles. I can wait for a hot drink, can you?" At his nod, she added, "I don't want them to return in the morning and find us. Can you shove these things into my pack? Then we should go."

Ryan took a long look at her, then unzipped her pack. He rummaged around inside and came up with a Ziploc that contained a set of her dry clothing. He crammed the blanket inside and closed her pack. He shoved his bat through the loops on the outside of his pack and tucked the bottom into the water bottle pouch on the side. Focus returned to his eyes. He looked less dazed.

He confirmed it when he spoke. "When we get across the road and away from the house, you should change. It's going to be a long night and I don't want you to get sick." He took the flashlight while she clutched the bag of dry clothes to her chest as they walked.

Her eyes filled with tears as they shuffled down to the road, across the paved surface, enough that her vision was blurry. She didn't want to cry, but couldn't help herself between the pain and the relief, her system was overwhelmed. They slid through the ditch and found a gap in the sagebrush where it thinned. Stopping beside the culvert that had saved her, he shone the light into its mouth, where two sets of crimson eyes gleamed.

She shuddered.

Ryan's voice was unsteady. "It was lucky you fit. You must have been terrified."

She took off her pack to change without speaking. She peeled off her wet clothing and used the somewhat dryish back of her T-shirt to rub herself; goosebumps covered her chilled flesh. After changing into dry, if not-quite-clean, clothes, she warmed up. She stuffed the wet clothing into the plastic bag, then shoved it into her pack and put on her jacket.

Before she put her pack on again, Ryan unclipped his and pulled her into an embrace. She always felt better when he did that. She felt him wince as her arms closed around him despite her care to be gentle, but he squeezed her against him as they shared their warmth and their strength. As he held her, the tension drained away until only the pain in her ankle remained, a hot flare in the night's chill.

"If they'd taken you, I don't know what I'd have done," he said into her hair. "I'm glad you're safe. I don't think I could do this without you."

CHAPTER 22: RYAN

Ryan and Kat walked all night, trudging into the sun as it came up the next morning. The sky paled, then an orange and pink glow spread along the horizon and bled into the dark gray sky. Movement required a great deal of effort. Ryan tried to be tough and not show how much he hurt, but every breath was agony. Daylight allowed him to get a proper look at Kat and her condition. He'd been worried all night. It wasn't like her to be so quiet.

While he was the one who'd taken a beating, she hadn't left the encounter with the Slains unscathed. Her eyes looked haunted and her limp had returned. She hadn't mentioned hurting herself, but she'd re-injured her ankle. He didn't know how far they'd traveled overnight, but ten miles was a reasonable estimate. Their progress had been slow, and it wasn't enough distance to set his mind at ease. He scanned the distant hillside to the north. They needed a safe place to stop soon.

He'd seen the distant lights of a house once near the beginning and they'd crossed a couple of packed dirt and gravel roads but had seen no sign of habitation for some time. The dry grasslands spread open, a drab sameness that stretched to the horizon with sparse greenery. At first, it had been a relief to walk in the thin grass where the footing was somewhat reliable, even in the dark, with fewer roots and stands of sagebrush to trip over. Without the black cloak of night, it seemed exposed. His back tensed, thinking of the danger from behind that could return.

Toward late morning, as the glowing orange orb of the sun disappeared behind gray-covered skies, they veered north toward a rocky ridge with a smattering of low evergreen trees and juniper bushes. The vegetation wouldn't provide a lot of protection or cover, but it was better than nothing. Ryan needed to stop and sleep, and Kat looked half-asleep on her feet. He wasn't sure where to find somewhere safe to rest. Twice they startled pronghorn antelope that bounded away, their white rumps flashing through the air before disappearing from sight.

The second time, Ryan changed course, following the animals.

The ground near the northern ridge was stony and hard, but the flat appearance was deceptive. It had layers and dips that weren't seen from the level surface of the plain. When he found a low point that he liked the look of, he dropped his pack. One of the deeper crevices could be used to set up their tent. They'd be seen from above, but not by a casual searcher on the scrub-filled grassland. They huddled below the level of the plain to cook, somewhat sheltered from the constant breeze.

Ryan took stock of what remained of their meager supplies. They had three days' worth of food, two canteens each, and their belongings in the backpacks. Everything else was gone, but at least they had the essentials. He boiled water in their remaining pot—the others had been lost with the bikes—while Kat spread her filthy, wet clothing from last night on the ground near the tent. She weighted each piece with a stone. Every move looked awkward as she avoided putting her full weight on her injured foot.

Kat caught him watching her as she finished with a wince.

"I want to look at your ankle."

She shrugged. "I wrapped it as best I could in the dark, but it wouldn't hurt to see how it's doing."

She sat across from him on the warm, crumbly black rocks and swung her foot into his lap. He undid her hiking shoe with deliberate care. The damp laces were difficult to loosen, but he was patient as he picked at the double knot. Kat braced herself as he slid the boot off, sucking in a pained breath as it came off her foot. Her wrapping job was adequate, but uneven and perhaps too loose—though not bad for having been done in the dark. He unwound the bandage to reveal the swollen purple ankle. One side had a new bruise in a mass of older green and yellow. Her ankle was a mess.

"What happened?" He looked up for an explanation, one eyebrow raised. Why hadn't she said something? He probed the new bruises, watching her reaction, trying to gauge the depth of her injury.

She sighed. "I did it when we first split up. I jumped through the ditch and over a patch of sagebrush. It was almost better until my awkward landing."

He wished he'd known, though it wouldn't have changed anything. They hadn't spoken much during the night as they'd saved their strength for hiking. He'd also been worried about sound carrying and giving their position away. Guilt wracked him. Perhaps he and Kat should have left the road sooner or cycled back to Kaycee, even if it had meant losing the day. If he hadn't insisted that they could circumvent the men at the barricade, they might not have lost the bikes or been injured.

"Do you want to talk about what happened? Lying in that metal drain was probably terrifying. You must have been trapped there for almost two hours. More, if I was unconscious longer."

Her bottom lip trembled and she chewed on it for a second. The expression in her eyes looked like she was gathering her strength to deny needing to share.

"Really, I want to know." He put conviction into his tone and squeezed her hand.

She told him about the cold water and the smell, and the men who'd spoken outside, and about the gigantic rat. He told her how the man at the house and his dog had turned him in the first time, and that he'd asked the man to watch out for her. Sharing their stories in the daylight helped him to banish his fear, and he hoped it did the same for her.

"Where do you hurt the most?" she said, tracing the lump on the side of his head.

He lifted his shirt to show the mottled bruises on both sides of his ribs. "Just bruised, nothing broken." It hurt like hell to take a deep breath, and he suspected running would be agony, but he'd heal. "That and my head. They knocked me out with the butt of a rifle."

She gasped and looked like she might cry. "Did you take Tylenol for the pain?"

He gave her a weary smile and shook his head. "I will." He got up and dug around in her pack for the first-aid kit so she wouldn't have to hop. He got Tylenol for himself and ibuprofen to reduce the swelling in her ankle. They gave each other rueful smiles and swallowed their pills with a scant mouthful of water. He rewrapped her ankle, and she covered it with only her thin inner sock. She left off her hiking shoe and set it by the tent.

Ryan checked his watch. It was ten a.m. "How's your battery? Can you set an alarm? I want to be on the move again by one." Without his phone, they'd have to depend on hers.

He didn't want to sleep more than a few hours before they continued. They could still have trouble with pursuit, and he worried about how long it would take to cross the grasslands on foot and about their water supply. Even if they located water, it would need to be treated. Their supply of water purification tablets was low, as was their fuel for boiling water.

In the national park, they shouldn't run across houses or people. Out here, they were alone with the antelope, prairie dogs, sage grouse, and the immense sky. He missed the mountains of the West Coast. He hadn't always paid attention to them, but they'd been a constant part of the skyline. What did they look like now after the eruptions?

Looking at his watch reminded him of the loss of his phone. Losing it didn't bother him as much as he'd have thought it would a couple of weeks ago. In the old days, he'd been inseparable from his phone and he would have purchased a new one at the first opportunity. He didn't feel desperate since he hadn't used it for almost a week except to check the time, but it was the only way his parents had to reach him and let him know if they were okay. He couldn't dwell on that right now. Even if they lived, he might not hear from them again. His mother's final message had read, *"Take your selfish ass to hell."* He'd read at it a dozen times, trying to take the sting from her words by desensitization. His efforts had been unsuccessful.

He didn't wish for mom and Roy to be dead, but whether or not they were was out of his control. He resigned himself to not knowing.

After a quick meal, which they ate cold and straight from the foil pouches, they lay down in the tent, the fly open to whatever breeze might rush through the crevice—which wasn't much. It was hot and stuffy inside the tent, and not very comfortable—though they'd spread their sleeping bags and Thermarests to pad the hard ground. Ryan drew Kat into place against his shoulder, his arm around her. He wanted to feel her next to him; her presence was a comfort, and he'd grown used to having her there. More than used to it, he needed her. He hoped she knew how important she'd become. They hadn't talked about it, but it was there, underneath their interactions.

"Lie against me. If it makes it easier to sleep, it's good. We need the rest." She turned and snuggled closer, her hand resting on his chest, over his heart. He placed his other hand on hers, feeling their connection and at peace.

Despite the sun rising overhead, he didn't have any trouble falling asleep.

Kat's alarm woke him three hours later. She slept on, unfazed by the sound. Her face was smudged with dirt and her frazzled hair needed to be washed. Even after she'd changed her clothes, she exuded an undertone of rotten drainage water, but he was thankful she was alive and unharmed. Luring the men away and taking a beating had been worth it to keep her from harm.

He smoothed the hair from her face and she twitched in her sleep. He hated to disturb her rest, but they needed to pack and go. Sliding out, he shook her by the shoulder just enough to wake her. When her eyelids first fluttered open, she looked confused, then realization dawned.

"It wasn't a dream, was it?" she said with a sigh. "We've got a lot of walking to do. Maybe a hundred miles." She didn't wait for an answer and rolled off the bed, deflated her mattress, and stuffed her sleeping bag into its tube. She undid her ponytail and smoothed it back once more in some semblance of order. There wasn't much else they could do to freshen up without more water.

"We do. There's half a thermos of tea left. We can drink it when we're walking. Maybe it'll give us the energy to get going. It should be hot and sunny this time of year, but the ashy skies may be a blessing in disguise if they give us some sun protection. I'm going to wear my hat, anyway." He pulled his ball cap from his pack and put it on over his grimy hair.

"How long do you think it will take to walk to the cabin?" She looked down at her filthy hands, examining her chipped nails.

"At least four days, maybe five," he said as he finished, tossed his packed bedding out of the tent flap, and tied his hiking shoes before standing up.

"What are you not telling me?" She tilted her head up to look at him as she exited.

"What makes you think I'm not telling you something?"

She sent him a look that let him know she didn't believe him. Her raised eyebrows could be so eloquent.

"You look worried and I don't think it's because of my foot. It'll slow me down, but not that much. Remember, I'm tougher than I look." She sat, and he checked the wrapping on her foot, taking care not to move it more than necessary. She stuffed her feet into her hiking shoes, preparing to leave.

They unclipped the tent as they talked, not needing to pull stakes. The ground had been too hard to bother and without wind, it hadn't been necessary. Working as a team, they folded and rolled the tent. She held the tent while he slid on the stuff sack.

She stared at him and repeated her question. "What else?"

"Water," he said at last. It was a relief to share his concern. "I don't know if there's drinkable water out there. We'll have to strain, boil, and purify what we find, and we don't have a lot of fuel."

"So, we tighten our belts and eat what we can without cooking. Save our water for drinking. If we get hungry, it'll just be for a few days. I can tough it out that long."

He admired her determination and grit. "You're right. We can do this." He gave her a smile and helped her to her feet.

• • •

The first full day of walking was tiring when they'd already started sore, tired, and hungry, but at least it was uneventful, as was the next night. Had they eluded Bob and the Slains? Sleep was harder to come by, though they were exhausted. Ryan's stomach rumbled as he lay in the dark, feeling empty. It shouldn't be hard to go without a proper meal just this once, but it was more difficult than he expected. He'd been spoiled his whole life because even when he was young and times had been rough at home, he'd been able to find something to eat, even if he'd had to cook it himself. A granola bar for lunch and a protein bar for dinner, with limited water to wash them down, was unsatisfying.

His mouth was parched when he woke the third morning and his skin was dry and scaly enough that he wanted to scratch until it hurt. It couldn't go on like this much longer. They'd have to watch for water as they hiked. The map showed a seasonal stream to the north, but the meandering creek bed looked too far away to be reasonable, plus it was in the wrong direction, Vita being southeast, not north. They still had more than a full canteen each, but at least two more days of walking at this pace to reach the main highway on the farmer's map.

Late on the third day, the weather changed.

All-day they'd plodded, their pace slower than the first day, a certain listlessness in their steps; ash kicked up at every step and they wore their masks to keep from inhaling it. He tracked the gray skies as they grew thicker, then darker, becoming a boiling mass of ominous black overhead. The air grew hot and muggy and he and Kat dripped with sweat, despite the infrequent gusts of cold air. The light changed color, no longer its regular shade, but an unhealthy yellowish haze that reminded Ryan of the sky before a hailstorm.

He cast his mind back to long ago. He'd been caught out once with his grandfather, who'd taken one look at the sky and told young Ryan to run for the truck. He'd sprinted, impressed with his aging grandfather's speed as they dashed for safety. They'd only just hopped inside the pickup when the first bits of hail bounced down, bits no bigger than peas. The first few hailstones seemed exciting to eleven-year-old Ryan, who'd been exhilarated by the storm.

Thirty seconds later, the hailstones were closer to the size of golf and ping pong balls and bounced off the metal truck with a horrendous roar. He'd been sure the ferocious pounding would dent the truck. Ryan had covered his ears and cowered in his seat. His grandfather had scooted closer and put a stringy arm around his grandson's bony shoulders while they waited for the onslaught to pass.

Ryan didn't remember how long it had taken, but by the time the hailstorm had relented, the bed of the truck was half-filled with chunks of ice and snow and the road had been covered with slick balls of ice, a couple of inches deep. His grandfather had shifted his truck into four-wheel drive and driven, bumping over the slippery hailstones.

Ryan hadn't thought of the storm in ages, but now the memory made the feeling that they needed to seek shelter urgent. He walked faster.

Seeing his attention and feeling his pace increase, Kat looked up, perhaps taking in the unearthly color of the heavens.

"I don't like the look of the sky," she said, a crease in her brows.

"Me either. Do you think we can make it to the trees ahead?"

"I can try. We might be near the other road. Where we're supposed to turn south."

Sure enough, what looked like a line cut across their path about two hundred yards ahead. If he'd been paying attention to something other than the sky, he would have noticed. Just beyond the road was another of the orange and gray rock bluffs that characterized Thunder Basin Grasslands Park, or what they'd seen of it.

She squinted and pointed. "Not much shelter in those low trees. Maybe we can find cover by the bluff."

A blast of cold air hit them and lightning rocketed through the sky.

He grabbed her hand and jogged. It would be torture for her with her sore ankle and his ribs felt like someone had bashed them with a hammer, but they needed to hurry. Each breath sent shooting pains through him, and her limp became more pronounced. He felt bad about towing her across the uneven ground, but not enough to stop. They scrambled through a shallow ditch and over the narrow highway and the rocks beyond.

Wind whipped Kat's hair and buffeted them sideways with a powerful gust. The storm was almost upon them. He aimed for a shadow near the base of the cliff as the first solid bits descended from the sky. The first hailstones were small. They bounced and peppered the ground, not much bigger than cooked rice. Maybe it wouldn't be so bad. They didn't seem to be a problem, though they made the ground slick with a thin layer of ice.

Ryan would have slowed, but he remembered the innocuous beginning to the storm with his grandfather. That had been before extreme weather from climate change, let alone the recent infusion of dust and volcanic ash into the atmosphere. Chances were that this storm would be substantial. The cliff ahead looked too steep to scale, but at the base was a shadow. It didn't look deep enough to be a cave, but perhaps a hollow where they could fit under an overhang. Hurdling over several boulders and around a stand of juniper bushes, they reached the bluff.

They were in luck.

When they pressed their backs against the rocky cliff, they almost fit underneath. Taking off their packs, they set them near their feet and squeezed deeper inside.

It wasn't a moment too soon.

The sky opened up, dropping a cascade of hailstones that grew in size. First peas, then marbles, then ping-pong balls, and larger. Many bounced over a foot in the air, ricocheting in all directions as they pelted the ground. Kat and Ryan watched with held breath at first while the storm wracked the countryside. He couldn't see beyond the sheets of hail, but this level of intensity couldn't last. He took Kat's hand and squeezed, holding it through the storm. A storm like this in semi-desert territory was another sign that the climate was unstable.

Errant hailstones bounced beneath their overhang, many with enough force to sting when they hit. Beside him, Kat jumped twice, wincing at the pain of the fast-moving ice. The worst part of the storm lasted only about fifteen minutes and the whole hailstorm moved past them in less than half an hour, leaving the ground white as far as he could see.

Kat held up her bare arm to show two red welts rising on her forearm. "Some storm." Her shaky voice seemed loud in the unearthly quiet that followed the roar of the hail. "I've never seen it hail like that. We can return to the road now that we roughly know where we are. If it seems safe."

"How far was this junction to the south?

"About thirty-five or forty miles from the road where they took the bikes," she said. "We came farther on foot. More like sixty-five miles. Depends how far north we are. Maybe seventy miles in total to the bunker."

It was frustrating knowing how close they were to xTerra and yet how much farther they had to walk. He calculated at least three more days, even if they stayed on the road where walking was easy. He would love to find, steal, or borrow a car, but the land was desolate and inhabitants were sparse. They could be at the bunker in under two hours if they drove, but there wasn't anyone or anything for miles.

Kat stepped from the shelter, moved along the bottom of the cliff near the small trees, and bent to collect a handful of broken branches.

"We should make a fire and melt some hail. We'll have to strain and purify the water, but it should help, right?"

He nodded, relieved she'd thought of an ingenious solution to one of their problems. He dug in her pack for the cooking pot and filled it to the brim with chunks of hail, trying to scoop the top layers that were less dirty. They planned to filter the water with the pump, but the less dirt and ash that he added, the better. He crushed the hailstones with the bottom of his water bottle to pack more inside.

Kat returned with an armload of firewood and a smile. She had an uncanny ability to stay positive and bounce back, even when things were tough. She was something special.

Focusing on the matter at hand, he searched for a bare patch of ground and used the far end of the overhang to build a fire. There wasn't enough wood to keep one burning long, but any fire was better than none and he was excited to augment their water supply. His hands were red with cold where he'd used his bare hands to scoop ice. Neither he nor Kat had been wearing jackets when they'd taken off at a run and they were both cool and damp, though the air temperature had returned to normal.

It was too early to stop for the night, but another thirty to forty-five minutes to melt, boil, and clean water—and also to get dry—wouldn't be wasted time. Ryan scavenged larger pieces of wood and added them to the pile.

He scooped away a few hailstones and removed a firestarter from his pack. Made with wax and dryer lint in a paper egg carton, it was an old trick of his grandfather's for starting a fire in bad weather or when you didn't have access to newspaper or kindling. There were two chunks left in an outer pocket of his pack. Layering sticks in a teepee shape over the firestarter, he lit a match and started the fire, watching the greedy orange flame spread with crackling noises. It wasn't long until the warmth seeped through his damp pants. He held his hands close and moved the pot beside the fire. One side of the metal container would heat and they could turn it until it boiled.

Kat reappeared with a large stack of branches from further away, throwing them down nearby. The welts on her arms had become circular purple bruises. He suspected he had half a dozen of his own. She unpacked her jacket, put it on, and passed his to him. As the ice melted, he added more to the pot.

She dunked the tube for the filter into the pot when the liquid was ready. She stretched a clean-looking sock over the mouth of the canteen to strain the gritty liquid.

"A sock?" he said, feeling his eyebrows shoot skyward.

She shrugged. "Do you have a better idea?"

He moved closer so he could help, taking over the pump while she held the ends. Between them, they filled both empty canteens and topped up another, so once again they had four full ones. With a better water supply, his shoulders relaxed. When they finished straining their gathered water, they refilled the pot with filtered water, and boiled some for a hot meal. The rich scent of the dehydrated beef stew when the water hit was intoxicating. It was all he could do not to rip into his dinner pouch before the five minutes were done.

While they waited to eat their late lunch, they refilled the pot a final time and replaced the water they'd used for their hot meal. Cleaning up and putting out the fire with the rest of the meltwater, they trudged toward the road while the embers hissed, white smoke rising into the air. He hoped it wouldn't give their position away to the Slains or anyone like them, but he couldn't leave an unattended fire burning. He didn't know how he was going to keep moving, but somehow, he put one foot in front of the other, south down Route 116.

CHAPTER 23: KAT

Kat and Ryan walked down the cracked and bumpy highway long into the evening. Kat's foot throbbed with every step, despite taking Tylenol at four-hour intervals. She grimaced, knowing the pain would keep her awake tonight, as it had last night. She didn't complain or let Ryan know how much it hurt, or let it slow them down further. The journey to South Dakota had already been extended too long.

She wished they could just be at the bunker already. Last night, she'd listened to every breath of wind as she lay in the tent. Also, to every stomach growl and scurrying rodent while she'd lain there unable to sleep, her ankle a hot source of discomfort.

It was after their non-existent dinner voices carried on the breeze from ahead. The sounds came from further up the road, past the next rolling hill. Heart thumping, she worried it might be the Slains brothers or another roadblock. They crept off the road and into the sharp grass and prickly sagebrush, preparing to make a detour. They could circle back to the road after they were past the danger zone.

She grabbed Ryan's arm when she saw a day-use picnic area shelter ahead with four picnic tables and a small brick building she guessed was a public washroom or rest area. Two dusty SUVs were parked in a gravel lot between their position and the shelter.

The delicious scent of grilling burgers wafted to them on the evening breeze. Kat's stomach gurgled and her mouth watered. A hamburger would be fantastic. She could almost taste it from the aroma. They'd only eaten one hot meal in the last three days because they'd been short on rations, and her body was feeling the lack of food.

"They look busy," said Ryan with a frown.

She hadn't paid attention to the people, just the grill. The important thing: food. She wasn't sure what Ryan meant at first, then it hit. The two men were far from their vehicles. It would be easy to sneak up and see if the keys had been left inside.

"Right. A car." She'd been distracted by the smell of food.

Kat didn't want to steal and Ryan wasn't a thief by nature, but the last few days had been difficult and people out here were looking after themselves first. Perhaps that was the right attitude. Only the strongest and smartest would survive. A car would change everything. Their trip could be over today.

They crept closer, crouching low to the ground, staying behind the bigger patches of pale green sagebrush. In the evening light, she was well-camouflaged in her dusty hiking clothes of faded olive and tan. If the men below expected trouble and looked up the slope past the cars, they might have seen them, but she and Ryan advanced unnoticed.

With each creeping footstep closer, she paid more attention, shoving the thought of food far away. Two tall men with dark hair and jeans joked while cooking on a portable grill on one of the picnic tables. Assorted condiments and a stack of paper plates sat beside them. There was a lot of food for just two people. Were there others in the concrete building? She looked around, making sure no one else was outside. Her throat tightened as she contemplated another situation where they were outnumbered. She'd rather keep moving.

The men spoke in clear voices that sounded relaxed and friendly. They didn't look dangerous, though she couldn't tell for certain anymore. Anyone could be a threat. A pang of guilt stabbed through her. This wasn't a good idea. One man stooped to grab a tennis ball and threw it for a golden retriever who raced back with the soggy ball to lay it at his feet. The dog pranced while he waited for a repeat throw.

"I'm going in for a closer look. Wait here," whispered Ryan.

She nodded and continued to watch the men. It looked like dinner was almost ready. There were hot dogs and burgers on the grill. Mouth watering, she could almost taste a burger with pickles, ketchup, and mustard.

The door to the bathroom flung open, hitting the side of the building with a crash, and Kat jumped, stifling her scream. Her heart pounded. Had she given herself away? Crouching lower, she held her breath, but it seemed the same below. A little boy, perhaps six years old, had burst from inside the building. He dried his hands on his jeans and handed a flashlight to the tall man at the BBQ.

"Daddy, are they ready yet? I'm starving. I bet I could eat five hotdogs." The boy looked up at the dark-haired man at the grill.

"Five?" his father said. "That's a lot of hot dogs, Buddy."

"Five," the boy repeated with a nod.

Kat's heart ached for them. The boy should be playing with Lego or thinking about first grade. He shouldn't be camping in this desolate place with nothing but dust and sagebrush. She brushed the hair out of her eyes. At least he had family and wasn't alone.

"You bet," his dad said, lifting a hot dog with his tongs and putting it in a bun on a paper plate. "Let's start with one at a time." He looked around. "Where's your mom?" He set the food down in front of his son.

"Still with Aunty Ella and the babies," said the boy, wrinkling his nose.

He climbed onto the bench seat and sat in front of his dinner, now facing away from Kat. His dad added a row of ketchup with a flourish, then the kid picked up his hot dog and took a huge bite.

Kat's mouth watered and she couldn't look away. If a hot dog looked fantastic, she must be desperate. Two weeks ago, she would have refused one without a second thought or regret. Now she was ready to steal from a six-year-old.

After the kid chewed the first gigantic bite, he put his dinner down and said, "Oops. I forgot to wait for everybody else."

Even at this distance, he was cute.

"You don't need to wait. You can have a head start since you're eating five hot dogs. Besides, we're camping."

The boy grinned up at his dad. "Did you make one for Sunny?"

"When everyone is eating, Uncle Luke will put down his dinner," said the man with a generous smile. "Don't you worry."

The man grinned as two petite blonde women joined them. One held the hand of a dancing preschooler with a wrinkled pink princess dress and a tiara framing her blonde ringlets, while the other carried a baby girl. The quiet man who'd been playing with the dog held out his hands and the baby chortled and dove into his arms.

The scene of the happy families made Kat's chest ache. This was a mini-vignette of their lives and she shouldn't be able to judge what they were like, but she did. They looked like good people. Her chest tightened. Stealing from them would be wrong. She and Ryan couldn't take their vehicle, the car seats, and their belongings inside. The family would be stranded or missing vital supplies for the children. She didn't want to get to xTerra this way. She'd rather walk, even on her sprained ankle.

She needed to stop Ryan.

She'd taken only half a dozen crouched steps when he looked back over his shoulder. She shook her head and mouthed, "Don't do it." He hesitated and crept back to her. His eyebrow raised.

"We can't do this," she repeated in a whisper. "They have kids. If anyone deserves a chance to get somewhere safe, it's them. I hope they make it and I can't be the one that wrecks that."

His tense shoulders loosened and dropped. "I didn't feel good about it either."

They backtracked to the road and walked on toward the junction of the other highway just beyond the picnic shelter. No more sneaking. They'd wasted enough time here. These people weren't a threat. That's what she kept telling herself, but her nerves were on edge. It felt strange to be in plain sight, knowing people would see them. They'd spent the last few days on the run and before that, skulking to maintain a low profile. Doubts and second thoughts crept in as they strode closer. Her steps faltered; it wasn't too late to sneak around.

"Hey, you two. On the road," shouted the father of the little boy. He trotted toward them and stopped halfway between them and the others.

Kat froze, her heart hammering. Was there going to be trouble?

"You two want some dinner? We've got extra."

Her first thought was that it was a trap. At this stage of their journey, she didn't welcome the idea of strangers. The last few days had left them raw and on guard.

Kat looked at Ryan, who shrugged. If this wasn't a trick, it was extra good luck.

He squeezed her hand. Her shoulders tensed—solid like iron—and she remained watchful. Still, she pasted on her best non-threatening smile as they strolled toward the happy family. The dog ran to greet them and licked Ryan's outstretched hand.

"We'd love a burger," said Kat. It felt strange to speak to someone new and suddenly she couldn't muster the energy for a show. She wanted to be herself. If they didn't like her, what did it matter? "We've been smelling them for miles."

The closest man grinned. "Nobody can resist my cooking," he said, winking at his wife. "I'm Christopher."

He was as tall as Ryan, if not taller, with dark hair and the palest blue eyes she'd ever seen. "That's my wife, Elizabeth."

Elizabeth smiled but looked nervous as she gripped her daughter's hand and stepped closer to her son at the picnic table.

How rough did she and Ryan look? Every scratch etched on Kat's skin; every bruise felt neon. For all that, Christopher was friendly, the others had more typical wary reactions, for which Kat couldn't blame them.

"That's Jayden and Allie," Christopher continued, pointing to his children. "We're with our friends, Luke, Ella, and little Jess." His spatula indicated each in turn.

His smile was friendly and warm. Kat's heart constricted for having considered stealing their car and was relieved they'd chosen to leave it. Would she have been able to live with herself if they'd gone through with something so low? They'd have been pond scum for stealing. Worse than scum. They'd be in the same league as the Slains.

"I'm Kat and this is Ryan." She was proud of keeping her voice friendly, but even.

"You two been on the road long? Or do you live around here?" The expression in Luke's startling deep blue eyes was more guarded and his face harder to read. She suspected he didn't miss much.

"We had to leave the car near Missoula—which was burning," said Ryan as he shook hands with the adults. "We switched to our bikes to get around the military roadblocks so we could keep going south, then east, instead of back to Spokane. We rode for a couple of days, holed up in a cabin to wait out the worst of the ashfall, but the bikes were stolen a few days ago at twilight. Since then, we've been on foot."

"Your journey has quite the story," said Ella, moving up beside her husband, resting her hand on his arm.

It looked like she was urging caution.

Kat shuffled her feet on the dusty ground, more aware than ever of how filthy and unkempt she must look despite her efforts to smooth her hair down and keep it braided. Her face grew warm at the thought. The other two women looked like they were camping, but without the air of desperation that must be in her own look.

"Where are you from?" Ryan asked.

"Portland." Christopher's face looked distressed. "My brother worked with someone high in the government who passed along a tip to leave. We had to make several detours, but we're almost at our destination." He looked at the sky where the sun had started to set, spreading brilliant colors onto the horizon. All the dust and ash in the air made for gorgeous sunsets. "If it wasn't for the kids, we'd push on tonight. As it is, we're going to camp one more night." He looked at his wife with a pointed look. "Some mothers are strict about things like dinner and bedtime." He grinned when his wife swatted his shoulder with a look that spoke of their familiarity and his common teasing. He had a warmth about him that was easy to like.

The only town in this direction was Edgemont, right outside the bunker complex, but it was a tiny dot on the map. It seemed improbable that such a small town was their destination. Were they going to xTerra as well? It would be quite the coincidence to meet others on their way to the same refuge, but she didn't know where else anyone would go when the land seemed so desolate and barren. They'd passed the last small town.

Ella brought two plates with buns and handed them to Kat and Ryan. Kat's hand shook as she took the plate. If the others noticed, nobody said anything. Christopher dropped a burger patty onto each of the buns. "Help yourself to the rest," he said, waving at the table. Their generosity blew Kat away and tears pricked her eyes. It was almost too kind.

Kat added cheese, ketchup, pickles, and mustard and a green salad. If you examined it, the lettuce was rusty, but it was the closest she'd been to produce in a week—ever since the apples ran out. She was about to dive in when she glimpsed her hands. They were filthy. She couldn't eat like this.

Feeling conspicuous, she put her plate back down. "Thank you, but I should wash up first." Overwhelmed by their kindness, her voice shook. Her throat closed, making it difficult to speak. These people were so generous and it was undeserved.

"Don't forget to scrub between your fingers too," said Jayden from where he sat finishing a second hot dog. He'd smeared his face and hands with ketchup. "I wanted five, but I can only eat two." He held up two reddened, goopy fingers.

"Jayden," said Elizabeth, her tone one of amused exasperation. She looked at Kat. "I don't know where he gets that from."

From the warm look she threw in Christopher's direction, Elizabeth had a solid idea.

"We'll go with you to wash up," Elizabeth said with a longer glance at her son. She sighed and held out her hand for Jayden, who took it and hopped down. She grabbed the lantern and headed for the bathroom, and Kat followed, leaving Ryan to talk with the men. It felt strange to go somewhere without him. They'd been inseparable for eleven days.

In the bathroom they stood at separate sinks, the lantern casting an eerie white light.

"We're almost to our destination too," Kat said as she washed her hands, scrubbing them with soap before rinsing. Once clean, she used them to splash water on her face. Her hands came away muddy. "Oh my. I'm a disaster." Her cheeks flamed.

"Where are you from?" Elizabeth washed Jayden with a wet facecloth. Her voice was soft and seemed non-judgmental.

"Seattle." Kat burst into tears and covered her mouth in horror. "I'm so sorry."

Jayden patted her arm in sympathy. "It's okay. We all get sad sometimes. I cried when we left my best friend."

"You must have left early too," said the other woman with pity shining in her eyes. "The coast sounds bad. We haven't heard from anyone since we left."

Kat took a deep breath and nodded. "On the twentieth. Only the day before. It's been eleven days on the road, but it feels longer."

"I know what you mean. We detoured into southern Idaho, trying to convince Luke's father to join us. We stayed for close to a week, but he wasn't interested in leaving his ranch. One of his teenage granddaughters had texted to say she'd gotten through the mountains but was on foot. He stayed, waiting for her to arrive. It might take her a while. He promised to join us, eventually." Her eyes looked sad.

They returned outside to find Luke and Ryan setting up a big tent while Christopher finished with the grill. Kat picked up her burger and ate, trying to savor the taste, though thoughts of home turned the food to sawdust in her mouth. She was quiet while the other women took turns eating, supervising the children, and packing up the extra food.

When Kat finished, she strolled over to join Ryan, who'd moved on to unpacking their tent and setting it up. Her questions must have been in her gaze.

"Safety in numbers. I mentioned our trouble with the Slains brothers who wanted me to join their militia and told how they got belligerent when I turned them down. These guys came via a more southern route and missed the blockades, but it doesn't hurt to be cautious. Besides, I didn't think you'd want to walk any further on that ankle today."

She nodded. "Thank you." Even this kindness from Ryan brought tears to her eyes. What was wrong with her? Perhaps the sleeplessness, uncertainty, and hunger were taking their toll.

Twilight fell and Ella retreated to one of the big tents with the baby, while Elizabeth took her two youngsters into the other to settle for the night. Quiet murmurs of bedtime stories and sleepy voices came through the thin walls of the tent. The homey sounds made Kat ache in a way that was new. Children were precious. Perhaps one day she would have her own. Even in this crazy mixed-up life, it might be possible.

In the parking area, Christopher rummaged around in the back of his vehicle as he packed the leftover food away for the night, leaving herself and Ryan alone with Luke.

"What happened to your ankle?" said Luke when she rejoined him near the table.

"I hurt it hiking a few weeks ago, but re-injured it running away from the men who took our bikes."

"That's when you were in a fight?" said Luke, turning to Ryan.

"You don't miss anything," said Ryan. "Yes. The men from the most recent roadblock. It wasn't so much a fight, as a beating." He related the short version of the story. "It was worth it, though. I was scared about what they wanted to do to her." He took Kat's hand. "Just a shot in the dark, but anyone here a doctor?"

"Christopher and his wife both have doctorates," said Luke, "but I'm your best bet for checking injuries. I've had some experience. But you're still walking on that ankle and you can breathe, so nothing's broken."

Luke looked at her again. She got the impression he was making a decision.

"I'm surprised you trusted anyone enough to just stroll into camp," said Christopher as he joined them with four cans of beer. He handed one to Ryan and another to Luke. Kat shook her head. She wasn't interested in drinking. Ryan put his down without opening it and Christopher set the unopened spare on the table beside it.

"They didn't," said Luke, surprising Kat, who'd thought their initial approach had been unnoticed.

Everyone looked at him, and he shrugged.

"They snuck down the hill to watch us first. When we looked safe, they circled back and hiked down the road while we were cooking."

"Why didn't you say something sooner?" said Ryan.

Kat wondered the same thing.

"I thought I'd see how the evening played out. You both moved like you were hurt and don't have guns." He turned to Ryan, "Though, from your size, I'm guessing you swing a mean bat."

His words implied that he'd seen them at a glance and that he was confident he could have eliminated them if they'd proven to be a problem.

"I want to put our cards on the table." Luke looked at Christopher, who nodded. "We're headed to xTerra and I'm guessing you are, too. Where else would anyone be going out here?"

Kat and Ryan shared a glance, and she nodded.

"Why are you telling us now?" said Kat. "You don't have room to take us with you. We're still going to be on foot. We appreciate dinner and all, but we can't travel with you." Their cars were crammed full of baggage and camping gear taking every bit of space not filled with car seats.

"I see I'm not the only one paying attention," said Luke with a slight smile. "But I want to answer your question. The world has gotten harder and there's strength in numbers. We're future neighbors and I wanted to see what you were like. I wanted to see if you were the kind of people I'd trust to live near my daughter."

That made sense. Kat wasn't sure that was the whole reason, but she didn't feel like pushing the issue. She was too tired.

"Do you mind if I borrow your lantern? I'm exhausted, but I want to wash my hair before bed. I still smell like culvert carcass and stagnant water."

"I wasn't going to say anything," teased Ryan with a wink.

"Go ahead," said Christopher. "We're all on the way to bed soon. Kids get up early." He drained the last of his beer, hefted the cooler, and headed for the cars to stow it for the evening. "Night all."

Kat picked up the light and went into the cold concrete bathroom and dunked her hair in the sink to wash it with handsoap. She needed to get the smell out or she might have trouble sleeping again, but it was awkward to tilt her head back far enough in the water to rinse the lather out. She was about to give up, when Ryan joined her, holding a cup from the table.

She tilted her head forward and let him rinse her hair with the cold water. She was shivering by the time he was finished, but at last, the smell was gone. When they were done, they switched, and she washed his hair. After a quick scrub in the important places, they were cleaner than they'd been in days. It helped to feel almost normal.

Ryan wrapped his arms around her from behind and nuzzled her neck. "Your skin smells delicious. Like candy." He kissed her throat and sent delicious tingles racing through her. "You want to wait until we're in xTerra, or can you be quiet tonight?"

"Is that a challenge? How about both?" she said, letting him lead her to their tent where it sat apart from the others, giving them space, but not so far that they weren't part of the group. He was right. Safety lay in numbers.

• • •

This was the first night Kat and Ryan had been intimate since she'd acknowledged her feelings for him. She didn't know if it was her imagination or the way her thoughts were skewed tonight, but it seemed they were careful with each other. She didn't want to hurt his ribs and kept her weight off him, and he seemed intensely aware of her ankle and was cautious about not bumping it.

From their first gentle kiss, her heart had filled with tenderness. His lips fit hers just the right way. She arched into his touch; everything about him was just what she needed. Every stroke of her face, every touch to her jaw. She loved the way he sucked in his breath when she touched her tongue inside his mouth and the heat of his body. Every nerve ending tingled, and his hands caressing her skin ignited a fire within. His whispers made her wet and squirm out of her clothes, eager to be naked.

She wasn't just having fun sex; she was making love with someone she cared about. The thought almost blew her away. She hadn't imagined falling so hard for anyone ever again. Ryan smoothed her hair from her face and she stopped trying to analyze everything and let herself enjoy every caress, every word, the sensation of his hard, muscled body, and the heat of his smooth skin on hers.

Knowing the others were camped nearby meant they tried to be quiet, but several times they burst into laughter when she covered her mouth to keep the sound in or he nibbled at her lip. With every motion, she ached for him and when he slid inside her, she pulled him tight and vowed to never let this excitement between them fade. She wanted this feeling of completion to last forever. When at last they'd exhausted themselves, she stayed in Ryan's sleeping bag, her head on his chest, his arms around her, and their legs entwined.

This was love. This was life.

CHAPTER 24: RYAN

Sometime later, Ryan startled awake, his heart pounding in the darkness. He listened through the flimsy tent walls. What woke him? Since they'd been on the road, his brain had been in overdrive, trying to feel safe and keep him alive. It must have registered a sound outside, something now quiet or imperceptible to his ear. Faint rustling sounds came from inside one of the other tents. Was that what he'd heard? He doubted it. The dog barked once and was shushed. He wasn't the only one awake.

Ryan glanced at Kat, who still slept, half in his sleeping bag with one leg out in the cool air, resting on her bedding. Lucky she was a sound sleeper. He slid out and into his cold pants, pulled on a shirt, and jammed his feet into his shoes. He wouldn't sleep without checking to see what had awakened him. Grabbing his baseball bat, he slid out into the cool night, trying not to disturb anyone.

The night was cloudy, but between the clouds, the sky was a deep navy rather than the true black of the dead of night. Morning approached and it smelled like it might rain. He listened, but there was nothing out of the ordinary, not even a gust of wind. It was still and quiet in the chill predawn. He'd hoped they might be safe tonight, but now they might face additional danger.

Ryan wouldn't always have said he had a lot to live for, but he was determined to live and make it to safety. Not only that, but his feelings for Kat had grown. Though he hadn't told her, when he'd woken up alone in the dark after being beaten, he'd had an epiphany. Kat filled a hole in his soul, one he hadn't known existed. He'd spent so much time ensuring that nobody hurt him, that he'd never been close to anyone, even keeping an arm's length from his closest friend. Nick hadn't pushed and had accepted the trust and friendship offered.

Ryan had become close to Kat since that night in the cabin when the volcanoes had erupted. She needed him as much as he needed her. They were a match. If he ever saw Nick again, he'd thank him.

She'd reached across that immense bed and placed a piece of her heart in his care and he'd accepted. It hadn't been conscious, but that night had been a turning point. There'd been healing in that, a trust that had developed between them. He hadn't decided to fall in love. That's just what had happened once he allowed himself to feel. Not only was he not going to push her away, like he had everyone else in his life, including Heather, but he also wasn't willing to let anyone or anything threaten their peace, their future.

Shivering, he turned, about to return to bed when stealthy unzipping sounds broke the silence and Luke emerged with Sunny, the leash in one hand, and a flashlight in the other. It was just a few moments more before Christopher joined them. Ryan wasn't the only one unable to get back to sleep, and his heart pounded harder.

The three of them looked at each other. It wasn't likely to be nothing when something had woken all of them. Sunny stared out into the empty grasslands and growled, a low sound, one that built into a menacing tone. Luke's hand rested on his dog's head, reassuring him, and the dog quieted but remained tense, staring west. Luke jerked his head to one side, and they moved away from their sleeping families to converse.

It was interesting how old gender-based roles reverted in an apocalypse; tonight, it was the men on patrol.

"He wouldn't wake me if it was nothing," Luke whispered

He meant the dog.

A distant glow of headlights appeared, coming from the west, not close enough they should have been disturbed, but somehow his brain had recognized something out of place. Someone was on the road, driving in their direction.

Ryan's grip on the bat tightened and his heart rate increased. "It might be nothing."

"It might not," said Christopher, his eyes narrowed to slits. "We didn't get this far by ignoring our gut instincts." There was no sign of the levity he'd shown earlier. This Christopher meant business.

Staring at the place where the lights had disappeared, Ryan admitted that if he'd been smart, he would have told Kat how he felt. She deserved to hear that he'd fallen in love. She might even feel the same. The feeling was still new and unspoken, but important and changed how he saw the world. From the moment of his discovery, he'd considered himself a two, not a one. All decisions were joint decisions. It would be awkward if she didn't feel the same way; sharing a bunker would be difficult. But he'd sensed a depth to her feelings, too.

Startling him from his reverie, Luke whispered. "You know how to use a gun?"

In the near dark, Luke's expression was difficult to see, but Ryan had no trouble mistaking his meaning. Luke was asking if Ryan would shoot someone if necessary. He swallowed. He'd been to the gun range a few times with guys from work, but he'd never shot at anything living.

"I wouldn't shoot my foot off, if that's what you're asking." Ryan kept his voice even. To reach safety in the bunker, he'd do a lot of things in the name of survival that he'd never have considered before the asteroid.

"It might be nothing," said Christopher, holding a handgun, the muzzle pointing toward the ground but ready for action.

Luke gave him a pointed look and raised his eyebrow, visible only because of their proximity. He removed a pistol from the small of his back and passed it to Ryan. It was heavier than he expected. Luke showed him where the safety was and produced another from somewhere on his person. Who slept with two guns?

The three of them crept further from the tents. Luke waved Ryan to a position by the washroom building, a dark lump extending toward the sky, blocking the horizon and his view of the road where the lights had disappeared.

"Hang back in the shadows as long as possible. If a threat gets past us, shoot. If you can get away with bashing a skull instead, that will also do." Luke's voice was steady and his eyes gleamed in the darkness, his gaze direct.

Ryan nodded. He wouldn't let anyone hurt Kat. Or himself. Or the others who'd been good to them. Thinking of the sleeping children heightened his resolve. Enough innocents had perished.

"Ella's awake in our tent. Don't go near it without saying first her name, then yours. She's a dead shot."

Ryan swallowed again and nodded. Somehow, he felt better knowing he wasn't the final defense. He appreciated the trust they were putting in him all the same. He and Kat must have passed a test at some point. Not everyone would trust a stranger with a gun near their families. He was glad that they didn't think he and Kat had lied or could work with their approaching visitors.

"We'll be near. At either end of the parking lot." Luke glided left into the darkness.

Ryan appreciated that someone had taken charge.

Christopher squeezed Ryan's arm on the way toward the right. Ryan couldn't make out their forms well as they blended into the shadows and stepped with silent feet. Ryan's heart hammered against his sore ribs, beating out a painful rhythm. The rest of the night was so quiet that it surprised him that his heartbeat wasn't audible. He took a deep breath. His ribs didn't hurt as much as before, but that could be the rush of adrenaline.

In the distance, a coyote yipped and was answered by another, closer one. Without the flashlight, Ryan saw next to nothing. Each tick of his watch took an eternity.

At first, nothing happened, but a low whine became discernible. He held his breath as the vehicle approached, rising from a dip on the highway where it had disappeared. Closer, it became clear that it wasn't a truck; it was a pair of motorbikes. Not loud like Harley's, but higher in pitch, maybe something smaller for off-road or for short-range. Without the roaring trucks, he wasn't sure it was the Slains.

In the silence, their high-pitched engines became loud.

It looked like the bikes were going to ride past the sleeping campsite, but when their headlights reflected on the parked vehicles, the bikes slowed. Their brake lights gleamed like beacons, and Ryan's heart sank. He wished they'd kept riding.

The bikes stopped just out of sight behind the washroom building. The engines kept running. What was going on? After a long minute, the motorbikes advanced again, continuing past the campsite at a creeping pace.

Turning around, the bikers stopped, parking on the road about a hundred yards past the junction where he and Kat had come from. His feeling of dread grew, his stomach churning. He didn't think he was done with the Slains. This might be their men on patrol, still searching for him and Kat. On foot, he and Kat had been pushed north and hadn't covered enough distance to be out of their reach.

Their glaring lights shut off one by one, and Ryan squeezed his eyes closed. He'd lost his night vision when he'd stared at the glow of their lights. Cursing to himself, he waited for them to readjust. He couldn't make out the riders in the poor light, but they were coming to investigate the camp. Holding his breath, he waited for someone to speak as the air became charged, expectant.

The murmur of voices on the road moved closer, then stopped. He strained at the darkness, but he couldn't see further than the parked cars. He broke out in a cold sweat and wiped his palms on his pants. His bat lay on the ground by his feet, the slick gun in his icy hands. He eased the safety off, just in case, gripping it with shaking hands.

"Can I help you, gentlemen?"

Luke's voice broke the silence, making Ryan's heart race.

The men on the road cursed and their footsteps grew louder. The pretense of sneaking into camp to investigate was gone.

"Perhaps you could help us instead," said a gravelly voice.

Ozzy's voice. Ryan ground his molars and raised the gun, aiming past the vehicles, searching for a hint of where to target. At least one bruise on his ribs was from Ozzy's boots, and he was pretty sure the other man had a black eye courtesy of his elbow. He wished he could let Luke and Christopher know that these were the same men who'd attacked. His fellow campers were smart and may have reached the same conclusion on their own.

"How's that?" called Luke. Sunny growled, then barked. "That's close enough. My dog doesn't like strangers."

"A couple of trespassers came through our place a few days ago. Perhaps you've seen them? A man and a woman. They'd be on foot."

Ryan couldn't hear a lie in his voice. The man was slick.

"Haven't seen anyone else for days." Luke's voice was steady. "Pretty quiet out here."

"That's how we'd like to keep it," said Ozzy. "This is our land. Frankly, I'm surprised to see you here. Most of the roads are blocked. Where're you headed?"

"East," said Luke. "Family in Michigan." He kept it short and sweet.

"You must have slipped through on backroads while we were searching for the other two. We don't appreciate strangers on our land."

"Pretty sure your land is a national park." Christopher's voice came from the right. He must be letting the men know Luke wasn't alone.

"That's the old world," said the biker, his voice coming closer. "This belongs to the Slains brothers now. I'm married to their sister, so that makes me one of them. If we want to get technical, you're also trespassing."

Why hadn't the other biker spoken? Were they still together? Ryan tensed, hoping Luke or Christopher had a better idea where the second man was. Ryan tried to keep track of everyone, not a straightforward task in the dark, but he couldn't see far in the still-dark morning.

"We'll be gone in the morning," said Luke. "You'll never have to see us again."

There was a soft crack behind the washroom building, like a twig breaking underfoot. Ryan held his breath. Someone, perhaps the missing biker, had circled around, trying to be sneaky. Perhaps to get the jump on the others from behind. He hoped Luke was also aware.

Ryan went with his strength. He put the safety back on his gun and tucked it into the waistband of his pants. Stooping, he picked up his bat. Its solidity felt reassuring in his hand. This was about to get real.

He waited for the man to step away from the shadow of the building and toward the cars. He was only two feet away, headed for where Luke's voice had originated. Ryan let him take another step, but he didn't want to let the man get any further. He stopped listening to Ozzy and the others speak and concentrated on being quiet as he got in range.

Lifting the bat, he swished it as hard as he could, aiming for the back of the other man's head. The bat whistled through the air, making a sickening thump on contact. The man dropped straight to the ground and didn't move. Direct hit. Ryan's arms tingled from the wooden bat's vibration.

"What the fuck?" growled Ozzy. "Kenny?"

There was no answer, and the man on the ground remained motionless. Ryan swallowed. What if he'd killed him?

Luke's voice called out. "That you, Ryan."

"Yes," said Ryan, proud of keeping his voice calm. "Home run."

A scream pierced the night and froze his blood.

Kat's voice.

He sprinted toward the tent, leaving the man on the ground. Ryan's fist curled around the bat, but before he'd gone more than a dozen yards, a shot rang out. His back muscles twitched, and he resisted the urge to drop to the ground as he rounded the corner and stopped. A man was down outside his tent. Ella stood over him, nudging him with her toe. His nostrils twitched at the scorched scent of gunfire that filled the air.

"Kat, you good?" said Ella.

Ryan's breath caught until her reply.

"Yes."

Before he could continue, chaos erupted. Three additional shots came from the area near the parked vehicles, followed by the thud of retreating boots on the road. One bike roared to life and illuminated the parking lot with its yellow glare. Through the gloom, Ryan made out the form of someone down in the dusty lot, a black pool of blood spreading outward. It wasn't Christopher or Luke, but a much smaller man. A third intruder down. There must have been two men on each bike, with the passengers getting off when the bikes had stopped out of sight. The motorbike thundered past them as it streaked westward, back where it had come from.

The sky remained dark, but a faint band of lighter sky showed on the horizon.

Ryan resumed at a walk. Not wanting to get shot, he said, "Ella, it's Ryan." His voice was unsteady.

She nodded, her eyes flicking to him, then back to the man lying on the ground.

He stepped over the body in his hurry to get to Kat. "You're okay?"

She popped out of the tent and threw herself into his arms. He squeezed and didn't let go.

"Call out," said Luke's voice as it came closer to the tents. "Was the first shot you, Ryan?"

"That was me, Honey," said Ella's calm voice. "We're all good. Man down and he's going to stay down." She bent down to check the man's pulse. Seeing Ryan's gaze, she shook her head and grimaced.

"I hit the other guy pretty hard." Ryan released Kat and stepped to his right to look toward the building. His man was still down and hadn't moved. "I think he's just unconscious, but someone should check him." He hoped his voice didn't sound as shaky as he felt. He reached for Kat, who stayed at his side.

"I'll do it. I shot the one in the parking lot," said Christopher. "He's dead. You and the kids good, Lizzie?"

"Yes, though that was more exciting than I prefer before breakfast and caffeine." Her muffled voice came through the tent wall.

Ryan agreed with her assessment.

"I should've guessed there'd be more than two guys," Luke clenched his fist. His tone seemed disgusted with himself.

"By the time I got a read on it, it was too late to share with anyone," said Christopher.

"Luckily, no harm's been done to us. The baby's sleeping and the kids are fine," said Elizabeth, as she stuck her head out of her tent. "That was some scream. You sure you're alright, Kat?"

"Yes. I woke up, and Ryan was gone. The next thing I knew, Bob Slains was climbing into my tent."

"That was smart thinking, shining the light in his face. He yelped, you screamed, so I shot him," said Ella. "I'm guessing he was your sick friend from the other day?"

Ryan couldn't believe the petite blonde was so calm. He'd underestimated her toughness.

"He was. We'd followed his trail of violence since the first day. Road closures and the fire at Missoula meant we were on the same route eastward. Turns out his family lives not too far from here."

Luke appeared out of nowhere wearing a long cloak like a Jedi, which must have helped him camouflage in the darkness. He crouched beside Ryan's intruder and checked if he was breathing and if he had a pulse.

"This one's alive. At least for now. We'll tie him up. Leave him in the washroom. We're breaking camp. Going to make a run for xTerra. I say we take the longer route but stay on the main highway where we won't get lost. We'll make better time. That guy on the bike might return with friends. If he's from the Wright area, he could be back inside an hour and a half. Maybe a little less." Luke checked the time.

"That's the one I call Ozzy," said Ryan, releasing Kat, who scrambled to get her boots. "There might be teams of men out there. It could take less time to be back with reinforcements in the trucks."

"We'll hope he has to go the full distance." Luke's gaze went back to the road.

"I don't love the Slains being this close to xTerra." Ryan followed Christopher toward the man he'd hit with the bat, who still lay sprawled on the hard-packed ground.

"Neither do I, but that's a problem for the future, not today," said Christopher as he patted the man's leather vest and removed a set of keys. He held them up with a jingle and tossed them to Ryan. "Looks like you've got wheels."

"Pack up quick. We'll make the run together. We can find room for your backpacks, even if we're loaded to the rafters," said Luke.

Ryan nodded, his hand clutching the keys. They bit his hand and he relaxed his grip. He passed the gun back to Luke, who took it with a nod. Christopher appeared with a length of rope in his hands. He peeled the unconscious man's boots off, stuffed his socks into his mouth, and tied both his wrists and ankles. Between the three of them, they hauled the man's prone form into the bathroom and secured him to a thick metal pipe. If his friends arrived, he'd be easy to free. He was still out cold and the back of his head was bloody, but they couldn't take chances if he awoke before they left. They didn't want him to know what direction they went. They dragged the other bodies behind the building and left them.

Returning outside, little Jayden stood outside his tent, rubbing his eyes. He wore ABC pajamas and clutched a gray stuffed dog to his chest. Ryan was impressed with his good behavior and grateful that the kids weren't crying after all the loud noises. Elizabeth and Ella had dressed, taken the little girls to their car seats, and fastened them into the cars—still sleeping. At least someone was still asleep.

Elizabeth took Jayden by the hand and led him to their vehicle. "Do up your buckle, sweetheart. We have another little drive."

"Is it time for breakfast yet?" Jayden's voice was sleepy and he let out a terrific yawn.

"Not yet. Go back to sleep if you can."

"I'm not tired," he said, still rubbing his eyes as he climbed into his car seat.

Ryan shot Kat an amused look, feeling his mouth twitch. The sun was coming up and even without the light of the flashlights, it was now possible to discern details as the night faded. The glow on the horizon became bright orange, the dark clouds lit from behind with brilliant color. In the other direction, black clouds loomed, tendrils reaching toward the grasslands. It was going to be wet. He glanced toward the tent area. Luke and Christopher broke one down, Ella the other, and Kat had stuffed the sleeping bags and tossed them out and was almost done with their tent. She'd had a head start since she hadn't helped with the remaining prisoner. He put the bat on the picnic table and ran to help.

With everyone working at full speed, they packed the camp in minutes. Not everything had to be pretty, just fit in the vehicles. With their bags packed, Ryan trotted up the road to check the motorbike. He'd ridden dirt bikes with Nick's family a few times in university. This one didn't look different, just bigger.

He started the bike and rode up the highway a few minutes, testing the balance, the feel, and how to change gears before returning. He wasn't crazy about riding it and would have been more confident on four wheels, but it was better than walking. If they didn't take chances or go too fast, he would be fine.

At least Kat could rest on the bike. She'd been restless and uncomfortable for several nights. Her ankle had worsened with every day of walking and he'd worried she was doing permanent damage. It had to be almost intolerable, and not once had she complained.

Impressed by how soon everyone was ready to leave, Ryan shook hands with Luke and Christopher, who climbed into their vehicles with their waiting families. Kat hopped on the back of the dirt bike, clutching his ribs too hard and sending shooting pains through his side when they first took off. He winced but kept the discomfort to himself as they fled toward shelter and xTerra, racing the clock and, if he wasn't mistaken, the weather.

CHAPTER 25: RYAN

Ryan expected trouble from behind at every turn, but so far, the road had remained empty. Now that they had wheels again, driving the highway seemed fast. Route 450 East was deserted; the pavement cracked and buckled in places, but no worse than the others. He watched out for holes, which got easier as the sun rose further and visibility improved. His shoulders and chest remained tight as they traveled. He wasn't an experienced biker, and riding this one took all his concentration.

Kat might have been a nervous passenger, but she didn't move or throw off the balance of the bike. She relaxed her grip after the first few miles and was light enough that he barely noticed she was there, other than warming his back.

At the small town of Newcastle, a village surrounded by cattle ranches, they turned south on Route 85. The signs said: Edgemont 65 miles. From there, xTerra was only twenty-five minutes away. They were so close. With the possibility that the Slains could pursue, it was hard for Ryan not to let his guard down. He wanted the journey to be over. Instead, sections of the highway worsened and Ryan had to slow the bike or risk wiping out on the rough patches.

Three times their convoy had to go off-road around downed power poles lying across the width of the highway. The electricity had been out where they'd camped, but he gave the poles a respectful distance just in case, avoiding the broken wires. They couldn't tell if something was live.

They'd almost made it to the turnoff at Edgemont when misfortune struck. The lead car, driven by Christopher, fishtailed across the road; it swerved back and forth and it seemed as if he was struggling to regain control. One of the rear tires had blown, perhaps punctured by something on the road. Christopher wrestled the car to a halt at the side of the narrow two-lane highway. Luke pulled over on the shoulder while Ryan parked in front.

Elizabeth emerged, pale and shaken, but everyone appeared to be okay.

"Mommy, is it time for breakfast yet?" said Jayden from the backseat. "I'm hungry."

"We've got to fix this," said Christopher as he climbed out, kicking the flat tire in disgust. "Damn. We're so close."

"You fix the tire. I'll feed the kids," said Elizabeth with a sigh.

Kat hopped off the bike to stretch while Ryan propped it up and did the same. She dug through their most accessible backpack in Luke and Ella's car and located the last two granola bars. He smiled his thanks, took a bite, and went to help with the blown tire.

"I'm going to stand watch," said Ella, scanning the surrounding landscape. The dark clouds loomed nearer and thunder rolled in the mountains to the north. "Up there." She pointed to a rise a hundred yards behind them that would have a view of the road back the way they'd come.

"You don't think they followed us?" said Kat, biting her lip.

"No idea," said Ella, "But I'm not taking chances when we're this close to our destination. I'll fire a signal shot if I see them while you're working." She checked her gun, grabbed a pair of binoculars, and set off through the tall grass.

Changing the flat was a bigger deal than it should have been, with kids inside and a full carload piled on top of the spare. He and Kat pitched in, organizing what Luke and Christopher removed so that they could reload everything afterward. He was impressed with how much they'd jammed inside, but that meant a mountain to cram back in. It was hard not to feel jealous of their wealth in supplies when he and Kat had started with so much more, but now had one bag each.

It didn't take long to change the tire, but the whole time Ryan glanced up and down the road, unable to relax, expecting the worst after their run of bad luck. Changing the tire didn't take everyone, and he had little to do except wait.

The delay cost them three quarters of an hour, most of which was spent unpacking and repacking. Part of him wanted to take Kat and rush ahead, but these people had been kind to them and were his future neighbors. It was also possible that the Slains might know a faster route, and beat them to the turnoff, if they'd figured out where they were headed. He and Kat should stay with the group where there was strength in numbers.

No sooner had they fixed the tire and returned everything to the vehicle, when the sky opened. The downpour that had threatened since dawn arrived with a vengeance. Ryan and Kat wore raingear and added their goggles, but it was going to be a wet, slippery ride.

A shot fired, and Ella came charging back through the tall grass. She shook her head before she jumped in her car. She unrolled the window to speak. "I couldn't see much because of the rain and fog. Visibility was poor. Right at the end, I thought I heard something. Might be them following. It was louder. They might have the trucks. I'd assume they're still coming and we've lost most of our head start."

"You go first," said Luke. "We'll follow. Make sure you're not left behind."

●　　　●　　　●

Back on the bikes, their progress at a crawl, they finally arrived at the bunker complex. The road ended at a tall gate in a metal fence that was over five meters high. It was too early to breathe a sigh of relief. They still had to get inside and find their bunker.

Since the last time Ryan had been here, they'd added a wooden watchtower beside the gate and several more rose from inside the wall around the perimeter, some still under construction. The precautions seemed appropriate for how the last twelve days had gone and the difficulties with people on the road, but he hoped they wouldn't have a problem.

"You'll have to enter one vehicle at a time," shouted someone from the closest tower. "Single-file, nice and slow." The man carried a rifle with a scope and aimed it downward.

Ryan understood, but being in the crosshairs made him twitchy. His heart drummed against his sore ribs as he took a deep breath. He'd long since memorized the code from the notebook he'd collected from work and shared it with Kat, determined that if something happened, they'd still be able to get into xTerra. With sweaty hands, he punched in the six-digit code.

At first, nothing happened. He glanced up at the gunman, his hand hovering over the keypad, about to re-enter the numbers, when a green light flashed.

With a whirring sound, the mechanism swung the gate open.

He and Kat rode through and were waved to a muddy lot next to an office building. The gate closed, then opened again as Luke entered a code. He and Ella drove inside and the gate closed. This was repeated a third time while Christopher and Elizabeth entered.

At the side of the building stood a covered carport with slots for dozens of cars. Once each of the cars parked, a guard punched a code on another keypad.

"Please remain in or on your vehicles until the gates are closed," called the guard by the gate. His gun remained trained on their group. "Someone will attend to you shortly." He spoke into a walkie-talkie and swiveled his gun toward the outside as the gate continued to close.

A flurry of action inside ensued as three additional guards ran up the wooden stairs at that tower and three more in one nearby. The newcomers seemed forgotten as the gate closed. What was going on?

With a roar of machinery, two loud vehicles pulled up outside with a spray of gravel. Seconds later, someone shouted outside the walls. "Open the damn gate." It was Ozzy.

From atop the tower, the original guard called down, still looking through his rifle scope, "Enter your code, and the gate will open."

"I don't have a fucking code. Open the gate. We have unfinished business with those you just let inside."

"The gate doesn't open unless you have a valid code."

"You mean to tell me that our trespassers have a code to this stupid town you've built inside?"

"I do. They had a code and if their story checks out, they're citizens of xTerra and beyond your jurisdiction."

"This isn't the last you've heard of us," called Ozzy.

From outside the wall, there were more sounds, like someone kicking the gate, several curses, and engines revving. From the noise, two trucks spun their wheels in the mud and gravel before departing.

The first guard spoke into his walkie-talkie once more and the extra riflemen climbed down and disappeared through the main doors. At each of the three closest towers, a watcher with binoculars remained, following the Slains' retreat.

Ryan breathed a sigh of relief. They'd outrun the Slains.

After the calm returned to the gate area, an older woman with frizzy blonde hair and a clipboard emerged from the office, followed by two men with rifles. Security here was a lot tighter than Ryan remembered. He swallowed his nervousness, hoping he had the right answers. He owned a bunker and had a code; it shouldn't be a problem. All at once, a scenario arose in his mind where a militant group had taken over the complex and might turn them away. It would suck to have come so far and fail, only to be homeless.

"You all in one bunker, or different ones?" The blonde's stare unnerved him.

"Three separate ones," said Ryan, his mouth becoming dry.

"Your name?" She didn't seem welcoming or friendly.

He could have used a smile or some reassurance. This lukewarm reception put him on edge.

"Ryan Griffiths." He wanted to give her the bunker number and proceed, but waited for her next question.

"Occupation?"

"Lawyer."

She wrote on her paper, but kept it angled away from him. "Have you been to Vita before?" She looked bored, barely flicking a glance at them since the first stare.

Ryan clenched his jaw. They sat shivering on the motorbike for stupid bureaucracy. His jeans were drenched and stuck to him and Kat must be soaked to the skin. Couldn't this be done faster or inside?

"I inherited it from my grandfather, Lewis Griffiths, about a year ago. He was a full-time resident. You might have known him." He waited for a reaction but got none. "I'd visited him here three times since 2020 when he bought his bunker. I've been here an additional three times on my own."

The woman made a clicking noise with her tongue and wrote something on her clipboard before looking up and turning to Kat, her bored expression intact.

"Your name?"

"Katana Sullivan." Kat looked at him, perhaps wondering if he'd been subjected to this level of scrutiny before. She'd dropped Mark's last name.

"Occupation?"

"Teacher."

The woman looked up. "Good. You're only the second teacher to arrive. Elementary or high school?"

"Elementary," said Kat. "But I have a major in Earth Sciences and a minor in Biology, so I'm qualified to teach high school Science. I just chose younger kids." The woman scrawled additional notes on the questionnaire.

"Have you been here before?"

Kat shot him a second wide-eyed look, like she didn't know how to answer. He gave her a small nod. She should just tell the truth. It would be okay. They were still sitting on the bike, so he reached his hand back and curled it around her calf. She relaxed at the squeeze.

"No, I'm Ryan's guest."

He watched her struggle to stay herself and not put on a fake smile or an act. He kept his hand on her leg.

He glanced over at Luke and Christopher's families. They had their own guards and clipboard people and were answering the same set of questions. No one had been asked to leave, so it appeared they'd all passed. At least so far. He overheard that Luke and Ella were private investigators and that Elizabeth and Christopher had worked at the Portland Museum of Natural History.

"You may proceed to orientation," said another guard by the door to the office building. "We encourage everyone to share contact information, see medical, and have a hot meal here before continuing to your bunker. We provide shuttle service via golf cart to your designated quarters. Living here can be isolating at first and we're expecting trouble any day."

Ryan breathed a sigh of relief about their reception, but wondered what the man meant about upcoming trouble. Here? Or outside the wall? He would rather relax than remain on high alert, but it was difficult to slow his brain, which had been in survival mode for so many days. Kat's lips had turned purplish-blue, and he wanted to get her inside. His questions could wait.

"Where's your luggage?" asked the woman with frizzy hair, turning toward the office.

"Our backpacks are in Luke and Ella's vehicle," said Ryan, gesturing to the black SUV on their left. "That's everything we have left."

She nodded and added that information to her checklist with a frown.

One of the others with a clipboard sauntered over, took her clipboard, and she left without another word.

"Don't mind Gillian, she's a grouch." said the woman who now carried all three clipboards. She gave them a small smile and glanced at their paperwork. "Oh, she forgot to ask your city of origin."

"Seattle," said Ryan.

The woman's eyebrows shot up to her hairline. "You too. Your group is the first who've arrived from the Pacific Northwest. That must have been quite the journey. We've given up on most of the West Coasters." Her eyes widened, and she covered her mouth before continuing. "We're going to have a lot of empty bunkers. A full third were owned by Californians." Her mouth flattened and she wiped a tear with the back of her hand. "Please, come in, you must be freezing."

Ryan slid off the bike as she continued to chatter.

"We're setting up an admittance council and a once-a-month meeting for those in the community. We have underground bunkers as homes, but we want this place to become its own town. We hope you'll be happy and productive residents."

The tension left his shoulders. Ryan smiled and waved to their new friends, who were organizing their children. "See you inside."

CHAPTER 26: KAT

Kat wanted off her foot, as the pain was excruciating. She'd clenched her jaw and borne the pain because there was no alternative. She'd hoped the ride on the bike would give it a rest, but the angle it had hung on the bike—with only her toes on a footpeg—hadn't helped. The throbbing had become almost unbearable. She gritted her teeth and hopped off the bike onto her good foot. She wanted to crumple to the ground and let her tears flow, but though they swam in her eyes, she held them inside a little longer.

Ryan moved to her side and wrapped his arm around her waist. "Lean on me."

She put her arm around him and let him support her into the building. It touched her he'd helped as a matter of course. Mark would've asked if she needed help in a way that would have seemed like she'd asked too much. Then he would have reminded her he was great for helping. If she had to talk, she was afraid the dam would break, and she'd be a blubbering mess. The end of their journey was in sight and she just needed to keep it together for a short time.

The lobby reminded Kat of a rec center with a bank of chairs, and an office, partitioned with plexiglass, and long hallways branching off on either side. A gray-haired woman dressed in camo stood at the counter area, three clipboards in hand. She looked up as they crossed the room and scanned the clipboards before she returned two to the counter.

"You must be Ryan and Kat, since you don't have children with you." She flashed them a wide smile, reminding Kat of her favorite grandmother who had passed several years ago, the perfect warm welcome. The familiarity made her feel more at ease than anyone else here.

Ryan guided Kat to a nearby chair, where she slumped as he stepped up to the counter. "She re-sprained her ankle and then walked on it for several days. We heard there would be a chance for medical care. Is someone available?"

Kat appreciated that he'd taken charge and that she didn't have to speak.

The woman nodded and picked up an old-fashioned corded phone, pushing buttons. When someone on the other end answered, she said, "Can I send someone down for medical treatment? A new arrival with a sprained ankle?" She smiled in their direction as she hung up. "Someone will be up to collect you ASAP."

"I can't believe your phones work. We heard cell towers and satellites were knocked out and damaged all over." Kat's voice sounded shaky, but now that help was coming, she wanted to make an effort.

"We're lucky," the woman said with another smile. "The phones are just for our bunker complex and connect to this building; they don't work with the outside. We use old-style phones that have to be plugged in. Cell phones would be useless."

"We haven't had a chance for much news," said Ryan as their friends entered, kids and dog in tow, and the lobby became crowded.

"Let's get everyone settled and checked out, then you can all do orientation and get the latest news updates," the woman said. "If you need anything else, just ask for Rose." She pointed to her name tag. I'll arrange a ride to your bunker.

"The doctor will see you now," said a young man wearing ripped jeans as he arrived with a wheelchair.

"We'll see you in a bit," said Ryan to Christopher and the gaggle of kids surrounding their new friends. Luke held Sunny's leash and waved to show he'd heard.

Kat hopped two steps and sat in the wheelchair. Her ankle was excruciating. Otherwise, she'd have felt embarrassed to be wheeled down the hall. It was such a relief to keep her weight off her foot, even if it continued to throb. Ryan walked beside the wheelchair, which made her more comfortable as they traveled down the hall. She didn't want to let him out of her sight.

Now that they were here, she didn't know their status. He cared about her and was kind, but did he want her in his bunker long-term? What if she got on his nerves? They'd have to try it and see. Their relationship might be different from it had been on the road. If it didn't work, she'd apply as a resident on her own. It sounded like there was space and that they welcomed the arrival of someone with her occupation. They wanted her to be part of their community.

In the medical center, the doctor squeezed, manipulated, and x-rayed her ankle. After she confirmed it hadn't broken, she rewrapped it in a cleaner tensor bandage. The doctor fussed over Kat and gave her painkillers to take at night. They also gave Kat crutches and strict instructions to stay off her foot.

Everything else was quick, and the doctor gave Ryan and herself a clean bill of health. The others arrived for their health check when she and Ryan finished. Kat sat at a table in a small cafe and savored a toasted bagel and a piping hot tea while she waited. Being there, doing something so mundane as enjoying food, seemed so anticlimactic, almost like the last twelve days hadn't happened. It seemed so ordinary here; it wasn't what she'd expected.

Less than an hour later, their new friends joined them and they pored over a map of the complex and bunker numbers. Luke and Ella were in 113, Christopher and Elizabeth were in 217, and she and Ryan were in 105.

"We won't be too far apart," said Elizabeth, examining the map. "It's nice to know a couple of people here already." She smiled and

Christopher took her hand. It was sweet that both other couples were so clear in their love for each other. What did they think of her and Ryan? Did they know that their relationship was new?

"I like the idea of connecting phones," said Kat. "I was a little worried that once we went into the bunkers, we'd be totally isolated. Cut off from everyone and everything else."

"Me too," said Ella. "This is much better."

"Sounds like they'll want you to teach in a school. At least eventually," said Ryan. "You okay with that?"

Kat nodded. "It'll feel normal. I miss teaching kids." Her eyes filled with tears at the thought of all those left behind, many of whom may have died. She didn't want to dwell on that. It would only lead to depression. She was lucky and alive.

"Ready for orientation and news?" said Christopher, taking Jayden by the hand. "The sooner we can get settled into our place for these two to have an N-A-P, the better."

"I don't need an N-A-P," said Jayden. "I'm big now and not tired."

Kat suppressed a smile. It would be fun to teach a smart kid like Jayden in the not-too-distant future. It would help her life feel a little more normal. She and Ryan followed the group to a meeting room near the office. She'd never used crutches before, but was getting used to how they worked.

They sat and watched a ten-minute video about Vita xTerra, probably an old sales promo video, but it gave her some idea of the amenities and features of the complex.

Afterward, a man in military-style khakis stepped to the front of the room. "The weather is supposed to continue to be erratic. Lots of storms. But, the biggest news is the imminent eruption of Mount Mazama, which could be any day. We've been told that the last time it exploded, it was spectacular."

"Every archaeological site in North America uses the Mazama layer as a reference," said Elizabeth. "Either newer than 7,700 years or older."

"That's more than most of us knew two weeks ago," the man said with a nod. "I'd been to Crater Lake but didn't know the name of the mountain that blew up to create it."

Kat had overheard that Elizabeth was Dr. Winters and had worked at a museum; she sounded like an authority on this subject. "I hope it isn't as big this time."

"I'm afraid it might be," said the man at the front with a grimace. "Worldwide, there have been two dozen volcanic eruptions in the last ten days and an ongoing series of massive earthquakes as tectonic plates shift because of the asteroid strike. It's like a domino effect. Earthquakes and tsunamis along the coastlines have plagued coastal regions all over the world, even those countries spared asteroid impacts."

Kat reached for Ryan's hand. This was the stuff of nightmares, even if it wasn't unexpected. Some of their greatest fears were being realized. It was unlikely that anyone from Europe or other countries would come to their rescue, at least no time in the immediate future. They'd arrived at the bunker in the nick of time.

"Yesterday, the military contacted the front office and warned us to prepare, to batten down the hatches. Mount Mazama has regrown and Crater Lake is gone, vaporized. The explosion will be the largest one yet, bigger than when Mount St. Helens and the others erupted the same night. The world might go to hell in a handbasket, but you aren't alone. At xTerra, we have three hundred and fifty bunkers worth of citizens and we want to work together to maintain some sort of civilization, even if it might be different than before. Some of us have prepared for years. We might be on our own, but we're together and alive."

Rose from the office stuck her head in the doorway. "The carts are here. You'll need to load your trailers with your luggage. Your vehicles can stay here in the car park where they're at least partly protected from the elements. They can be moved to the long-term storage facility in a few days. Ryan and Kat, yours is ready to take you home as soon as you collect your bags."

The word "home" sounded like heaven.

"I'll come now," said Luke, standing up and pushing in his chair. "Since your backpacks are in our car." He leaned over and kissed Ella where she sat with their sleeping daughter in her arms. "I can unload and get you when our cart is ready."

Ella smiled and nodded.

"You want to stay with the kids or unload the car?" Christopher asked his wife.

Elizabeth laughed. "If you don't mind, I'll join you in a few minutes. I'd like to finish my tea." Their little ones were drawing in coloring books with crayons she'd pulled out of her purse, giving her a moment's peace.

Outside, Luke unloaded their backpacks and set them in the front seat of the waiting Polaris, next to the driver, leaving the back seat free for Kat and Ryan. Luke and Christopher shook Ryan's hand, and each gave Kat a quick hug.

"Don't be strangers," Christopher said with a smile as he and Luke turned back toward their loaded SUVs.

Ryan took her crutches and helped her aboard. Her heart fluttered as they drove the smooth gravel roadway toward bunker 105.

The grounds were more extensive than she'd imagined from the description online. Ryan had said that there were about five hundred bunkers. But seeing that many all together was larger than she'd expected. There were five hundred seventy-five concrete and steel bunkers on this site, arranged in long rows in five sections. This had been a military base until 1967, when it had been decommissioned.

In recent history, it had been converted to survival bunkers of about 2400 square feet. The promos had called it long-term glamping and to expect that level of comfort. Adequate, but not luxurious. The grounds were reported to be three-quarters the size of Manhattan, and the far wall was too distant to be seen. The complex had been designed to withstand almost any catastrophe. Climate change, nuclear blast, and perhaps, an asteroid strike. They could survive up to five years sealed inside a bunker. Longer, perhaps. No matter how bad it was outside, it seemed this place gave them a real chance at survival.

Big black numbers on a neon yellow sign over the entrance identified Bunker 105. The resident who'd driven them opened steel doors and drove into the waiting shed. He passed the keys to Ryan after he'd deposited their bags by the door.

"I'll walk. I'm just in 102," said their driver. "Name's Jerry. You can call me anytime if you have questions. Good luck settling in."

"Thanks for picking us up," said Kat.

"Yes, thank you," said Ryan.

It didn't seem adequate after the silent ride where she maybe should have made small talk to be polite, but hadn't because she'd been afraid it would have sounded awkward. After so many days of not speaking, it was odd to be with someone different.

Jerry winked and didn't seem offended. He shook their hands. "Lewis was a good guy. He'd be glad you made it." They watched him walk back the way they'd come, his feet quiet on the paved pathway.

"Shall we?" Ryan helped Kat out of the cart and slid the shed door closed with a scraping sound. They walked up to the numbered keypad by the door, where a steel plate had been slid aside.

"Would you like to do the honors?" said Ryan.

He had a strange look in his eyes that she couldn't interpret. She wished she could read his expression. Was he regretting his decision to share a bunker, even if it had a lot of space? Her heart caught at the idea. That was nonsense. She shook her head.

He punched in the entry code, waited for a clicking sound, and opened the thick steel door. He slid the panel behind its protective cover once more. A motion-sensor light flicked on in the area just inside the door and Ryan tossed the backpacks inside.

Kat bit her lip and took three swinging steps forward on her crutches to follow, but Ryan blocked her way. She stopped right in front of him near the threshold. He held out his hand for her crutches. She didn't know what was going on in his head, but handed over the crutches. He leaned the crutches against the inside wall.

Without warning, he scooped her up into his arms and cradled her against his chest as he carried her inside. "This isn't my place. It's ours."

His romantic gesture warmed her heart and allayed her fears.

He carried her through the first section of the house, down the hall. "Storage, laundry, gym, and pantry," he said as they passed two doors on each side of the passage. He stopped to flip a light switch and illuminated a long room in front of her with an arched ceiling, with the high point in the center.

The main living area held two sectional couches, a dining room with a table for six, and a kitchen with an island eating area and three additional stools. This place looked much more than functional; it looked comfortable and lived in, with throw rugs and blankets on the furniture. This didn't seem like somewhere for a rustic vacation. It looked like a home.

"There are three bedrooms, two bathrooms, and an office in the back." He set her on one of the soft couches and said, "Can you wait here a second?"

She was confused by the way he wouldn't meet her eyes. On the road, she'd learned to read most of his expressions, but since arriving, he'd been different. Was he up to something?

"Sure." She leaned back with a deep sigh, keeping her sore foot propped up in front of her. She sank into the couch for a minute before noticing the nearby electrical outlet.

While she waited, she plugged in her phone. She'd thrown it into her pack days ago and forgotten about it until she was in the golf cart. Right away, it pinged with a notification. Her heart racing, she snatched it up.

She had a cached message, one that must have arrived before her phone lost power and they'd crossed through a section with coverage.

The message was from her mother. *"We're sorry we didn't believe you. Hope you made it somewhere safe."*

Kat covered her face with her hands and let out a sob. They didn't hate her. The message was old, and she didn't know if they were still alive, but closure was something. It was good news. She pulled herself together while she waited for Ryan to return.

A couple of minutes later, Ryan brought her crutches and leaned them on the wall only a step away. She appreciated his thoughtfulness, even if he was acting odd. He went back for the backpacks and closed the outer door, sealing them inside with a clang. He carried the luggage down the hall, through the hallway into the back, but she couldn't see if he went into more than one room. When he returned, he looked to be empty-handed, his hands jammed deep in his pockets.

It was time to find out what the situation was. She'd waited long enough and curiosity was killing her. "Did you put my stuff in my room?" she blurted. "A room of my own?"

Ryan stopped walking; his face still unreadable. "Would you rather have your own room? Not share?" he looked surprised. That might be a good sign.

"That's not what I meant," she said, speaking more carefully. "I just don't want to impose. We haven't talked about what would happen once we arrived, though perhaps we should have." She chewed on her lip, but kept her eyes on his face.

Ryan took one hand from his pocket, but kept it balled in a fist. He dropped to one knee. "Maybe this will clear up a few things." His voice was full of emotion, his gaze intent on her face.

Kat held her breath. This couldn't be what it seemed like. Time slowed around them as she met his beautiful, mismatched eyes.

"I had an epiphany the other night." He wiped his forehead with the back of his hand. "I woke up beaten and bloody and you were gone and I didn't think beyond getting up to find you. I was scared for you and frantic that they might have found you after I'd been knocked out."

She hadn't known what he'd thought that night, but she'd been having similar thoughts in the drainage pipe. She rested her hand on his warm arm while he spoke. He shot her a crooked smile that melted her heart.

"I tried to look for you, but I passed out again. I'd decided that I wanted to marry you. To have you with me always. I know this might seem rash, but I don't just want to share my bunker with you. I want to share my life. You've claimed my heart. I should have told you sooner."

Tears rolled down her flushed cheeks, and she nodded, an enormous lump in her throat preventing her from answering.

"So that's a yes," he said, the corner of his mouth twitching. "I never thought to see you speechless." He opened his fist and held out his cupped hand. Inside lay a diamond ring.

"This was my grandmother's. My grandfather left it for me with the bunker. I never saw a reason to take it anywhere else. The last four days, all I've thought about is getting here to ask you to marry me."

"You don't care that I'm different," she said. "That I'm neurodivergent."

"That's what I like about you best," he said. "I love you just how you are."

"I love you," she said, feeling as though her heart would burst. "I've known since the same night."

She held out her left hand.

With trembling hands, he slipped the cold metal band onto her ring finger. It was a perfect fit. She dropped to her knees in front of him and his mouth captured hers. It was several minutes before thought returned.

They still knelt on the floor, his forehead resting on hers when the ground shuddered, and a bright orange light flashed above the hallway leading to the door. Another light flashed by the door.

He let out a deep breath as the earth continued to shake. "Mount Mazama," he said. "But here, we're safe together."

She wrapped her arms around him and kissed him again as he pulled her close. This was where she wanted to be and who she wanted to live her life with. She'd never take living for granted again.

ACKNOWLEDGMENTS

Who knew that a chance encounter with a long-lost friend would bring me here, to having my first published book? I'd like to thank Michelle Rothery, who asked an innocent question in July 2017, "How's your writing?" It had stalled out. After she asked, I started writing again, and we met every few weeks to discuss our projects over bottomless cups of tea.

That fall, Michelle dragged me to an author's night where she introduced to the second of my early writing support partners, Nic Farrell. We listened to Jack Whyte, Diana Gabaldon, Michael Slade, Robyn Harding, and Eileen Cook talk about writing. I'd like to thank them too for their inspiration. They said the right words at the right time. I rushed home and canceled all of my gaming subscriptions, freeing up time to write.

By the time the Surrey International Writer's Conference rolled around in 2019, it was my second time attending. With Nic and Michelle's encouragement, I felt just brave enough to sign up for my first blue pencil session. I shook like a leaf, barely coherent, so I'd like to thank Owen Laukkanen for his patience, his suggestions, and for giving me confidence in my story.

I'd also like to thank writer Jenn Sommersby for answering my early rounds of questions and for steering me to the right places for answers, in particular the online writing community, The Creative

Academy for Writers, which has been pivotal to my progress. Through this community, I found beta readers, resources, and encouragement, so thank you to everyone at TCA.

I'd also like to thank the most patient beta reader, Deborah Lambert. We met over dinner at my first Surrey Conference and that winter she worked her way through the 235-thousand-word tome that was my first story. Her comments improved my writing, even if at first, I had to look things up online to understand. I also appreciated her beta reading a later manuscript.

A huge thanks to Eileen Cook for being an excellent teacher, my first editor, a reader, and head cheerleader when I need it most. She has become the experienced author friend who I turn to for advice.

Other beta readers that I'd like to thank are Johanna Haas, Leslie Wibberley, Bonnie Jacoby, Brian Munro, Jacqui Paul, Kayla Kurin, Lynette Van Steinberg, Joy Ellenhall, Michele Amitrani, and Wendy Turner. Some read a few chapters, others a manuscript or two, some a query or synopsis (or seven), but whatever the length, their feedback was appreciated. A special thanks to two beta readers, Ben and Tracy, who have become something more.

To Ben Brockway, who befriended me on Twitter after we'd submitted to the same agent. He's read everything I've written in the last two and a half years, pointing out things that frustrate me and sometimes make me cry. I realize every manuscript needs a little tough love. He also suggested that I submit to Black Rose Writing and was the first person to call and congratulate me on the contract offer. He's given invaluable feedback on pitches, active writing, and how to fix obvious plot holes (his words, not mine). Arguing has improved my writing and along the way, he's become a friend.

I can't say enough about Tracy Thillmann. She volunteered to read my dark fairytale in the spring of 2020 and set a new benchmark for beta readers with helpful suggestions and positive feedback. I asked her to join my floundering writing group. Now we have a critique partnership and she's met with me every week for two years, selflessly giving her time and energy. Tracy has become not just a critique partner and trusted friend, but my editor. She hears my author voice and supports my stories in a myriad of ways. Every author needs a Tracy.

A special thanks to my friend Julie Beyea, who stayed up late at night to finish reading my stories, and my mom, Cheryl Jennings, who has read everything I've shared over the last two years. I'd also like to thank my former running coach, Chris Kuhn, who showed confidence that I would have published books one day. From the beginning, these people made me feel like an author.

I'd also like to thank the team at Black Rose Writing for believing my story was worthy of publication. I've appreciated the weekly information packets and the ability to connect with their other authors for tips and reviews. Thank you to their writers that read and reviewed *The Edge of Life*, including Gail Ward Olmsted, Jeff Ulin, Jefferson Blackburn-Smith, and Mina Alexia.

Last but not least, is my family. I'd like to thank my husband Rob for listening to endless story ideas and for not being offended when I almost never use his suggestions. He's given me time and support by doing the lion's share of the household chores, so I can write. I'd also like to thank my daughters, Laurel and Hayley Dabb, for reading synopses, query letters, and occasionally, opening pages (even if once I had to pay them). For them, and for my step-kid, Kayla too, thank you for your belief and support.

I couldn't have done it without all of you.

ABOUT THE AUTHOR

Lena Gibson is a storyteller as an elementary school teacher and keeper of the family lore. She holds a First-Class Honors degree in Archaeology, with minors in History, Biology, Geography, and Environmental Education from Simon Fraser University.

A voracious reader from age eight onward, Lena seeks wonderful books in which to escape. Because of her passion for different genres, she combines elements of many in her writing. As an adult newly recognized with autism, she often creates characters that reflect her experience.

When Lena isn't writing, she reads, practices karate, and drinks a ton of tea. She resides in New Westminster, Canada with her family and their fuzzy overlord, Ash, the fluffiest of gray cats.

https://lenagibsonauthor.wordpress.com

ABOUT THE AUTHOR

NOTE FROM THE AUTHOR

Word-of-mouth is crucial for any author to succeed. If you enjoyed *The Edge of Life*, please leave a review online—anywhere you are able. Even if it's just a sentence or two. It would make all the difference and would be very much appreciated.

Thanks!
Lena Gibson

We hope you enjoyed reading this title from:

BLACK ❁ ROSE
writing™

www.blackrosewriting.com

Subscribe to our mailing list – *The Rosevine* – and receive **FREE** books, daily deals, and stay current with news about upcoming releases and our hottest authors.
Scan the QR code below to sign up.

Already a subscriber? Please accept a sincere thank you for being a fan of Black Rose Writing authors.

View other Black Rose Writing titles at www.blackrosewriting.com/books and use promo code **PRINT** to receive a **20% discount** when purchasing.

CPSIA information can be obtained
at www.ICGtesting.com
Printed in the USA
BVHW080240201222
654602BV00004B/4

9 781685 131715